Wartime at Woolworths

~

Elaine Everest was born and brought up in north-west Kent and has written widely for women's magazines – both short stories and features – as well as fiction and non-fiction books for the past twenty-one years. A qualified tutor, she runs The Write Place creative writing school in Hextable, Kent. Elaine lives with her husband, Michael, and their Polish Lowland Sheepdog, Henry, in Swanley, Kent. *Wartime at Woolworths* is the fourth book in her Woolworths series.

You can say hello to Elaine on
Twitter @ElaineEverest or
Facebook at www.facebook.com/ElaineEverestAuthor

Elaine Everest

Wartime at Woolworths

PAN BOOKS

First published 2018 by Pan Books
an imprint of Pan Macmillan
20 New Wharf Road, London N1 9RR
Associated companies throughout the world
www.panmacmillan.com

ISBN 978-1-5098-4367-1

1 3 5 7 9 8 6 4 2

A CIP catalogue record for this book is available from the British Library.

Typeset by Palimpsest Book Production Ltd, Falkirk, Stirlingshire
Printed and bound by CPI Group (UK) Ltd, Croydon, CR0 4YY

Visit www.panmacmillan.com to read more about all our books
and to buy them. You will also find features, author interviews and
news of any author events, and you can sign up for e-newsletters
so that you're always first to hear about our new releases.

To the people of Erith, and those
who remember 'the good old days'

Prologue

November 1944

'You really need to be home putting your feet up,' Betty Billington tutted at her friend, Sarah Gilbert. 'How long is it until this baby's due? I really can't keep up with all the baby news amongst my friends,' she added, a slight twinge of sadness in her voice. She so longed to be like her younger friends who were able to bring new lives into the world, but as quickly as those thoughts had come to mind she pushed them away again.

'I have two months to go, as you well know, Betty. You seem to be so forgetful these days,' Sarah joshed.

Another sign of my advancing years, Betty thought before giving herself a quiet shake to remember to stop being so miserable. She had much to be grateful for. With the war now in its fifth year she was blessed to know that her friends and family were still alive, despite Hitler's attempts to prove otherwise. 'I do feel you should be at home all the same, rather than here giving me a hand. Not that I'm not grateful,' she added quickly.

'Betty, if I don't feel the ticket, I'll take myself off home but believe me, it's a joy to be here helping do the staff payroll with you. Georgina is well taken care of at Gwyneth's house and being child-free and here adding up rows of numbers is pure joy.'

Betty nodded, fighting back the tears threatening to fall. Gosh, what had come over her?

'At least put your feet up.' Betty pushed a wooden chair close to her friend, who eased her legs into a horizontal position. 'Your ankles are a tad puffy. You should take more care, you know,' she advised.

'That's because I've been queuing for an age at the butcher's rather than carrying this lump round with me. I swear it must be a boy – he was playing football against my ribs all night long. Little Georgina was a dream to carry compared to this little wriggler.'

'Surely someone else could have queued for you?' Betty scolded.

'It was quicker to go there myself, as is so often the way. Plus, I'd heard a rumour they had some stewing steak in – I can't remember the last time I enjoyed a good stew.'

'And did he have any?' Betty asked as she pulled a large leather-bound ledger from a shelf and opened it on the desk in front of Sarah.

'It had all gone by the time I reached the counter but he did have some sausages and put in an extra one "for the baby", as he said,' she added with a grin. 'There are perks to being an expectant mother.'

'What has it come to that we're pleased to receive an extra sausage from the butcher?' Betty declared as she checked she had enough brown envelopes in which to put the staff's wages. 'Would you mind very much writing the names on the envelopes? The list is here,' she said, pointing to the row of names neatly written in the ledger. 'I just need to put through a telephone call to head office. The delivery of cups and saucers has still not arrived and I'd hate to disappoint our customers. It's strange to think that we are so happy to see a few pieces of crockery on the counters. As for saucepans, I can't remember the last time we had a shining display of pots and pans to sell. I'm not surprised people are travelling over to New Cross in order to pick up a pan before they're sold out. Why, if I hadn't heard that little snippet of information from head office, Maureen wouldn't have been able to go there to replenish her battered pans that survived the roof of her house collapsing.'

Sarah giggled as she reached for Betty's fountain pen and dipped it into the pot of black ink, then felt she should explain when Betty gave her a questioning frown. 'All this talk of pots and pans reminds me when Alan proposed to me as he stood atop the pots and pans counter. It seems such an age ago now,' she added wistfully.

Betty smiled. 'It's one of my most memorable moments of working here at Woolworths. Then Maureen burst into song and the customers joined in,' she added with glee. 'Such happy times we had before this damnable war started.'

'At least I still have the set of pans that Mr Benfield gave us as a wedding present. It was a struggle but I held on to them for grim life when the Scouts came to the door collecting utensils to build spitfires.'

'Dear Mr Benfield,' Betty smiled, reflecting on her predecessor who had left the employ of F. W. Woolworth to

3

join the army. 'I was most upset to hear that he'd succumbed to measles whilst serving in the pay corps. It doesn't seem right that a serving soldier should pass away from something our children suffer with.' She ran her hand gently across the leather-bound ledger. 'He taught me so much about running this store. Why, the first pages in this ledger contain his copperplate handwriting. I tried to be as neat in my early endeavours to enter the numbers of hours and pay earned by our staff, but try as I might, my handwriting isn't as good as his.'

Sarah nodded, hoping against hope that Betty did not notice the large ink stain she'd left in the ledger when the temperamental fountain pen had leaked onto the lined pages. She hurriedly reached for blotting paper, doing her utmost to stem the flow. Mr Benfield would not have been amused.

'Now, I must crack on and make that telephone call, then perhaps we could spare five minutes to go to the staff canteen for a cup of tea and a slice of the bread I can smell? Be with you in a minute.'

Sarah smiled to herself as she copied names and numbers onto the front of each envelope before blotting the ink and placing them in alphabetical order. Sarah thought about how much she enjoyed helping Betty in her small office above the bustling Woolworths store. To be able to pop in to help out with paperwork made her feel she was still part of the happy band of Woolies workers. Was it really six years since she had first stood with a group of eager young women in this very office listening to Betty Billington giving her serious talk about the responsibility of being a member of staff and how they would all be given an arithmetic test? It was also the day that she met Alan Gilbert and her glorious romance began as the dark days of war grew steadily closer. Who would have thought that Alan would now be a pilot in the RAF and that they would be the proud parents of beautiful four-year-old Georgina, with another child on the way? Sarah placed a protective hand over her swollen stomach. A son would be lovely. A son who looked just like his father and who would live in peaceful times rather than this awful war. Why, if what her nan, Ruby, said was true, the war could be over by Christmas. There again, she said the same every year.

With a smile on her face, she looked to where Betty was deep in conversation on the black Bakelite telephone. Her boss seemed to have a glow about her, which Sarah put down to being married to the handsome Douglas. Yes, it would be contentment. Something that all newly-wed women felt in those first few years after their wedding.

Betty suddenly stopped talking and frowned at what she was being told. A look of horror crossed her face. 'Oh my God!' she exclaimed. 'It can't be true.'

Making a hurried goodbye, after asking to be kept informed, Betty replaced the heavy receiver in its cradle and turned to Sarah. 'There's been an incident at the Woolworths branch in New Cross. We don't know if it's a gas explosion or ... or, enemy action.' She sunk down onto the spare seat opposite Sarah.

The young woman's face had turned a ghostly shade of white. 'Is it serious ... are there casualties?' Sarah whispered, afraid of what the reply would be.

Betty nodded her head slowly. 'There must be ...'

'Must?' Sarah asked, hardly daring to breathe. 'What do you mean, must?'

'There's nothing left of the store . . .'

'But Mum and Maureen were going there.' She looked at the clock on the wall opposite the desk. 'They could have been in the store . . .'

Betty reached across the desk and took Sarah's trembling hand. 'Please, please don't get upset. You have to think of your baby. Anything could have delayed your mum and Maureen getting to their destination on time.'

As the women stared at one another, their fellow co-worker, Freda, rushed through the office door. She was still wearing the uniform of a dispatch rider in the Auxiliary Fire Service. Without making an apology for her hasty arrival, she blurted out, 'I've just heard at the fire station that New Cross Woolworths has taken a hit. Our lads have to go up there to help out. I'm on my way there now. Betty, I thought you ought to know . . .' She looked at the two shocked faces. 'I take it you've heard already?'

Sarah nodded slowly, a sense of foreboding consuming every fibre of her body. 'Mum and Maureen are there.' She heaved her feet from where they were resting and, using the edge of the desk, she pulled herself to her feet. 'I need to go and find my mum. I'll come with you, Freda.'

1

March 1943

'Don't look now but that woman's watching us again. I swear every time I visit Ruby's house the bloomin' woman's curtains are twitching,' Maisie declared as she pulled her pram close to the front wall of number thirteen and kicked the brake to stop.

'Whatever are you talking about?' Sarah asked, bumping her daughter Georgina's pushchair up the small step and pushing it close to the bay window of the Victorian terraced house. 'Wait a minute, darling, let me lift you out and you can go in and see Myfi. She'll be home from school by now,' she told her daughter, who was demanding to be freed from the reins that were keeping her secure. 'My, you are growing into a big girl. It must be all those carrots you eat,' she puffed as she lifted her daughter free of the blanket that covered her. 'Now, run along and knock on the door, there's a good girl.' Sarah turned back to where her best friend, Maisie, was lifting baby Ruby from her pram. 'Here, let me take her while you sort yourself out,' she offered, taking the sleeping baby and holding her close. 'She's such a little sweetheart. I could just eat her up,' she said, inhaling the aroma of baby milk and soap flakes that reminded her so much of when Georgina had been that size.

'You wouldn't say that if it was you she'd been keeping up most of last night. I'm fair whacked today. If it wasn't for Freda telling us we had to get round here on the double to hear Gwyneth's news, I'd not have ventured outside me front door today.'

Sarah smiled at her elegant friend. Her appearance was as immaculate as usual. Considering the country had been at war for well over three years, she looked as smartly turned out as any society hostess on the covers of the latest magazines. Even though Maisie complained about being constantly exhausted, she never once had a hair out of place or her lips not perfectly painted with the bright red lipstick she never left home without. 'Now tell me, what are you going on about?'

'Over the road at number sixteen. Yer nan told me a new family 'ad moved in but all I've seen of her is when she stares at us from behind those grubby nets. Don't look,' Maisie hissed as Sarah peered towards the house. 'Come on, let's get inside and find out what all the fuss is about, and I'm dying for a cup of something hot, this wind is blowing right through me. Be quick, mind, your Georgie looks as though she's got her arm stuck in the letter box.'

Sarah handed back baby Ruby and hurried to extricate her daughter just as the door opened and Freda came out to help them, quickly followed by Myfi and Nelson the dog. 'Come on in, we've been waiting an age for you,'

Freda said, sweeping the squealing Georgina up into her arms. You'll never guess what's happening?'

'Don't tell me that Mike Jackson has finally proposed to our Gwyneth?' Maisie laughed and quickly apologized as she saw the crestfallen look on their friend's face. 'C'mon, Freda, it's been on the cards for ages.'

'Well, just don't let on. Pretend you're surprised, Maisie.'

Maisie promised she would as she followed her friends into the house and turned to close the door. Sure enough, the curtains moved again as the woman over the road observed the happy group.

'Put that bloody curtain down, woman. Why you want to be forever watching those load of snobs is beyond me?' Harry Singleton growled from his armchair.

'They look like nice people. I don't think they're snobs; well, not like our old neighbours,' his wife, Enid, answered meekly. 'They seem to be friendly enough and I'm sure I've seen a couple of them working in Woolworths. You ought to go and speak to them.'

'And a fat load of good working at that place ever did me – a bad back was all I got out of it and now we haven't got a brass farthing to call our own.'

Enid Singleton knew well when her belligerent husband was beginning to lose his temper and often it meant she'd be at the sharp end of his harsh words. She also knew that they'd had to move away a bit sharpish. 'The doctor did say that, given time, you'll be fine so let's hope you'll be back on your feet before too long,' she said, hoping to cheer him up.

Harry glared at his wife. 'Don't you think I'd be fighting the bastard Krauts if I could stand for longer than ten minutes at a time? Do you honestly believe I like being beholden to a woman to care for me and to earn a crust?' He looked at the mahogany mantle clock. 'It's time you had a bit of grub on the table. A man could starve around here,' he muttered, opening his newspaper to the back page and shaking it dismissively.

Enid hobbled off as fast as she could to the small kitchen at the back of the house. She thought it convenient that Harry's bad back seemed fine whenever he took a walk to the New Light for a pint or two. Here on Alexandra Road, the air smelt cleaner than it had in the streets around their old home and she felt a lurch of excitement in her stomach at what the future held, as long as their past never caught up with them. It might even be possible to bring home their two boys, who had been evacuated in 1939. She tightened the ties around her pinny and peered into her stone pantry at the paltry supplies. But even if she was struggling, the piece of paper tucked into her pocket offered some hope. It was so lucky she'd walked past Woolworths just as the card advertising for a cleaner had been placed in the window. Even opening the door to the stone pantry and viewing only one egg, a couple of slices of bread and a few potatoes couldn't dampen her happiness. Yes, she'd soon be able to put more food on the table and possibly send a few bob to the kids. If it weren't for her Harry, life would be on the up.

*

'So, why have we been summoned here?' Maisie asked as she passed baby Ruby to her namesake before settling on the arm of the settee in Ruby's best room. 'It must be something important if you've put us all in here,' she grinned, looking round Ruby's front room at the faces of the Caselton family, each person balancing a cup and saucer on their knees whilst all speaking at once to catch up on news. Ruby's lodgers, Freda Smith and Gwyneth Jones, along with Gwyneth's daughter, Myfi, were grinning fit to burst.

Sergeant Mike Jackson stood nervously, trying to listen to Gwyneth and Freda's conversation while his father, Bob, attempted to get his attention. 'We really need to get locals involved in the allotment society. There are some allotments going begging and they're starting to become overgrown. Do you think you could have a word down at the police station and get the lads to put out the word that we need more people to get involved in the "grow your own" campaign?'

Mike nodded his head, not taking in his father's words. There were bigger things on his mind at the moment.

Ruby rocked the young baby in her arms and stroked the little girl's button nose. She'd been chuffed to bits when Maisie and her husband, David Carlisle, had announced they would be naming their first-born Ruby Freda Carlisle. Personally, she felt her name was a little old-fashioned and would have preferred to see the girl named after Princess Elizabeth or Princess Margaret, but it was an honour she wore with pride and she had already declared the baby to be as precious to her as her own children and grandchildren. 'Come on, Mike, let's get the formalities out of the way then we can have another cuppa and a slice of the seed cake I made special for the occasion,' she said loudly, putting a stop to all the chit-chat in the crowded room.

Mike Jackson coughed politely before holding out his hand to Gwyneth, who got to her feet and took her place by his side. 'The thing is . . .'

'Come on, cough it out,' Maisie urged the shy man.

'The thing is . . .' Mike said again, trying to clear his throat and loosen the top button of his police uniform. At that moment he felt rather sick and the room was closing in on him. 'The thing is . . .'

Gwyneth patted his arm. 'The thing is, Mike has asked me for my hand in marriage and I've accepted,' she announced proudly in her lilting Welsh voice.

'I said yes too,' young Myfi declared from the floor, where she had been sitting playing on the rag rug with Sarah's daughter, Georgina, which caused the roomful of friends and family to erupt into laughter at the same time as shouting their congratulations.

George Caselton slapped his friend on the back. 'You kept that a secret, you dark horse,' he exclaimed. He was pleased for his friend, who had remained a bachelor for many a long year. 'You've made a good choice in Gwyneth.'

'I'm sure Gwyneth did some of the choosing as well, George,' Irene Caselton reprimanded her husband. 'Many congratulations,' she said, giving both a polite kiss on the cheek.

'Thank you,' Gwyneth replied politely. She had never felt comfortable in Irene's company as the older woman always gave off an air of being more important than anyone else in the room. George Caselton, on the other hand, was a different kettle of fish and was as warm and welcoming as his mother, Ruby, and daughter, Sarah. 'Mike asked me a little while ago but he wanted to do things properly and ask my father first.'

'Even though you've been married before?' Irene asked, arching her eyebrows. 'Was it not a wasteful journey to go to Wales in wartime?'

'It wasn't possible for us to travel to my parents' home, even though I longed to see them. It's been a while since Myfi has seen her grandparents, but as Mike has to work I wrote a letter and we gave them a time when we would telephone so that Mike could ask my father for my hand, which is the correct thing to do.'

'Why, you should have said, old man. You could have used the telephone in our house,' George said.

Mike and Gwyneth murmured their thanks but both thought it would have been an extremely uncomfortable experience with Irene present. Huddled together in a public telephone box had been most romantic.

'So when's the big day?' Maisie called across the room.

'We need to find a home of our own first,' Mike started to explain.

'It needs to be close to the town for Mike to get to the police station and Myfi loves her school so I'd not want to take her away now she's settled and happy,' his bride-to-be continued. 'We thought that the autumn would be as good a time as any and would give us time to get a few things together and be prepared. That's if you don't mind Myfi and me lodging here for a while longer, Ruby?' she asked the elderly woman, who was collecting cups and placing them on the wooden tray held by Bob Jackson.

'You're welcome to stay here for as long as you like,' Ruby replied, giving the woman a gentle smile. 'I won't say I'll not miss you and the girl but you need your own home as there will be children of your own before too long, and a blessing they are too,' she said, looking to where Freda was now holding Maisie's baby.

'Steady on, Mrs C,' Mike stuttered as his face turned a mild shade of pink. 'I'm getting on a bit to be thinking of babies and such like.'

'Well, Gwyneth is still in her prime so don't dismiss having half a dozen or so,' Maisie hooted with laughter.

Gwyneth fell silent, and stared down at the floor. Granted, she and Mike had not discussed having a family but she knew that her life would not be complete without children she could call her own. For all intents and purposes Myfi was her daughter, even though her dearly departed twin sister had given birth to the child, but she so wanted to be able to have Mike's babies. They needed to have a quiet chat, and very soon.

'You know, Ruby,' Bob said as he followed Ruby to the kitchen carrying the wooden tray laden with crockery, 'it would make life simpler for Mike and Gwyneth if we married sooner rather than later. I could move in here with you and let them have the house to themselves.'

'Now's not the time to talk of such things, Bob. I've got a houseful of people dying for a cup of tea,' Ruby said, avoiding his gaze.

*

Enid took a deep breath and pushed open one of the dark-wood-framed doors of the Erith Woolworths store. Why was she so nervous? Not only had she shopped a few times in this very store since moving to the town but she had worked in one of the East End branches for many years with her Harry. However, this time was different: she desperately needed a job, not only to keep their heads above water due to her husband's injury but also to help keep her sane and give her life an interest away from him. She'd made a point of checking where the staff door was after receiving a letter with an appointment for her interview from someone called Betty Billington. It made her smile to think she could have a female boss; times were indeed changing if women could have such important jobs.

Taking a deep breath and checking her reflection in the mirror tiles that decorated a pillar close to the first counter, she felt happy her hat was on straight and that the wisps of greying hair were clipped back tidily before pushing open the door marked 'staff only'.

'Come in, Mrs Singleton,' Betty said as she opened the door to the last of the ladies due for interviews that day.

'Now, tell me a little about yourself,' Betty said after Enid had taken a seat to one side of the desk. 'Your letter says that you have worked for Woolworths in the past,' she prompted.

'Yes, ma'am,' Enid replied nervously. 'I worked for ten years at the Canning Town branch of Woolies . . . I mean Woolworths,' she corrected herself. 'My husband also worked there.'

Betty nodded. She could see the woman was very nervous, gripping a shabby bag on her lap and fiddling with

15

the handle between her fingers as she answered. 'Can you tell me what you did whilst in your last job?'

Enid felt so nervous. She hoped no one would ever find out why she had left the East End of London and Woolworths. All she wanted was a quiet life and to be able to put food on the table – and for her Harry to be a little kinder to her. 'I was a cleaner, ma'am, and I also helped out in the kitchen when the cook was busy or off sick. She was a martyr to her bad feet.'

Betty tried not to smile. 'We most certainly could use your services in this store, Mrs Singleton. May I ask if you ever worked as a sales lady on the shop floor?'

Enid wriggled a little uncomfortably. 'I'm not that good with numbers or spelling and I know as how Woolworths like to employ clever people to work on their counters, ma'am. Besides, I've got this gammy leg since having polio as a kid. It's always been a dream of mine to serve on the counters, though. But I'm happy enough to have any job.'

Betty nodded thoughtfully. She prided herself on being a good judge of character. 'Never say never, Enid. If someone had told me that I'd be managing this store one day, I'd have laughed out loud. Women are the backbone of this country and we can all play our part in bringing this war to an end.'

For all of her forty-two years Enid had never felt so inspired in her life. Perhaps working here would give her life more purpose. 'I hope so, ma'am,' she answered politely.

'Do you have a family, Enid?' Betty asked, trying to find out a little more about the woman.

Enid's face lit up. 'I have two boys, Fred and Wilf. They were evacuated but I've managed to see them a couple of times. I'm just so pleased they're safe and by jingo, they're growing up fast,' she said proudly.

'Your husband is in the forces?' Betty prompted.

The look of joy left Enid's face. 'No, he's an invalid. He would like to join the army but it's not possible at the moment.'

'I'm sorry to hear that,' Betty responded. 'Let me out-line the hours I'd like you to work and then we will need you to complete a form so we have some records. By the way, do you have any references?'

Enid looked flustered. 'Er, no. We lost everything in the bombing.'

Betty thought that she'd be able to write to the Canning Town branch for details of Enid Singleton so assured the woman it would not be a problem. Reaching into her desk, she pulled out a file and handed a form to her along with a pencil. 'Are you able to compete this? It's just a little information for my records.'

Enid shook her head, a look of panic crossing her face. 'No, I told you I'm no good with numbers and words.'

Betty got to her feet and put a comforting hand on the woman's shoulder. 'Please don't be distressed. I'll call one of my girls to help you.' She left Enid and opened the door, calling to a staff member who was passing by on her way to the staffroom. 'Freda dear, can you spare me a few minutes, please?'

'Certainly, Miss Billington,' Freda said politely, noti-cing there was someone in the office. Betty was only referred to by her first name when the women were outside of work or talking privately. She entered the office and gave the woman a broad smile as a way of offering a hello.

'Freda, I wondered if you would take Enid to the staffroom and help her to complete her paperwork? I'm sure a cup of tea and one of Maureen's cakes would be most welcome.'

'Certainly, Miss Billington. Maisie has popped in to see everyone; she has baby Ruby with her. Shall I ask her to come up to see you – that's if you aren't too busy?'

'I'd be upset if she didn't spare me five minutes. I can always find time to see my latest goddaughter. We are a very close family here,' she explained to Enid. 'Who doesn't enjoy a cuddle with a baby?'

Enid nodded politely and got up to follow Freda. Although she was overjoyed to be starting a new job, the thought of mixing with strangers was terrifying.

'Here you are,' Freda said as she put a large mug of steaming tea in front of Enid and slid a plate holding a generous slice of gypsy tart alongside it. 'It's on the house,' she added as Freda noticed Enid reaching for her purse. 'Our cook Maureen said welcome to the store. Well, you're almost staff and we don't charge our friends before they've earned their first pay packet. Mind you, you'd best make the most of it, as we don't often find the ingredients for the gypsy tart these days. No doubt Maisie had a hand in this. She seems to know people who can lay their hands on most things.'

Enid turned in her seat to call her thanks to the

dark-haired woman who was pouring out tea whilst speaking to a pretty blonde girl holding a baby. 'Oh, it's the posh lady,' she exclaimed before turning bright red. 'I'm sorry, I didn't mean to sound rude. I've seen her before with her pram and she's always so well turned out.'

Freda frowned for a moment. 'I thought I'd seen you before. Aren't you the lady who's not long moved in over the road? I've spotted you at your window.' She didn't like to add that Enid had been the topic of conversation on more than one occasion as the inhabitants of number thirteen had discussed the lady who watched from behind her net curtains. Her landlady, Ruby, had twice knocked to welcome the family to the road but the door had never been answered.

'I've not long moved into rooms in Alexandra Road,' Enid answered. 'It's just the old man and me as my two boys have been evacuated to the country.'

Freda called out to Maisie. 'Can you join us for a minute? There's someone I'd like you to meet. You too, Maureen.'

Maisie sat down at the table after passing her baby to Freda while Maureen wandered over still wiping her hands on her pinny.

'This is Enid. She's just moved into rooms opposite Ruby's house. She's going to be joining us here at Woolworths.'

The two women murmured words of welcome.

'I'll be back to work 'ere as soon as I'm able,' Maisie said as she raised her pencilled eyebrows at Freda to acknowledge she knew Enid to be the lady from behind the net curtains.

Enid was astounded. 'You work at Woolies? I thought you'd have had a posh job somewhere.' She looked to where the cherubic baby was sleeping soundly in Freda's arms.

'What, me? Blimey, girl, there's nothing posh about me,' Maisie said as she burst into laughter. 'I'm more than 'appy to work 'ere with me mates.' She then went on to explain how they'd all met at the store before the outbreak of war and who had lived at number thirteen. 'Even Maureen 'ere had a room there when the roof of 'er house caved in last year. Number thirteen welcomes all waifs and strays.'

'Where are you from?' Maureen asked as she waved to a staff member waiting at the serving counter to acknowledge she'd spotted her there. She had also been briefed about the lady opposite who watched the world go by from behind her curtains and had found it funny when the girls came up with suggestions about the unknown occupants of the house.

'I'm from Canning Town, born and bred,' Enid said proudly, before adding quickly, 'We was bombed out and my husband wanted to get away from the area.'

Maisie liked the look of Enid straight away. She seemed a little timid but that would change once she got to know everybody. 'Just let me pop in and see Betty . . . I mean Mrs Billington, then I can walk back wiv you. I'm going round to see Ruby as I've some wool to drop in to her before I head fer me own place. I take it you've all but finished up here?'

Enid felt a little shocked by the suddenness of not only being accepted by the women but that someone so smartly turned out should wish to speak with her. 'I thought you called her Miss Billington?' she said to Freda.

'I did, but I keep forgetting that now she's Mrs Billington,' Freda laughed, seeing Enid's confused look. 'I'll let Maisie explain that when she walks home with you.' Handing the baby back to her mother, Freda picked up the form that lay on the table. 'Why don't I fill in the questions for you while you eat your gypsy tart and finish your tea, then you'll be ready to head off with Maisie?' She'd seen the woman giving the sheet of paper a worried look and guessed that possibly Enid wasn't up to completing it.

'And I'll love you and leave you to get back to work or else there'll be a right ruckus over there,' Maureen said. 'It's been good to meet you, Enid, and I'm sure we'll see much more of each other before too long.'

Maisie bumped her large Silver Cross pram off the high pavement and hurried across the road as a brewer's dray turned the corner nearby on its way to the pubs down by the river. She was keen to get home as soon as possible as David was off duty and she wanted to make the most of having him around for a few days. He was always in London or travelling away from home doing something or other for the RAF. She was never certain what it was but one thing was for sure, she was grateful that he didn't have to fly a plane like Sarah's husband did. She could think of nothing worse. Once she'd introduced Enid to Ruby and whoever else was at number thirteen she'd get herself off to her own place to see David.

Thinking of Enid made her slow down to accommodate the slower pace of the woman with the limp. 'I'm sorry, ducks, I was miles away and there's you trying to keep up wiv me. What must you think?'

'It's not a worry. I can get about quite well with my gammy leg. It's never held me back,' she explained, although she never mentioned the merciless bullying she'd received as a child as she wasn't able to join in so much with the other kids in her street and had tired easily.

'All the same, I feel bad for hurrying you. You will come in and meet Ruby, won't yer? I know she'll be happy to meet a new neighbour.'

'I'd like that,' the woman answered, even though she knew Harry would have something to say about her mixing with the locals. He wanted to keep himself to himself in this town.

'Were you upset to leave your 'ometown?' Maisie enquired.

'In a way I was, but then again I may be able to get the boys back home a bit quicker now we aren't in the East End of London anymore. It seems so peaceful around here.' She looked sideways at the pretty young woman and frowned.

'What's up?' Maisie asked, noticing Enid's stare. ''Ave I got a smut on me nose or something?'

'Sorry,' Enid replied, feeling embarrassed. 'It's just that you remind me of someone I used to work with. If she wasn't a good bit older, you could be sisters,' she said before frowning. 'There again, it was a few years ago when I first joined Woolworths. She retired last year when her husband was poorly. I thought she might have returned to work but I never did see her again. Perhaps she moved away,' she added thoughtfully.

'Poor cow looking like me,' Maisie grinned. 'What was 'er name?'

Enid thought for a moment. 'Queenie . . . Queenie Dawson.'

Maisie froze. That was her mum's name. What was she doing in Canning Town and did Enid say Queenie's husband . . . her dad . . . was poorly? She couldn't make sense of what she'd been told. She needed to get home and think about things.

'Do you know the name?' Enid asked, noticing how Maisie had lost her happy smile.

'You could say that,' was all Maisie would say as she turned into the bottom of Alexandra Road. 'Look, there's Ruby at her gate. Watch out, though. She's talking to Vera Munro from up the road and Vera's the nosiest woman on earth. She's got a tongue like a razor blade as well.'

Enid absorbed Maisie's words. Perhaps Harry's idea to move away from the East End wasn't such a good idea after all? Friendly work colleagues could lead to all kinds of problems without having nosy neighbours as well.

2

'Let me get this straight,' David Carlisle said as he ran his fingers through his hair whilst pacing the floor in front of Maisie, who was bouncing their baby on her lap. 'You want to go racing off to goodness knows where—'

'Canning Town, David. It's in the East End of London.'

'You want to go racing off to Canning Town to look for parents that you've not thought about for God knows how many years? Maisie, whatever hare-brained scheme will you think of next?'

Maisie knew that her adored husband was referring to when she decided to head back to Erith rather than give birth to their child at his mother's home. 'It's not hare-brained, David. Since this little one has come along I've got to thinking about how she has a family she don't know. I want her to know all her grandparents.'

David shook his head in disbelief as he sat down in the armchair opposite his wife and reached out to take his daughter's small hand. 'Maisie, our little princess only just recognizes us, let alone strangers. I know it may still be a few years yet, but can't this wait until the war is over and we can travel around London without fear of being bombed to smithereens?'

'Don't yer think I wanna know how they are? Enid told me Dad had been poorly and by the time this war's over, both me parents could be six feet under. It's all right for you, you've got a family,' she huffed, feeling close to tears. Enid's mention of her mum the day before had made her think about her past and how she had walked away from her parents after being accused of playing a part in the death of her little sister, Sheila. 'And what's all this about the war taking years to finish? You kept that quiet,' she added stubbornly, sticking out her chin.

David raised his hands in surrender. 'I give up,' he sighed. 'If you really need to rush off to London, then do as you please. You'll get your own way whatever I say, you usually do. But you will not take our daughter with you, do you understand?'

Maisie nodded her head in agreement. She knew when it was best not to argue with her husband. She loved him too much to disobey him over something as important as their daughter's safety. She had imagined walking into her parents' home and showing off her child and her wedding ring but perhaps that could wait for another time. It was best she reached out to them first. They could meet David and little Ruby another time. 'And the war?' she asked.

'My darling wife, however important you think my part is in this war, I do not have the ear of Winston Churchill, or Adolf Hitler come to that. Now, how do you intend to find your parents, or are you planning on walking the streets of London until you find them?'

Maisie felt her stomach lurch at his words. She knew he'd voiced them in all innocence but she was still ashamed of some parts of her life that she'd only shared with a few of her closest friends. If David knew everything, it would be the end of their marriage. Of that she was sure. 'I'm going to ask Betty to help. Enid told me that someone going by mum's name, and who looked like me, had worked at the Canning Town branch of Woolworths. I'm sure that with her contacts she can find an address for me. What do you think?' she asked, hoping that David would be impressed with her plan.

'Possibly Betty can advise you,' he said carefully. 'However, if she cannot help you, please don't go rushing off on a wild goose chase. And if Betty does have useful information, I insist that we discuss this carefully and, when you are ready to travel to London, you take someone with you. There is no urgency.'

'Would you—'

David held up his hand and smiled. 'No, my darling wife, as much as I love you I refuse to join in with—'

'My hare-brained schemes?' Maisie said with a grin. She had a gut feeling that her trip to the East End of London would reap success. 'I'll ask one of the girls ter go wiv me.'

'But not at the moment, Maisie,' her husband said as a serious expression crossed his handsome face.

'Why ever not? If Betty can 'elp me, then there's nothing stopping me going at once.'

'I have my reasons,' he said.

'Don't tell me, Hitler's tipped you the wink that he's

visiting the East End after all?' she grinned as she ribbed him about his earlier comment.

'Let's just say it's something like that,' he answered warily. 'Please don't go rushing off without thinking about this, Maisie.'

'I've not decided when or if I'm going yet. But you know me. Once I get a bee in me bonnet I'm likely to do anything, but I promise I'll leave our Ruby here if that makes you 'appier?'

'Slightly happier,' he said seriously, 'but I'd rather you were home here with me.'

Gwyneth slipped her gloved hand into Mike's as they stood staring out over the River Thames to the bank on the other side of the river. The tide was out and ahead she could see a stretch of water with its steel-grey ships and barrage balloons bobbing overhead. But as twilight cast its glow over the river, she thought it was the most romantic place on earth. She'd taken to walking down to the nearby police station to meet Mike when he came off duty. For a few minutes they could be alone together, away from the busy households in Alexandra Road. 'I like this river,' she whispered almost to herself. 'I imagine the ships heading overseas to goodness knows where and then returning home. Or the small tugs going upstream to the port of London and the bright lights and excitement.'

Mike pulled her into his arms. When they were alone like this he was no longer the shy police sergeant; Gwyneth brought out the protector in him. 'Only you can see the magic in this dirty old river,' he smiled down to her. 'Do you know that as a young boy I swam out from this mudbank along with George Caselton? Our mothers gave us what for when we returned home stinking to high heaven.'

Gwyneth smiled. 'I can't imagine you as a small boy.'

'Our parents called us a pair of mudlarks as we always came home with old clay pipes and suchlike we found in the muddy banks. I do believe my haul is still in Dad's garden shed. I'll show you sometime.'

'It looks as though I shall need eyes in the back of my head when our children come along,' Gwyneth chuckled as she snuggled close. There was a nip in the air and she was starting to shiver. She felt his body freeze for a few seconds before he relaxed and held her closer.

'I cherish these moments we have together,' he said before gently brushing her lips with kisses.

Gwyneth sighed. Whenever she mentioned children Mike would change the subject or simply ignore what had been said. Before too long she would need to have this out with him but for now she'd enjoy his kisses. It could wait for another day.

'I'm sorry, Maisie. I'm not sure I can help you with your request,' Betty Billington said to her friend as they sat across the table from each other in Hedley Mitchell's tea rooms just over the road from the Woolworths store. It hurt her not to be able to assist her friend.

In the corner of the room a string quartet was playing a Strauss melody whilst waitresses in black-and-white uniforms scurried about supplying tea and hot water to waiting customers. If it wasn't for the absence of savoury fillings for sandwiches and the usual abundance of pastries, one would hardly know there was a war on, Maisie thought to herself. But try as she might, Maisie's thoughts could not escape the harsh realities of war, as she peered through the crisscross of sticky paper on the windows to catch a glimpse of a woman weeping as her uniformed companion was saying his goodbyes. She nodded quietly. 'It was a silly idea ter even ask you. I'm sorry, Betty. I 'spose I was grasping at straws thinking I could make amends with my parents after all these years.'

Betty was thoughtful. 'Are you sure that it was your mother who worked at the Canning Town branch?'

Maisie shrugged her shoulders. 'I've no reason ter doubt her. There can't be many women called Queenie Dawson who look like me. I just thought it'd be nice for our Ruby to know she had grandparents other than David's mum and dad. Don't get me wrong, they've been pretty decent to me, considering how I legged it ter get back here last Christmas before she was born.'

'How about another pot of tea?'

Maisie nodded. 'Yes please. So, in a way you're the only person who can 'elp me to find me parents,' she added, looking hopefully at Betty.

'Perhaps it is time to build bridges with your family, Maisie, but I'd be in trouble with head office if I gave you information about Woolworths employees. As it is, I'd have to write to the personnel department and ask for your mother's address and they would no doubt want me to explain why I was making the enquiry.'

'I don't want ter get you in trouble,' Maisie said. 'P'raps

it's plain daft of me to want to see them after all this time. They may show me the door but at least I'd have done something,' she added sadly.

'Are you sure they moved away from . . . Bermondsey, was it?'

'Yes. I wrote to let them know when I married my first 'usband and the people who lived in their house answered to say they'd moved away from the area but didn't know where to. I wasn't that bothered at the time as I'd done me best and thought it wasn't ter be but now, with our little Ruby being 'ere, I 'ad this foolish idea of us all being one 'appy family,' she said, looking sad. 'But I never thought they'd move north of the Thames. That seems a bit on the strange side.'

Betty waved to get the notice of the waitress, the full weight of Maisie's dilemma bearing down on her. She too had cut links with her parents when she left home to start work at Woolworths but at least she knew where they were and could send the occasional postcard. How she would dearly have loved her parents to know that she was happily married. But they were long gone. There must be a way she could help Maisie? 'I know!' she finally exclaimed, making the young woman who was clearing their table, ready for the fresh pot of tea, jump out of her skin. 'I know what we can do.'

Maisie grinned in delight as Betty told her she would give a letter of introduction to the manager of the Canning Town branch of Woolworths explaining how Maisie was a valued staff member and friend and hoped her colleague could help her in her search for her family. Jumping to her feet, Maisie rushed round the small tea table and hugged Betty, again startling the same waitress, who was approaching with a laden tray. 'Aw, Betty, I don't know what ter say. This means the world ter me,' she exclaimed, reaching into her brown suede handbag for a handkerchief. 'Are you sure you won't get into trouble?'

Betty smiled and reached for the teapot after thanking the worried waitress. 'I'm doing nothing wrong. A letter of introduction is simply a formal way for a person to be introduced to a mutual friend or colleague. I'll type the letter myself when I get back to the office. Now, drink your tea while it's still hot. I may even attempt to eat one of these biscuits,' she added, looking at the slightly burnt objects that had been placed on the table, even though her stomach lurched at the thought.

'I can't wait to tell David,' Maisie grinned.

'I'm sorry, Maisie, but I'm putting my foot down over this. You're not taking our daughter up to the East End of London and putting her in danger,' David said, slamming his newspaper down by the side of his armchair. 'I thought we'd already discussed this?'

Maisie sighed. She'd cooked her husband a decent meal, although the small piece of steak was as tough as old boots and could possibly have been horsemeat. She'd hoped that after a long day at his desk in London doing God knows what for the RAF she could put him in a good frame of mind before breaking her news.

'I mean it, Maisie, so don't look at me like that. I will not be changing my mind over this,' David fumed.

'But—'

David raised his hand. 'I'll not be swayed on this. What if there's an air raid? Where will you go with a pram and a young baby? It's sheer lunacy. I'm amazed you're even considering taking our child into danger.'

'I want her to meet my parents and for them ter know I'm happily married and settled,' she said quietly, feeling stinging tears threatening to fall. She wasn't one for crying but David's words had really hurt. She held her head high but her chin started to quiver uncontrollably. 'I'm sorry you think so badly of me,' she gulped before turning to walk away.

David leapt from his chair as he saw how distressed his wife was. 'Oh my darling, please don't cry,' he said, pulling her into his arms. 'I don't wish to see either of you in danger. How do you think I'd feel if I waved you off only to hear that the Luftwaffe had taken you from me?'

He caressed her hair as she clung to him and sobbed. 'I'm sorry, David. I'm a bloody fool,' she said when at last she could speak. 'I just had this longing to see my mum and show her our baby. I wanted to tell her how I'd made good . . . and I wanted her to say she's proud of me.'

David sat back in the armchair and pulled his wife onto his lap. Maisie felt safe and secure. 'Maisie love, why not wait a couple of weeks and by then I can get a few days off and accompany you? Then you can impress your mother with your handsome RAF officer husband,' he grinned cheekily. 'But please don't travel with Ruby. London is such a dangerous place right now. I couldn't bear it if anything happened . . .' The smile left his face as he gazed into her eyes. 'Promise me?'

Maisie thought for a moment. 'I promise I won't take

our daughter to London,' she whispered before kissing him deeply. 'I love you, David Carlisle,' she said as he returned her kiss and all thoughts of her parents and Canning Town were swept away by their passion.

'Of course I'll have the little poppet and don't you come rushing back. I've looked after more than my fair share of babies in my time,' Ruby said before returning to coo over her sleeping namesake.

'Are you off somewhere interesting?' Freda asked as she walked into Ruby's front room rubbing the sleep from her eyes. 'You look smart,' she added, admiring Maisie's tweed two-piece suit and jaunty brown felt hat. 'Going somewhere posh with David?'

Maisie shrugged her shoulders. 'Oh, this? It's something I've had at the back of my wardrobe since before the war.' She looked excitedly from Ruby to Freda. 'I'm going up the East End to look fer me parents. Enid reckons Mum was working at Woolies in the East End not long ago.'

Ruby frowned. 'On your own?'

'Why not?' Maisie replied defiantly. 'It's perfectly safe.'

'So safe you're leaving your baby with me?' Ruby answered back quickly. 'Does David know about this?'

'He knows I won't take the little one up ter London,' she replied, trying hard not to look Ruby in the eye. She didn't want to lie to the woman who had been like a mother to her.

Ruby folded her arms over her chest and huffed. 'I thought as much. You and your mad ideas; I'd feel better if you didn't go alone. What are you up to today?' she said to Freda, who was watching the conversation between her friend and her landlady.

'What, me? Nothing really. I've got the day off and I was going to give Bob a hand down the allotment. I'm due at the fire station this evening for a late shift but the past few nights it's been quiet so I might just polish my motor-bike,' she explained.

'Well, get yourself dressed. You can go with Maisie and keep an eye on her for me,' Ruby instructed the young woman. 'You,' she said, giving Maisie a light-hearted glare, as Freda hurried up to her bedroom to change, 'you can come into the kitchen and help yourself to a bowl of por-ridge. It's none too warm out there and I'll feel better knowing the pair of you have gone out with a bit of grub inside you. There's no knowing when you'll get to eat again.'

'What about Bob and the allotment?' Freda called down the steep staircase.

'I'll be helping him so there's no need to worry your-self. Now hurry up or the breakfast will get cold,' Ruby scolded. She was looking forward to walking young Ruby down to where her family shared an allotment with Bob Jackson and his son, Mike. She made a note to bring back a few vegetables for her friend Vera. The woman hadn't looked herself for the past week or so. Even if she was a bit of a curmudgeonly woman, Ruby had a soft spot for her as they'd known each other for many a year. Besides, Vera hadn't had the best of lives. She'd have to get to the bottom of what was bothering her before it festered too long and Vera started to upset people again.

Ruby laughed to herself as she headed to the kitchen. It would be lovely to have a bit of peace and quiet for a few days. What with this blooming war and all the toing and froing in her house, she never knew what would happen next. As it was, she had a feeling in her water about Maisie going to look for her family and she feared the consequences. The girl had been through a lot in her short life and Ruby didn't like to think she was heading into more trouble.

Across the road Enid watched from behind her net curtain as Freda and Maisie left number thirteen. She'd heard that the blonde woman wanted to go and find her mum and hoped beyond hope that mentioning she'd seen Queenie Dawson when she worked at Woolies wouldn't open up a can of worms for Enid and her husband. That would never do.

'That hit the spot nicely,' Bob declared as he drank the last of the tea Ruby had passed to him only minutes before.

'Why don't you park yourself for a few minutes and rest your bones? It can't be comfortable leaning your elbow on that garden spade,' Ruby said from where she sat on a plank of wood Bob had placed on a pile of bricks to form a bench. 'You've been working since breakfast time. Here, I've got a bite to eat for you. I must say, you've done a good job down here. I'm not much of a gardener but even I can see you've made a difference.'

Bob joined Ruby on the bench, passing back the empty mug after throwing the dregs over a nearby compost heap.

'You do look after me well,' he grinned as she delved into her shopping bag and pulled out a sandwich wrapped in a clean tea towel. 'What have we here?' he asked, rubbing his earth-covered hands together.

'It's only meat paste with a touch of pickle but it'll fill your stomach for now,' Ruby answered, wrinkling her nose at his grubby state. 'Is there somewhere to wash yourself before you eat?'

'Only the water butt and there's a layer of slime on top. My next job is to empty it out and give the inside a good scrub before the next rainfall. Mind you, that oil drum is so old it may well fall apart if I'm not careful. I'll have to ask the lads down the docks if they've got something to replace it with,' he said, biting into the sandwich.

Ruby shook her head before getting to her feet to check on the baby. 'She's not an ounce of trouble, bless her,' she said, checking the baby was tucked in tightly under her blankets in the pram. Although there was a watery sun in the sky, the March air had quite a nip to it. 'I don't know how you can work out here in just your shirtsleeves, Bob Jackson. You'll catch your death one of these days,' she chided him as she took the makeshift seat next to him.

Bob laughed and cuffed away stray crumbs of the grey-coloured National bread from his mouth using the back of his hand. 'You'd miss me if I did, Ruby.'

'No doubt I would but don't push your luck,' she joshed.

They sat in companionable silence until Bob finished the last mouthful. 'I've been meaning to have a bit of a word with you,' he said seriously. 'I've had an idea and wanted to run it past you first . . .'

Ruby held her breath. She hoped he wasn't about to bring up the subject of them getting married again. He'd hinted at it a few times since Gwyneth and Mike became serious and she knew it would make sense as then he could move into number thirteen with her and the couple could live across the road in Mike's house. But, if truth be known, she wasn't so sure she should have accepted Bob's ring last Christmas or promised to be his wife. She'd ducked and dived whenever she felt he was about to broach the subject but here, alone in the quiet allotment close to Erith recreational ground, she couldn't think of a way to tell him. Perhaps she should suggest they remained good friends for now . . . 'Bob, I—'

He raised his hand. 'Let me get this said before I lose my nerve.'

Ruby frowned. He wasn't one for being nervous.

'I've been pondering on this for a while now and think it's time we got a pig . . .'

Ruby burst out laughing. There was her thinking she had to fight off his attention and all the time he'd been hankering after getting a pig.

'I don't think it's a laughing matter, Ruby. You wouldn't say no to a nice slice of roast pork with some crispy crackling on top, would you?'

Ruby's mouth watered at the thought. 'I most definitely would not say no to that.'

'I'm thinking we could start a pig club. One of the lads at the police station started a club with his family. There's a bit of red tape to be got through but I reckon it's worthwhile.'

'Where would we keep it? I know some people are

keeping animals in their gardens but if you'd bothered to read the deeds to Mike's house, it says that no one can keep pigs in Alexandra Road. Not that we've got the room,' she added.

'I've already checked it out. The small print also says we can't run an alehouse but I know of a few who brew their own,' he grinned. 'I wondered about speaking to your Pat? If we cut her and John into the club, perhaps they'd have room for it on the farm where they live?'

'I don't know, Bob. That old chap they work for can be a miserable bugger. I'd not want them to jeopardize John's job or the home that goes with it. Where would they go with all those kiddies?'

Bob smiled to himself. Trust Ruby to overthink the situation. 'We're only talking about one pig, Ruby. I wondered about asking Maureen, your George and Irene, as well as Maisie and David to join us, and perhaps that new couple who've moved in across the road from you. What do you think?'

'I do believe you've already planned the whole thing, Bob,' she answered, getting to her feet. 'But with all your planning you've forgotten one person.'

'Who's that?' he asked. 'I included Sarah and Alan in with Maureen as they live with her.'

'You've left out Vera. If we don't include her, she'll only moan and invite herself to eat at my house so we may as well let her join us. Besides, I'll never hear the end of it if we don't.'

Bob took a well-worn notebook from the pocket of his work trousers and licked the end of the stub of pencil he had behind one ear. 'Consider her included. At this rate it's going to have to be an exceedingly large pig,' he grinned.

'Well, I can't sit about chatting all day. I need to get this young lady back home – she's been out long enough. Can you spare any vegetables to pad out a stew for tonight's meal? I'd be ever so grateful,' she said, eying the barren-looking patch of land.

'I'm ahead of you there,' Bob said, walking over to the small shed on the corner of the plot made up of a hotch-potch of old doors and planks of wood. 'I was going to ask Freda to take them back with her but she hasn't turned up yet. Still in bed, I suppose?'

Ruby slapped her hand to her mouth. 'I completely forgot to tell you. Freda's going up to London with Maisie; that's why I'm caring for this little one today. Sorry, Bob.'

'Not to worry. I'm sure a shopping trip is preferable to digging over a patch of land on a cold March day.'

'Oh, she's not shopping. In fact, I told her to go with Maisie to make sure she doesn't get into any scrapes. That girl can attract problems like I don't know what.' Ruby went on to explain to Bob how Maisie was intent on find-ing her parents and was taking herself off to Canning Town on a whim.

'Canning Town, eh?' Bob said thoughtfully. 'That'll be a trip and a half. Let's hope Adolf doesn't have any plans on for today so they get back home before it gets dark. I wonder what David has to say about all this?'

'I get the impression he doesn't know so we can expect fireworks at some point.' Ruby sighed. 'But that's their business. I said I'd look after the nipper here and I'm more than glad to do so,' she added, picking up her bag where Bob had collected together a few sorry-looking vegetables. 'I just want those girls home and safe, and as soon as possible.'

3

Freda and Maisie settled down in their seats as the train left Erith station and headed towards Woolwich.

'When did you last see your mum?' Freda asked as she picked up a newspaper left on the seat beside her.

'It's been quite a while,' Maisie replied, wiping the window with her glove. She swore out loud as she spotted the grime it had left and attempted to rub away the mark. 'It was before I married my Joe.' She didn't wish to say any more, fearing her young friend would be startled by what her past life had been like. She'd never told her friend all of what happened before she knew them. Coming to Erith had been the start of a new life, even if she did lose her first husband soon after at the hands of the Germans. 'Let's just say I think it's about time I put the past behind me and got to know them again. There's also my brother, Fred. I'd like to see him. Why, he could have a family of his own by now and Ruby could have cousins. Little Ruby needs to know all her family. If meeting Sarah and her family has taught me anything, it's that we need our family around us.'

'We are very lucky indeed,' Freda agreed. 'Do you have any other family?'

Maisie shrugged her shoulders. 'Quite a few aunts and uncles; Mum and Dad both come from large families. Not that I've seen any of them. They're scattered all over the place,' she added quickly. 'How about you? Do you plan to see your mum again any day soon?'

Freda shook her head sadly. 'My brother Lenny reckons he'll head up to Birmingham and see Mum next time he's on leave but God knows when that'll be. His ship always seems to be on the other side of the world.'

'Wouldn't you like to see her again?'

Freda stared out of the window, not taking in the scenery as she was consumed by thoughts of her past life before she headed to Erith and her new life.

Freda remained silent, leading Maisie to ask, 'Was it that bad?'

Freda nodded, unable to speak, and was thankful when the train pulled into Abbey Wood station and a group of women entered the carriage. Deep down she ached to see her mum but with that bully of a second husband around she dared not return home. All she could think about was a time when her dad was still alive – yes, they had been poor but they had also been happy.

Both Freda and Maisie remained deep in thought as they continued their journey. Eventually the train arrived at their destination, Woolwich Arsenal.

'We'd best be lively or the train will set off before we're on the platform,' Maisie urged as she picked up her bag and gloves from the seat next to her and reached for her jacket that had been laid carefully on the parcel rack above their heads. 'I was miles away there. If we don't get off here, we'll have to stay on the train until we get to

Charing Cross and then get the underground train back to the East End.'

Freda shuddered as she grabbed her things and followed Maisie onto the platform, assisted by a man waiting to take her seat. She nodded her thanks before hurrying to catch up with her friend who was already striding off down the platform. 'Thank goodness we did get off. I can't think of anything worse than being on the underground. What if something happened?'

'Like what?' Maisie grinned as she reached into her handbag for her ticket. 'You are a funny thing. Are you sure you'll be okay walking through the foot tunnel under the Thames?'

'I hadn't thought of that,' Freda said, looking glum.

Maisie slowed down and looked at her young friend. 'You do look a bit green about the gills. I tell you what, let's hurry through and then look for a cafe on the other side and have a cuppa? I'll treat you to a fried egg sandwich as well.'

Freda grinned. 'You're on,' she declared as the two women headed to the entrance of the foot tunnel at a brisk pace, overtaking people in front of them. Freda knew there was as much chance of enjoying a fried egg sandwich as there was of finding hens' teeth but she knew Maisie meant well and a cup of tea would go down very well indeed.

'Betty, you look exhausted,' Sarah said as she entered the Woolworths manager's small office. 'Do you think you're going down with something?'

Betty gave a wan smile as she looked up at Sarah. 'I do hope not. I seem to have lost all my energy of late. Goodness knows what's come over me,' she said wearily, indicating to Sarah to take a seat on the other side of her desk. 'Between you and me, I'm finding it hard to keep up with work and my home life.'

Sarah checked the door to the office was firmly shut and sat down opposite her boss and good friend. 'I've been thinking I could take on some extra hours now that Alan is away on duty. In fact, that's what I popped in to discuss with you,' she offered.

Betty reached for the staff rota she'd been marking up and looked at the days where she was short of sales and warehouse staff. 'I could certainly do with the help but can you spare the time?'

Sarah nodded her head enthusiastically. 'I've had a word with Nan and she said she could have Georgina for a few extra hours, and with Mum living nearby, she's always saying she doesn't see enough of her granddaughter. I thought I'd bite the bullet and ask if she'd like to help out one day a week,' she grinned.

Betty looked slightly shocked. 'I'm pleased you're closer to your mum these days, Sarah, but I'm surprised you've reached the point of asking her to care for Georgina. I know myself how tiring a child can be and my stepdaughters are much older than your little poppet.'

'I've got my reasons for wanting to work more hours and if that means Mum having Georgie more often, then so be it,' Sarah said, lifting her chin defiantly.

Betty reached across the desk and patted Sarah's hand. 'Good for you. I do like to see a woman play a part in their marriage that goes beyond caring for a child. Now tell me, what are you up to?'

Sarah grinned. 'I've been thinking of when the war ends and how our lives will be. Alan and I would really like to have more children and we can't expect his mum to keep putting us up. She only has that two-up, two-down in Crayford Road and it isn't for us to take over her home with little ones.'

Betty agreed. She knew Maureen Gilbert well and how much she loved her son and his family dearly, but would they be as happy if they were crammed together under one tiny roof? 'Maureen has been good to you,' she said, nodding to Sarah to continue. 'So, what's your plan?'

'I thought that if I could put a little away each week, then by the time the war ended we would be in a position to rent our own house and Alan would be able to start back at Woolworths without worrying about money,' she said with a smile.

Betty thought for a moment. 'Sarah, do you honestly believe that Alan will be happy to return to Woolworths and perhaps one day manage his own store? He has seen a world outside of this small town, and that can change a person. I also wonder how a man would feel knowing it was his wife's wages that had paid for their home? The war has changed things a lot but even so, a man is head of the household and as such should have the say in what happens in his family.'

'I'd thought of that,' Sarah said. 'Alan is a proud man and would hate to think I was the one who had paid the deposit to rent a new home or a few sticks of furniture.

So, instead I shall say that I've been careful with the money he sends home to me.'

'That's an excellent idea,' Betty said. 'Let's just hope that this war is over soon and Alan is home with you for good.'

'Nan says it will be over by Christmas but she's been saying that since 1939 and it hasn't ended yet,' Sarah laughed.

Betty joined in with the laughter, thinking that as much as her dear friend hoped that life would go back to the way it had been before the start of war, she knew that wouldn't be the case. Men had tasted life away from their homes and women had become free of the restraints of the kitchen. Life was certain to be different.

'I wonder if Gwyneth would be interested in working a few more hours, what with planning for her wedding?' Sarah suggested. 'It would fill in a few gaps in your rota if she agreed.'

'I'll pop down to the shop floor and catch her for a word now,' Betty said, getting to her feet and reaching to a shelf behind her desk. 'If you could check these stock sheets for me in case I've added up a column incorrectly, it would be a weight off my shoulders. Oh my . . .' she added, putting a hand to her forehead before slumping back into her chair.

'Betty, whatever is wrong?' Sarah said in distress as she rushed to her friend's side and placed her hand on Betty's shoulder.

'I came over faint for a moment,' Betty said. 'I'm fine now.'

'No you're not,' Sarah said, noting how pale Betty

looked. 'Why, you're as white as a ghost and you're trembling all over. You really ought to see a doctor.'

Betty smiled and took Sarah's hand, giving it a squeeze. 'I do believe I know what he'll say,' she added with a whisper, a pink spot appearing on her cheeks showing her embarrassment. 'I do believe Douglas and I are expecting a little visitor.'

Sarah frowned. Whatever did Betty mean? Then she too went a little pink as she realized what she was being told.

'Oh my! Why, that's wonderful news, Betty. I'm thrilled for you. What does Douglas say?'

'I've not told him yet. I do have an appointment to see my doctor later today and thought it best not to say anything until I know for sure. You know what men are like and Douglas is such a dear he's bound to make a fuss.'

'Would you like me to accompany you?' Sarah said at once. Betty's shock news had made her think about the Woolworths manager having a child. Wasn't she too old? She'd never given Betty's age a thought until now.

'I'd be so grateful if you would. I'd been a little afraid you would laugh at my news, what with me being so much older than you,' Betty said shyly.

'I'd not given it a thought,' Sarah answered at once, hoping that her face had not shown otherwise. 'Now, let me get you a cup of tea and you're to take things easy until we go to see your doctor.'

'Are you sure you don't mind me leaving baby Ruby with you while I pop down to see Vera?' Ruby asked Bob as he stood at the kitchen sink wearing one of Ruby's aprons while he washed up the plates from their dinner. It wasn't as much to keep him dry as to cover his dirty gardening clothes.

'Off you go, the baby's as right as rain with me. Don't forget I helped out when I had one of me own,' he told her with a grin.

'Who is now a strapping police sergeant about to be married and with a ready-made family. You might be a bit out of practice,' she laughed.

'Be off with you, woman. If she wakes and starts to cry, I'll push the pram down to you if I can't cope. How's that?'

'You do that, Bob,' Ruby grinned, wondering how long it would be before he came hurrying up to Vera's house with a wailing baby. There again, she'd just been fed so would be out for the count for a good while. Ruby wasn't one for giving a kiddie National Dried Milk but little Ruby seemed to be thriving on it. She collected the vegetables she'd set aside from what she'd brought home from their allotment along with a dish of what Freda called 'lucky pie' – you'd be lucky if you found a lump of meat in it – and headed out the front door.

Vera's house was further up Alexandra Road and a mirror image to Ruby's home. However, the similarity ended there, as anyone walking into Ruby's house would be faced with a warm welcome and a cosy home whereas Vera's was full of knick-knacks and had a cold atmosphere. She knocked on the door, wondering with a sinking heart what tales of woe Vera would relate to her today.

'Hello, Ruby, come on in. Excuse the mess. I've not

been up to doing much housework lately,' Vera said as she led the way through to the living room.

Ruby was surprised as usually all guests were shown into the bay-windowed front room where Vera could show off her latest ornament or photograph of her grand-daughter. Vera seldom took her through to the back of the house and Ruby was shocked by the general air of neglect to her friend's house. The gloom of the room was not helped by the part-closed curtains which blocked out what there was of the early March light.

'I'll let some light in, shall I?' Ruby said, putting the veg and pie down on a cluttered table and heading to the single window. Pulling back the green cotton fabric, she was even more surprised to see that the nets needed a wash and the window a good going-over with vinegar and newspaper. Vera wasn't one to let standards drop. Something must be amiss.

'Are you all right?' she asked her friend, who had sat down at the table without offering Ruby a seat. 'I've not seen much of you lately so thought I'd pay a visit. There's some pie here and Bob brought back more veg than I can use and I thought you'd be grateful.'

'I am, Ruby,' Vera said as she took the clean tea towel off the pie tin to look at the contents. She licked her lips.

Ruby was puzzled. Usually Vera would criticize the food before taking it anyway. She wasn't one to accept anything gratefully. Something didn't add up here. 'Shall I put the kettle on and stick this in the oven to warm?' Ruby asked, starting to slide the enamel dish away from Vera.

'No, I'll eat it as it is,' Vera said, pulling the dish close and breaking off a piece of the potato crust.

'Then I'll stick the kettle on and make us a cuppa. Perhaps you'd like a fork?' she called over her shoulder.

What met Ruby in the small kitchen made her want to weep. She placed the filled kettle on the gas stove but try as she might, there was no getting a light underneath. 'What's up with your gas?' she called out as she turned to open the cupboard where Vera kept the tea caddy. Not only was the caddy empty but there wasn't a crumb of food to be seen. Becoming more puzzled by the minute, Ruby checked the stone pantry, thinking there would at least be some milk or perhaps a slice or two of bacon or cheese in the meat safe. Again, there wasn't any food to be found. 'What's going on?' she asked, marching back into the living room to see Vera licking the empty dish clean.

Vera looked up at Ruby and slowly her face crumpled. She put her head in her hands as muffled words came tumbling out. 'I don't have a penny to my name. If there were still poorhouses, I'd be living in one right now. I'm destitute, Ruby, and I don't know what to do.'

'Well, I'll be buggered,' Ruby said as she pulled a chair from the table and sat opposite the trembling woman. 'What happened to the bit of pension you got from your Don's firm when he died?'

'The dairy got bombed out six months back and there's no money for the likes of me. It wasn't much but it put food on the table,' Vera said, looking at the empty dish. 'It was good of you to bring that down for me. I've not eaten properly for over a week now as I've not had a coin to put into the meter, not that I have anything to put on the hob.'

Ruby couldn't believe what she was hearing. Was this really happening in the street where she lived and to someone she considered to be a friend, however irritating Vera could be at times? Had she missed something? Perhaps Vera had tried to tell her and she'd been so caught up in her own life that it had washed past her?

'I haven't told anybody, I'm that ashamed that I couldn't manage on my own.' Vera started to cry, wiping her face on a grubby apron. 'I've not even been able to heat a drop of water to wash my clothes.'

Ruby left her seat and held her friend while she cried. 'Well, you've told me now and a trouble shared is a trouble halved, as my Eddie used to say. We can sort this out so don't you go fretting yourself. First, you're going to come home with me. I'll get the tin bath in and you can have a nice soak while I make us a cuppa. Then you're going to tell me everything.'

Vera nodded. 'That's good of you, Ruby, but I don't want anyone else knowing my problems.'

'Don't you worry. There'll be no one home to bother us. Gwyneth's at work and Freda's gone out with Maisie for the day. Once we get back to number thirteen I'll relieve Bob of baby Ruby and we'll have the house to ourselves.'

'You'll not say anything about my . . . about my problem, will you?'

'I hardly know what your problem is yet so don't you worry. Now, get yourself a clean set of clothes and your dressing gown and we'll get cracking. In fact, you can stay the night with me. It's blooming chilly in here and I'll not rest in my bed knowing you're catching your death up the other end of the road.'

'It was the coalman. He wouldn't give me any more tick. I burnt a few bits of wood from the garden but they soon ran out . . .' Vera muttered as she headed to the foot of the stairs before stopping. 'Thank you, Ruby,' she added, then turned and hurried up the stairs.

It was then that Ruby knew Vera really had problems, as she'd never said thank you before and hadn't asked what Maisie and Freda were up to.

Whatever next? she thought to herself.

'Blimey, I didn't expect to have that put in front of me,' Freda said as she wiped her mouth with her handkerchief. 'A full fry-up! Even Ruby hasn't managed that in the past few years. Wherever did he get the bacon, let alone proper eggs?'

Maisie, who had just finished a sausage sandwich and was busy lighting a cigarette, grinned at her friend. 'You're in the middle of the docklands now, Freda. People can get hold of almost anything down here. That's if you know the right people.' She winked as she tapped the side of her nose.

The girls had hurried down the hundred steps and through the pedestrian foot tunnel under the Thames as fast as they could, what with Freda being a little worried that the river would burst through and drown them both. Even though Maisie had laughed at her friend's fear, she couldn't help but jump as droplets of water ran down the tiled walls and both had breathed a sigh of relief when they'd stepped out into the grey morning daylight of north Woolwich, slightly breathless from the climb up the circular staircase. Maisie had steered Freda along a short footpath that brought them to the busy Thames where they'd found the rather shabby-looking cafe.

'Have you got any idea how we get to Canning Town from here?' Freda asked.

'Leave it with me. I'll ask the chap behind the counter when I pay him,' Maisie said, stubbing out her cigarette and picking up the scrap of paper that had been left on the table when he brought out their food.

'Please, let me pay something. I swear I ate twice as much as you,' Freda said, reaching for her handbag.

'No, this is on me. You'd not be 'ere if it wasn't for me and my hare-brained scheme, as David calls it. Finish your tea and I'll see you outside.'

Freda gulped down the remains of the strong brew and went outside. She'd love to have stood and watched the ships being loaded and the cranes at work. No wonder Hitler was intent on bombing the docks so often, what with so much going on there. She shivered as she pulled on her woollen mittens and tightened the matching scarf around her neck. She could feel the start of a chilly drizzle and hoped the rain didn't come down with any force.

'Ready?' Maisie asked as she joined her. 'We've only got to walk up to the road and there'll be a bus stop where we can get one of two buses that'll take us within walking distance of Woolies. We'll be there within half an hour.' Maisie put up her umbrella and the two girls linked arms and hurried to the bus stop.

*

'It's so good of you to accompany me,' Betty said as she sat beside Sarah in the busy waiting room.

'Don't be daft. What's a friend for if not to lend a hand when a friend is in need?' Sarah said, giving a small giggle. 'I sound like Freda with her Brownie pack.'

'I'm glad you're here,' Betty said with a nervous smile. 'This is not something I expected to be seeing a doctor about at my time of life. I feel like a fraud.'

'Don't be daft, Betty. You should be excited to welcome a baby into the world at . . .'

'At my time of life?'

'I didn't mean . . .' Sarah stumbled over her words.

'Sarah, my dear, I've been thinking the same as you. Why me and why now?'

'Could it be because you're now married?' Sarah giggled, her cheeks turning a delicate shade of pink.

'That could well be the answer,' Betty agreed, joining in with Sarah's mirth. 'However, I'm not sure what my stepdaughters will think of this. Clemmie has been more than a little hard to live with these days.'

'It must be difficult for the girls to accept another woman as their mother.'

'I sat them down and had a chat about the part I would play in their lives. I made it quite clear that I would not be replacing their mother and I would help them keep her memory alive. I've placed Clementine's portrait on the wall in their bedroom and they've both shared out her jewellery and personal items. On her birthday and the anniversary of her death I encourage Douglas to take the girls to visit her grave and to have some time together. I don't see what more I can do.'

Sarah was saved from commenting on Betty's predicament as at that moment her friend's name was called out and she headed to an oak door at the side of the waiting room to see her doctor.

Sarah watched Betty disappear from view and hoped with all her heart that her friend would have good news. How they would cope with Betty giving up work if she was expecting was another question. What if head office sent some horrid person to take charge of the Erith store? She may just decide to stop working if that was the case and devote herself to her daughter and home. She'd still be able to do her war work until she and Alan were blessed with an addition to their happy little family.

It didn't seem like five minutes since she'd been sitting in another doctor's surgery waiting for Maisie to emerge with her good news that a baby was on the way. She could still see her face now. How they'd celebrated, and look at her now: the proud mother of baby Ruby Freda Carlisle. There's nothing more special than news of another life coming into the world and even Hitler and this bloody war couldn't stop that joy. She dug into her shopping bag and pulled out her knitting as she smiled to herself. Hadn't she done exactly the same while waiting for Maisie when she was in seeing her doctor? Sarah sat contentedly knitting what would be a navy blue cardigan for Georgina. She had some scraps of wool in her sewing box and thought about embroidering a few daisies down the front to brighten it up. She could do another for Gwyneth's daughter, Myfi. The two girls were close friends, even though there was five years between their ages.

She was deep in thought as her needles click-clacked

away and the arm she was knitting had grown several inches when the door to the doctor's room opened and an ashen-faced Betty appeared. She quietly thanked the doctor and headed towards the door to the street. Sarah leapt to her feet, stuffing her knitting into her bag, not caring if stitches slipped from the needles, and hurried after her friend. This didn't look like good news.

4

'Now, is the water hot enough? I'll put the kettle on so you can have a top-up,' Ruby said as she dipped a finger into the tin bath she'd earlier placed in front of the coal fire in her living room. 'If we hang your towels over the clothes horse alongside your dressing gown, they'll be nice and warm for when you're ready to climb out. It'll also give you some privacy in case any of the girls come bursting in unannounced.'

Vera looked alarmed and stopped unbuttoning her cardigan. 'Are they likely to?'

'Not to my knowledge but you never know in this house with so many people coming and going. I'm not expecting Maisie and Freda back anytime early so you should be all right. I've told Bob to scarper as well.' She smiled. The mere mention of Vera and the tin bath was enough to see him racing back up the allotment. 'Now, I'm going to sit in the front room for a while and listen to the radio. You have the room to yourself and I shan't come back through until you give me a shout. Then we can have a bite to eat and a little chat.'

'Thank you, Ruby, you're a good friend and that's not a

word of a lie,' Vera said as she again started to unbutton her cardigan. Ruby headed to the front room, pulling the door closed behind her.

She picked up her knitting and settled down to concentrate on the tricky heel of a pair of grey socks she was making for Bob. He seemed to go through them quicker than a dose of salts. As the needles worked their magic, she began to wonder about Vera and her predicament. Their husbands had been great friends, serving together in the last war and often drinking together down the working men's club. Even in retirement they met up to play bowls and while away their time. If truth were known, it was their husbands, Eddie and Don, who had been friends. Ruby had tolerated Vera and classed her more as someone who lived in Alexandra Road than a friend and confidante. It had only been when the two men passed away within months of each other that she had begun to look beyond the busybody persona and saw a very lonely woman. Vera might brag at times about her granddaughter but in truth the girl was not home very often and had little interest in her grandmother. Vera had never been well-off but the solid three-bedroom house was now in her name and from what Ruby was led to understand, Vera had a few bob tucked away, which was more than many other widowed women of a similar age. What on earth had happened for Vera to have retreated into her shell as she had? Ruby felt it was her duty to find out what had left her in such a predicament.

*

'Ta, ducks,' Maisie called over her shoulder as the bus pulled away, leaving the two friends on the pavement of the busy street.

'That was good of the conductress to tell us where to get off,' Freda said. 'We could have been sitting on the bus for God knows how long. She said it was a little way up here. Or was it down there?' She sighed, putting her hands on her hips and staring about in bewilderment. 'Can you remember where Woolies is?' she asked Maisie, who was checking her face in the mirror of a small gold compact.

'I'll be blowed if I know. I've never been ter Canning Town in me life, even though I'm supposed to 'ave family living nearby. We'd best ask,' she said, closing the compact and putting it away in her handbag before marching into a nearby tobacconist's shop. She emerged a couple of minutes later and headed up the street with Freda close on her heels. 'It's only a few hundred yards up here. If we'd stepped into the road, we would have seen it.'

'And most likely got run over,' Freda puffed as her short legs worked overtime to keep up with her friend. Canning Town was much busier than Erith, with horses and carts as well as the occasional trades van making deliveries to the shops and businesses. 'Did you happen to ask if there was an air-raid shelter nearby? I wouldn't like us to get caught out if a siren should sound.'

'Don't be daft,' Maisie grinned at her chum as she slowed down to allow her to catch up. 'We'll just follow everyone else. Mind you, I doubt if the Luftwaffe are going to return anytime soon. There's not much left to bomb, is there?'

Freda agreed. 'They've taken a bit of a bashing. I suppose it being so close to the docks. We've got off light compared to this town. Look, there's Woolworths up ahead. Do you want to go straight in or take a few minutes to prepare yourself?'

'Let's get it over with. I didn't come all this way to stand about dithering,' Maisie said as she boldly marched through the double doors of the store and stopped dead, causing Freda to almost walk into her. 'Blimey, we could be back in Erith,' she declared, looking at the polished mahogany counters and wooden floors. 'They've even got the same light fittings.'

Freda grinned as she looked around her. 'We only need Betty and Sarah to appear and it'll be exactly like Erith. Do you suppose the staff area is in the same place?'

'We won't find out standing here. Let's ask someone.'

'There's a cleaner over there, let's ask her,' Freda pointed. The store may look the same as their own workplace but she felt intimidated by the busy staff behind the counters and didn't wish to approach them. Did Maisie and her other colleagues look as efficient?

'Excuse me, love,' Maisie said to the woman who was busy polishing one of the many glass doors that fronted the shop. 'I'm here to see a Miss Cuthbertson. Would you know where I can find 'er?'

The woman gave Maisie a sideways look and, without stopping what she was doing, nodded to a door marked 'staff'. 'You'll find her majesty in there somewhere,' she muttered.

'It's the manager I'm after, not the Queen,' Maisie said with a smile.

'Well, this one acts like the blooming Queen with all her orders and rules. I've seen four managers run this place since I started work here and she's the worst of the lot. I've told my old man I've had enough. It would be more peaceful working in munitions and that's where I'm off to come payday. She can scrub the bloody floors and polish the windows herself for all I care,' she added, turning back to her polishing.

The girls thanked her, trying hard not to giggle. They walked through the door and that was where the similarity to their own workplace stopped. There were no stairs to start with, and they were faced with a busy storeroom area. 'Now where do we go?' Freda said, feeling a little afraid. She had been wondering why someone would call the manager 'her majesty?' Did it mean she was posh? But then Betty was a bit on the posh side and she was a lovely boss? She no longer felt as though she wanted to giggle.

'What are you doing in here? You do know we don't like civilians behind the scenes?' a female voice rattled across the room, sounding rather like a parade-ground sergeant major.

Freda felt her chin almost hit the ground as she spotted a tall rotund woman holding a broom dressed in what could be either a boiler suit or a very severe siren suit. She was nothing like the backroom staff at their Woolies.

'Er, we're looking for the manager, Miss Cuthbertson. Can you tell us where she is, love?' Maisie said, trying to be as friendly as possible.

'I'm Cuthbertson,' the woman boomed, walking towards them. 'What do you want?'

Freda heard Maisie whisper, 'Bugger,' almost underneath her breath before she delved into her bag and pulled out the letter of introduction that Betty had typed out neatly and placed into an envelope embossed with the Woolworths name. 'We've come from the Erith, Kent, store. Our manager, Mrs Billington, has written this,' she said, holding out the envelope.

'Follow me,' the woman said as she marched off, leading them through several doors and along corridors until they reached a room bearing exactly the same sign that adorned Betty's office, 'manageress'. They followed the woman inside. That was where any similarities ended as Miss Cuthbertson's domain was filled with heap upon heap of files and cardboard boxes full of stock. She noticed Freda's startled look and barked, 'There's a war on, don't you know? It's all hands to the pumps. I have no time for women who sit on their backsides in offices. We need to roll up our sleeves and work as hard as the menfolk do. Now is not the time for shillyshallying.'

Freda nodded. She much preferred Betty's way of running a store and knew that head office approved of her working methods. Didn't the last area manager say as much? She wished she was back in Erith right now and felt sorry for the staff of this branch of Woolworths.

Miss Cuthbertson scanned the letter without inviting the girls to sit down. Not that there was a chair without something stacked on it. She gazed at Maisie and frowned. 'You do have the look of Queenie Dawson about you.'

'So you know my mum?' Maisie asked with hope building up inside her. She hadn't realized just how much she hoped this woman could help her.

'I wouldn't say I knew her that well but I knew of her. She worked here when I first came to this branch. I have no idea what became of her.'

Maisie's heart plummeted. She'd hoped for better news. 'Would you possibly have an address in your filing cabinet?' she asked.

Miss Cuthbert frowned. 'Even though you have this letter I'm not at liberty to give out information about former employees, I'm sorry.'

Maisie shrugged her shoulders. 'It's not your fault. I don't want anyone to get into trouble. In a way, I'm just clutching at straws 'ere.'

Freda stepped forward. She wasn't going to leave this room until Maisie knew where her Mum lived, and she held her chin up defiantly. 'Would it hurt that much for her to be given an inkling as to where her parents lived . . . a street name perhaps? Maisie could ask around and then you wouldn't be to blame . . . ?'

The woman stared at Freda for a moment, summing up her words. 'I'm sorry, it's more than my job's worth. Now, if you'll excuse me, I have a store to run.' She opened the door, indicating that the girls should leave.

Freda had never felt so angry in her life. 'But she only wants to find her mum. What's wrong with that? How can you be so hard-hearted?'

Freda quaked in her boots as Miss Cuthbertson turned and gave her a hard stare. 'Young lady, I can assure you I am not a hard-hearted woman. However, I do have the welfare of my staff to consider and that includes past staff as well. How would you feel if the manageress of your store gave your personal details freely to anyone who came calling?'

Freda frowned. 'That's not the same thing at all. Mrs Billington detailed Maisie's problem in her letter. Surely you can help somehow?'

Maisie took her young friend by the arm. 'Come on, Freda. We're wasting our time here. Let's try our luck somewhere else.'

'But where are we going to try our luck?' Freda asked as she hurried after Maisie.

'Where we should have started ten minutes ago,' Maisie said as they stepped into the bustling shop area. She headed to where the cleaning lady was still buffing the glass doors.

'I've got no idea what you are going on about,' Freda grumbled.

'Excuse me,' Maisie said, tapping the woman on the shoulder.

'I take it she gave you short shrift?' the older woman asked, throwing her cleaning cloth to the ground and stretching her back with a groan.

'You could say that,' Maisie said in her sweetest voice. 'I'm looking for my mum. She used to work here a while back. You may know her? The name's Dawson ... Queenie Dawson. Would you remember her by any chance?'

Freda started to grin. Maisie never missed a trick. It was a shame they hadn't thought to ask this woman first, then they wouldn't have had to face Miss Cuthbertson.

The woman thought for a moment. 'D'yer mean Queenie what lives down Bethnal Green way? Come to think of it, you look a bit like her,' she said, giving Maisie a hard stare.

'That's her,' Maisie said, hoping that in fact her parents did live near Bethnal Green. 'Do you 'appen to know the road or the house where she lives?' she added, crossing her fingers that the woman did indeed know.

She thought for a moment. 'No . . . it's gone. But no doubt her or her old man would drink down the Salmon and Ball pub, you could ask there.'

'The Salmon and Ball? Where would that be?'

'Where do you come from? Everyone knows that pub. It's opposite the underground station. You know, the one that ain't open yet, not that I'd go down those things. I'll stay out in the sunlight,' she added, turning back to her cleaning.

'We've come from Kent,' Maisie said with a grin, 'that's why we don't know our way around.'

The woman looked back over her shoulder as she picked up her cloth. 'I thought you was a bit on the posh side.'

Maisie had already started to walk towards the door following other shoppers, who were avoiding the clean-ing lady as she worked, but Freda held back. 'I wonder if you know someone else? Enid Singleton? She used to work here along with her husband. You may recall her, as she walks with a limp?'

'She didn't go by that name when I knew her,' the woman said with a haughty look. 'You want to keep clear of that one. Nothing but trouble, I can tell you.'

Freda turned and hurried after Maisie, who was now

holding the door open waiting for her friend. Whatever did the woman mean?

'I feel so much better for that,' Vera said as she sat down with her cup of tea in Ruby's front room.

'You've got a bit of colour back in your cheeks as well,' Ruby nodded. Vera looked comfortable wrapped up in her dressing gown with a towel around her head.

'Now, tuck into that sandwich while we have our chat. It's only Spam but it'll fill your stomach. I've put a bit of the chutney in that we made last summer.' She could almost see Vera's mouth start to water as she put her cup and saucer down beside her and tucked into the grey sandwich.

'I'll be glad when we have white bread again,' Ruby sighed.

'That doesn't bother me,' Vera said through a full mouthful. 'This is delicious.'

Ruby shook her head. This wasn't the Vera she knew. By now she would usually have commented on the thickness of the Spam, the colour of the bread and how her own chutney was better than anyone else's at the WVS. 'Now, why not tell me what's led to this sorry state of affairs? Correct me if I'm wrong but I thought your Don had left you without too many problems. I know he was always careful with money.'

'He was and I'm better off than most as I've got a roof over my head as well as the bit of old-age pension. I won't say that my Sadie's rent didn't come in handy when she lived with me but then I had to help her out with a, erm . . . problem and things started to go downhill pretty fast.'

Ruby frowned. 'Why didn't you say something to me? I could have helped you out. I don't like to think of anyone struggling when I can do something. I don't have much myself but I'll not see anyone suffer.'

Vera shook her head violently, causing the towel to slip onto her shoulders and strands of grey hair to fall over her eyes. 'No, I don't want to be beholden to anyone. It's not in my nature. Borrowing money is a sure way to lose a friend. I'd rather starve first.'

'And you damn near have,' Ruby said angrily, and she leant over and took the empty plate from Vera so she could sort herself out. 'It's time to put your cards on the table so we can see a way to sort out your problems, and no, it won't be lending you money if that's not what you want. We've got the place to ourselves apart from baby Ruby so we can come up with a plan for the future. First, you need to trust me and tell me what's up with your grand-daughter. I take it a man's involved somewhere along the line? I promise to keep things to myself unless you say otherwise.'

Vera thought for a moment. 'You're a good woman, Ruby Caselton. I trust you to know my problem, even though I'm ashamed to tell it.'

Ruby checked the teapot on the tea tray she'd carried into the room. 'This has gone cold. Let me make a fresh brew and then we can chat more. I have a slice or two of sponge cake in the pantry that our Sarah brought round. Why don't we polish that off at the same time?'

Vera gave a weak smile. 'You're truly blessed with your

family. I don't know what I've done that mine have turned out so bad. I really don't know,' she added, searching for a cotton handkerchief in the pocket of her dressing gown to wipe away the tears that were forming.

'Well, you can stop that for a start. You're made of sterner stuff and all you need is a plan and you'll soon be as right as rain,' Ruby huffed as she walked from the room, trying hard to blink back her own tears. However annoying Vera could be at times, it wasn't fair that at her age she was in this dire situation. Poor thing clearly hadn't eaten properly for days and was living in a cold house in early March. 'Once we've sorted out your problems you can help me empty this tin bath before Nelson decides to play in it. Thank goodness the baby isn't crawling yet or she'd be in it like a flash,' she called back. As sad as she was about Vera's predicament, she didn't take to having a messy home.

'There's the Salmon and Ball, but I'm not sure about going in on our own?' Freda said as they walked along Bethnal Green Road.

'Don't be daft. You walk into the Prince of Wales on your own when we meet there,' Maisie laughed. 'Besides, you ride a bloody big motorbike, and that's a man's job. You can't chicken out now.'

Freda shrugged her shoulders and ignored the jibe about her motorbike. 'That's different, I know the landlord and his wife and they know me. It's not considered ladylike to go into a pub without being accompanied by a man. I'm not so sure about walking into this pub.'

Maisie pushed past her friend. 'Then follow me. I've not come all this way ter give up now. There might be someone inside here who knows where my parents are living. Besides, me feet are killing me, it's started to drizzle again and I could kill for a drop of gin.'

Freda fell in step behind Maisie and kept her head down. She hadn't felt so uncomfortable in a long while. She just hoped Maisie didn't drink too much, as she had no idea how to get back to the foot tunnel and the safety of the south side of the Thames and knew she'd have a problem steering her mate in the right direction.

Inside the public bar it was gloomy and the air was thick with cigarette smoke. Maisie walked straight up to the bar and rapped her fingernails on the wooden surface to get the attention of the barman. 'A gin and a small sherry if you please, barman,' she said loudly above the muffled noise of those enjoying a last drink before the pub closed for the afternoon.

'Another five minutes and I'll be calling last orders,' a surly barman said, looking Maisie up and down.

'You'd best make that two gins and two small sherries then,' she replied, giving him a steely stare.

'I'm not so sure I can drink that much,' Freda whispered.

'Shh, I need to ask some questions and I can't do that if we don't have a drink in our hands,' she said, reaching into her handbag for her purse. 'Now, why don't you go and sit at that table over there and I'll bring the drinks over?'

Freda did as she was told and sat on one of two rather battered bentwood chairs set around a small table. The surface was sticky and had seen better days so she decided, as she removed her gloves, to place them straight into her handbag, after which she kept the bag on her lap, gripping tightly to the handles. She spent the time waiting for Maisie looking around at the pub and the people whiling away a Wednesday afternoon. It seemed a strange time of day to be drinking but then it took all sorts to make the world go round, as Ruby was often telling them. Over in the corner an elderly man was playing a piano. She strained her ears to make out what the tune was but gave up after a while. Going by the number of empty pint pots on the top of the piano, he most likely didn't have much of an idea of the tune either. Freda could see a young soldier sitting with a couple who looked like his parents. From across the bar she was aware the woman was wiping a tear from her eye and the man kept slapping the lad on the back with pride. There was a knapsack on the floor at the soldier's feet so no doubt he was heading to camp after being called up. Freda hoped fervently that he would return to the fold of his loving family before too long.

'Ta, love,' Maisie said as she lifted the tray with their drinks and carried it over to where Freda was sitting. She placed the tray on the table and handed a glass of sherry to Freda. 'I asked the barman if he knew of my parents but he wasn't much help as he's not long moved to the area.'

'Perhaps someone else would know them,' Freda said as she sipped her drink and grimaced. 'I think I'd have preferred a half pint of bitter than this,' she said, pulling another face. 'I was watching that couple over there. I think their son's going off to war. His mother seems very upset.'

Maisie turned round to look. 'It must be heartbreaking to have ter see them off. I'm not sure I could do that with our Ruby. I'd lock her in the coal shed rather than let her go off to fight the Hun.'

'This war is the one reason I'm glad I'm not married and don't have kids,' Freda said sadly. 'You just don't know, do you?'

Maisie plonked her glass down on the tray, which made the glasses rattle alarmingly. 'We're a right couple of miserable buggers. It's time we livened things up,' she said, getting to her feet and marching over to the piano.

Freda watched as Maisie leant over the pianist and chatted to the man. There was much shrugging on his part and much waving of hands by Maisie before she turned to the drinkers and called out loudly, 'There's a young lad over there who, by the look of things, is heading off to war. Let's give him a bit of a send-off and his mum and dad something to remember about today rather than tears.' She gave the pianist a nudge and he started to play.

'*Wish me luck as you wave me goodbye. Cheerio, here I go on my way* . . .' she sang with gusto. Before she'd finished the first verse everyone had put down their drinks and joined in.

There were cheers and cries for more so Maisie had a quick chat with the pianist and once again began to sing. '*Any time you're Lambeth way, any evening, any day* . . .'

Freda smiled before joining in. 'The Lambeth Walk' was one of her favourite songs. She would have loved to get up and dance but as no one else had she didn't like to be the only one and instead clapped her hands and tapped her feet to the jolly tunes. One of the elderly men who'd been playing dominoes reached into his pocket and pulled out two spoons, which he began to tap against his body in time to the music. Freda was fascinated. She'd heard of people playing the spoons but had never seen it happen. What a fun afternoon this was turning into.

After finishing with a rousing rendition of '*Maybe it's because I'm a Londoner*', Maisie went to speak to the young soldier and his family and then headed back to Freda, stopping to shake hands and chat to drinkers along the way. 'We're in luck,' she said as she knocked back the remains of her first glass of gin. 'Someone told me where me mum lives. Finish that and we'll get cracking,' she said, picking up her second glass.

'However did you manage to find that out?' Freda asked as she did her best to knock back the sherry. It was worse than taking medicine. Next time she'd ask for a lemonade, although she'd have preferred a cup of tea.

'Everybody loves a sing-song. I chose a few songs that would lift the spirits and endear me to the drinkers. After that they were willing to speak to me even though I'm a stranger to them,' Maisie grinned as she picked up her handbag. 'Come on. I'll buy you a bag of chips otherwise you're going to be staggering all over the place. I've never met anyone who can't hold their drink like you,' she said, grabbing Freda's arm as she took a few wobbly steps towards the pub door.

'You crafty so-and-so,' Freda said, alarmed at how she slurred her words after just two drinks. 'Lead me to the chip shop and don't spare the horses.'

5

'She's settled down now,' Ruby said, coming back into the front room where Vera had started to doze off in front of the coal fire. 'She only wanted her nappy changed.'

'I don't know how you can do all that,' Vera huffed, showing a little of her old spark. 'Why, I was glad to see the back of nappies and the like once mine were old enough.'

Ruby smiled. She'd usually have bitten back but she was just so glad that Vera was almost her usual self. All it took was a bit of food and a soak. If only the world's woes could be solved so easily. 'Now, let's put our heads together and see what we can do about your predicament,' she said, settling herself down in the armchair closest to the fire and stretching out her feet towards the heat. 'My, that feels good.'

Any bravado that Vera had shown only minutes ago suddenly disappeared. 'I really don't know where to start.'

'What about at the beginning? Tell me why you've no money. Surely your pension is enough to see you through from week to week, and didn't you have a bit put by after your old man passed away?' Ruby prompted.

Vera looked sad. 'I did and usually my old-age pension's enough, I was glad of that when I turned seventy, but when our Sadie came crying on my doorstep I couldn't not help her out, but that wasn't the end of it . . .' Vera clamped her lips into a tight, thin line and stared ahead, lost in her own thoughts.

Ruby frowned. 'Whatever do you mean?' As far as Ruby knew, Vera's granddaughter lived a charmed life in the perfect job and with a boss to whom she was romantically attached. Vera had even hinted at wedding bells sounding on the horizon. Something serious must have happened for Vera to get into this state and not to ask for help.

'Look, Vera, you can tell me to mind my own business but you'll be six foot under within the year if you carry on like this,' she said gently. 'I really want to help you.'

Vera, still lost in her thoughts, snapped back. 'I'm ashamed of her bringing trouble like that to my doorstep. Whatever it costs, I'll find the money just to keep her away.'

Ruby was troubled. 'Whatever Sadie has done can't be so serious that you would almost starve to death and be sitting in a freezing cold house. Please tell me what's happened so that I can help you?' she begged, moving from her cosy place by the fire and sitting next to Vera on the sofa.

Vera nodded her head slowly and sighed. 'You know me, Ruby. I set myself high standards to live by and expect my family to do the same. When that daughter of mine went off the straight and narrow I washed my hands of her and thought I'd done a good job bringing up my grand-daughter.'

'You have, Vera. Why, you've told us all about that wonderful job she has in London working for someone important.' She didn't add that Vera had bragged mercilessly and was always reminding her that Ruby's own granddaughter only worked in Woolworths and was no way as bright as her offspring. Now wasn't the time. 'Didn't you mention something about an engagement to her boss?'

'That's all over and done with,' Vera muttered bitterly. 'No decent man would touch her with a bargepole now. She's gone and got herself in the family way and he's gone back to his wife and won't take responsibility for what he's done. She came crying on my doorstep and I sent her packing.'

Ruby was always of the opinion it took two to tango but wasn't about to put her thoughts into words at that moment. 'Oh, the poor girl. You didn't mention he was a married man,' she said, trying to pick her words carefully so as not to infer that Sadie had been foolish.

'She kept that small detail to herself. She's no better than she ought to be,' Vera snapped back.

Ruby was confused. 'But the money . . . how are you out of pocket . . . did she steal from you?' Ruby stared at Vera, willing her to speak and tell her what had happened. What she'd tried to keep secret until the cold and lack of food had made her vulnerable.

'She's brought the family name into disrepute,' Vera said, jutting her chin out in defiance. 'I've worked hard to make my name respected, especially after my daughter, Sadie's mum, was such a . . . such a . . . tart. There, I've said it. She was nothing short of a streetwalker and a bloody prostitute. But we sent her packing and brought her daughter up ourselves and now look what she's been and done. She's no better than her mother. There's bad blood there but I don't know where it's come from as me and my Don came from decent families.'

Ruby gasped. She'd never heard Vera speak like this before. 'I don't want to poke my nose in where it's not wanted, Vera, but are you sure about all this? I mean, you couldn't have made a mistake, could you? Your Sadie has a respectable job and her future's mapped out, what with being engaged to marry a man who, from what you've said, will make very good husband material.'

'Oh, he's that all right. The only thing is he's someone else's suitable husband material,' she said with a catch in her voice. 'Someone who not only married him but has given him three young kiddies. Now there's a fourth baby on the way and his wife has nothing to do with it.'

'So you gave her money to help her out. Well, you did the right thing there. Who can we go to in times of trouble if not our family? I suppose you just overstretched your-self but we can soon sort that out and it'll be lovely for you to have a great-grandchild to show off. Will Sadie come and live with you—'

Vera glared at Ruby, stopping her excited chatter. 'You've got it all wrong. I don't want her round here with her bas-tard child. I gave her all I could so that she would stay away. If it takes more money to save my family name, then I'll pawn my wedding ring rather than have her walk up this street with her belly full of a married man's child and have everyone in the street laughing at me behind my back.'

*

'Betty, Betty . . . wait for me,' Sarah called out as she hurried to catch up with her boss, who raced from the doctor's surgery without looking in her direction. 'Slow down, you'll make yourself ill. You don't want to do that,' she puffed as she caught the woman up.

Betty turned to face Sarah, who was surprised by Betty's tear-stained face. 'You mean it's not good for the baby? Don't worry about that, there isn't one. I was just being foolish. It was just my age. The doctor told me that at my age I should get used to not feeling on top form and perhaps I should consider giving up a man's job running the Woolworths store.'

Sarah was shocked by her bluntness. 'Look, this isn't something we should be chatting about in the street. Besides, it's starting to drizzle again and it's none too warm. Why not come back to my place and you can warm yourself and we can have a chat? Maureen can keep Georgina busy so she doesn't bother us. What do you say?' she pleaded. Betty looked dreadful and nothing like the self-assured boss who ruled her staff with a rod of iron. She looked like a woman who had been told she'd never have a family of her own and could not accept the truth.

'I don't want Maureen to see me like this,' Betty said, reaching into her coat pocket for a handkerchief to wipe her eyes. 'I'll catch a bus and head off home. Douglas will be expecting me,' she added.

'Don't be silly. You told me earlier that he's off to the Home Guard this evening and the girls are well looked after by your housekeeper. If you don't want Maureen to see you, let's go round to Nan's instead. She may even have a few words of advice for you.'

Betty thought for a couple of seconds and then agreed. 'Thank you, if you don't think I'll be bothering Ruby. I always value whatever she has to say and I must admit to needing a cup of tea,' she said as the two women fell into step beside each other and headed towards Alexandra Road.

'Nan will love to see you, Betty. Her door is always open wide to family and friends.'

'She's a good woman,' Betty agreed before falling silent as they crossed Manor Road, weaving their way through a group of men on bicycles. The afternoon was leading into early evening and workers were heading home from their day jobs to prepare for a few hours' war work, be it fire watching, Home Guard duties, air-raid precautions or simply knitting by the fireside prepared to dash to their Anderson shelters if the air-raid sirens should sound. 'I never thought for one moment that I'd get the chance to marry and possibly be a mother. To be honest, it never bothered me . . . until now. Now I feel as though I've been robbed of something wonderful. You're a lucky girl, Sarah,' she added wistfully.

Sarah had no idea what to say to her friend. She knew she was lucky to have a husband and a beautiful daughter and had taken it for granted that her life would be the same as that of many other young women who had a wonderful courtship, marriage and then a family. It must be truly awful for women of Betty's age who had lost loved ones in the Great War and faced a life of spinsterhood and little to look forward to in later life. She knew that Betty was one of the few women of her age who thought progressively of a career to fill the void left by not having a family. Sarah knew that would not suit her, even though she loved her work at Woolworths. She was proud to be a supervisor, although things would be sure to change once the war was over – whenever that would be.

'Here we are, Nan will be pleased to see you,' Sarah said as they walked up the path of number thirteen and she pulled at the string attached to the letter box to retrieve the front door key to let them inside. 'My goodness, whatever is all this noise?' she said as the sound of a wailing baby and a sobbing woman met them when they entered the house. In the background Alvar Lidell could be heard reading the news on the wireless.

'Oh my goodness,' Betty exclaimed.

'Nan, it's me and Betty, where are you?'

'In the front room, love, come and give me a hand. You couldn't have arrived at a better time.'

Sarah quickly pulled off her coat and hung it on the hall stand before heading into her nan's best room, where she found her with her arm round Vera from up the road who was sobbing uncontrollably. 'Whatever's wrong with Vera and why is she in her dressing gown?' a puzzled Sarah asked.

'She's had a bit of an upset and with her house being on the cold side I thought she could stay here for the night. Will you help me to get her upstairs and tucked up in bed and then I'll make us some cocoa? I'll add a drop of that rum Freda's brother Lenny brought home on his last leave. That would go down well, eh?' she said as she helped Vera to her feet and gave Sarah a wink. 'Grab her other side, love. Betty, will you see what's up with baby Ruby, please. She probably just needs a cuddle.'

Betty stood for a moment watching as the two women assisted Vera up the steep staircase until baby Ruby's insistent wails gave her no choice but to head into the living room and look into the pram where the child had been sleeping.

'There, there, little one, whatever is the problem?' she cooed as she lifted the red-faced baby out of the pram and held her close. The baby's distressed cries subsided as Betty walked up and down the room whispering soothing words whilst rubbing her back. She tried to brush all thought of never being able to do this for her own child away from her mind, but it was hard. Perhaps if only for a few minutes she could dream that this was her and Douglas's own child conceived out of love and so very much wanted. Never before had she grieved so much for something she never thought she wanted. As baby Ruby's tears subsided so Betty's own tears fell silently onto the hand-knitted cardigan of the sweet-smelling baby. Oh, how she'd give up everything just to be able to hold her own child. What a fool she'd been not to make the effort to socialize with people of her own age after Charlie had died. She could have been married for years and her children would be grown up by now. She scolded herself for her thoughts. If her life had taken another path, then she never would have met her handsome Douglas and been so blissfully happy. Or, she was until her thoughts had turned to babies.

'You have the magic touch,' Ruby said as she entered the room and headed to the kitchen.

Betty jumped. She'd been so deep in thought she'd not heard the older woman come downstairs. Placing the placated baby back in her pram, she tried hard to stem her own tears, but Ruby was no fool.

'Oh, Betty dear, whatever is the problem. It seems as though everyone in this house is turning on the water-works today. Let me stick the kettle on the hob and we can sit down and have a little chat. That's if you want to talk?' Ruby said. She was not one to probe but knew Betty well enough to see she was upset.

Betty nodded and tucked a blanket around the now sleeping baby before heading into Ruby's front room and taking a seat by the fire. She loved visiting the Caselton home where she was always made so welcome.

Ruby came in wiping her hands on her pinny and sat down opposite Betty just as Sarah appeared. 'Is it all right for me to join you?' she asked, having overheard her nan's words as she came downstairs.

'Of course you can,' Betty said. 'I'd be offended if you didn't.' She went on to explain to Ruby what had occurred earlier when she visited her doctor not expecting to hear his blunt words.

Ruby listened patiently, only making the occasional tutting sound as she disagreed with what Betty was say-ing. Sarah slipped from the room to make cocoa, which she silently handed to the two women, keen not to stop Betty talking of her need to have a child of her own. When she fell silent Ruby reached for her drink and sipped the hot liquid.

'What do you think, Nan?' Sarah asked.

'What I think is that this doctor is a bumbling idiot telling our Betty that she's barren.'

Sarah gasped. 'Nan, how can you say such things?'

'I can say it because it's true. How many men do you know who had a baby? He may have his clever medical books to read but only a woman knows what it's truly like. How old are you, Betty, that's if you don't mind me asking?'

'I don't mind at all, Ruby. I'll be forty-five on my next birthday. I was eighteen when my Charlie died at Passchendaele and the plans we had for our life together faded away to nothing.'

'So young,' Sarah murmured. 'A few years younger than I was when I married Alan.'

Ruby nodded her head. 'A crying shame that so many menfolk perished in the mud and what for, when we're at war once more?'

'We'll keep sending our boys to war until this country is free, Ruby,' Betty replied.

Ruby sniffed. 'Cannon fodder, but that's neither here nor there at the moment. You, young lady – for you are still young – should not be defeated by one bumbling fool of a doctor. I take it everything's working as it should be?'

Sarah felt herself blush. Should her nan be asking such questions? 'Nan, honestly!'

Betty looked Ruby in the eye and smiled. 'Everything is working correctly, thank you very much, Ruby.'

Ruby leant over and patted her knee. 'Mark my words, you'll be fine, but I wish I could say the same about Vera and that granddaughter of hers.'

'That's a big house,' Freda said, looking up at the imposing Victorian dwelling in front of them. 'There's a cellar as well by the looks of it. Your family must be doing well for themselves.'

Maisie snorted with laughter. 'You silly cow, the place looks so run-down it'll fall down as soon as Hitler waves a feather at it. I thought you said you'd sobered up after eating all those chips?' She took a scrap of paper from her pocket and peered at the words. 'They have rooms on the top floor. Come on, we've got a bit of climbing to do.'

Freda gave a hiccup. Perhaps eating those chips as well as a large pickled onion wasn't such a good idea if she had to climb up into the rafters of the house. 'Can we take our time or I might be sick,' she asked as Maisie strode ahead.

'I'm not hanging about for you. I've got a baby waiting for me at home and an 'usband who'll be annoyed if he knows what I'm up to so we need to get a move on. I didn't realize it would take us so long ter find where they lived. That woman at Canning Town Woolies wasn't any 'elp whatsoever. Come on, hurry yourself.'

Freda did her best to keep up with Maisie as they climbed the numerous staircases up to the top floor. Several times people came out of their doors to check who was there and went back inside when they saw the two girls. As they climbed higher and higher so the stair carpet became more threadbare and the banisters even more rickety due to age, and also no doubt the bombing. The constant bombing of the East End had caused plaster on the ceiling and walls to crack and fall away. Maisie sighed to herself. She had half expected to see her parents living in squalor but when actually faced with it, she was becoming sadder and sadder the higher she climbed in the old building.

'I think this is it,' Freda wheezed as they stopped for a breather in front of one door at the top of the final staircase.

'Well, we can't get any bleeding higher. There aren't any more stairs,' Maisie snapped back. She was beginning to fear what state the rooms would be in once they stepped over the threshold. Rather tentatively, she knocked on the door.

It seemed an age before the door creaked open and Maisie was faced with a woman she'd not seen in years. 'Hello, Mum, aren't you going to invite me in?'

Freda followed Maisie into the room. It seemed to be comfortable enough, although the few coals letting off a small glow in the grate didn't do enough to heat the room. Curtains were already drawn against the impending night sky, making the room appear to be gloomy. The woman who'd let them in stood in the middle of the room, hands on hips. Freda could see how Enid had recognized the likeness in Maisie as apart from being slightly shorter, and displaying the ravages of what she assumed was a hard life, the women were incredibly alike. Queenie was grey-haired whilst Maisie sported her usual blonde locks.

'Who's that lady, Nanna?' a small voice asked from the sofa.

'We don't know you,' echoed another child's voice, the owner of which seemed to be tucked up underneath a blanket.

Ignoring the children, Queenie Dawson pointed to a couple of chairs set by a small table. 'You'd best park yourselves there. I'd not take your coat off if I was you,' she said to Freda, who had started to unbutton her overcoat. 'You'll catch your death. We get drafts from all sides being up this high.'

Maisie stood in the centre of the room glancing about. 'Where's Dad?' she asked as she looked for signs of her father.

Queenie laughed bitterly. 'You're a year too late. If you want ter see 'im, you'd best get yourself off to the Mile End cemetery. It was 'is heart,' she added, watching Maisie's shocked expression. 'We 'ad no way of letting you know as we 'ad no idea where you were, what with you not keeping in touch with yer family.'

'I wrote a letter to your old address to let you know what I was up to but you never replied,' Maisie said as she sat down on a nearby seat. 'It's a bit of a shock ter suddenly be told your dad's dead and buried.'

The older woman's expression softened for a second or two. 'The daft old bugger always did 'ave a soft spot fer you, even when you was a kiddie. He asked about you in his final days. Never a word for me, oh no, it was all about you as usual.'

Maisie sat quietly, still trying to take in the news that her dad was no longer with them. Without being cruel she'd have preferred it to be the other way round. Her mum had never really liked her. It had all been for her younger sister, Sheila, and since Maisie was the cause of the child's death their relationship had become unbearable and was the reason she'd run away from home. 'I'm sorry,' was all she could whisper before clearing her throat that ached from trying not to cry. 'I'm sorry that I never saw 'im before he passed away. Was it quick?'

Queenie glared at her daughter. 'If you can call coughing up yer lungs fer months on end quick, then I suppose it was. But why should you care? Never once did you give a damn about any of us.'

Freda flinched. She needed to say something before the woman flew at Maisie and chances were that Maisie would retaliate. She held out her hand. 'We've not been intro-duced. I'm Maisie's friend, Freda. We work together at Erith Woolworths.'

The woman ignored Freda's outstretched hand, instead roaring with harsh laughter. 'Woolworths, you say? Well, blow me down. Fer all yer airs and graces you 'aven't gone far in the world, 'ave you?'

It was Freda's turn to be indignant. She adored Maisie and secretly wished to be more like her. 'Maisie was our supervisor,' she replied. 'They thought very highly of her at Woolworths.'

'Did they? Not working there anymore then? Got the sack, did you? Found out about you, did they?' Queenie mocked, getting closer to her daughter's face until Maisie flinched at the last couple of words.

Maisie failed to respond but Freda could see there was sadness in her eyes. 'Maisie will go back. Our manager wants her back as soon as baby Ruby is old enough to be left with someone for a few hours every day. Not that she has to, with her husband being an important man in the RAF.' Freda felt as though she'd done a round in the boxing ring and waited for Queenie to throw the next punch. But then Maisie spoke.

'I'm sorry that Dad has passed away and that I wasn't here for him. I can't make that right and I can't put right what 'appened with our Sheila. But you've got to remember that I was no more than a kid at the time and you've got to take some of the blame for leaving her with me. Our Fred never seemed to get any blame and he's two years older than me. You made it impossible fer me to stay with you all and that's the reason I ran away, Mum. Anything could 'ave appened to me in those first years and ter be honest, I went through some 'orrid times. Then I met my Joe and my life started ter make sense again.'

Queenie stared at her daughter for what seemed a lifetime to Freda as she watched with bated breath to see what would be said. 'So yer 'usband's in the RAF, is he?'

'No, Joe died at Dunkirk. I remarried and David and me've got a good life and a little girl.' She reached into her handbag and pulled out a small photograph of Ruby. 'You can 'ave this,' she added, holding it out to her mum.

Queenie took the proffered photograph and peered closely, the light in the room not being that good. 'She looks like you did at that age, poor little blighter,' she said but her words bore no malice.

Maisie laughed. 'It's good to know she got her looks from me and not my 'usband. Not that he's ugly,' she added proudly.

As the tension in the room dissipated Maisie noticed the two young girls huddled under a blanket on the sofa. 'Who do these belong to? Not taking in kiddies for money, are you?' A leopard can't change its spots, she thought to herself. Her mum never did have time for any child, preferring to spend her time and cash down the local boozer when she wasn't at work.

'They're Fred's,' was all she said, not even glancing towards the two children.

'Where is he?' Maisie asked. 'I take it he's got a wife as well . . . ?'

When Queenie didn't answer, instead reaching for a packet of cigarettes and lighting one from the embers of the fire, not bothering to offer one to her daughter or Freda, Maisie thought the worst. 'No, please don't say our Fred's . . . our Fred's gone too?' she asked, aware that the two girls were listening and could become distraught.

'If you mean is he in the army somewhere in North Africa, then yes he has. He doesn't even know I've been landed wiv these two little perishers.'

Freda flinched. She'd become used to Maisie's language over the past few years but Queenie's choice of words, and in front of two young children, was more than colourful. She glanced at the two girls and smiled and was rewarded with two cheeky grins back. No doubt they'd grown up around Queenie and her choice of phrases and knew no better.

'Thank God fer that. I thought you was going to say he'd popped 'is clogs. So, where's the mother?'

'Mothers,' Queenie corrected her daughter. 'Our Fred's been a bit of a lad in his time,' she said almost proudly. 'The older one lost her mum during the Blitz and when Fred married his wife, Cynthia, she took on the kid. Then she 'ad her own one before she went.'

'Went?' Freda asked, so wrapped up in this fascinating tale that she forgot for one moment that Queenie was talking to Maisie.

'Went and legged it with some Yank. She dumped these two off on me and Fred don't even know I've got 'em or that Cynthia's done a runner.'

'Haven't you written to him?' Maisie asked, knowing that her brother would be devastated that his wife had left him.

'I'm not one for letter writing,' Queenie said, going to a coat stand in the corner of the room. 'Now, if you'll excuse me, it's time I was down the underground before all the best places ter sleep have been taken.'

Freda was horrified. 'You sleep down the underground? What about the trains?'

Queenie looked at Freda as if seeing her for the first time. 'We go ter Bethnal Green station as it's just down the road. They don't 'ave any trains running through there as it's not long been built. You should come too if you know what's good fer you.'

'All the same,' Freda faltered, thinking of being enclosed below ground while the Luftwaffe did its worst up above. She felt quite sick just thinking about being in such a situation. 'If it's all right, I'd rather stay here. Or, perhaps we should think about heading for home, Maisie?' she said, hoping her friend would agree.

'We can stay a little while longer. Perhaps walk with you down to the underground station. We should be able to get a bus down there that'll take us back to the Woolwich foot tunnel.'

Freda nodded, hoping that the air-raid sirens wouldn't go off before they were on their way home.

'Come on, you two, or I'll leave you behind,' Queenie said, grabbing a bundle of rolled-up blankets by the door along with a shopping bag and leaving before the two little girls had scrambled from beneath the blanket.

'Oi, you can't go out like that,' Maisie bellowed, making

the two youngsters halt in their tracks. 'Let's get your shoes on. Do you have any shoes? What about jumpers and coats?' She was met by blank stares from the two girls before they scampered out of the room, returning seconds later holding the required clothing and pushing their feet into scuffed shoes.

'Well done,' Maisie smiled. 'Now, button up your coats and show us the way to the shelter. It might also help if you can tell us your names. Your nanna seems to have forgotten that little detail.'

'I'm Bessie,' the taller, dark-haired, pretty child replied with a shy smile. 'I'm nine.'

'Blimey,' Maisie whispered to Freda. 'Our Fred didn't hang about 'aving her.'

'She's Claudette,' Bessie said, pointing to the younger chubby child. 'Her mum named her after the actress. She's six.'

The younger girl grinned up at Maisie with a toothless smile whilst trying to buckle up her shoe.

'That's a name to live up to,' Maisie said, trying not to laugh out loud. 'Come 'ere, ducks. Let me do that for you.'

'I think we are all set to go. Now, run ahead a little and see if you can spot your nanna but don't go out of sight, will you?'

'We won't,' they both chanted and dashed out of the door and down the stairs just as the air-raid siren started to wail. Freda and Maisie were hard pushed to keep up with the two children as they ran as fast as they could down the many flights of stairs.

Out in the street they joined other locals who seemed to be hurrying in the same direction holding an assortment of possessions. They spotted one woman carrying a cage containing a canary while another person had tucked a small dog inside her coat with just its nose peeping out.

'Bloody 'ell. Keep those kids in your eyesight, Freda. I'll be blowed if I can see 'em.'

Freda stepped out into the road, just avoiding a man on a pushbike who gave her a mouthful of colourful language. 'They're just up ahead and it looks like the entrance to the underground station isn't far off. I can see your mum as well. Once we've seen them down safely can we go? I'd rather not follow them . . .'

Freda's last words were blocked out by a massive whooshing noise close by and in the distance ack-ack guns could be heard firing into the night sky.

'It's a bomb,' a woman screamed and the crowd surged forward, followed by more screams.

'Whatever's happening?' Maisie called to Freda, who was slightly ahead of her and being pulled forward in the surge of people.

'I'm not sure. It looks as though something's happened in the crowd,' Freda shouted back. 'Oh my God, there are so many people and it looks as though they're falling on the steps down to the underground. The kids and your mum are there somewhere in the crush. We've got to help them, Maisie, or they could be hurt.'

6

Looking back, Freda couldn't understand how she'd escaped with her life. As she tried to reach out for the two girls, she was gradually sucked into the crowd of people falling down the steep steps into the near blackness of the underground station. Her worst nightmare was coming true. She tried to call out to Maisie for help but her voice joined those of people screaming before they fell silent. A single light overhead gave a small glow, which was just enough to see those around her slipping underneath those who were fighting to stand. She knew that under her own feet it wasn't steps that she was now standing on but most certainly people who had fallen ahead of her. She'd not gone very far down the steps into the underground. If only she could hold on to something, but there was nothing but people trying to save themselves.

Bessie and Claudette must be close by, but where was Queenie? Thoughts rushed through Freda's head as she tried to stay upright. This was worse than when a lad had thrown her into the deep end of Erith baths and she'd done her best to tread water until Alan and Sarah dived in to save her. She spotted Claudette and reached out, shouting her name. All at once it seemed to Freda that the child popped up out of the heaving bodies, followed by Bessie. As she grabbed their coats and pulled with all her might she spotted Queenie. As quickly as she'd seen the woman she disappeared again but then Freda too felt hands pulling at her hair and coat as she was plucked from the sea of people.

'Thank God,' Maisie sobbed as they all collapsed onto the pavement, assisted by those at the top of the stairs. 'I thought you'd all been killed. Thank goodness I was far enough behind you to be able to help pull you back. However did you get hold of the girls?' she asked as she cuddled them close, all of them sitting on the wet pavement oblivious to the cold and the light drizzle, and to the fact that for all intents and purposes there could still be an air raid as the all-clear had yet to sound.

Freda frowned as she thought hard about what had just happened. 'Someone pushed them up out of the crowd. If they hadn't done that, they'd both have been . . .' She looked at the two girls who were wide-eyed with shock. 'They'd have both been badly injured by now.'

Maisie cuffed her eyes with the back of her gloved hand, not caring about her make-up or the fact her carefully pinned hair was falling in damp strands around her face. She was aware they were in the way as strangers tried to help those closest to the top of the staircase that led down to the platform of the underground station. 'We need to get the girls back to their home. Will you do that while I look for Mum? I'm going ter give her a hand as well. I can't just walk away without 'elping.'

Freda nodded. She was trying hard not to scream out

loud in terror as she thought about being trapped and so helpless. She prayed she would never find herself in that situation again. Looking after Bessie and Claudette would keep her busy and her mind off the horror. 'Come on, girls, let's get you home and fed, shall we?'

'What about the air raid?' Bessie asked. 'Nanna said we're never to go outside until the all-clear and we're to go down into a shelter.'

'I'm hungry,' Claudette added, looking dolefully towards Maisie. 'And I've lost my shoes.'

Maisie looked around her. The child was right. It would be foolhardy to take them back to their home on the top floor of the old house. They'd be sitting targets for the Luftwaffe. 'Look, there's a shelter sign over there next to the pub,' she said to Freda. 'Take the girls there and I'll find you when I'm done here. I'll bring Mum with me.'

Claudette started to grizzle. 'I'm hungry.'

Freda helped them both to their feet before picking up the shoeless Claudette. 'Let's go over there and I reckon we'll find something to eat, don't you?' She looked back to Maisie who was staring towards the entrance to the underground station. 'Maisie, it was your mum who helped the girls,' she said in no more than a whisper. 'I'm not sure . . .'

Maisie nodded her head but said nothing for a few seconds. She held out her handbag to Freda. 'Hang on to this for me. I'll see you later.'

Freda followed a steady stream of people who were heading towards the shelter. She walked past the Salmon and Ball pub, where just this afternoon she'd sat drinking that awful sherry – it seemed an age away – and went under the arches beneath the overhead railway line. It was like another world as there were willing hands to find them a seat and very soon they were drinking hot cocoa and being offered doorstep-sized sandwiches that pacified young Claudette, who was still claiming she was hungry and was now oblivious to the fact she was not wearing shoes. Thankfully a kindly lady from the WVS who searched amongst a pile of clothing and found a second-hand pair that fitted the child perfectly soon rectified that. Wrapped up snugly in army-issue blankets, the girls were quite happy and didn't seem any the worse for what could have been the end of their young lives. Inside the shelter people were trying to keep spirits high for the children while all the time eyes were turning to the exit with thoughts of what was happening outside. Occasionally people came in and there were huddled whispers but all in all spirits were good and youngsters were kept unaware of the horrific situation across the road.

Checking her wristwatch, Freda could see that it had been over two hours since she'd left Maisie and she was becoming worried about her friend. She was in no doubt that Queenie Dawson had perished in the sea of bodies and her last thoughtless act had been for her two grandchildren. Freda thought back to how Maisie had coped with the loss of her first husband, Joe, and knew her friend should not be alone. She had a quick word with a woman sitting close by who was more than happy to keep an eye on the two children, before buttoning up her coat and heading out into the night air. Walking out of the shelter, she first spotted a telephone box and checked her purse for coins before looking further along the road. Freda was not prepared for what met her eyes. In the dim glow of a myriad of torchlights was a scene she'd remember until the day she died.

'Please, love, can you spare me a couple of coppers? I need to let Dad know that we've lost Mum. He's still at work down on the docks.'

Freda turned round to see a young man with a tear-streaked face. She was next in the queue to use the public telephone and didn't want to miss the chance of contacting someone back in Erith who could help them and also to say they were safe. She still wasn't sure what had happened. Was it a bomb? Opening her purse, she took out two coins and handed them over. 'That leaves me with two and that's enough for my phone call. Look, why don't you go in front of me? Your need is greater than mine.'

The young man smiled weakly and took the proffered money. 'You're a diamond, love, cheers. He needs to be here to see her before they take the bodies away or he won't believe me when I tell him what's happened. This is going to kill him but he needs to know.'

Freda followed his gaze as he looked over the road to where row upon row of blankets covered the bodies of people who'd been pulled from the stairway. Beside some bodies were distraught friends and family whilst others lay silent and alone. She couldn't see any sign of Maisie. Once she'd made her telephone call she'd have to go and look for her, not that Freda relished the thought of walking amongst so many bodies. There must be dozens of them. A sense of numbness washed over her as she stood waiting. The young man was talking animatedly although she couldn't hear what he had to say.

She saw him insert the second coin and continue to talk before waiting and running his free hand over his face in despair. Without a second thought she tapped on a glass panel in the door and he pushed it open. 'You may need this,' she said, handing over another penny. One would be enough for her to reach home. She'd thought it best to contact Erith police station. If Mike weren't on duty, they could pass a message to him to let Ruby and David know where they'd got to. They'd be beside themselves with worry by now.

'Bless you, love,' he mouthed before the heavy door closed and he continued his conversation.

Freda turned her back on the horrific scene and faced a brick wall while she thought what they should do next. Locals seemed loath to head for home not knowing what to do about family and friends who'd suffered. In the short term Bessie and Claudette needed to be cared for and put to bed, but what about when they awoke and were told that their nanna had died? How would they react and who would care for them?

She nodded to the young man as he left the telephone box and stopped to thank her, before she stepped inside the stuffy box herself and pulled out the number she needed to get through to Erith police station. After giving her number to the operator she put her coin into the slot and was relieved to find Mike at his place of work. She managed to explain as quickly as possible where they were and the situation they found themselves in before her money ran out.

*

Ruby jumped with a start to someone hammering on her front door. She'd wheeled the baby's pram into the front room where it was warm and the pair of them had snoozed for the past couple of hours as they waited for Maisie and Freda to come home. She'd not heard a word from Vera since they put her to bed with a cup of cocoa heavily laced with rum. Betty and Sarah had helped to empty the tin bath and put the living room to rights before going home to their families. Glancing at the clock Eddie had been given on his retirement that now had pride of place on the mantelpiece, she was surprised to see it was almost midnight. Whatever had happened to those two girls and who the hell was that banging on her door at this time of night? The noise was enough to wake up the whole street.

Trying to stretch her stiff limbs as she headed to the door, Ruby called out, 'Hang on a minute, I'm coming as fast as I can.'

She switched off the hall light and pulled back the heavy blackout curtain before turning a stiff lock and opening the door. She could see the outline of a man in uniform and automatically recognized Maisie's husband David. 'Hello, David, has Maisie sent you to collect young Ruby? Get yourself indoors so I can turn the light on.'

'You mean she's not here?' David said in none too happy a voice.

'You've not seen her?' Ruby replied as she led him into the front room where his daughter was beginning to cry. 'She's been as good as gold,' she said, lifting the child from her pram and handing her over to David.

David smiled at his daughter and rocked her to and fro

in his arms before taking a seat as Ruby filled him in on where Maisie was. 'I told her not to go off on her hare-brained schemes to find her family but would she listen? At least she listened enough not to take our child with her. Goodness knows why she's not home yet. I don't like her walking about God knows where this late at night, and alone too,' he said, looking more worried now that his annoyance had subsided.

'Freda's with her and she's not one to do anything rash. If Maisie has found her parents, they've most likely forgotten the time, what with catching up on news and all that. I'll get you a cuppa and then change the little one's nappy before you head off home.'

Ruby had no sooner got to her feet when there was more hammering on her front door. 'That's probably them now but goodness knows why Freda can't use her key,' she muttered.

David watched the front room door as it opened, expecting to see a contrite Maisie. Instead in walked an out-of-breath Mike Jackson.

'It's a bit on the late side to come courting, isn't it?' David grinned before seeing the confused look on the police sergeant's face.

'Gwyneth and Myfi are down in Wales visiting her family. Dad treated them to tickets. No, it's you and Ruby I've come to see.'

'Oh my . . .' Ruby said, gripping his arm. 'Is it Maisie and Freda?'

Mike nodded his head and led her to a seat. 'Both are fine but they've been caught up in something,' he said, looking around him.

Ruby frowned. 'You're safe in my house, Mike. My walls haven't got ears so cough up whatever it is you've come to tell us. It won't go any further.'

They all jumped as the door opened and Vera stood there yawning. 'How can a woman get a good night's sleep around here with so much noise? What have I missed?' she said, quizzically looking from the RAF officer to the police sergeant.

'Feeling a bit better, Vera?' Ruby asked, wondering how whatever it was that Mike was about to tell them could be kept silent with the biggest gossip in Erith now standing in her front room. 'Sit yourself down here, we may need your advice. Then you can help me make everyone a cup of tea.' She winked at Mike who nodded back. What better to stop Vera gossiping than to make her feel she had a part to play?

Mike explained that he was on duty at the police station down by the river when the phone call had come in from Freda. 'She wanted you all to know that they're both fine but something's happened over at Bethnal Green underground station. Her coins had run out by then and I wasn't able to call her back.'

David put the now sleeping baby back into her pram. 'Do you think it was an air raid, Mike?'

Mike looked uncomfortable. 'I made some enquiries before I left and whatever happened is hush-hush. It never happened,' he said, staring hard at Vera.

'Don't be daft. If something happened, it must have happened. Why are you talking like this, Mike Jackson? Have you been down the Prince of Wales having one too many?' she glared back.

'What I'm trying to tell you is that whatever has happened at Bethnal Green is not to be spoken about. It would do morale no good and Hitler could jump on the news and make much of it to the detriment of this war. Do you understand, Vera?'

Vera puffed herself up and continued to glare at the police officer. 'I can keep a secret as much as the next person. Your secret is safe with me,' she added primly.

Ruby ignored Vera's comments. 'Tell us what's happened, Mike? I'm worried about the girls.'

'I don't know any more than what I've already said, but I can tell you that Freda and Maisie are fine. I did make a call over to the local police station but no one answered. I was wondering if you could pull a few strings?' Mike said, looking at David.

'I was thinking the very same thing. Is the phone box on the corner working?'

'It was this morning. I spotted someone using it when I walked past,' Ruby said.

David checked he had enough coppers for the phone and headed to the door. 'I'll not be long. Why don't you make us all a cup of tea, Vera? I know I could do with one and no doubt Mike could too.'

Vera beamed at the two men. 'Would you like a bite to eat?'

'Tea will be fine, thank you,' David said, giving Ruby a crafty wink. 'We don't want to eat Ruby out of house and home. Are you coming, Mike?'

'Leave the tea for now, Vera, and sit yourself back down. They'll be more than a little while making their enquiries. I want to have another word now that you're more like your old self,' Ruby said as the two men closed the front door behind them.

Vera frowned but did as she was told. 'I'm still not the full ticket,' she said, trying hard to make her voice tremble but not quite succeeding.

'That's as may be but there's something puzzling me about your granddaughter.'

'What do you mean? I've washed my hands of her. I've no longer got a granddaughter.'

'Now, don't be daft, Vera. You can't ignore the girl because of what she's done. Why, if I'd done that, I'd not have any family left.'

Vera's eyes grew wide with interest. 'What have your lot been up to then?'

Ruby could have kicked herself for saying such a silly thing. 'That's neither here nor there. What I'm trying to say is that Sadie is your own flesh and blood. She's all you've got left of your old man and I bet whether it be a boy or a girl that Sadie gives birth to, there's a big chance it'll take after your Don in some way or another. It would be like turning your back on your own husband. Apart from that, this kiddie's going to have some posh blood running around in its veins, what with having such an important man as his father.' Ruby had no idea who the baby's father was but felt that if she appealed to the snobbery that lay just under the surface of Vera's skin, it might just make her think.

Vera gave Ruby a look that meant she was thinking on what her friend had just said. 'You've got a point there. You never know, the baby's father may end up acknowledging the child and then we'd be related.'

Ruby would have given herself a pat on the back if she could reach. After all these years she could read Vera like a book. 'I'm not saying it would solve your financial situation at the moment but if you could make amends with your Sadie, then you could face the rest of the world together . . .'

'You've got a point there.' Vera started to smile. 'We could always tell the nosy neighbours that the kid's well-to-do father works away on official war business and that's why she's come home to live with her gran.'

Ruby felt her face starting to twitch as she tried not to laugh out loud. 'It's up to you what you want to tell people.'

'You won't go telling everyone about my business, will you? You know I can't abide gossips,' Vera spat back.

Ruby should have felt annoyed with Vera's words but she was too relieved to see her old friend turning back into her usual self. 'Your secret's safe with me but you'll need to tell her of your plans. Where is she living? I'll come with you to see her if you like, if you think it would help.'

Vera's face dropped. 'All she said was that it's somewhere down West Street near The Ship, temporary like, and she was planning to go and stay with a friend once she had some money. Will you really help me find her?'

Ruby sighed. What had she let herself in for? That part of the town was not very nice and no self-respecting woman would walk down the street in daylight, let alone during the blackout. Whatever was Vera's granddaughter living down there for? 'Of course I will. Now, get that kettle on before David and Mike walk back through the door. I want to hear what they have to say and we can't do that while we're fiddling about with cups and saucers.'

Wandering back down the road searching for Maisie, Freda did her utmost not to look towards the bodies lined up along the pavement, or to count them. Even so, she could tell by the size of the shapes underneath the rough coverings that it was children, as well as adults, who had perished. In the haste to get to those who might still be alive some had not been covered very well and the sight of protruding limbs greatly distressed her. Turning the corner of the road, she spotted Maisie kneeling next to the part-covered body of Queenie Dawson. She was holding her mum's hand and had the photograph of her daughter Ruby in the other. Approaching quietly, so as not to disturb her friend, Freda could hear what Maisie was saying.

'I'm going to put this in your pocket, Mum, so you can take it with you. You'd have loved our Ruby. Already she shows signs of being a proper Dawson with her cheeky smile and loud voice. You'd have adored her but I'll not let her forget she had a nan and granddad who lived in the East End. I promise you that.'

Freda knelt down beside her friend and put her arm around her. Maisie seemed unaware that Freda had joined them.

'I'm so glad I got ter see you, Mum. I promise I'll take care of Bessie and Claudette until our Fred is 'ome again. Give Dad a big kiss for me, won't yer?' she added as her voice started to crack.

'Maisie,' Freda said gently, 'Maisie, I think it's time we took the girls home and put them to bed. Your mum wouldn't have wanted them out at this time of night, would she?'

Maisie chuckled softly. 'Did you hear that, Mum? Freda doesn't know how you and Dad would leave us to roam the streets while you was down the boozer until all hours and we turned out all right, didn't we? We could have got up to all sorts, and often did. Do you remember when the coppers brought us 'ome after our Fred kicked a ball through the Co-op window? Dad didn't half give 'im what for. He couldn't sit down fer a week.'

'Maisie . . .'

'Give me 'alf a mo and I'll be with you. I just want ter say goodbye,' she replied, still not taking her eyes off Queenie. 'Let me just straighten your hair a little bit, Mum,' Maisie said as she gently stroked a few stray hairs from Queenie's face. 'There, that's better, isn't it?' She leant over and kissed her mum's cheek. 'You're wiv Dad and our Sheila now. Give them both my love,' she whispered as she got to her feet.

'We'll take good care of her,' a voice said from just behind, making both the girls jump. A policeman and an ARP warden stood close by as a covered lorry pulled up at the edge of the pavement. Freda could see that they wanted to place Queenie's body inside with many others. 'Do you know her name and address?' the policeman asked. 'We need it for our records. Would you know anyone else who might have been going down the steps to the underground? It could help us identify some of these poor buggers.'

'I'm sorry, this is the first time I've been 'ere,' Maisie explained as she gave her details, along with Queenie's. 'I'll be taking my nieces, Bessie and Claudette, 'ome ter live with me until we can get word to my brother, Fred. Mum said he was in North Africa with the army but I don't know any more than that. He'll need ter know about this and where he can collect his two nippers. Can you find 'im?'

'I don't know about that, miss, but I'll jot it all down and pass it to the authorities. We'll do all we can to help you.'

Maisie thanked the men before turning her back on what they were about to do and starting to walk away.

Freda stopped to have a word with the police officer. 'You will check that she's . . . that she's dead, won't you?'

The ARP warden nodded sombrely before the policeman could answer.

Freda hurried to catch up with her friend. 'I've left the kids under the arches by the pub. Someone's keeping an eye on them. They don't seem any the worse for what's happened to them,' she explained, hoping it would give Maisie some kind of peace of mind. 'I've also let Mike Jackson know where we are so he can tell your David.'

Maisie nodded, whilst walking briskly across the road staring straight ahead and not glancing at Freda, who was doing her best to keep up with Maisie's long strides. 'It's when the nightmares begin that worries me.'

Freda was unsure whether she meant her own or the children's.

7

May 1943

Irene Caselton slowly exhaled the smoke from her cigarette before addressing her daughter, Sarah, as they sat in the garden of Irene's comfortable bungalow in Crayford. 'I have no idea how Maisie can cope with three youngsters to take care of. However is she going to make Gwyneth's wedding gown, let alone finish all the dressmaking orders she's been given?'

Sarah, who was busy ensuring her daughter, Georgina, didn't pick Irene's prized roses, silently fumed. 'Have you thought about trying to sew yourself, Mum? It would take the pressure off Maisie a little? You do tend to load her up with your mending and such like.'

'Darling, you know I don't have a clue about such things.'

Sarah tucked her complaining daughter under one arm and returned to sit in the garden seat out of the May sunshine. 'Alan's mum said that the pair of you always used to make your own clothes when you first started working together. She said you were a whizz on the Singer and could dash off an outfit in no time.'

Irene gave a little laugh. 'That was a lifetime ago. I'm surprised she can recall such things. I'm not sure your father would like to see me as some little housewife making her own clothes and darning his socks. He's doing well in his work and needs a wife who can be by his side, not up to her teeth in pins and needles and smelling of sewing machine oil when he returns home each day.'

'Mum, Dad is just a working-class man who holds down an important job just like many other people in the war. Why, Maisie's David has an extremely important job in the RAF, even if we don't know what it is, and Maisie has three youngsters to care for, she does her war work and does very well with her sewing business. You do very little by her standards. I'm surprised you've not been called up for war work considering you're still young enough.'

Irene flinched. Her daughter's words had hit home and more than dented the armour she wore as she tried to shake off the humble roots of her childhood. 'As it happens, I have received a letter. That's why I invited you to visit today so that I could ask your advice.' She stubbed out her cigarette in an ornate glass ashtray and delved into a tan leather handbag by her side before thrusting the letter towards her daughter.

Sarah put Georgina to the ground amongst her dolls and pulled the letter from its official-looking envelope. After carefully reading the three paragraphs she returned it to Irene. 'Do you plan to attend the appointment at the labour exchange? It seems you've conveniently missed two others. Mum, you do realize you could get yourself into awfully serious trouble with the authorities by not doing your bit for the war effort?'

Irene flapped her hand in the air, dismissing her daughter's comment. 'I'm still helping out with the WVS and wasn't it me who suggested the fundraising dinner dance at the golf club?'

Sarah was astounded at her mother's attitude. 'And no doubt when Hitler and his troops come marching through Kent you'll arrange a dinner dance to welcome him!'

'Honestly, Sarah, there's no need to speak to me like that.'

'Mum, people are beginning to talk about you. Even Nan does more than you and look at how old she is. You should be ashamed of yourself. In fact, I don't want to have anything to do with you until you pull your finger out and do something to help us win this war. Why, my Alan is goodness knows where with the RAF while you're putting our family to shame. We won't stay for tea, if it's all the same to you, and until you come to your senses you can forget about looking after Georgina.'

'But darling . . .' Irene called out as Sarah lifted a protesting Georgina into her pushchair before heading out of the side gate.

Irene made no attempt to run after her daughter. It would have made no difference and she knew that deep down she agreed with Sarah. She was not pulling her weight in this war. If only she could go back to those days when she'd first met George and had been such good friends with Maureen Gilbert. What had happened that she'd changed so much? Everything she'd done since their marriage was only undertaken in order to help further George's career. She'd educated herself in the ways of the other wives and done her best to mix with only the important people at Vickers. If she fitted in, then so did George, even though he only cared for his job and wasn't one for social interaction. She'd done it all for the best and now it had blown back in her face. What a fool she'd been, and now she could lose the friendship of her daughter and perhaps never be able to care for her adorable grand-daughter again. With time heavy on her hands, she looked forward to when she had the little girl alone and could read her fairy stories and teach her nursery rhymes. The child was like a sponge, absorbing information, and she had shown a keen interest in the garden, which was Irene's pride and joy. Why, she'd even created a small space where the child could dig and plant a few bulbs. She was planning on showing her how to grow vegetables this year. Spending time with Georgina had made Irene realize that she was a very lonely woman. She had made a few acquaintances at the golf club down the road but with George working such long hours at the factory they never got to attend functions very often – not that her husband was keen on such things. Her mother-in-law was as busy with war work as her daughter and all her young friends. Irene knew that it was her aloofness and her ambition to be better than those she grew up with that had caused her to be in this situation.

She reached for the letter and read it carefully word for word. It was time she stopped this silly act and pulled her weight. She might not have another chance to put things right. Heading back into the house, she looked at the time.

There was a bus due shortly that would get her into Erith. She knew there was one person who could advise her, but she would need to hurry.

Betty yawned. It had been a long day and there was still three hours before she could lock the doors of the Erith store and head for home. Her next job, after an exhausting meeting with the store's supervisors, was to walk the shop floor and see that everything was ticking over, as it should do. This was something she did at least once every day and it gave her a chance to have a word with all the staff and also customers who stopped to ask questions about supplies. This was where she discovered the needs of those who spent their hard-earned money in Woolworths – the people of Erith would soon complain if things were not to their liking.

Betty wondered if the changes she was about to implement by moving stock to other counters and reducing sections where items were low would meet approval. Several of her supervisors were none too happy and this had led to a rather heated meeting. She hoped that she wasn't about to make a mistake. The last thing she wanted was a stressful working life. She smiled to herself as she thought of her husband, Douglas. Quiet and dependable, he supported his wife's need to work and since their marriage at Christmas, had done as much as possible to make her change of circumstances as easy as possible. From being a spinster all her life she was suddenly not just a wife but also a stepmother to two young girls who worshipped the memory of their mother. The younger child,

Dorothy, was a delight and Betty simply adored the child. However, the older girl, Clemmie, was not only named after her late mother but was the spitting image of the portrait that had hung over the fireplace in Douglas's home. Fortunately for Betty, who felt the eyes of his late wife were boring into her at all times, she had been able to move this to the girls' bedroom. To step into someone else's home and also be a newcomer to the family had been hard for Betty. For Clemmie, who had never been comfortable with her father's new wife, it was an excuse to sulk and be as obstructive as possible. When would her life be peaceful and calm? The tonic her doctor had given her when she stupidly thought she was expecting Douglas's child had done the trick and she was more like her old self, albeit with a fresh set of worries. She seemed to do nothing but worry of late when in the past any problem would have washed over her like water off a duck's back. Obviously another sign of my impending dotage, she thought, laughing to herself as she closed her office door and headed downstairs to the shop floor to start her daily inspection.

'Hello, Betty.'

Betty turned with a startled jump. It was unusual for customers to call her by her Christian name. She smiled as she saw who it was. 'Why, hello, Irene, I've not seen you in the store for a while. If you're looking for Sarah, she's not working today.' She was surprised by the forlorn look that crossed the woman's face.

'No, I wondered if you would allow me to have a word with Maureen Gilbert? I won't keep her from her work. If it's a problem, I can catch her when she finishes?'

Betty could see that Irene Caselton was troubled. She hoped it wasn't anything to do with Sarah or Alan or, God forbid, young Georgina. Glancing up at the large clock on the wall of the store, she smiled kindly at the woman. 'I don't see why not. Afternoon tea breaks have finished. Maureen will be clearing up the canteen. If you're lucky, the teapot may still be hot and no doubt Maureen will be able to offer you a biscuit. I've no idea how she does it but she always seems to have a cake or biscuit tucked away somewhere. Go on up. You know the way.'

Irene gave her a watery smile before thanking Betty politely and heading for the stairs to the staff area.

Betty watched her disappear through the door before continuing with her duties. There was something not right with Irene Caselton. She didn't seem her usual self at all.

Maureen Gilbert finished wiping down the last of the tables in the Woolworths staff canteen and stepped back to admire her work. The lino on the floor had also had a good going-over with a mop and hot soapy water and although rather shabby, Maureen knew it was clean enough to eat her dinner off. She took a pride in the canteen, not only with cleanliness but also in being able to provide a hot meal for all the staff. She knew that a few of the workers were finding it hard to make ends meet and would go without for the sake of their children. So, she kept an eye on them all and always had a little something for them to take home in the way of leftovers, as well as ensuring there was a good meal inside them to keep them going for the rest of the day. She looked up at the tap on the door and was surprised to see Irene standing there.

'Sorry to intrude,' Irene said, stepping carefully on the pages of newspaper Maureen had laid on the wet floor as a pathway from the door to the counter. There was always a late customer and she didn't want muddy shoes from the warehouse staff messing up her clean floor. Those men could make a mess standing still in their stockinged feet.

'Whatever brings you here?' Maureen said. A staff canteen was not usually a place that Irene Caselton frequented. 'There's not something wrong, is there?' she asked, putting her hand to her chest where her heart had suddenly started beating twenty to the dozen.

'No, please don't alarm yourself, Maureen. The children are all fine and no news is good news, as they say, as far as Alan is concerned. It was you I wanted to have a chat with. That's if I may interrupt your hard work for a few minutes?'

Maureen frowned. Irene might well say she only wanted a chat but it was unheard of for her to approach any of them for a simple chat. 'Sit yourself down. I'm about done here and ready for a cup of tea myself. Would you like a biscuit? I did some baking earlier and there are a few left in the tin.'

'Tea would be fine but please save your biscuits for the staff. They work hard so should have the treats. I just need to ask for your advice . . . and to give you an apology.'

Maureen raised her eyebrows in surprise as she shuffled on the sheets of newspaper towards the counter where she kept the large brown teapot. Irene apologizing? This was a turn-up for the books. Whatever was it that

Irene wished to apologize for? To her knowledge they'd not had cross words or fallen out. In fact, they had little to do with each other these days. If it wasn't for her son, Alan, being married to Irene's daughter, Sarah, and the women sharing a young granddaughter, they'd have nothing whatsoever in common.

Maureen carried two cups of hot tea to the table and sat opposite Irene. 'Is something bothering you, Irene?' she asked, concentrating on stirring her tea and trying not to make eye contact.

'I've been an utter fool for many years and I've come here not only to apologize for becoming such a snob but to also ask you for advice. We used to be such good friends before we met and married our husbands. It has taken my daughter to point out to me that I need to change or I could lose everything I hold dear.'

Maureen couldn't believe her ears. What had made Irene confess such a thing? 'I hope Sarah hasn't been upsetting you?' she finally asked after trying hard to think of the right thing to say.

'No, she's a good girl. I don't deserve such a daughter. She brought me to my senses. Goodness knows why George has put up with me for so long . . .'

'George is a good man and you're putting yourself down, Irene. You've made a good home for him and given him a lovely daughter. Any man would be proud to have you for a wife.'

'Only if they were looking to climb the social ladder – I'm one of those women who push their husbands,' she said, sniffing into a delicate lawn handkerchief. 'You know I don't have any proper friends. Oh, I can sit on committees and organize social gatherings, but I have no one I can confide in or simply have a nice chat with.'

Maureen felt her heart break as she saw her old friend reappearing from behind the smart clothes and perfect make-up. She replaced her cup on its saucer and reached out to hold Irene's hand. 'I'm still your friend, Irene. We've just walked separate paths for a few years. I'll always be here for you . . . as long as you don't expect me to join you for a game of golf,' she added with a cheeky grin.

Irene had the good grace to laugh. 'You always were a tonic, Maureen. You could always lift my moods.'

'Now, as a friend, what was that advice you wanted to ask about?'

'I want to do some war work,' Irene explained, reaching for her handbag to find the letter she'd earlier shown to her daughter.

'I thought you helped run the WVS?' Maureen asked, remembering that Irene's earlier endeavours to organize the women of Erith had not gone to plan.

'No, I mean a proper job. Something to help end the war.'

'Whatever do you mean?'

Irene slid the letter across the table and didn't speak until Maureen had read the words typed on the page. 'I've been thinking while I was on the bus. There were some women going home after their shift and I could hear them chatting. They seemed such a happy bunch and I want to be just like them. I want to get a job on the railway.'

'What, drive a train do you mean?'

'Yes, or be a ticket collector or perhaps a porter. Whatever I do, it will free up a man to do important war work. It's the only way that I can see for me to really help to end this war. By rolling up my sleeves and setting to I just know I can make a difference. I fear for the future for our granddaughter and young friends if we don't sort Hitler out once and for all.'

Maureen nodded her head thoughtfully. 'I've felt as helpless as you. I know I do my bits and pieces of fund-raising but when I think of my Alan up in the skies in those planes it brings it home to me that I'm not as active as I should be.'

'We seem to be too old to join the forces and too young to sit at home and knit socks for the troops.'

Maureen chuckled. 'Don't let Ruby hear you say that. She'd take Hitler on single-handed if she could.'

The women sat drinking their tea in companionable silence.

'I'm going to walk round to the labour exchange when I leave here to find out what I need to do about applying for a job. I wondered if you'd come with me for moral support? I'm as nervous as I was when I went for my first job as a young girl.'

'I'll do more than that,' Maureen replied with a glint in her eye. 'I'll find out about signing up myself. It's time we fought for a brighter future for our granddaughter.'

'I can't say I'm not pleased about having you join me but what about your job here? What will Betty do about the staff canteen? I know George will have something to say about my decision, but I can handle him.'

'I'm sure Betty will find someone to replace me. There are enough women out there who can pour tea and wash floors,' Maureen replied, even though she felt bad about letting down Betty Billington.

'Maisie, have you seen the state of my uniform jacket? It has sticky marks on the sleeves and I need to be off in a few minutes,' David Carlisle huffed as he walked into the small kitchen of the rooms they rented in a large house in Avenue Road. He wrinkled his nose at the sight that met his eyes. 'I hope that's not our dinner?'

Maisie turned and grinned. Wrapped up in a voluminous pinafore with a scarf covering her hair, she wiped the steam from her face with her hand before tucking away a stray curl that had escaped the hair covering. 'Any more of yer lip and you will get this on a plate along wiv a few spuds and carrots. If I don't get Ruby's nappies boiled and on the line, she'll have run out by teatime. Now, what did I hear you moaning about?' she asked, hands on hips and looking her handsome RAF husband up and down.

David felt slightly ashamed. 'The sleeve of my jacket appears to be a little sticky.'

Maisie laughed and reached for the dishcloth and gave the offending mark a good scrub. 'There you are. Now go off and try to win the war without getting grubby,' she snorted with laughter.

'I love you, Maisie Carlisle,' he said, sweeping his wife up in his arms and swinging her around the room before gently kissing her lips.

'I think you're a bit of all right too,' she replied and was about to return his kiss when two little girls could be heard giggling in the doorway. Maisie shrugged her shoulders and tidied the scarf on her head. 'What are you two up ter? I bet it's a bit of no good or you'd not be laughing like that.'

'Just you and David kissing each other; it's a bit soppy, ain't it?' Bessie grinned.

'You won't be saying that in ten years' time,' David replied, pulling on his jacket and straightening his tie. 'Now, who wants to come to the front door and wave me off?' he said to the two young children.

'Me, me,' they chorused and danced ahead of him out of the door to their front room and along the corridor to the stairs that led down to a communal front door.

'See you tonight,' she said, giving her husband a lingering last kiss before he followed the girls. 'Tell the pair of them to come straight back upstairs.'

She smiled to herself as she checked the nappies boiling away in the bucket on the stove before turning off the gas and reaching for a cloth to use to grip the hot handle and take the bucket to the sink. Who'd have thought that Bessie and Claudette would settle so well into life here in Erith? When she thought back to that awful day when she only expected to see her parents again . . . First to hear that Dad had died, then to lose her mum almost in front of her eyes would be more than many women could cope with. Maisie knew that since becoming a mother she had grown so much stronger and thinking back to that awful moment when she sat holding her mum's hand on that cold pavement, she knew she had to be strong for the sake of those two girls.

Going back to her mum's flat had been strange because

the place had felt so empty. With Freda's help she'd fed the girls and put them to bed where they'd dropped off within minutes and seemed none the worse for their ordeal. Not knowing when, or if, she'd return there, Maisie had pottered around the few rooms tidying up and putting away her mum's possessions. She'd found an old suitcase and packed the few clothes the little girls owned and also an envelope of official-looking paperwork that might be needed to sort out Queenie's affairs.

Using the last of the milk Freda had found in a small pantry, they'd sat drinking cocoa without saying a word until there was a quiet knock at the door. Rushing to open it, she'd fallen into her husband's arms. They would all be safe now. Waking the girls and dressing them warmly, they'd gone out into the night air to find Mike Jackson waiting by a lorry she recognized as belonging to the farm where Ruby's daughter Pat worked. The girls were settled in the cab with Freda while Maisie and David retired to sit on sacking at the back of the vehicle. Snuggling up to her husband, Maisie had told him all that had happened as they'd headed back in the darkness towards Erith and home.

Bessie and Claudette kept an eye on young Ruby while Maisie hung the nappies on the line. There was a stiff breeze and she stepped back to admire the row of white running the length of the garden. She had an errand to run before settling down for an afternoon of sewing. These days Maisie found her time taken up making clothes for the children, as all three had grown at an alarming rate in the past two months. Although adept at making something out of nothing, even Maisie was finding it hard to turn old clothes into items that were useful for the girls. There were four girls to consider, as she'd never forget Sarah's daughter, Georgina, when producing pretty frocks and outfits. As she positioned the clothes prop and double-checked the washing she remembered that there was Gwyneth's wedding gown to consider too. Apart from asking Maisie if she could make her bridal gown, Gwyneth had given no indication of the style, or indeed the colour. It wouldn't be that long before Gwyneth would be getting hitched to Mike Jackson. Perhaps she should forget about enjoying an afternoon of sewing and visit number thirteen instead? She'd hate to have to rush making such an import-ant gown. There was also the girls' schooling to consider before the school board man came knocking at their door. Maisie grimaced as she picked up the wash basket and headed indoors. What happened to those far-off days of visiting the pub and going dancing and having a good laugh with her chums?

Climbing the steep stairs back to their rooms, she came across Bessie with a tea towel in her hand. 'I've done the washing-up,' she declared proudly.

'And I've dusted the front room,' little Claudette announced with a cheeky grin.

'Why, girls, that's a lovely thing to do for your Auntie Maisie, thank you both,' she said, putting down her wash basket and sweeping them up in a big hug.

'Nanna Queenie said we had to work for our keep,' Bessie said seriously.

'We don't want you to go away as well,' Claudette chipped in, her chin wobbling slightly as she gave Maisie a sad look.

Maisie was thinking about what a cow her mum had been, making those young kiddies work for their keep, when she stopped and thought for a moment. The girls had seen many people leaving them in their short lives and she really didn't want them to suffer any more than possible. She wanted these little ones to remain with her until they grew up and made their own way in the world. Her brother was sure to agree – going by the little she'd heard about him from her mum and the girls – if they ever heard from him again. 'I promise you I ain't going anywhere, my loves,' she said, giving them both a big kiss. 'Now, how about we fetch our coats then go and visit Ruby? You never know, Myfi and Georgina might be there?'

The children didn't need a second bidding and were downstairs waiting just inside the front door as Maisie followed carrying baby Ruby and placed her in her pram. She checked she had her handbag and they set off on the short walk down the avenue, over the railway bridge past the Prince of Wales pub and the Odeon cinema into Manor Road before crossing over into Alexandra Road. It was still a walk that Maisie enjoyed as Ruby's house felt so much like home.

'Come in, come in,' Ruby beamed as the two little girls stood on her doorstep. 'My, I think you've grown since the last time I saw you. I have some visitors who would love to see you,' she said, leading them into the house.

'I'm sorry, Ruby. We can visit another time. I only popped by on the off chance Gwyneth was home and we could sort out her wedding dress. We can come another time if you've got visitors?' Maisie said with an apologetic look on her face.

'Don't be daft, girl. Get yourself inside and take the weight off your feet. You look exhausted. It's only Vera from up the road and Irene and Maureen. Not really proper visitors. More like family really. Vera will be off in a minute. She just came down to give me some news.'

Maisie raised her eyebrows at the way Ruby spoke.

'I'll tell you all about it when we're alone,' she whispered as she lifted her namesake from Maisie's arms and carried her into the front room.

There was a time when the front room of number thirteen was only used on high days and holidays. Ruby would keep the green velvet curtains closed so the sun didn't fade the furnishings and the door was firmly shut against visitors. It was from this room that her darling Eddie had taken his final journey up to Saint Paulinus churchyard and his final resting place. However, with the comings and goings of Sarah and her friends over the past few years she'd gladly opened up the room again and it was used more often. Today her daughter-in-law, Irene, was sitting chatting nineteen to the dozen with Maureen and Vera could be heard from the kitchen talking to the two little girls.

Maisie was lost for words. Ruby's mouth twitched as she tried not to laugh at her expression. 'Maureen and Irene have come to tell me something and to ask my advice on the best way to break their news to George. Sit yourself down and I'll get you a cup. This tea should be all right,' she said as she passed the baby to Maureen and then felt the teapot on the sideboard.

'I've brought in some hot water,' Vera said, appearing at the door. 'Hello, Maisie, those two girls are a credit to you and isn't young Ruby growing fast?' she beamed.

Maisie could not think of a word to say. She would have pinched herself to check she wasn't dreaming if it wouldn't have appeared to be rude.

'I'll get off and leave you to it, Ruby. I want to get the bedrooms ready and air the bedding before my guests arrive,' Vera said, taking her coat from where she'd left it on the back of a chair. 'The girls are sitting in the other room with a biscuit each,' Vera added as an afterthought before picking up her gas mask and bidding them all goodbye.

Maisie sat with her mouth open and tried to think of something to say to Sarah's mother and mother-in-law. 'You both look excited. Has someone opened a jar of jam?' she asked.

'You and your sayings,' Irene tittered. 'If that means are we happy, I suppose we are. We've made life-changing decisions.'

'Oh my,' was all Maisie could think to say as she took a gulp of the hot tea Ruby had just handed her and spent the next few minutes coughing and spluttering.

8

Maisie was incredulous. 'Vera is going to take in paying guests?'

'Yes,' Ruby beamed. 'It's the perfect solution to her problems. Vera was nervous about having unsuitable people living under her roof but she did agree it would be the ideal way for her to have a few bob coming in every week. I had a word with George as I thought there must be people working at Vickers who'd like to sleep in a bed with clean sheets and eat a home-cooked meal in the evenings. George came up trumps. He was pleased to be able to recommend Vera to a couple of his colleagues.'

'That's really good of you, Ruby. Do you think he'll be as happy when he knows his wife's going to be working on the railway and doing the work of a man that could well be dangerous with what's carried by rail these days?' she said as she thought back to when the nearby Slades Green train depot had almost been blown sky high when incendiary bombs had landed on a goods train in the siding that was packed with high explosives.

The two women were sitting in the front room after Irene and Maureen had left for their homes. The girls were helping Bob, who'd arrived to work on the vegetable plot at the end of the garden as well as check on the contents of the pig bin. Now the pig club had been formed and the animal was in residence down the Green at the farm where Pat and her family lived, Bob was relentlessly reminding Ruby to save scraps of food to fatten up the animal. 'It's best that Irene has that out with George herself. I won't say I'm not surprised. I didn't think she had it in her to do such work but it seems she's felt guilty for some time about not pulling her weight. With our Sarah giving her what for she decided it was time to do something about it. However, it's not for me to say.'

'Good for her,' Maisie said. 'But it's right that Irene tells George herself. I'm not being funny, but she probably knows how George ticks more than you do these days. Look at how she's led him a merry dance with all her high and mighty goings-on.'

'My George will still need convincing that this isn't some mad whim but that's down to him. I'll not poke my nose into their business.'

'All the same, I'd like to be a fly on the wall when she breaks her news to 'im,' Maisie laughed.

Ruby joined in with the laughter before a worried look came over her face. 'Mind you, it's our Sarah I'm worried for. Her Alan's off goodness knows where and there's her mum and mother in-law wanting to take on men's work at their time of life. The girl will be worried sick.'

'She has you, Ruby, as well as the rest of us. We can rally round and keep her spirits up, never fear. If this war 'as taught us anything, it's that we've grown a thick skin as far as the future's concerned.'

Ruby smiled at the woman sitting nursing her baby. Maisie had changed in so many ways from the woman she'd first met when Sarah had brought her friend home to meet the family back in 1938. The perfectly coiffured hair was just as perfect, although her face showed signs of weariness, but she was just as beautifully turned out and still never left home without a dab of perfume and her lips painted red. Ruby sniffed appreciatively. 'That's a lovely perfume.'

'David's mum sent it down to me. She said it didn't suit her. Lovely, in it?' she said, holding out her wrist for Ruby to sniff. 'It's called Evening in Paris. David reckons she only sent it as she doesn't like the smell of baby sick on me.'

Ruby roared with laughter. 'I'm sure that's not the case. Now, joking aside and while you're here, there's something I want to discuss with you.'

'I ain't got room to take in any more kids if that's what you are going ter ask me?' Maisie said with a grin.

'Three's enough for now, unless you're thinking of having a brother or sister for young Ruby?'

'God, give me a chance. It only feels like yesterday that this little one came along. I'm not ruling out having another but for now I'm happy with my three,' Maisie added.

'The girls will stay with you?'

Maisie's face took on a serious look. 'I never thought I'd hear myself saying this but I love them like they're my own. We've got so much in common, what with experiencing life wiv my mother,' she grinned. 'They're a delight ter live with. Would you believe they did the washing-up and young Claudette even tried to dust the front room, bless her. If I can just keep them safe and have them well fed and wiv clothes on their backs, then I'll be 'appy.'

'What about your brother, is there any news on his whereabouts?'

Maisie lifted young Ruby onto her shoulder and rubbed her back. She was rewarded with a loud burp. 'There's a good girl . . . David's put out some feelers to find Fred but we've not heard a dickie bird yet. I do 'ope he's fine but all the time we don't hear then I get ter keep the girls.'

'That's why I thought you'd like to hear about a house that's come up for sale. It's got three bedrooms and a large garden for the children and it's not far from your friends . . .'

Maisie gave a delighted whoop, which startled the baby. 'We've been looking about the area but wiv bomb damage there isn't many houses to be had. Come on, do tell . . . where is it and why's it up for sale?'

'It's one of the two double-fronted houses at the top of the road. Old Miss Denton is going to live with her nephew in the country and she's decided to sell up. She told me yesterday in case I knew of someone who could afford to buy a house. Not everyone can afford to. Even the furniture's up for grabs.'

'Oh Ruby, it would be like a dream come true. I'll 'ave ter speak to David as he's the one who knows about our finances. I just get me housekeeping and try not ter go overboard.' Maisie leant over and kissed Ruby on the cheek. 'Thank you fer thinking of us but wouldn't Sarah be interested in the 'ouse?'

'She's happy living with Maureen and one day that house will go to Alan no doubt. Now, how about staying for a bite to eat with Bob and me? Gwyneth and Myfi are going to the pictures with Mike and Freda's on duty at the fire station until late. You're more than welcome.'

Maisie looked at the clock over the mantelpiece. 'Oh my gawd, look at the time. Thanks, Ruby, but I'd best get back. I've a load of things to be getting on with and I've a line full of washing that'll be ready ter bring in. I did want ter see Gwyneth about her wedding dress but it'll have to wait for another day. What I was going to ask was if you still had that box of my old bits and bobs stored in the loft? There are a couple of things that I'll not fit into anymore that I was thinking of cutting down to make some outfits from for all the girls.'

Ruby clapped her hand to her mouth. 'I completely forget to tell you. Gwyneth left a parcel for you. She meant to drop it round to your place but with all the overtime she's doing at the moment for Betty she's not had time. It's some fabric she brought back from Wales that she'd mentioned to you.'

'I do feel guilty not being able to put in a few hours at Woolworths. I suppose Betty'll not be too 'appy at losing Maureen as well?'

'That had crossed my mind too,' Ruby nodded.

'And Gwyneth may give up work when she's married and the babies start to come along,' Maisie added. 'Blimey, there'll be no one left at Woolies save a few old timers.'

'I'm not sure that Gwyneth's ready to get married as fast as they first planned.'

Maisie was surprised at Ruby's words. 'Oh no, they've

not had a falling-out, have they? Her and Mike are made fer each other.'

Ruby shook her head. 'I don't know quite what's wrong but she's been quiet when I mention weddings. I'm thinking she wants her own home. After all, the pair of them are older than most couples and having kiddies must be on the near horizon. I can't see as it'd be anything else that's worrying her.'

'Hello, love,' Bob said, sticking his head round the door. 'I'll not come right in as I'm covered in muck from the garden. The girls are washing their hands. They got messy helping me.'

'Oh Bob,' Ruby scolded. 'Why couldn't you keep an eye on them? They looked so pretty in their matching frocks. I'd best go and see what state they've got themselves into. The parcel from Gwyneth is under the sideboard, Maisie. She's put a note inside as the plan was for Mike to drop it over to you. You get it while I sort out what trouble Bob's caused and fetch the girl's coats.'

'Don't worry yourself, Ruby, it'll all come out in the wash,' Maisie called after the older woman as she grinned at Bob, who was looking glum. 'It'll be worse when you two get hitched and you're under her thumb,' she laughed, seeing his expression.

'Whenever that'll be,' he sighed.

'Don't forget to clear up your bits and pieces in the garden, Bob, and those scraps will have to go down to our Pat's or they'll be off before that poor pig gets to eat them and perhaps help Maisie home with that parcel,' Ruby called out.

Maisie laughed at Bob's dejected look. 'She means well,

Bob. I'll be fine with the parcel. It'll go on the pram just fine. Just give me a hand bumping the pram down the step and we'll be on our way. P'rps it's time you sat down with Ruby and had a word about things, eh? I'd thought the pair of you would be hitched by now.'

'A word? I don't think I'll get one in edgeways,' he said glumly. 'As for our wedding, it seems to me that every-one else comes first around here. But you're right, love. I'll do just that. I'll have a word with Ruby and get things sorted once and for all. Yes, I'll do that right now,' he muttered to himself, helping Maisie out of the door of number thirteen as the girls ran past him excitedly, catching Maisie up at the same time as she turned to wave goodbye.

'It's lovely to see her so happy,' Ruby said as she ush-ered Bob back inside the house. 'That house'll be perfect for her. I'll take a walk up the road and let Miss Denton know that Maisie's interested before someone else gets in first.' She stopped by the hall stand and reached for her coat.

Bob took her hand and led her into the front room. 'Just wait a few minutes, woman, I want to have a word with you before you go shooting off up the road,' he said firmly, pushing her into the nearest armchair.

'Get off, you silly bugger,' Ruby laughed half-heartedly. She had a good idea what he was going to say and she wasn't in the right mood to listen now. 'Can't this wait until later?'

'No it can't, Ruby,' he insisted, taking a seat close to the door so she had no way of leaving the room. 'You've been avoiding me for months and I want to know where I stand? You agreed to marry me but we're no further forward than we were when I put that ring on your finger at Christmas. I agreed we had no need to rush but I thought that at least we'd have some kind of understanding? Now, with Mike wanting to marry Gwyneth and them needing somewhere to call their own, it makes sense for them to have the house over the road and for us to live here as man and wife.'

Ruby looked at the ring on her finger. It was almost the same as the one her first husband, Eddie, had given her so many years ago which she'd passed on to Freda on the occasion of her twenty-first birthday. She couldn't think what to say to this dear man. 'Bob . . . I just don't know if it's the right thing to do . . .' There, she'd said it out loud. 'I'm fond of you . . .'

Bob was angry. 'But you don't want to marry me. Is that it?'

'I do . . . I do . . . please believe me. It's just that my Eddie . . .'

'Your husband Eddie's gone, love, just as my wife has gone. We will always love them but life has moved on. I thought you cared for me, Ruby?'

Ruby reached out and stroked his stubbly cheek. 'I care for you very much, Bob, and I'd not have accepted your proposal if I didn't. It's just that lately I've felt as though I never really said goodbye to my Eddie. Do you think I'm daft?'

Bob took her hand and stroked it gently, his anger disappearing as quickly as it had appeared. 'You daft thing, of course I understand. Are you saying that once

Eddie gives you a sign you'll be ready to marry me?' he asked, hoping against hope that she would agree.

'Yes, I do believe that if the time was right Eddie would send me a sign, but will you wait, Bob?'

'I'll wait, Ruby, but I'll not wait forever. I'm not prepared to be your odd job man or to sit at your table without being the man of the house.'

'And I'd not let you, Bob Jackson,' she said, gently kissing his cheek. 'I don't deserve someone like you.'

'That works both ways, my love. I don't deserve someone like you. We were lucky both having had long and good marriages. Isn't that enough to tell us we should try a second marriage?'

Ruby wanted more than anything to tell Bob to book the church and get things moving but still she held back. 'It should be, Bob, but I just need . . .'

'You need your Eddie's approval. In that case we'll wait for him to let you know. I don't want you dashing off to that spiritual church over Dartford way, though. I don't really hold with such things.'

Ruby nodded her head. She'd best burn the advertisement she'd cut from the *Erith Observer* showing the times of service at the church before Bob came across it. Perhaps there was another way to receive the sign she so desperately wanted. 'I'll not do that, Bob. Now, how about a cup of tea while I sort out our dinner? Pat dropped off some nice fresh eggs this morning and we can have some bubble and squeak with them.'

Bob rubbed his hands together. It had taken a lot out of him to force Ruby to discuss their future. He was ready for his dinner. 'That sounds grand,' he smiled.

Ruby picked up the teacups left from when Maisie had visited and headed to the kitchen. She looked at the framed photograph of her with Eddie on their wedding day that hung on the wall. 'Come on, Eddie, give me your blessing,' she whispered.

'Whatever is wrong with everyone? There seem to be so many glum faces today,' Freda said as she accepted a cup of tea from Sarah and sat down at a small table in the corner of the staff canteen. 'Even Maureen looks as though she lost a pound and found a penny. That's not like her.'

They looked across to where Maureen was wiping down the serving counter without putting in an ounce of effort.

'She's been in to see Betty and what she thought would be a little chat and a pat on the back for signing up for war work turned into a bit of a barney. As I passed her office door I overheard Betty begging her to stay at Woolworths, at least until she could find a decent replacement. I didn't hang about as I knew that Mum and Maureen had been given a start date by the railway. They can't get enough staff up there by all accounts so they both got taken on at the interview and could have started that very afternoon if they'd wanted to. Maureen explained she had to work her notice and Mum said as how she had to talk Dad round.'

'Blimey, I'd not want to do either of those things. Was your dad happy about your mum going off to work? It surprised me, I can tell you,' Freda grinned.

'With Ernest Bevin announcing that all women under

the age of fifty are to be called up to work he couldn't really argue with her. I'm surprised you've not had a letter, seeing as you work at Woolies full-time and you're over twenty-one and don't have a family to care for,' Sarah said, feeling a little sorry for her dad, George, who would be coming home to an empty house and no food on the table once her mum started shift work. 'I bet that Mr Bevan hasn't sent his wife out to work building planes or making bombs,' she huffed.

Freda was staring at Sarah. 'What do you want me to do? Get myself knocked up with the first Yank who comes into Woolworths, to help bring the next generation into the world, or perhaps I should let down Betty just like Maureen has and go off and join the Land Army? I'll have you know I was worried the government would think I wasn't pulling my weight and I went up to the labour exchange and had a word about it. I was told I was doing more than enough, what with my dispatch riding duties for the Fire Service and if I'm needed to do more work, I'll be joining the Fire Service full-time as I'm trained and all.'

'I'm sorry, please don't be angry with me, Freda. I'm not myself today, what with all this going on with Mum and Maureen, and then the news.'

Freda gave her chum a quick smile. She wasn't one to take offence and could see that Sarah wasn't her usual self. She had dark shadows under her eyes and her usually shining chestnut hair hung about her face as if it hadn't seen a hairbrush all day. 'What's been going on? I've not listened to the radio in days and had to miss going to the pictures because I was covering for another dispatch rider,' she added, reaching across the table for a discarded newspaper. 'Crikey, our boys did some damage to those German dams, didn't they?'

Sarah nodded her head but looked sad, her hand reaching for the silver sixpence that hung around her neck. 'So many lives have been lost on both sides. It makes me wonder if it's all worth it?'

Freda was shocked by Sarah's thoughts. 'If it brings about the end of the war, then it's most definitely worth it,' she exclaimed excitedly, making the table rock from side to side as she shook the newspaper out to read the rest of the front page and grabbing her cup to stop the tea slopping into its saucer.

Sarah stood up and looked down at her young friend. 'But what about Alan? What about the pilots that were giving support to the Dambuster planes? My husband could be lying dead somewhere over in Germany right now. Look, you can see how many planes have been lost. There will be children just like my Georgina drowned in the floods caused by our bombs. How can you sit there and act so pleased that our country has done this to women and babies? I thought I knew you, Freda Smith. I thought you were a friend. I'm not so sure now,' she sobbed and rushed from the canteen, leaving curious colleagues watching Freda, who didn't know what to do.

'Why don't you come and help me for a few minutes?' Maureen Gilbert said, coming over to where a dazed Freda was still sitting. 'I'll take these cups and get you a fresh brew. These are stone cold.'

'You don't hate me as well, do you?' Freda said, following the older woman behind the serving counter and fighting hard to remain composed as her bottom lip trembled and tears were close to falling. 'I didn't mean to upset Sarah. We've often cheered over the news and she's never acted like this before. I should have thought before I opened my big mouth.'

Maureen pulled a stool close to the counter and indicated for Freda to sit down. 'It's one thing after another at the moment, love, just you think about it. Her mum's doing something out of character for the first time in her life. Our Alan's God knows where, and she doesn't see so much of her friends since Maisie's taken in those girls and you're either here or dashing off on that motorbike of yours. She doesn't hate you, ducks. She's just as mixed up as most women are right now. Perhaps it's time the three of you had a bit of fun for once rather than trying to win this war by yourselves? Put your thinking cap on and see what you can come up with. Me and Irene will muck in and look after the kids if you want to kick up your heels for a few hours.'

Freda flung her arms around Maureen's neck and gave her a hug. 'I wish I was as wise as you, Maureen. You make any problem easy to overcome,' she grinned, all thought of tears forgotten.

'If you've been around as long as I have, you too would get to learn a thing or two as well. Besides, I know my Alan is fine. I can feel it in my water. A mother knows when her babies are in trouble and I'm sure he'll come home safe and sound, you mark my words.'

'I hope you're right. He's like a big brother to me. I miss him when he's not about.'

'I'll tell you a little secret,' Maureen said, giving Freda

a cheeky wink. 'Alan told me that if anything should happen to him, then I'm to let you have Bessie.'

Freda's eyes opened wide. 'But he loves that motorbike. It was his dad's.'

'And that's how I know he's coming back. Do you think he'd let a slip of a girl ride off on Bessie? Why, he almost had kittens when he taught you how to ride.'

Freda hooted with laughter. 'I do remember that day and he was so nervous.'

'So, we've got nothing to worry about,' Maureen said, patting her shoulder.

'I should go and speak to Sarah and apologize. She must be in such a state.'

'Let her stew for a while. It won't hurt her. She can be a little dramatic at times. She has her mother to blame for that,' Maureen laughed.

'You used to be friends with Irene when you were kids, didn't you?'

'We were about the age you are now but she got some high and mighty ideas once she set her cap at our George and that was it. Once they married she was off to pastures new. It's taken this war for her to come to her senses, so no damage done.'

Freda was puzzled. 'You said *our George*. Did you know him before you met Irene?'

Maureen smiled and her eyes took on a faraway gaze. 'Not so you'd say. He was walking out with me when he met Irene. Their eyes met and the rest was history, as it says in those books you've always got your nose in.'

'Oh,' was all Freda could think to say.

'Yes, things could have been so different,' Maureen said

softly before pulling herself together. 'Now, let's get you that hot cup of tea and I'd best make one for Betty as well. She's none too pleased with me for handing in my notice, I can tell you.'

'Would you like me to take it to her? I really ought to get back downstairs or I'll be in trouble for taking too long on my tea break. The bell went a few minutes ago as it is.'

Maureen opened a cupboard door and pulled out a battered tin. Forcing off the tight lid, she took out a heaped teaspoon of sugar. 'I keep it for special occasions and I reckon Betty could do with a cup of sweet tea right now after the news I gave her. She looked a bit on the pale side. I'm sure I heard her mutter something about rats deserting a sinking ship . . .'

Freda looked puzzled. 'What do you mean?'

'Never you mind. Here, take this to Betty before it gets cold and don't forget to arrange that night out for the three of you.'

Betty looked at the staff rota in front of her. However much she scribbled all over it and moved staff from the counters upstairs to the staff canteen and storeroom, there was no denying she was short-staffed and would soon be without someone who could knock up a hot meal for her hardworking staff. 'Bloody war work,' she muttered to herself. 'Isn't running a shop as important in wartime? Everyone needs Woolworths.'

She looked up at the sound of a gentle tap on the door and Freda came in carrying a steaming cup of tea. 'Just what I could do with,' she smiled. 'Thank you for thinking of me.'

'It was Maureen, not me. She thought you'd like one. She'd have brought it herself but she's busy,' Freda said, thinking she needed to speak up for Maureen.

Betty gave a small tinkling laugh. 'Did she? That's very good of her. She will be missed very much. Goodness knows who'll be cooking the staff lunches next week,' she added, clearing a small place on the cluttered desk so that Freda could lay the cup and saucer down. 'I'd do it myself but I can just about make a sandwich and boil an egg.'

Freda knew that to be untrue, as she'd stayed with Betty on a few occasions when she'd been on late duty at the fire station close to Betty's house in nearby Cross Street. That had been before Betty married Douglas and moved into his house in Bexleyheath. Betty was a good cook but it wouldn't be right for the store manager to be frying sausages or creating meals out of hardly anything as Maureen always managed to do. She peered at the rota on Betty's desk. 'It does look as though you have a problem,' she said, trying to read the chart upside down.

'I'd be grateful for any suggestions. I'd place an advert in the *Erith Observer* but I've missed this week's paper and we need someone to start almost at once. Perhaps a card in the window would reap rewards? It did find me two store cleaners when I needed them.'

'Why don't I ask all the counter staff if they can cook and would like to move upstairs?' Freda suggested tentatively.

Betty nodded. 'That's a good idea, although I can hardly spare one of my ladies as we're short-staffed on the shop floor as well. What a pickle this is. At the moment I feel as though I could walk away from Woolworths and join Maureen in her big adventure.'

Freda had never seen her boss in such a state. Betty was the one person who could be relied upon to remain calm and collected in any situation. 'Let me have that word with the girls. You never know, we may just come up with something.'

Betty reached for the telephone that had started to ring. 'Thank you, Freda, that would be most helpful.'

Freda left Betty's office intent on finding someone who could take on Maureen's duties, but first she needed to collect the newspaper that had been left in the canteen. An idea had just crossed her mind about how she could treat her chums.

9
~

'Oh Douglas, not again,' Betty said after listening to her husband's news that he would be working late. 'We never seem to spend any time together as a family. It's been a fortnight now that you've not reached home until the girls are in bed. We do miss you, but apart from that you look so tired all the time. Something has got to change, you can't carry on like this.'

'Unless you can miraculously find me some extra staff, I'm afraid it will be some time before I'm home in time to join you for dinner,' he apologized.

'With the funeral service being a reserved occupation you'd think finding employees wouldn't be a problem,' Betty sighed. 'I take it another of your men has joined the services?'

'Yes, two this week and both off to join the army. If only I could pay them more, they wouldn't have the lure of leaving to join up.'

'You can't blame them for wanting some excitement, I suppose,' she replied, thinking how lucky she was that unlike Sarah, she knew her husband would remain safe and be home for dinner each night, regardless of whatever time that would be.

'That reminds me: would you let Bob Jackson know that I'll not get to the Home Guard meeting this evening? It's a damn nuisance as we're having training on how to make Molotov cocktails.'

Betty smiled to herself. What was it with men that they enjoyed such things? 'I will, Douglas, and please do try to find some more staff before your family forget what you look like.'

'I'll do my utmost to rectify the situation, my darling wife. Perhaps you could loan me a few of your Woolworths girls?'

'Don't you lay a finger on my staff. To use one of Ruby's sayings, it would be easier to find hen's teeth at the moment than to fill all the vacant positions in this store. Maureen gave notice this morning. She's off to do her bit for the war by working on the railway, along with Irene Caselton, would you believe?'

'My goodness, that is a surprise. I suppose that puts an end to a slice of cake when I visit you at work?'

Betty laughed. 'That's the least of my worries.'

After saying goodbye to her husband Betty placed the heavy Bakelite receiver down and sighed. It would be another difficult evening alone with the girls. She could think of nothing less appealing. Clemmie was becoming more challenging by the day. It was as if a rebellion was building and very soon would erupt, splitting the Billington family. At times she still felt like the outsider living in a home that she took no part in choosing, caring for another woman's children. 'Oh Betty, whatever have you undertaken?' she muttered to herself before tackling the pile of paperwork in front of her that never seemed to decrease. The cup of tea, brought in by Freda, went untouched on her desk.

Freda headed downstairs into the Woolies store. The sun was shining through the sticky paper covering the floor-to-ceiling shop windows. Dust motes could be seen in the beams of light. Freda frowned and took a close look at the floor and the dust that lay close to the wooden skirting boards. She could see there was no longer a high shine on the counters closest to her. The standard of cleanliness Betty expected of her store seemed to have slipped. She might not be able to do anything about the shortage of staff but it shouldn't be that hard to use a bit of elbow grease and have the store spick and span again before head office got to hear that standards had dropped. Calling out to two assistants who weren't serving at that moment, she decided to get cracking. 'Dora, can you find out where the cleaner is and have her come down here, please? Rachael, find the polishing cloths and put a shine back on this counter, would you?'

Both women nodded and set to with their tasks. Freda might be younger than many of the Woolworths staff members but she was admired as a hard worker and no one would think to question what she was up to.

'Did you want me?' Enid Singleton said, appearing by Freda's side.

'I did, Enid. I was wondering why the floors were so dirty. Haven't they been swept lately?'

Enid shrugged her shoulders. 'They looked all right this morning.'

'And the wooden counters don't seem to have a decent shine on them. Aren't you supposed to polish them every day?'

Enid shrugged her shoulders. 'I can't be everywhere at the same time.'

'By the state of this store I'm wondering if you've been anywhere lately. You know how understaffed we are at the moment and we all need to pull together. Do you think you could get this place looking shipshape again before Mrs Billington notices?'

Enid nodded and limped away slowly, dragging a broom behind her.

'A little faster, please, Enid,' Freda called after the woman but was ignored. Not one to be ignored when there was work to be done, she raced after the woman and caught her up by the entrance to the staff area. 'I say, Enid, do you have a problem with your work?'

Enid turned and looked at the younger woman. Freda could see she had tears in her eyes. 'I'm sorry,' she whispered, wiping her face with a grubby hand. 'I've not been sleeping that well lately and everything's got a bit on top of me. Please don't get me sacked. I'll catch up, I promise I will.'

'Don't go upsetting yourself, Enid. This is easily fixed. A little elbow grease and everything will soon be as right as rain. Now, how long have you got left at work before you clock off?'

'Two hours,' the woman replied, starting to look a little brighter. 'I'll work hard, I promise.'

Freda gave her a bright smile. 'Perhaps start with the floor and if it quiets down, you can put a shine on the woodwork around the counters. I'll have some of the girls polish the glasswork and the mirrors on the pillars. Now, I have to leave you, because I need to find out if any of the girls can cook, as we need a replacement for Maureen. Mrs Billington is almost at her wit's end trying to replace her,' she added as she pulled a notebook from her pocket and walked off through a crowd of shoppers.

Enid looked downcast. 'Don't bother asking me. No one ever asks me,' she muttered, angrily kicking her broom.

Betty let herself into the house. It was gone eight o'clock and yet again she was late. Knowing that Douglas wouldn't be home made her stay just a little later than usual. She'd even caught up with reports that head office was waiting on, which wasn't a bad thing. She hung her coat and gas mask on the large oak hall stand and placed her handbag on the floor close to the umbrella stand. She checked the blackout curtain was pulled tightly over the front door before walking down the hall to the kitchen.

'Good evening, Mrs Billington, your dinner's keeping warm in the oven and the kettle is on the boil. Would you like me to make you a cup of tea before I leave?' their housekeeper said as she started to remove her apron.

Betty felt guilty. All the time she was dragging her heels not wanting to get home to the girls and here was the poor woman waiting patiently for her to arrive when she had her own home and husband to get home to and feed. 'I'm so sorry; I'll do my best to be home earlier in future. I'll have a word with Douglas about someone sitting with the girls in the evening when we're working late. It's not fair of us to presume on your time so much. Give my apologies to your husband.'

The woman nodded politely, although her lips were pursed into a thin line. 'It was no trouble to sit with the girls. They are a credit to you and your husband. My Percy is down the Black Prince this evening with his darts team so he won't have missed me, although I'd appreciate getting off on time tomorrow as my daughter's intended is visiting. We have a wedding in the offing,' she added proudly, pinning a navy felt hat to her grey hair.

'How absolutely wonderful,' Betty beamed. 'You must let me donate something to the proceedings, you being such a good friend to our little family.'

'I won't say no. It's not been easy arranging a wedding, what with rationing and Neville being away at sea so often. I'd like to put on a nice spread to show his family that our Doris comes from a good family, like. In fact, Doris wondered if Clementine and Dorothy would be her bridesmaids, what with me knowing them since they were small children. The first Mrs Billington was such a dear woman and the girls have been so brave about things,' she added, reaching for her coat. 'I'll bid you goodnight.'

'Goodnight,' Betty said in a whisper as she followed the woman, turning out the hall light before opening the front door.

'I take it Mr Billington will be home late again this evening?' the housekeeper enquired as she stood on the doormat.

'Yes, it's a busy time in his business, as you can appreciate. We're both rather busy at the moment.'

Even in the semi-darkness Betty could see the woman

nod her head slightly. 'The first Mrs Billington didn't hold with her husband staying out late. She insisted he was home each night for dinner. There again, she didn't work in trade. She was a lady,' she added before heading off down the garden path.

'She was a blooming saint from the way you're always going on about her,' Betty muttered to herself as she checked the door was closed and dragged the blackout across it aggressively.

'Are you angry about something?' a voice said.

Betty spun round to see Douglas's eldest daughter sitting on the bottom step of the staircase, her hands folded primly on her lap. 'Good evening, Clemmie, I'm very well, thank you. Should you not be preparing yourself for bed? You do have school in the morning.'

The girl tossed her long ringlets and stared at Betty haughtily. 'Daddy said I could wait up for him. I'm not a child, Betty.'

Betty sighed. It had been a long day and she was pretty sure her husband had said no such thing. 'As you please, but I suggest you bathe and put your nightclothes on so that once you've seen him you can go straight upstairs.'

They both stared at each other for what to Betty felt like a long time before the girl got to her feet and slowly climbed the stairs to her room. She'd just disappeared from sight when there was a shriek followed by a child's cry. 'I'll tell Betty you hit me,' she heard the younger child cry out.

'You can tell her whatever you want, Dorothy, I don't care what she thinks; she isn't our mother. She's just some shop girl who got her claws into Daddy. Mummy was a lady and you must never forget that.'

Betty held on to the banister rail, ready to go up and sort Clemmie out once and for all. She was becoming spiteful and often made her younger sister cry. But would it make any difference? She'd tried being pleasant and bringing home treats but the girl was becoming progressively more aggressive in her behaviour when alone with her stepmother. When Douglas was at home she was sweetness personified. No, she would bide her time and show this young girl that she was not going to give up on her new family whatever it took.

'Welcome to our new 'ome,' Maisie announced, throwing open the front door to Freda and Ruby and pulling them inside. 'Mind where you step, the floor's still a bit wet. I've got some rugs to put on the linoleum once it's dry. I 'aven't stopped all day long. Who'd 'ave thought that moving a few bits and pieces from our old place would have taken so long? Thank goodness David was 'ome and able to help me out or I wouldn't have even been able ter put the kids' beds together before it got dark.'

'Where are they?' Ruby asked as she looked around the front room that she'd walked into as she followed Maisie. 'This is a nice room. It's a bit smaller than mine but very nice all the same,' she said, running her hand across the back of a large sofa. 'This looks new.'

'David's gone ter pick them up from school and take them up the swings so as ter give me a while to get things straight. Everything is here but I just need ter make the beds and put the crocks away. Park yerself down and I'll put the kettle on. It's nice, isn't it?' she said, noticing Ruby admiring the sofa. 'David's mum sent it down on the back of a lorry, would yer believe? There was also some beds and two chests of drawers for the girls now they have a room to themselves. I was going ter buy the furniture in the second-hand department at Mitchell's but there's no need now. I'll use the coupons ter make some curtains instead, as long as I have enough.'

'This is comfy,' Ruby said, almost bouncing up and down on the seat. 'I could doze off here in front of the fire listening to Vera Lynn on the wireless of an evening. Yes, this would do me very nicely.'

'You're welcome to visit as much as you like, Ruby. You opened your home to me when I 'ad nowhere to go and as far as I'm concerned what's mine is yours.'

Ruby felt choked at Maisie's kind words. 'I'd not see any of our Sarah's friends without a place to put their head down. Besides, you're part of the family now, just like Freda here.'

Freda had been standing quietly by the door. 'One big happy family,' she said without much enthusiasm. 'I thought Sarah would have been here to help seeing as she wasn't working today.'

'Did I hear my name being mentioned?' a voice said from the back room before Sarah appeared holding a bucket and cloth. She was wearing an oversized wrap-around apron and her shoulder-length hair was caught up in a bright flowered headscarf to keep it clean. 'Hello, you two, have you come to give us a hand? I've run a cloth over the washing line and swept the garden path. You're all ready for wash day,' she grinned. 'The Anderson shelter looks snug and not too damp so you've struck lucky there. Fingers crossed you'll not have cause to use it for much longer.'

'Let's hope so,' Ruby said as she pulled herself up off her seat and walked over to the window, sizing it up with her hands on her hips. 'I've got some curtains I reckon will fit these windows. I went mad a few years ago and bought some new ones for all of downstairs and put the old sets in the loft. As long as the mice haven't got at them they should be all right for you for now. Even though you've not got a bay window like me I think they'd fit. You can have them as a moving-in present.'

Maisie gave Ruby a hug. 'You're sure about that, Ruby? You may need them again someday. It only needs bloody Hitler ter send the Luftwaffe over and drop a bomb and you could lose your windows and ruin your curtains.'

They all laughed at Maisie's enthusiasm. 'If Hitler ruins my curtains, I'll pop up the road and get the others back from you,' Ruby roared with laughter.

While Maisie and Ruby were standing by the window discussing curtains, Freda looked shyly at Sarah. In the couple of days since they'd had their falling-out in the Woolworths canteen she'd avoided Sarah while she planned how to make things up to her friend for her silly words. 'I'm sorry for what I said, Sarah. I wasn't thinking and I feel awful that it could spoil our friendship.'

Sarah, who had felt equally bad for being so short with her best friend, punched her gently on the arm. 'Don't be daft. I was just as much to blame and more than a little selfish. Let's forget all about it, shall we?'

'I'd rather not if it's all the same to you,' Freda said as she opened her handbag and pulled out two envelopes. 'Maureen reminded me that we used to have so much fun together before weddings and children came along and perhaps, with the war and everything, we'd forgotten how much we meant to each other, so I thought I'd treat the three of us to a night out. Here you are,' she said, handing an envelope each to Maisie and Sarah.

'Tickets to see *Show Boat* in the West End,' Maisie shrieked. 'Oh my goodness, Freda, you are a sweetheart,' she said, holding the ticket to her chest and jumping up and down with glee.

'You know you didn't have to do this,' Sarah said, hugging her young friend. 'But as you have, I'd like to treat us to a meal at the Lyon's Corner House.'

'And I'll buy the cocktails. It's time you expanded your taste in alcohol and they taste far better than sherry,' Maisie grinned, reminding Freda of the afternoon they'd spent in the pub in Bethnal Green.

'As for me, I'll be comfortable right here with a bottle of stout to keep me company,' Ruby said, settling back down on the leather sofa. 'I take it you girls would like me to look after the children for the evening?'

'Ruby, you're a gem,' Maisie exclaimed, throwing herself down next to the older woman and giving her a big kiss on the cheek. 'I bless the day I came to Erith and met you all.'

Ruby, accompanied by her granddaughter, Sarah, along with her lodger, Freda, walked back down Alexandra Road after a busy time helping Maisie make beds and turn the house into a home for her young family. It was fast

approaching teatime; she was glad she'd thought to prepare a meat and potato pie that would only require
warming up in the oven when she got indoors. 'So what's
this about the pair of you falling out? If you weren't grown
women, I'd have banged your heads together and told you
to grow up.'

'It was nothing, Nan, honest.'

'Best forgotten,' Freda added quickly.

'The pair of you don't get off that light. Come on, out
with it,' Ruby demanded.

'I made a comment about the raids on the dams in
Germany and how many German people would have
been killed and how most would have been women and
children,' Sarah explained.

Ruby stopped walking to catch her breath. 'And what
did you have to say about this that made the pair of you
fall out?'

Sarah hung her head. 'I was angry as I thought that
Alan could have been flying on that mission protecting
the men carrying the bombs.'

Ruby thought for a second or two. 'So who thought
they were right?'

'I thought it was right for me to say what I thought,'
Freda said quietly, before explaining her view.

'I believe I'm right with my view,' Sarah said, jutting
her chin out defiantly.

'You're both right. I also think that the pair of you agree
with each other's views, even though you'll not say as
much. We don't want Alan injured . . . or worse. We love
him dearly and for that reason we want this war over and

done with as soon as possible and if that means blowing up all of Germany, then so be it.'

Freda started to speak. 'But, Ruby—'

Ruby raised her hand to silence the young woman. 'However, none of us want to see anyone hurt, especially women and young kiddies, but that's war for you and most likely all those hundreds of miles away there are women just like us having the same conversation. War is not nice. I've been through it once and didn't expect it to happen again in my lifetime. So we've got to put up with it and cope as best we can. Let's not fall out over it, shall we? What do you say?'

The girls both nodded in agreement and linked arms with Ruby as they started walking down the street. Ruby didn't say that she'd kept her copy of the *Daily Telegraph* that contained the article and put it away at the bottom of her wardrobe along with other newspapers. She knew that Alan would like to read the news when he finally got home, whether he be flying over Germany, bombing Burma or teaching younger lads how to fly planes. There was also an advertisement about ration books that she needed to cut out and read.

The women walked on in silence until Ruby spoke. 'Who'd have thought it?' she said out loud.

'Thought what, Nan?'

'That our Maisie would have become such a home bird, and with three kiddies as well.'

'To be fair, she did always want to have children. She made that plain enough the first time we ever met her. I was rather embarrassed by the way she put it and I'd only met her an hour before,' Freda giggled.

'She's a good mum,' Sarah said. 'Bessie and Claudette are fortunate to have been rescued that evening in Bethnal Green. My blood runs cold just thinking what could have happened if you and Maisie hadn't been there to pluck those girls out of the crush of bodies.'

Freda nodded. 'I still wake up at night in a cold sweat after dreaming of being pulled down with all those other poor people. If we'd been a few minutes earlier, it could have been us that died along with Maisie's mum. What I don't understand is how there was nothing in the newspapers about it. Not even a mention on the Pathé News. If it wasn't for going to Queenie's funeral with Maisie, we could have thought we'd imagined the whole thing.'

'Yes, I thought the same,' Sarah agreed. 'But wasn't it the same with the oil bomb landing on Bexleyheath Woolworths? Not a mention of it and the police, as well as head office, told us we weren't to talk about it because of national security.'

'The last thing we want is Hitler finding out as he'd say he was winning the war with so many deaths. Best it's kept quiet. Those who are grieving know the truth,' Ruby said. 'What I want to know is if anyone's going to turn up and lay claim to those two little girls? It will break Maisie's heart to lose them now. Has she heard from that brother of hers? You'd have thought he'd have at least sent a postcard to his own kids,' she huffed.

'All I know is that David helped Maisie send a letter to the army after Queenie's death to let him know that the girls are safe with her. But who knows if the letter reached him, wherever his unit is in North Africa. It's supposed to be a big place,' Freda said.

Ruby stopped at the gate of number thirteen. 'Then again, he may not be bothered about them kiddies. He's been a bit of a lad from the little Maisie's told us. Now, have you got time for a quick cuppa before you head for home, Sarah?'

'If it is quick. Maureen's off out to her whist drive this evening and she's been a star looking after Georgie for me. I'm going to miss her help once she starts shift work on the railway,' Sarah said as she followed Ruby and Freda up the short path to the house.

'I still can't imagine your mum working. You say she wants to be a train guard? At least the trains will all run on time. God forbid anyone, including the Luftwaffe, who tries to stop her trains not keeping to the timetable,' Ruby laughed. 'Why, I . . .' She stopped dead as she walked into the front room, causing Freda to bump into her. 'Whatever's wrong, Gwyneth?' Ruby asked, rushing to her pretty Welsh lodger who was sobbing into her handkerchief. Her adopted daughter, Myfi, stood close by with an arm around Gwyneth and was equally distressed.

'I'm not going to be a bridesmaid,' the little girl cried, running to Ruby, who swept her up in a big hug.

'My, my, whatever is this all about?' she asked, stroking the girl's head and holding her close while she cried.

'I'll put the kettle on,' Freda said and disappeared out of the room as Sarah went to sit next to Gwyneth and put her arm around the woman's shoulder.

'What must you think of us?' Gwyneth said as she blew her nose and gave the women a weak smile. 'I didn't mean for you to come home to all of this. I had a few words with Mike and he left,' she added, looking worried. 'I said some harsh things, forgetting that Myfi could overhear from the next room.'

Ruby knelt down in front of the little girl and wiped her eyes using a clean handkerchief from her coat pocket. 'Now, young lady, you are not to get yourself upset like this. I take it you overheard your mummy?'

Myfi nodded her head, her face still quivering from the bout of crying, and looked at Ruby with her large green eyes.

'Sometimes people say things that they don't always mean when they're upset or when they think they're alone. I'd be very surprised if your mummy didn't wear that lovely dress we've been talking about so much and marry Mike just as we've been planning. Now, why don't you go and help Freda make the tea. I know you've been practising how to do it for your Brownie badge and it's the right time to show us how good you are. You could also tell Freda that there are a few biscuits tucked away in the tin at the back of the pantry. I was saving them for a special occasion and there's nothing more special than getting over a few tears.'

Ruby used the arm of a nearby chair to help her to stand up. 'I should think twice about getting down on my knees. It's a bugger to get up again,' she sighed as, with a slight stagger, she sat down in an armchair. 'Push the door to, Sarah, there's a love, then we can talk without little ears listening in.' She waited while Sarah closed the door and went back to sit beside the dark-haired woman, who seemed a little more composed than she had a few minutes before. She thought how so much had happened within these brick walls – sadness, happiness and a little

E L A I N E   E V E R E S T

too much grief. No doubt it would be the same in Maisie's house up the top end of the road, given time. Such was life. 'Now, why don't you tell us what all this is about and then we can see how to put things straight again, if only so that a little girl can walk down the aisle behind her mother?'

'This has been brewing for a while . . . well, it has for me. Mike seemed oblivious to what was bothering me. I've tried to talk to him but he either didn't understand or chose to ignore me.'

'Well, I'll be blown if I understand what your problem is . . .' Ruby said with exasperation.

'Give her time, Nan. Gwyneth needs to explain in her own time. Go on, love,' Sarah said, taking the woman's hand and giving it a squeeze.

'As much as I love her, Myfi's not my own child and I always dreamt that one day, if I should find the right man and marry, there would eventually be children. I'd hoped for three or four. When I met Mike and we fell in love I thought my life was complete. I hinted about our family a few times and Mike always managed not to answer. To begin with I thought he was shy. He's older than me and it's hard for some men to talk about love and such things.'

'You're right there, love. My Eddie was a decent husband and father but wasn't much of one for romance or talking about his feelings. I knew it was here in his heart,' Ruby said, placing her hand over her heart, 'but he'd have died rather than put it into words. In fact, he did,' she added, looking sad. 'Your Mike is no doubt just the same.'

'No, it's more than that,' Gwyneth said, her voice rising

as she became distressed. 'This afternoon he met me from work and we walked home together, collecting Myfi from her school on the way. I was telling him about meeting the vicar to arrange for the banns to be read and he suggested that until we have a place to live we shouldn't think of booking the church. He did say that we may be able to rent the rooms up the avenue where Maisie and David lived and that's when I got upset. I told him it was point-less moving into a place like that, as nice as it is, when we would most likely have to move within a year when a baby came along. We all know that Maisie didn't have room to swing a cat in her old home and we'd be in the same position when the kiddies arrived.'

Ruby thought Gwyneth was jumping the gun some-what but decided to keep quiet when she saw Sarah raise her eyebrows at her. Her granddaughter knew her far too well. 'Go on, love,' she urged instead.

'We'd just reached home and I let Myfi open the door and go ahead when he stopped me and . . . and . . .' She pulled her handkerchief from where she tucked it into the sleeve of her cardigan. 'He told me he thought we should consider carefully if we should have children . . .' She blew her nose and tried hard not to start to cry again. 'He told me he was happy with the way things were with us, having Myfi, and that we could adopt her properly and live together happily, just the three of us.'

Sarah was surprised to hear Gwyneth's words. Mike had never struck her as being a man who didn't want children. 'Are you sure this is what he said, Gwyneth, and you couldn't have been mistaken?'

Gwyneth shook her head violently. 'Oh no, he made his

feelings extremely clear and so did I. I put my foot down. No children of our own means there's no wedding for him. As far as I'm concerned I never want to see the man again.'

10

Betty yawned as she got up from her desk and wandered over to pull up the sash window in her office. A blast of warm air filtered in along with the sounds of people down in the street below. It was a Saturday and trade was brisk in the store downstairs. She'd hardly slept, what with waiting up for Douglas and then tossing and turning worrying about her eldest stepdaughter, Clemmie. Whatever she did, the girl wasn't happy and she seemed to take pleasure in making Betty feel uncomfortable in her own home. Douglas seemed oblivious to what was happening under his own roof. She would just have to bite the bullet and have a word with him. She turned sharply as someone knocked on her door.

'Come in.'

Freda stepped in holding a cloth money bag weighted with coins. 'I'm sorry to bother you, Betty. I'm finishing off the collection for Maureen. She leaves Woolies the day after tomorrow and I've still not thought about what to buy her as a leaving present. I wondered if you'd like to contribute?'

'My goodness, is it that soon? I thought we had another

week before she left. Oh my, I've still to find someone who can work in the staff canteen and cook decent meals for our workers. I take it you had no luck asking the counter staff?' Betty said as she reached for the handbag that was tucked under her desk and pulled out her purse.

'Not yet. A couple of them showed some interest but it came to nothing. I've put a postcard up on the wall in the staffroom and said to speak to you.'

'That's a good idea. I've notified the labour exchange that we're looking for a cook but, like you, I've yet to be successful. Oh dear,' she said, looking into her purse. 'I could have sworn . . .'

'Is there something wrong?' Freda asked, stepping closer to the desk.

'I could have sworn I had two half crowns in my purse. They were there last night when I paid my bus fare.' She shook her head in disbelief.

'You didn't spend them this morning on your way to work?'

'No, Douglas had an appointment in Erith so he kindly drove me to work.' She didn't add that it was in a hearse. 'I'll go up to the bank at lunchtime and withdraw some money. Put me down for five shillings and collect it this afternoon, otherwise I may forget that as well,' she said, looking bemused.

Freda gave Betty a wary look. Betty didn't seem to be on top form lately. Perhaps she was taking on too much now she had a husband as well as a busy job? 'I'll catch you later. There's no rush,' she grinned, trying to hide her thoughts as someone else knocked on the door. 'I'll leave you to it.'

Freda left the door open as she went out and Betty looked up to see who had knocked. 'Please do come in,' she called out after waiting to see who would appear. She was surprised to see the cleaner, Enid.

'Can you spare me a minute, Mrs Billington?'

'Hello, Enid,' Betty said. She had no idea what the woman wanted but with her mind still on the money that had vanished from her purse she was in no mood to listen to the problems of her staff.

Enid limped into the room and took the chair opposite Betty. 'I've come about the job.'

'The job? Are you not happy with your cleaning job?' Betty asked. She had meant to have a chat with the woman but it had slipped her mind. She was aware that

hall where the women now met. It
running the rag rug group as well
e do and mend' ladies. She stepped

discuss your work at the moment but if you'd like to come back later in the day, I can see you then,' she said, smiling at the woman, who seemed very nervous.

'It's about the cook's job. I want to give it a go. I see the advert in the canteen and no one's taken it down so I thought I could give it a go.'

Betty stared at the woman. For some reason she'd never really taken to her and her first thought was to wonder if her cooking was as good as her cleaning of the store. She was saved by the sudden wailing of an air-raid siren as it built to a crescendo that blocked out every other sound. Even now, after nearly four years of war, the sound was enough to make her want to curl up in a ball and hide.

'Mrs Billington, we need to go down into the cellar,'

Enid said, standing up and moving as quickly as she could out of the office with her limp.

Betty followed, stopping only to lock the office door and check the upstairs storeroom and canteen were empty, before going down to the shop floor and the entrance to the cellar. Her head was still buzzing with her problems. Would Enid be a suitable cook, and whatever was young Clemmie up to? Betty was sure of one thing, and that was that her stepdaughter was behind the money that was missing from her purse.

Ruby straightened her WVS uniform and reached for her matching green hat. She had a busy afternoon ahead of her at Christ Church ████████████ was Maisie's afternoon ████████████ as overseeing the 'mak ████████████ out of her front door and looked up the road to see Maisie heading towards her, young Ruby's pram laden down with clothes and a box.

'I hope young Ruby's safe under that lot?' she asked with concern.

Maisie hooted with laughter. 'David's home so he's got her fer the afternoon. The girls are at school so he shouldn't have any problems. He reckons he's going to sort out the garden and think about planting some veg once he's had a chat wiv Bob about what to put and where.'

'Let's hope her ladyship sleeps through then or he'll not get much done. Men and their big ideas, eh?' Ruby smiled.

'As long as David remembers to change the little one's nappy and give her a bottle I don't care what he does. By the way, what's going on with Gwyneth? I really need to get cracking on wiv her wedding dress. I caught her at Woolies yesterday, when I went in for some black thread, and she said she had no time and then avoided speaking to me.'

Ruby helped Maisie to steer the pram around the sharp bend into Manor Road, putting her hand on the load to stop it slipping. 'Her and Mike have had a bit of a barney. She reckons the wedding's off. She was in a right state the other night and so was Myfi as she overheard them arguing.'

'Blimey, I didn't think Mike was one fer arguing. He don't seem the type. Dependable and honest is how I think of 'im. What do you reckon is the problem? I like the pair of them and it would be perfect fer them to settle down with some kiddies of their own. Myfi needs brothers and sisters and the pair of them would make ideal parents.'

'I was hoping to have a word with Mike to see if I could help out in any way,' Ruby explained. She didn't want to mention that Gwyneth had refused to live in the rooms that Maisie and David had just vacated in case it offended her. Besides, it was not her place to share what she'd been told in confidence.

'Why don't you go down and see 'im at the police station? He's on duty now as David bumped into 'im earlier as he headed off ter work.'

'What, and be late for our meeting? They'll have my

guts for garters if I'm not on time,' Ruby said, although she thought Maisie's idea was a good one.

'Go straight there now and I'll cover for you. They'll hardly know you're gone before you're back. If yer know what I mean?' she grinned.

'I do and I will,' Ruby laughed.

The two women parted company at the junction of Pier Road and the High Street, with Ruby hurrying past the many shops in the High Street towards the riverfront where the police station backed onto the Thames beside the jetty. She noticed a queue at the fishmonger's and thought about making fish and chips for tea. She had a bit of flour for the batter, although it would have to be dried egg in the mix as her Pat hadn't been by lately with any spare eggs from the farm where she worked. It was a bright sunny day with people making the most of the sunshine. Not perturbed by the earlier air-raid warning, there were families making the most of the lovely day, taking in the air and watching the world go by on the river, albeit mainly ships painted a dreary gun-metal grey.

Pushing open the heavy double doors, she went up to the counter where, apart from someone reporting a lost dog, things seemed to be quiet. No major crime in Erith today, Ruby smiled to herself. It was Mike himself who came out of a side room to serve her.

After exchanging pleasantries Ruby got to the point. 'Mike, I wondered if we could have a quiet word in private?' she asked, giving the police sergeant a serious look.

Mike frowned. 'I hope there's nothing wrong, Ruby?' he replied, showing her through to a small room to the right of the high counter.

'I've not broken the law, if that's what you mean, but I do know of a young woman with a broken heart living in my house. I don't want to poke my nose in where it's not wanted,' Ruby said, taking the seat offered to her by a worried-looking Mike. 'It's just that if I can help in any way, I feel it's my responsibility to enquire, being as how Gwyneth's parents live a long way off and me being affianced to your dad, like.'

A small smile crossed Mike's face at Ruby's quaint way of speaking as he sat opposite her and rubbed his hands through his hair. 'You're the nearest thing to a mother that I have right now, Ruby. I need to speak to someone. I'm that muddled that I fear I'll lose Gwyneth for good if I'm not careful. I dare not speak to Dad as he'll tell me to pull myself together and act like a man.'

Ruby laughed. She could imagine her Bob doing just that. 'You can tell me whatever you want. It'll go no further. So what is it that's worrying you? I take it this isn't just a case of cold feet, lad?'

'I wish it was, Ruby. It's more a mix of a few things that, when added together, have me worried sick about committing to Gwyneth.'

'And Myfi – you can't forget the child. The pair of them come as a package.'

'I'd have it no other way. I already think of her as a daughter. She's the apple of my eye. No, it's the thought of having children with Gwyneth that has me tied up in knots, along with giving her a good home.'

Ruby nodded thoughtfully. 'She mentioned you'd said about taking on those rooms that Maisie and David rented until recently.'

'I can't understand how I put my foot in it. Maisie made it a good home and with Avenue Road being one of the best in town, facing out over the farm like it does and backing onto the recreation ground, it would be just right for Myfi to enjoy.' He shook his head in despair. 'I thought it would suit us down to the ground.'

'The problem is that Gwyneth sees the future more clearly than you. The pair of you are older than the usual young couples setting out in life. I get the feeling that Gwyneth wants children and that she'd like them to come along pretty soon.'

Mike looked embarrassed and ran his finger round the collar of his uniform jacket as his face turned a beetroot colour. 'That's the other problem. I reckon I'm too old for babies. If anything happens to me in this war, I don't want to leave Gwyneth not being able to cope. It's a lot to consider.'

It was Ruby's turn to go red in the face but this time it was with anger. 'Mike Jackson, that is the most selfish thing I've ever heard in my life. Why, any one of us could be wiped out by a bomb, step under a bus or drop stone dead at any time. We can't worry about the future but we can plan to be happy. You, my lad, can make Gwyneth a very happy woman, as well as a certain little girl who is dying to be a bridesmaid.'

Mike looked shamefaced. 'I'd not thought of it like that,' he admitted. 'In truth I've always fancied myself as a dad.'

'As for your living accommodation, that's soon mended. Bob can move in with me, then you'll have the house to yourself.'

'What, you'll be marrying Dad? That's jolly good news and about time too.'

Ruby held her hands up in horror. 'Hold on there, Mike. I didn't say anything of the sort. Please don't start putting ideas into his head, will you? There will be a spare room going begging once Gwyneth and the youngster move out. He can kip down in there. What will you do about the room you let out? Surely you won't want a stranger under your roof once you're married.'

'God, Ruby, I've not given that any thought,' Mike said, looking worried. 'I can't really kick the bloke out. He's not got any family around here.'

Ruby stopped to think. It was good of Mike and his dad to give a room to Mike's colleague but what could they do with him now things were changing? 'Don't worry about that for now. I'll have a think about it. There's bound to be somewhere he can put his head down that's clean and respectable. What you need to do next is to have a chat with Gwyneth and clear the air before she packs her bags and goes home to Wales.'

Mike looked pale with shock. 'She wouldn't do that, would she?'

Ruby shrugged her shoulders. 'The way she was talking it was on the cards. I suggest you sort out your differences sooner rather than later. If you're off duty this evening, why not take her somewhere nice? Erith Dance Studio has got a social on. You can pick tickets up at the door. I'll look after Myfi; she's a good kid and no trouble at all. She enjoys playing board games and is eager to learn how to play crib. Freda's off to London to see a show with Sarah and Maisie so we'll have the place to ourselves, apart from Nelson that is – that dog dotes on Myfi, as she does on him. I can see you having a dog as a lodger once you're married.'

Mike stood up and gave Ruby a big kiss on her cheek. 'You're a good woman, Ruby Caselton.'

Ruby left the police station as pleased as punch that she'd been able to put Mike's mind at rest and help the situation. She liked a good wedding and Gwyneth and Mike would make a handsome couple. The only fly in the ointment would be Bob living under her roof. Despite her telling him she wasn't ready to marry until she was sure her Eddie would approve, he was still pestering her to name the day. 'Well, he'll just have to wait until I'm good and ready,' she muttered to herself. 'If Bob's that keen to marry, he can pop up the road to Vera and ask her. She'd not turn him down.'

Freda sat entranced as she watched the stage. *Show Boat* was such a splendid musical. She'd sat, almost shedding tears, as the emotional and powerful 'Old Man River' was sung by one solo male singer in the middle of the stage and the next minute was tapping her toes along to the more lively show tunes. Perhaps it was the cocktail that Maisie had treated them to before the show that had her in such a merry mood or just the delight of forgetting the war for a few hours, even though she still had her gas mask close to hand to be on the safe side. She knew that many people had stopped carrying the cumbersome masks but surely the government would not have distrib-uted them without cause? No, Freda intended to carry hers in the handbag-style box that Maisie had covered in a pretty scrap of fabric until the day the war ended.

'Thank you so much for this wonderful treat,' Sarah said to their young friend as they filed out of the building amongst the happy throng of theatregoers. 'I shall remember this evening for as long as I live.'

Maisie reached for her cigarettes and inhaled deeply, blowing out a cloud of smoke. 'I must admit it was very good. The costumes were fantastic considering the designers have the same constraints put on them as we do when making clothing. I suppose some dresses would have been used from other productions. Make do and mend never seems to stop, does it?' she said in a bitter voice. 'If there's one thing that gets me down about this war, it's having to make do when I love to kit the kiddies out in new clothes without counting coupons and unpicking and remaking clothes. Bloody Hitler,' she grinned at the girls, at the same time as nodding to a nearby bar. 'Come on, I need another drink. David gave me some money to contribute to the treat so let's blow the lot on cocktails. What do yer fancy?' she asked, throwing her cigarette to the pavement and stubbing it out with the toes of one of her best brown suede shoes. 'I'm going to 'ave a Singapore Sling if they 'aven't run out of gin.'

'I'd prefer a cup of tea,' Sarah whispered to Freda as they followed Maisie through the boarded-up doors of the bar, 'but I'll not be a spoilsport. Let's make a pact not to drink too much in case we miss our train. Betty won't be happy if we don't turn up at work. It's Maureen's last day and she still hasn't found someone to replace her in the canteen. Here, there's a table in the corner,' she called out to Maisie, who was forging ahead through the crowd around the busy bar. 'It looks like the fleet's in,' she grinned to Freda as they reached the crowd and the sound of happy drinkers became deafening.

'Along with the RAF and half the army. This place is packed out. I'm going to grab that table before someone beats us too it,' Freda shouted so that Sarah could hear her. 'Keep an eye on Maisie so she doesn't buy the strong stuff and get us drunk.'

'You'll be lucky, darling, they water it all down in here,' a chirpy sailor winked at her. 'On yer own, are you?'

Freda knew his sort and wasn't keen for his attention. 'I'm with my mates. My husband's at home looking after our ten kids. Where's your wife?' The sailor muttered something unpleasant and turned back to his friends. She was still smiling to herself when Maisie and Sarah appeared with the drinks. Times had changed. Two years ago she'd not have said boo to a goose, let alone sent a sailor off with his tail between his legs.

'What shall we toast to?' Maisie said, raising her glass above her head.

'Friendship?' Sarah suggested.

'We always toast to that. It goes without saying, doesn't it?' Maisie replied, still holding her glass up for the toast.

'Then let it be finding a good cook for the staff canteen or we'll die of hunger,' Sarah suggested.

'You can't toast to looking for a cook,' Maisie scoffed as her arm started to tremble.

'Besides, Betty is giving Enid from over the road a trial. I don't hold out much hope as she's next to useless as a cleaner but beggars can't be choosers,' Freda chipped in.

'God save us all,' Maisie declared and took a swig from her glass.

'I'm not sure I can manage another dance,' Gwyneth said, leaning over to rub her foot.

Mike looked glum. 'Goodness, I didn't step on your toes again, did I? My feet are more used to plodding the beat than dancing.'

Gwyneth gave him a tender smile. 'Oh Mike. You're a wonderful dancer. I could stay in your arms forever. It's just that I've been on my feet all day and these dance shoes Maisie lent me are a little tight.'

'Why didn't you say? Here, sit yourself down and I'll fetch you a drink while you rest. I shall find you the best dancing shoes money can buy, then you'll be able to dance with me to your heart's content at our wedding,' he declared as he led her to a vacant seat at the side of the dance floor.

A shadow crossed Gwyneth's face. 'Mike, I'm still not sure . . . I know I agreed to go dancing with you but as for a future together . . .' She looked down at the engagement ring Mike had placed on her finger not so very long ago.

Mike bent down and took her hands in his. 'Darling, things have changed. I have so much I want to say to you.' He looked round at the crowded dance studio. 'We can't talk here. Do you think your feet could stand me taking you for a short walk?'

Gwyneth nodded her head. She'd hear Mike out. As she'd near enough made up her mind to return to Wales with Myfi to live with her parents after changing her mind about the wedding, it was only fair she say goodbye to him properly. She hated disappointing the man she adored so much but there was no point in walking into a future together when both had different thoughts on how the marriage should proceed.

'I'll get our coats,' Mike grinned.

Gwyneth walked slowly through the dancing couples, avoiding looking at the happy faces. She would miss Mike so much it felt as though her heart was breaking, even though she had not yet told him she was leaving Erith. She met him at the entrance and he slipped her coat around her bare shoulders. She'd worn a pretty navy blue dance frock that was scattered with tiny yellow rosebuds. The darkness suited her black hair and sparkling eyes, although at the moment they portrayed only sadness.

'Here, take my arm or you'll trip in the darkness,' Mike said as they crossed from where Erith Dance Studios was situated and walked in companionable silence up Pier Road.

'It's hard to believe this town can be so busy during the day and then so quiet at night,' Gwyneth sighed. 'You can't even see the barrage balloons up the Thames.'

'We'll see them soon enough when the enemy approach. Our searchlights don't miss a thing.'

Gwyneth shuddered. 'I hate this war and what it's doing to people's lives. It took Myfi's mother, my twin sister, from us,' she said bitterly.

'Myfi's got you now and you're a fine mother. No one could ever argue with that.'

'It's not the same, though, is it?' She spun to look at him. Even though their faces were just inches from each other Mike couldn't see if she was angry or upset. Taking a torch from his pocket, he led Gwyneth to steps in front of the door of the Woolworths store and placed his coat down, encouraging her to sit on the top step before propping his torch against a window which gave off a small glow of light.

'Gwyneth, I've been a bloody fool. I've thought everything through and come to a decision.'

'So have I, Mike. I've decided to return to the Valleys. There's been too much heartache away from home. It's time Myfi returned to Wales and her roots. There's nothing here for either of us.'

Mike couldn't believe what he was hearing. 'Gwyneth, we had words. I know what I said wasn't what you wanted to hear but believe me, I only meant to do what was best for you and Myfi. I've not been married before and to be honest, the whole business petrifies me.'

Gwyneth rested her elbows on her knees and covered her face with her hands. After a moment she looked up at Mike and gave him a watery smile. 'Mike, don't you think it petrifies me as well? I've had a violent marriage and I've seen my sister killed and Myfi left on her own. When I met you it was like coming home after a long time alone at sea. You've been gentle and kind and above all, I found I loved you.'

Mike reached out and took her hand. 'I've never stopped loving you, Gwyneth. I could kick myself for being such a buffoon. I wanted a home for us and never thought for one moment that it wouldn't be big enough for a proper family . . .'

'You mean, you do want children?'

'I want to adopt Myfi and I also want our babies, if we should be blessed with them. I've been a bit of a fool about us having kiddies, thinking I was too old, but I've come to my senses.'

Gwyneth couldn't believe what she was hearing. 'More than one baby?'

'A hundred babies if that's what you want, my love,' he said, kissing the palm of her hand. 'Just don't run off to Wales and leave me alone. Promise me that.'

'I promise I'll never leave you, Mike,' was all she could say before he pulled her close and kissed her gently.

'I could kick myself for almost losing you,' he said. Gwyneth returned his kiss and for a few moments they didn't speak.

'I don't mind moving into the rooms up the Avenue. Maisie made them really homely.'

'It's too late. They've been taken,' Mike replied, his voice still husky after their shared kisses.

Gwyneth was disappointed. 'So we're still left without a home?'

'I have a lovely home ready for you across the road from Ruby.'

'But that's the home you share with your dad and you have a lodger from the police station,' she said, trying not to sound disappointed, but then gave herself a stern talking-to. She had Mike back and shouldn't expect too much, especially not in wartime. 'Don't worry, we can look for somewhere together. We should be grateful that we have each other,' she told him firmly so that he under-stood she was happy with her lot.

Mike roared with laughter. 'Oh my love, you don't

understand. Dad will move in with Ruby and we can find somewhere else for the lodger to live, even if it means him kipping in a cell down the station.'

'That would be perfect,' she sighed.

Gwyneth was just snuggling into Mike's arms when they heard hurried footsteps and then someone bellowing, 'Put that light out!'

'God, I forgot Dad was on ARP duty,' Mike said, grabbing the torch to switch it off and pulling Gwyneth to her feet.

'What the hell's going on here? You could have alerted half the German air force to come and bomb us,' Bob roared as he arrived in front of them gasping for breath.

'Hello, Dad, you'll be pleased to hear the wedding's back on.'

11
~

'How pleasant it is for us all to sit down to dinner together,' Betty smiled at Douglas and the two girls as she dished vegetables onto their plates from her best serving dish. She'd pulled out all the stops seeing as how it felt like a special occasion.

Clemmie slouched sullenly in her seat, stabbing at potatoes on her plate. 'Sit up properly and eat your dinner,' Douglas reprimanded her.

'I don't like fish,' the girl replied, giving Betty a hateful glare. 'Everyone knows I really hate fish.' She threw her fork down on the table, giving a grin as it bounced across the white linen tablecloth leaving food marks in its trail.

Betty gripped her knife and fork and tried hard not to look annoyed. She knew from past experience that this was exactly the reaction Clemmie wished to see. Were all eleven-year-old girls like this? Would things improve when Clemmie reached her twelfth or thirteenth birthday? It was her birthday in a few days. Perhaps she should plan something nice for her? Betty thought to herself as she tried to keep the talk pleasant around the table while Douglas picked up the offending cutlery and handed it back to his daughter. She took it begrudgingly but did start to eat her food.

'So, Dorothy, how was school today? Did you have your reading test?'

The younger girl swallowed a mouthful of food and nodded. 'Yes, Betty, I read three pages of *Peter Pan* to Miss Peebles and she said I was coming along nicely.'

Betty tried not to grin. The girl was no trouble at all. Things had got so bad in the house of late that she often wished Dorothy had been an only child. She wondered, if she had been expecting a baby, rather than going through 'later life' as her doctor had laughingly suggested, if the baby would have been as temperamental as Clemmie? God forbid, she almost said aloud. 'That is good news, Dorothy. There's nothing better than to be able to read and enjoy a story. I'm fond of reading myself. By the way, girls, I wondered if either of you had come across two half crowns? I seemed to have misplaced them. One minute they were in my purse and then I must have taken the money out and left them somewhere. Rather silly of me but it is a lot of money to lose. I was hoping to use them for a special treat.'

Douglas raised his eyebrows but didn't speak. Betty knew she would be quizzed later.

'Oh dear,' Dorothy said in a sad voice, 'does that mean we won't have our treat now?'

'I'm afraid so. Money doesn't grow on trees, as well you both know. Money has to be earned or given as a gift.' Betty found only Dorothy was interested as Clemmie was finally tucking into her meal with gusto . . .

'What was all that about at dinner?' Douglas asked later

when the girls had gone to bed and they were enjoying a cup of cocoa sitting by the last embers of the fire. It had turned cold during the evening and Betty had lit the pre-pared fire on a whim.

'Oh, something and nothing. I seem to be getting a little forgetful these days and thought I might have mis-laid the money. No doubt it'll turn up soon enough.'

'And the treat?'

'It's Clemmie's twelfth birthday soon and we should celebrate the occasion as a family. What did you do last year? Did she have a party with her friends? I'd not like to repeat what you did unless you feel she would enjoy it.'

Douglas put his newspaper down and thought for a moment. 'I do believe she requested a new coat with a fur collar. Yes, we went shopping for a blue coat and we found a matching hat and gloves. Come to think of it, I've not seen her wear it since her birthday tea.'

Betty frowned. 'Are you sure you have that right, my love? Little girls don't often request clothing for their eleventh birthday.'

Douglas again put his newspaper down on his lap. 'I'm right; she wanted a coat as her two friends had similar garments. We went up to the West End, as there was a certain store where the coat could be purchased. She was most particular about it and wore the coat home and to school the next day. It is strange that I've not seen her wear it since.'

'Perhaps she's grown out of it. If that's the case, I'll have Maisie alter it to fit Dorothy. Waste not want not.'

'Why didn't I think of that?' Douglas said, giving up all hope of reading his newspaper.

'Because, dear husband, that is what a wife is for. You are the breadwinner. Now, perhaps you can update me on how your business is running? Have you found new staff so we can have the pleasure of your company at the dinner table every evening?'

'I'd hoped to have attracted new staff by now, but with Fothergill's Funeral Service undercutting us and paying higher staff wages the business is worse off than ever. It means I'm going to have to be a hands-on undertaker for a while longer and catch up with paperwork after the last interment of the day. So I'm afraid that means more late nights for the foreseeable future.'

'Oh, what a terrible bore,' Betty sighed, picking up her *Woman's Weekly* magazine and flicking through the pages. An article about women supporting their menfolk during wartime caught her attention. 'I do believe I have the answer,' she declared.

'Unless you can have a word in Hermann Göring's ear and have him organize the Luftwaffe to drop a hundred-ton bomb on Fothergill's, I'm not sure how you can help, my dear,' Douglas sighed.

'I'm afraid my days as a femme fatale are well and truly over, Douglas,' Betty chuckled, 'but I'm a dab hand at paperwork. Instead of coming home straight from Woolworths each evening I intend to head to your office and get stuck in with the paperwork. We can get through this together, I'm sure of that,' she smiled, reaching across and patting his hand. 'I'll go upstairs and collect Clemmie's coat while I think of it. Maisie is bound to come into the store and if I have the coat in my office, I can hand it over to her. I'll take Dorothy's winter coat so she'll be able to take measurements.'

Creeping into the girls' room so as not to wake them, she opened the large oak wardrobe that almost covered one wall of the bedroom. It was a piece of furniture that had once belonged to their mother. Betty shivered as she opened one of the doors as she could smell what she believed must have been Clementine's perfume. Reaching into the back of the wardrobe, past rows of pretty dresses and outfits that the girls must most certainly have grown out of, Betty thought it was time they had a sort-out. Maisie's two nieces would be in need of clothes and she knew that young Myfi might also fit into some, being that much smaller in size in comparison to Dorothy, who was prone to being a chubby little girl. She spotted the blue coat and reached for the hanger, bringing the garment out into the room that was lit by a small nightlight. Her shocked gasp woke Dorothy, whose bed was closest to where Betty stood. 'I knew someone would find out one day. I told Clemmie she should have thrown the coat away,' the child said, still groggy with sleep.

Betty checked the curtains were drawn before switching on the light, causing Clemmie to wake with a start. 'What is this all about?' Betty demanded, holding up the smart woollen coat that had a cut from hem to waistband and a slash across one cuff that was now hanging off.

'I told you you'd be found out one day, Clem,' Dorothy said before hiding under the bed covers.

Betty threw the coat over the bottom of Dorothy's bed and turned back to the wardrobe. 'Do you have any more damaged clothes hiding in there . . . ?' She froze as the sound of coins hit the linoleum-covered floor and two half crowns rolled towards her. She stamped on them to stop them rolling away before shouting at Clemmie. 'Explain this, please!'

Clemmie stared at Betty. The indolence had disappeared and been replaced with a look of fear.

Dorothy peered from behind a silky green eiderdown. 'You have to tell Betty, Clem. She can help you.'

Betty frowned. Whatever was going on here? Moving towards Clemmie's bed, she was surprised to see her flinch. 'I won't hurt you,' she said gently, sitting on the edge of the bed. 'I'd never do anything to hurt you, Clemmie. Why don't you sit up and tell me all about it?' As she spoke she was aware that Dorothy had climbed from her bed and was now sitting close to her sister, sucking her thumb. 'Please tell me what happened to your coat? You have no need to worry about it. I'm sure Maisie can help us to fix it.'

'I hate the coat, I hate it,' the girl started to sob, at which point her sister joined in. It was some seconds before the younger sister put her arms around the elder and whispered loudly. 'Tell Betty. I know she'll make things all right again. Please, Clemmie, please.'

Betty watched the two sisters, feeling honoured to be part of their world. She could see that for a long time it had been just the two of them looking out for each other. Douglas would have been oblivious to what went on in a little girl's life and as good as she was, the woman who was there for them every day was only a housekeeper paid to feed the family and keep the house clean. Something had happened that meant they could only trust each other.

'You call tell me everything. I promise not to be angry. I want to help you both,' she pleaded, reaching out to touch both of the girls.

Dorothy spoke first. 'It's that horrid Cecily Fitzsimons. She's been absolutely horrid to our Clem.'

'Is this true, Clemmie? Was it Cecily who damaged your coat?'

Clemmie shook her head. 'No, I did it.'

'But why? It's such a pretty coat. You must have looked so smart in it. I believe your daddy bought you a hat and gloves to match, what happened to them?'

'We hid them in my toy box,' Dorothy volunteered. 'They're covered in mud. The other girls threw Clem's hat in a muddy puddle and then laughed at her.'

Betty's head was buzzing. None of this made sense. It was getting late and the girls had school in the morning and Betty had a busy day at Woolworths. She longed to climb into her bed and just sleep but knew there would be two little girls who would lie awake all night worrying. 'I tell you what we'll do. I'm going downstairs to make us all a cup of cocoa. I'll bring it up here with the biscuit tin and we can snuggle down and have a good chat. What do you think of that?'

Dorothy grinned and climbed in beside her sister, who looked at Betty with her large brown eyes. 'You'll let us drink cocoa in bed? We may spill it on the covers.'

'It'll be fun and the covers can be washed. I'll be two ticks,' she said, tucking Clemmie's pink eiderdown around the two girls and leaving the room.

She'd not got as far as the head of the stairs when she

heard Dorothy declare, 'I told you Betty would be a good mummy.'

Betty thought her heart would break. Whatever had happened with these two little girls that they had secrets they thought they had to hide from everyone else?

She was soon back upstairs and, as good as her word, had milky cocoa and biscuits. The girls giggled when Betty draped them both with a clean tea towel before handing them their drinks. They drank and chatted about nothing in particular until the empty cups were back on the tray and Betty had wiped their mouths. 'Now, I want you to start at the beginning and tell me everything that has happened with this . . . Cecily?'

'Yes, it is Cecily. She's the one being horrid to our Clem,' Dorothy said, full of confidence now that she knew Betty was going to help them.

'Why don't we let Clemmie tell us the story, shall we?' she said, reaching out to hold the girls' hands.

'When we started at the new school my teacher sat me next to Cecily. She was everybody's friend,' Clemmie started after taking a big breath. 'We used to play together at playtimes and I would sit next to her in the school shelter when there was an air raid. We held hands when we were scared.'

'Cecily used to tell us about the ghosts in the shelter,' Dorothy piped in before putting her hand over her mouth, knowing she'd been told to let Clemmie talk.

'Did she try to frighten you?' Betty asked.

'Yes, she would pinch me if I didn't let her see my answers in our arithmetic lessons. She said that mummy's ghost would come and get us and she would be a nasty ghost who would hurt us.'

'Darlings, for one thing, there is no such thing as ghosts and for another, your mummy would never hurt you. She loved you both very much.' She looked up to where Clementine's portrait hung on the wall staring down at them. Perhaps she would have it moved tomorrow.

'That's when she told Clemmie that she wasn't to ask for toys for her birthday last year and was to ask for a blue coat just like the one she wore.'

'Then why was your coat damaged?' Betty asked, not understanding where the conversation was going.

'I wore it to school and also the hat and gloves and Cecily said I'd copied her and all the other girls laughed at me. Cecily said they weren't to speak to me.'

'They didn't talk to us for a whole week,' Dorothy added as her chin started to wobble. Betty sat closer to the girls and hugged them both.

She thought her heart would break. When she'd first met Douglas he'd told her proudly how he had put both the girls into a private school run by two genteel ladies and how excited the girls had been to meet new friends. It was a weight off his mind while he was working to know they were in safe hands. 'Your daddy doesn't know about this?'

Both girls shook their heads and looked fearful. 'Cecily said if we told Daddy then Mummy's ghost would get Mr Hitler to kill him and we would be orphans. She said that to be her friend again Clemmie had to cut up her coat and wear it home.'

Betty was livid. What a spiteful child. She wanted to

march up to the school tomorrow morning and give the headmistress a piece of her mind for allowing such things to go on under her roof.

'So you cut up your coat, Clemmie?'

Clemmie looked fearful but didn't speak.

'Under the circumstances I'd have probably done the same, but what about your hat and gloves?'

'When Clem put her coat on the others girls made fun of her and pulled off her hat and threw it into a puddle.'

'My gloves got muddy when I rescued my hat,' Clemmie said dolefully. 'I did like my hat and that's when I started to cry and Cecily pushed me over.'

'Cecily and her friends don't speak to us anymore. We sit on our own and try not to look at them so they don't call us names.'

'How does the money come into this?' Betty asked, wondering about the two half crowns that had been taken from her purse.

'That was my idea,' Dorothy said. 'We were going to run away so Cecily couldn't be nasty to us anymore as she said you would die too if you were our mummy. We wanted the money to buy a train ticket that would take us to the seaside.'

'We were going to hide in the tunnels in Ramsgate,' Clemmie volunteered proudly.

Relieved the girls trusted her enough to share their problem, Betty had to inwardly smile at their plans. The girls had been fascinated when Ruby's intended, Bob, had told them all about the tunnels under the streets of the seaside town where people hid when the air raids were at their height. Bob had explained about the bunk beds lined up along the sides of the tunnels where people slept and the girls could talk of nothing else for days. Betty had an inkling that the deep hole she'd found behind the rhubarb plants had something to do with young Dorothy planning her own tunnel. 'You know that you're too young to go off on adventures to the seaside alone? If you'd have told me, I might have been able to go with you,' she said, keeping a straight face. 'I enjoyed an adventure when I was your age. When were you planning to come home?'

'When Cecily stopped being horrid,' Clemmie admitted.

'Your father and I would have missed you terribly,' Betty said, doing her utmost to look sad.

Dorothy slipped her hand into Betty's. 'Sorry. You can come with us if you want?' she added excitedly. 'We will need more money for your train ticket, though.'

'I have a better idea,' Betty said. 'Why don't you both come to work with me tomorrow? Your father and I will deal with the problem of Cecily and her pranks. You're not to worry about the damaged coat, Clemmie.'

Dorothy looked delighted for a couple of seconds before asking, 'Will we get told off for not going to school?'

'I'll deal with your school. You get yourselves off to sleep. You're both working girls tomorrow and you need your beauty sleep.'

They snuggled into their beds as Betty went downstairs to tell her husband what she proposed to do for the two girls.

*

'This liver and bacon is as tough as old boots,' Freda said, trying to cut through the unappetizing food on her plate.

'The mashed potato is no better. Slops with lumps in is a better description. I do wonder if Enid has ever cooked for more than her family before?'

'I can't eat this,' Freda said, pushing the plate away. 'We have half an hour before we're due back downstairs. I'm going to walk round the corner and treat myself to a bag of chips. Fancy coming with me?'

Sarah didn't need any second bidding. 'Just let me stick my head in Betty's office and tell her I'm off out in case she needs me. She has her hands full today, what with having her daughters with her.'

'That does seem rather strange. So unlike Betty to mix her home life with work.'

Sarah frowned. 'Once married a woman does have to put her family first. You'll understand one day, Freda.'

Freda chuckled. 'Then I hope I never marry or have children as I can't think of anything worse.'

Sarah was shocked. 'But you help run the Brownies and Girl Guides. You love organizing activities with the girls.'

'It doesn't mean I want a houseful of children. If I ever have a family, it will be on my terms. Maisie doesn't appear to be downtrodden by her David and look at Betty still running a busy Woolworths store. If Betty has brought the children to work, it must be for a reason rather than her wanting to be close to them all day long.'

'One day I'll remind you of that when you're up to your eyes in dirty nappies,' Sarah grinned as she knocked on the office door.

'Oh, girls, how did your lunch go? Is Enid coping?'

Betty asked as soon as they entered the room. 'As bad as that?' she asked as Freda wrinkled her nose.

'So bad we thought we'd walk down to the fish and chip shop for a portion of chips. That should keep us going until we close up shop for the day,' Sarah said, giving Betty an apologetic smile. 'I just hope Enid will do better tomorrow.'

'She's told me it's toad in the hole. Can that be spoilt?'

Freda grinned. 'We'll soon find out. At least the chip shop will do a roaring trade. Would you like us to bring you something back?'

'That does sound tempting but I'd best wave the flag for Woolworths for today. It wouldn't do for staff to see me avoiding the canteen on Enid's first day.' She noticed Clemmie and Dorothy's disappointed faces. 'You've been very good this morning, girls, and I think just this once you can have chips for your lunch.' She delved into her bag and took out her purse, giving both girls a few coins. 'Stay close to Freda and Sarah and be good,' she warned as the delighted girls jumped to their feet and followed the two women out of the office.

Watching them go, she reached for the telephone and dialled the number to connect her to Douglas's business. It seemed to take an age before the telephone was answered and passed to her husband. She chatted for a couple of minutes, assuring him that the girls were no problem for today, and then outlined an idea that had been forming about the girls and the family's future life. 'Douglas, I know we have a perfectly adequate home at the present but I feel a change would suit the girls as they could attend a new school and . . . well, I'd feel like a new bride living in her own home with her husband. We would all be together on a new adventure.'

Betty waited to hear what Douglas had to say. The home she'd seen advertised was situated closer to Erith and would also be convenient for Douglas to get to his business each day. The idea had been bubbling in her mind for a while and when she spotted an advertisement in the *Erith Observer* yesterday she knew it was the ideal property for their family. With the events of last night she'd forgotten to mention the possible move. She knew that if she waited until she was home this evening and the girls were settled for the night, she would lose her nerve and not tell Douglas of her idea. The benefit of having a telephone at one's disposal made the chance for a quiet chat so much easier. 'Douglas, what do you think?'

Her husband roared with laughter. 'You seem to have our lives mapped out, Betty. I can't see any problem with renting a property while I put our current home on the market. Yes, it's a splendid idea. It will also remove the influence of that damn child Cecily on our daughters. Perhaps we could view the house this coming weekend?'

Betty agreed and wished her husband a good afternoon before taking herself off to the staff canteen to test out Enid's liver and bacon. She grimaced at the thought and wished she'd agreed to join the girls to eat chips soaked in salt and vinegar out of newspaper wrapping. But no, she had a job to do and if Enid wasn't too busy, she wanted to have a quiet word with her.

*

'You're late tonight,' was the only greeting Enid received as she walked through the front door of the rooms they rented in Alexandra Road. She could see from the dirty plate and cup on the floor beside his armchair that Harry Singleton hadn't moved far for most of the day. 'You should have put our tea on by now,' he moaned.

'I told you I'd be working longer hours now I've taken over the kitchen duties. I could slip off earlier when I was just a cleaner but now I've got responsibilities. It wouldn't have hurt you to put a few potatoes on to boil. We'd have been eating a bit earlier and you wouldn't have been so grumpy,' she added for good measure as she took a parcel from her shopping bag and carefully placed it on the table.

'What you got there? Is it fish? I could just fancy a bit of fish for a change,' he said, sniffing the air as Enid started to undo the layer of newspaper she'd carefully wrapped around the food.

'When would I have had chance to queue for fish? No, there was a bit of grub left over so I thought waste not want not. We may as well put it to good use.'

Harry wrinkled his nose in disgust. 'Liver? I'd rather go without, thank you very much.'

Enid ignored his jibes. It was always the same. He'd not refused a meal yet and wasn't likely to, she thought as she rummaged through a box under the sink where she kept their vegetables. The spuds had started to sprout but she deftly cut those bits off and sliced each into four pieces and covered them in the hot water left in the kettle. The lazy so-and-so had managed to boil water for his cup of tea. There was a bit of cabbage left too. Pulling off the yellowing outer leaves, she chopped the remains up and threw it into a pot ready for a quick boil once the spuds were done. As she moved around the small kitchen clearing up the debris from Harry's day she thought to herself that Ruby Caselton over the road wouldn't be having to poke round in a pile of veg that was on the turn just to sort out an evening meal. She'd heard her talking about that Bob Jackson's pig club and how the members put their scraps into a bin that was collected to feed the animal. Her mouth watered as she thought about roast pork. What she wouldn't give to have a roast pork dinner to sit down to right now.

Tipping the cold liver and bacon into a frying pan, she lit the gas underneath and added a drop of hot water to the food to create a watery gravy. Once it was bubbling she dished up the meal and carried the two plates to the table. 'Get yourself up here and eat it while it's hot,' she said to her husband, who was frowning at a letter he held in his hand. 'What you got there?'

'It's a letter. It came this afternoon. Seems they want me down the labour exchange for an interview as they think I'm fit for going into the services. They must be joking.'

Enid's face twitched as she saw the beads of nervous sweat forming on Harry's brow. 'Your bad back does seem better in recent weeks.'

He scowled at her. 'It's all right for you with your comfortable job at Woolworths cooking a bit of grub and pushing a broom about. A man has to work hard and it's his duty to be fit to fight for his country. I'm not up to it and I'll have to tell 'em so.'

'Didn't Doctor Graham say as you only need to get

some exercise and you'll be fighting fit before you know it? He did suggest you joined the Home Guard.'

Harry Singleton sighed as he made a show of walking to the dinner table. 'If I could do so, I would, even if it means that retired copper Bob Jackson telling me what to do. I'm not one to shirk my duties.'

'It's a shame you aren't in a reserved occupation,' Enid suggested as she sat opposite her husband. 'At least then you wouldn't get called up to fight in the services.'

'Fat chance I've got of getting into a reserved occupation,' he said, chewing on a particularly rubbery piece of liver. 'Don't you think I'd have done that if I could?'

Enid put down her knife and fork and smiled sweetly at her husband. 'I may just be able to help you there. My manager told me her husband is looking for an odd job man to work in his business,' she smiled sweetly.

'Oh yeah? How does that get me out of going off to fight?'

'He's an undertaker.'

Harry Singleton smiled thoughtfully as he continued to eat his meal.

12

July 1943

'Who was it suggested we go and work for the railway?' Maureen asked as she kicked off one of her black leather work shoes and leant over to rub her toes. 'My feet are killing me. Do you think this job will ever get easier?'

Irene joined Maureen on the small bench and yawned. 'I hate to be the killjoy but we both thought working on the railway would help us win the war. All I've done in the past month is learn the timetable of all trains from the coast up to London and found out that handling baskets of carrier pigeons makes me sneeze. I had a hell of a time getting feathers off my uniform,' she declared, checking her railway-issue jacket and brushing off imaginary marks. 'George thought I'd been attacked by a flock of birds when I returned home and he wouldn't stop chuckling all evening.'

Maureen grinned to herself. George was a good sort and at times his wife could be a little po-faced. There was never much merriment in their house unless young Georgina visited her grandparents. Maureen would love to have seen him with a smile on his face. Just because there was a war on it didn't mean they couldn't have a laugh or two. 'How's it going with your George at Vickers? Is he still busy?'

'Busy? I never see him to ask about his day. We seem to be like ships that pass in the night, what with his long hours and my shift work. It'll be even worse once we have to do night shifts when we're completely trained.'

'It could be worse,' Maureen said. 'At least you know he's only a few streets away from home. Sarah's at her wit's end not having seen our Alan all these months. I must say, I'm missing him as well.'

'Has Sarah not received a letter recently?' Irene asked as she combed her hair and repositioned her uniform cap.

'There was a letter for both of us a couple of weeks ago but we couldn't make anything out from what he wrote. We even steamed off the stamps to see if he'd left a clue. It was something that Freda's brother does while he's away at sea. Then the letters arrived out of order and she never did find out what he was trying to say. The way the war's panning out at the moment he could be almost anywhere in the world.'

'At least he's safe,' Irene said.

'How do you make that out?'

'If he was a prisoner of war, the letters would come via the Red Cross. I heard someone at my WI meeting saying that's how she heard about her son.'

'God forbid,' Maureen shuddered. 'I just wish we could get back to normal. I for one will be happy when I'm back in the kitchen of Woolworths cooking for the staff.'

Irene looked down her nose. 'You'd go back there?'

'Betty came round to see if there was any chance of me coming back. It seems the new cook isn't up to scratch. But I can't just drop things here and go running back, can I?'

'It's up to you. You're over the age of fifty so not obliged to do war work like I am. However, I thought you'd have wanted to do something more worthwhile.'

Maureen tried not to grin. She was less than two years older than Irene. 'Years ago I had the chance to sing with a dance band but our Alan was still at school and it didn't seem the right thing to do. Perhaps I'd have been another Gracie Fields or Vera Lynn singing to cheer up the troops.'

'Anything would be better than working on this station platform in all weathers. I suppose even peeling potatoes in the Woolworths staff canteen sounds enticing.'

Maureen didn't answer. She missed her old job more than she'd ever thought she would. From what Sarah had said the new cook wasn't up to much and they'd started to take their own food into work rather than eat what Enid was cooking. She'd promised Betty that as soon as she had a free day in between her shifts she'd visit the store and give Enid a tip or two. She looked up, breaking away from her thoughts, as the stationmaster walked into the waiting room where they'd been resting.

'Come on, you two. Whoever said a woman could do a man's job was talking out of his backside. Caselton, there's a train due in shortly and we need those bloody birds loaded or they'll not get to the coast. Gilbert, you can take a turn in the ticket office. Look sharp now,' he grunted as he left.

'Oh no,' Irene sighed. 'I just hope there's a strong guard on the train who can help me. I almost let a flock of birds out yesterday when a basket fell open.'

Maureen laughed as she bid Irene goodbye. A few hours in the ticket office was all right with her. It was a little pokey but draft-free and she got to chat with passengers. Working on their local station meant she knew many of the travellers and the rest of the shift would pass quickly enough.

Settling herself onto a stool, she peered out through the small glass screen and started to sing, '*A room with a view and you . . .*' She was rather partial to a Noël Coward song.

'I recognize that voice,' Ruby Caselton said as she appeared at the small window. 'What's all this, music while you work?'

Maureen stopped singing and peered back at Ruby. 'Hello there. I find it passes the time in between selling tickets. I'm also fond of, "*Oh! Mr Porter, what shall I do . . .*"'

'Ha! I wondered where Georgina had got that from. She tends to sing the same few words over and over again.'

'Bless her, she's such a little wonder, but then I would say that being as she's my only grandchild at the moment. If our Alan doesn't come home soon, it's unlikely we'll see any more little ones from the pair of them.'

'I may just have news for you. Sarah gave me this to pass on to you, as she knew I'd most likely bump into you this afternoon. She's that excited but I'll leave you to read your news,' Ruby said, passing over an envelope with Alan's handwriting on the front.

'Oh my,' Maureen beamed, clutching the letter to her

chest. 'If you don't mind, I'll take a quick look at what he has to say. There doesn't seem to be anyone queuing behind you. Are you off to Dartford or taking yourself up to London?' Maureen asked distractedly as she tore open the envelope.

'You won't find me going off to London. I thought I'd go to Dartford as it's market day and the train's quicker than the bus. Two stops and I'll be there. I might even have time to pop into the Co-op and have a look about.'

Maureen nodded her head but Ruby could see she wasn't listening to a word that was being said. Her face turned pale before she looked up at Ruby. 'He's coming home. My boy's coming home. He's reckons he'll be here on leave in time for Mike and Gwyneth's wedding.'

'A return to Charlton, please, love,' a man said, leaning past Ruby and dropping a couple of coins onto the brass plate screwed to the counter below the serving hatch.

Maureen gave him a small smile, passing a ticket and a couple of coppers in change back through the gap. 'Over the other side in two minutes, mate. You'd best hurry.' The man tipped the edge of his cap before rushing off towards the stairs that took passengers over the track to the other side of the line.

'He'll have to put a spurt on if he wants to get the train,' Ruby observed as she watched the man stop to catch his breath at the top of the stairs.

'He'll be all right. Irene's over on that side, she'll hold the train for him.' They both looked across the rails to where Irene was standing with her hands on her hips by a stack of wicker pigeon baskets. She was looking to where the signals had just changed and a train was slowly approaching the platform.

Ruby waved before the train obliterated the view of her daughter-in-law. 'I'd best get my ticket before I forget it,' she said, turning back to hand her money over the counter. 'Is there anything you want me to pick up for you while I'm in Dartford?'

Maureen cocked her head to one side and gave some thought to the question. 'A rich husband wouldn't come amiss,' she laughed.

'I'll keep it in mind but it's not the kind of thing you'd usually see on the shelf of the Co-op, or Woolworths come to that,' she laughed before her face took on a serious expression. 'Would you marry again?'

'It's never really crossed my mind. I'm happy enough with my lot. I miss my old man but I have family and friends around me so life is as good as it can be at the moment. Why do you ask?' she said, seeing the smile slip from Ruby's face. 'Are you having second thoughts about Bob's proposal?'

Ruby shrugged her shoulders. 'I think I've been a bit of a fool. I should have left things as they were but it's too late now.'

'It's never too late, Ruby. Bob will be disappointed but if you're honest with him, he'll get over it. He's a decent bloke,' Maureen said, looking concerned for the older woman. Ruby was always the one who could sort things out for others and here she was unsure of her own future. Anyone would tell her that Bob was perfect for her but Ruby needed to know for herself.

'Bob's planning to move into my place so that Gwyneth

and Mike have Mike's house to themselves after the wedding. He'll have Gwyneth's room. I said I don't want no hanky-panky in my house so you needn't raise your eyebrows like that, Maureen Gilbert,' she added, noticing Maureen's shocked expression. 'If I change my mind now, then it may stop the wedding and we already know that Gwyneth's had a few wobbles. I'd never be able to live with myself if the girl didn't marry Mike.'

'I can see your predicament,' Maureen said. 'If you make it clear to all and sundry that Bob is just your lodger for now, then you shouldn't have any problems. Bob's not daft. If he can see the pair of you aren't getting along as you should, then he may do the honourable thing and let you off your promise,' she advised.

'That could work. Thank you, Maureen,' Ruby said with a sigh. 'I know I should have spoken to someone sooner rather than having bottled this up for so long.'

'What would make you sure you were meant to marry Bob?' Maureen said, stopping only to sell a train ticket to an elderly woman.

'You're going to think I'm daft – I know Bob did when I explained it to him, but he accepted what I had to say. But that was a while ago now and I can't keep putting him off, can I?'

'You can tell me, Ruby. I'll not think you're daft. You're the most sane person I've ever known.'

Ruby turned to check there wasn't anyone nearby then leant in close to the window to the ticket office and in a half-whisper said, 'I'm waiting for my Eddie to give me a sign that he approves of me marrying again. I don't expect him to appear in front of me and speak but there must be a way that I know he's all right with me remarrying.'

Maureen nodded her head slowly. 'Yes, I can see what you mean. Give it time, Ruby. Something is bound to happen,' was all she could advise, although she decided that if there was a way she could help Ruby with her problem, then she would.

Ruby gave out a sigh of relief. 'I knew you'd understand. Now, I'd best get myself up the platform a bit or I'll have a long walk when I get off the other end. I'll see you later, Maureen, and thank you for the chat. I really do appreciate it.'

Ruby walked slowly up the platform towards the stairs that led to the bridge taking travellers to the other side of the track. She spotted Irene helping someone down the steps. It would be rude of her not to stop and say hello. As the couple reached the bottom of the steps she could see that Irene was holding a small suitcase in one hand and the arm of a heavily pregnant young woman wearing a voluminous smock top with the other. 'There you are, my dear. Are you sure you wouldn't like me to find you a seat for a little while until you catch your breath?'

The woman assured Irene she was fine although she looked a little flushed around the cheeks, and after taking her suitcase she walked slowly towards the door that led out of the station and towards Erith town, giving Ruby a puzzled look as she passed by.

'I never expected to see her come back to Erith so soon. Not in that condition,' Ruby said as she gave Irene a quick kiss on the cheek.

Irene frowned. 'Do you know her? She seemed very well spoken and polite,' she added in surprise.

Ruby laughed. 'I do know people who speak properly, Irene. Do you mean to say you didn't recognize her?'

'Should I?'

'That's Vera's granddaughter. The one who had the important job in London. I mentioned to you how they'd fallen out when Vera had her little misfortunes a few months ago.' She hadn't told her daughter-in-law the full story and the circumstances of Sadie's problems. 'I'm pleased to see they've made up and the girl's come home to see her nan. I'm surprised that Vera never told me about it, though.'

'I have no idea what you are going on about, mother-in-law,' Irene said primly. 'The girl never mentioned Vera or Alexandra Road. In fact, she asked directions to another part of Erith.'

'Then perhaps she's found somewhere to live on her own. I must admit, I'd find it hard to live under the same roof as Vera. I doubt she'd be too keen on a young baby living with her. She's never been much of one for kiddies. It's good to see a young girl providing for herself and not relying on relatives.' Perhaps she's made it up with the man she was carrying on with and he has provided for her, Ruby thought to herself. But wasn't he married?

'I need to get on with my work,' Irene said with not a little irritation in her voice. 'I do believe you have the wrong person. As I said, this one is not heading to Alexandra Road as she's walking to the other side of town to Oakhurst House in Lesney Park Road. You know that's the home for unmarried mothers, don't you?' she added with a small smirk. 'That would be a turn-up for the books, wouldn't it? Vera wouldn't like people to know her well-to-do granddaughter was going to that establishment.'

Irene left Ruby standing alone on the platform as her train slowly pulled into the station surrounded by a cloud of steam and a lot of hissing. Ruby felt numb as she climbed aboard. Even if Vera made up her differences with her granddaughter, she was never likely to set eyes on her great-grandchild. At the church-run maternity home that Irene had mentioned the babies were taken away and adopted as soon as they were born. Was this why Sadie was back in Erith?

'You look as pretty as a picture,' Freda said, admiring the flowing silk skirt edged with lace as Gwyneth turned around in her wedding gown. The girls were at Maisie's house where the front room had been turned into a dressmaker's workshop as preparations stormed ahead for Gwyneth and Mike's big day. 'No one would guess it was second-hand. It fits you perfectly.'

'You'll be bleeding all over the blooming dress if you don't stand still,' Maisie grumbled from one side of her mouth, the other being full of pins. 'Let me just check the neckline looks right. I had to unpick and remake the bodice as it was so large.'

'I don't know how to start to thank you,' Gwyneth said, her voice breaking with emotion. 'Myfi looks adorable in her bridesmaid's dress, as does little Georgina.'

'I just hope that Georgie behaves. She is rather young

to have such a responsible position at your wedding. I dread to think what she'll get up to,' Sarah said from the settee where she was stitching lace edging to a peach-coloured dress. A larger version was spread out on a nearby armchair.

'I've been thinking about that,' Gwyneth said, standing very still as Maisie made a couple of stitches on the edge of the sweetheart neckline and stepped back to approve of her handiwork. 'I want the three of you to be my bridesmaids, as well as Bessie and Claudette. You've all been such good friends to us since we came to live in Erith and I really want to share my happy days with you all.'

Freda, Sarah and Maisie all looked at each other in surprise. 'I'd adore to be your bridesmaid,' Sarah said, 'but that means another three full-sized dresses and two for the girls. Even if we had the fabric, I'm not sure even Maisie could work that sort of miracle in six weeks.'

All eyes turned to Maisie who had yet to answer. 'I do believe it can be done. How do you feel if Sarah and Freda wear the bridesmaids' dresses they had for my wedding?'

'Mine will need taking out a little,' Freda said. 'What about you, Maisie? You can't very well wear your wedding dress,' she grinned.

'I have the gown I wore when Sarah and Alan were married.'

Gwyneth clapped her hands together in delight. 'How wonderful. I can't wait for my wedding day.'

'Hold on,' Freda said. 'What about Bessie and Claudette? What will they wear?'

Gwyneth's face fell. 'We can't really leave them out, can we?'

'We don't 'ave to,' Maisie said with a secret smile. 'Freda, you get the kettle on and, Sarah, help Gwyneth out of that dress. I'll just be a couple of ticks,' she said, putting down her needle and thread and dashing from the room.

'Goodness knows what Maisie's up to,' Sarah said as she undid the row of small buttons down the back of the dress and helped Gwyneth step from the silky skirts of her bridal gown. 'You're going to make a beautiful bride,' she sighed as she carefully hung the dress on the wooden picture rail that circled the wall of the room.

'I wish I'd seen you and Alan marry,' Gwyneth said. 'I've seen the photograph that Ruby has on her sideboard. It must have been such a wonderful day.'

Sarah gave a wry grin. 'It was memorable for many reasons. We married the day war was declared.'

'Oh my goodness,' Gwyneth said, placing her hand over her mouth to stifle a giggle. 'I shouldn't laugh but in years to come what a tale you'll be able to tell your grand-children.'

'And we'll have an anniversary I hope Alan will never forget,' Sarah said.

'He'll be home to see Mike make me his wife. You must be looking forward to seeing him after all these months?'

'We're hoping that by the time Alan heads off to wher-ever the Air Force decides to send him there may even be a little brother or sister for Georgie in the offing,' Maisie announced, entering the room, her arms filled with a froth of blue organza.

'Oh my,' Gwyneth said, as much in shock from Maisie's

words as she was to see what the woman was carrying. 'Whatever do you have there?'

'I didn't know you still had this dress,' Sarah said, reaching out and gently stroking the fabric and trying to ignore what Maisie had intimated, even though her cheeks were starting to turn pink with embarrassment. 'Didn't you wear this dress the first time David took you out dancing? You've never worn it since.'

Maisie shook out the dress and held it up to herself. The colour suited her blonde hair and English complexion. 'Ter be honest, I've never really liked it. The bodice was on the tight side and I'll not get into it again now I've had the baby. It's not as if I can pass it on to you lot as we are all of a similar size,' she said, looking at Sarah and Gwyneth who both nodded in agreement.

'More's the pity. The colour reminds me of cornflowers,' Sarah said.

'It'll make two nice frocks for Bessie and Claudette. They can have the same style as Myfi and Georgina's dresses.'

'Oh, but Maisie, I can't have you cutting up your beautiful dress for me,' Gwyneth said, although she too reached out to stroke the dress.

'I do believe there'll be enough left to get a little dress out of it for the baby as well. What a colourful group of bridesmaids we're going ter make,' she said, reaching for her scissors.

'I'll be followed down the aisle by a rainbow. I honestly don't know how to thank you, Maisie,' Gwyneth said, giving her a kiss on the cheek. 'There's my parents thinking we're going to have a quiet wedding because of the war. They won't expect to see all this finery. It's all so exciting. If there's anything I can ever do for you . . .'

'You can start by helping Freda with that tea. I'm fair parched,' Maisie said with a wink to her friends.

Sarah gave a smile to the young woman standing at her counter. 'May I help you?'

The girl gazed up from where she was looking through knitting patterns and shook her head. 'I'm just looking, thank you,' she said wistfully.

'This is a nice pattern and easy to follow. I knitted the cardigan and bootees when I was expecting my daughter and I'm all fingers and thumbs when it comes to knitting. You can't have long to wait now, can you?' she added, looking at the size of the girl in front of her.

The girl placed her hand on her stomach and winced. 'I'm overdue by a week.'

'How wonderful, you must be so excited?'

'I'll not bother with this,' the girl said as she turned away from Sarah.

'Wait a moment . . . don't I know you? Aren't you Vera's Munro's granddaughter? I'm Sarah Gilbert, Ruby Caselton's granddaughter. How are you?'

'I'm sorry, I've got to go,' the young girl said and disappeared into the crowd of shoppers.

How strange, Sarah thought to herself as she went to serve a waiting customer. I'll have to ask Nan when I go to collect Georgie. Glancing up at the large clock on the wall of the store as she placed a customer's purchases into a brown paper bag, she noted her shift finished in another two hours.

Sarah let herself into her nan's house by pulling the string attached to the letter box until the she could reach the key. Nothing much changes, she thought to herself. She found Ruby sitting at the kitchen table drinking tea with Vera from up the road.

'Hello, Sarah love, the pot's still warm if you want to get yourself a cup and saucer. I've just put Georgina down for a nap. She's been helping Bob in the garden. He's given her a trowel and a couple of bulbs to plant. She loved helping him. I've washed her hands and face,' she added, seeing Sarah's grin. 'Bob said he'll replant the bulbs when she's gone home as most likely they've gone in upside down.'

Sarah laughed. 'I'll have to write to Alan and tell him that his daughter is now a gardener. That'll please him no end, as he'd rather spend his time tinkering with his old motorbike and getting greasy than planting things. How are you, Vera?' she asked before taking a sip of her tea. 'You must be so pleased to have Sadie back home with you?'

Ruby almost choked on her tea and did her utmost to stare at Sarah to alert her not to continue with the conversation. It was too late.

'My granddaughter is not living with me. I have no idea where she's living. I have a very respectable lodger at the moment. He's a police constable and known to Bob and Mike so comes highly recommended. I have no idea why you should think that Sadie is living under my roof,' she said, looking deeply offended.

ELAINE EVEREST

'I'm sorry, Vera . . . I had no idea . . .' she stuttered as she caught her nan pulling a strange face at her. 'I'll not say another word on the subject.'

They all drank their tea in silence until Vera spoke. 'What makes you think our Sadie is in town?'

'I spoke to her not an hour ago in Woolworths. She seemed . . . she seemed very well,' Sarah added, not liking to mention the girl's pregnancy in case Vera was unaware.

'If you mean she's in the family way and not married, then I'd not say that's looking well. I'd call it a sin,' Vera huffed. 'Besides, she's living miles away and not likely to be staying around here to shame her family.'

'I spotted her yesterday at the train station, Vera,' Ruby said, not happy with the way the conversation was going. 'She had a suitcase with her and was asking the way to Oakhurst.'

'Oh no,' Vera started to wail. 'Why would she come back and make me a laughing stock of the town? Whatever will people be saying about me?' she cried.

Sarah was alarmed. She hadn't meant to cause a problem by mentioning Vera's granddaughter. The woman had always spoken highly of the girl and how well she was doing. There was many a time that Vera had put Sadie up as a shining example of a hard-working girl and mentioned that she would never stoop to working in Woolworths like Sarah and her friends. 'Perhaps I'll collect Georgina and take her home,' Sarah said. 'Vera, I didn't mean to upset you, I'm sorry.'

Vera nodded as she wiped her eyes. 'You meant no harm. You're not to know what that girl's done to her old nan. If only she was a good girl like you. There's no need for you to go home on my account. You deserve an explanation.'

'I think this needs a fresh brew. I'll put the kettle on,' Ruby said as she got to her feet. 'I'll take Bob's out to him. I don't think we need him interrupting us while we chat,' she said, raising her eyebrows at Sarah as she went over to the stove and lit the gas.

When a fresh pot of tea was placed on the table and Ruby had delivered a mug out to Bob in the garden, she nodded to Vera. 'Perhaps start at the beginning so our Sarah knows what's been going on,' she urged the woman.

Vera cleared her throat and started to explain what had happened for her to send her granddaughter away. Ruby nodded her encouragement, already knowing the story. 'She lied to me,' she said to Sarah. 'I fell hook, line and sinker for her tales about her being engaged to her boss and him planning to marry her. Oh yes, he was very well thought of in his official job and was worth a penny or two but it turns out he had a wife and children. When Sadie came sobbing to me that she was expecting his baby and he'd sacked her and accused her of carrying another man's child, I sent her packing. I thought she was a good girl. She let me down. I washed my hands of her,' she said as the tears started once more.

Ruby was shocked. 'You didn't tell me she'd lost her job. I thought at least the blighter would have seen her all right.'

'I've no idea what happened after she walked out of my front door. She said she was all right for money. No doubt had another fancy man to look out for her. Her sort always do. I gave her my savings to make sure she never darkened my door again.'

'The poor girl,' Sarah said. She'd always found Sadie to be a snooty madam but no one deserved to be treated like that by a man. For her nan to turn her back on her only granddaughter was not something Sarah could understand. 'I couldn't think of anything worse than being alone while facing giving birth. She must have come back to Erith to be close to her home.'

Vera gave her a sharp look. 'Are you saying I've done wrong?'

Ruby took command. 'Now, now, Vera, there's no need to snap at our Sarah. How was the girl when you spoke to her, love?'

Sarah thought for a moment. 'We only spoke for a few moments as the counter I was working on was busy. Everyone seems to want knitting patterns at the moment. I didn't realize who it was to begin with and she said very little but I thought she was very thin in the face and withdrawn. Once she knew who I was she wanted to leave. I did think it strange that she was looking at knitting patterns but in a wistful kind of way.'

'She probably had no need of knitted baby clothes,' Ruby said.

'What do you mean, Nan? We all know you can't have too many knitted items for a baby.'

'There's no need when the girl won't be keeping the child. Many of the girls up at Oakhurst have their babies taken away for adoption,' Ruby said, giving Vera a sly look. 'What a to-do: your pregnant granddaughter back in Erith and living at a home for unmarried mothers, then to have her baby taken away. If people weren't talking about you before, they will after this, Vera. It's a shame you can't forgive her before the gossiping starts . . .'

Sarah watched Vera's face as the woman absorbed Ruby's words. She knew her nan could be crafty but this took the biscuit.

Vera stood up, looking angry. 'No one is going to take away my great-grandchild or talk about my family. I'll see to that,' she declared, reaching for her coat and marching from the house.

Ruby looked at Sarah and grinned. 'I thought that would make her see sense. I'd best go after her in case she causes a rumpus up at the unmarried mothers' home. You know what she can be like.'

'I know what you can be like as well, Nan,' Sarah giggled. With luck, Vera would have her granddaughter home and safe before the baby was born.

13

'Oh Douglas, I had no idea that things were this bad. Who'd have thought that a funeral director's business could lose money like this,' Betty said after opening the first of the ledgers on the large oak desk in Douglas's office. She stared in horror at the bank balance. 'I just wish I could have helped you earlier than this but with Woolworths and the family . . .'

Douglas reached over the desk and squeezed her arm. 'My dear wife, you work harder than many men that I know. I'm grateful for the time you can spare to help me. In truth, it's my fault the business isn't doing as well as it should.'

'Don't say that, you can't be in two places at the same time, and if you don't have the staff to turn out for the funerals, then it's only right you attend to the deceased and their family rather than sit behind a desk and add up pounds, shillings and pence all day. I'll put all the paperwork straight and then we can sit down together and look at the whole picture.'

Douglas stepped round the desk and kissed Betty soundly on the lips.

'Douglas, please, not here, someone may walk in. It's not very businesslike for an undertaker to be kissing his staff,' she grinned.

'Perhaps I should lock the door for a while,' he suggested.

Betty pushed him away and laughed. 'No wonder the business isn't doing so well if this is what you get up to when my back's turned. Now, be off with you and let me get on. We have three hours before the girls are home for their tea. I also want to speak to you about our new home. I can collect the keys at the weekend so we can take a look and see what needs doing. It won't cost a lot,' she added, seeing him glance down at the cashbook.

'Whatever would I do without you?' he declared, stealing another kiss before Betty could scold him. 'I'm off to visit the Gregson family about tomorrow's funeral. Can you hold the fort?'

'My dear husband, I'll be fine. You have six members of staff. I have more than five times that at Woolworths, plus a store full of customers most days. I don't think there'll be a problem, do you?'

'As long as the guests in the back room don't misbehave,' he grinned, nodding to where Betty knew the deceased were prepared for their funerals.

'Oh, be off with you, Douglas Billington,' she replied, giving him a stern look over the rims of the spectacles she wore when doing close work. 'You do not scare me,' although she decided to not venture into the room on her own.

Once Douglas left the office she settled down to bring the records up to date, first going through the chequebook and entering all expenses into the cashbook as well as all the sums of money paid into the bank. Satisfied she'd entered all she could, she reached for a pile of statements from the bank and ticked off the transactions one by one. After a while she sat back, puzzled. None of the figures seemed to match up. She made a note of the differences so that she could discuss the problem with Douglas and moved on to a large pile of invoices that required checking and paying. Being a meticulous person, Betty checked the calculations for goods ordered on each invoice and also that they added up to the correct total. As she worked through the pile she spotted a repeating problem and started to place certain invoices to one side, stopping only to stretch her aching arms and stiff neck. The pile of invoices containing queries worried her and she picked them up and read through each one. Had Douglas really used this many coffin handles in the past six months? If business was brisk enough to use this much stock over such a short period, then how come the bank balance was so low? This was most confusing. Walking over to a filing cabinet, she pulled out a beautifully gold-tooled leather-bound book. This was where Douglas kept a meticulous record of every service that Oborne and Butterfield had provided during the time he'd owned the business and many years before. After an hour of making notes and referring to the pile of invoices, she placed her fountain pen down and gave a sigh. Douglas had a serious problem. Somehow money was going missing, as was the stock. Add that to Fothergill's undercutting their prices and if they were not careful, Douglas would lose his business. Once he returned she would have to have a serious discussion with her husband.

Betty was deep in thought when a noise and voices from the back room gave her a start. She thought she was alone as all the staff should be out with Douglas working on a funeral. Looking around, she spotted Douglas's furled umbrella by the coat stand. Holding it firmly, she moved quietly to the door and threw it back and, speaking in a loud voice, called 'Who's there?'

Ignoring the hairs on the back of her neck standing on end, she peered into the gloomy room that backed onto the yard where the staff worked. 'Speak up. Who's there?'

After a few whispers and a cough a man approached her slowly. 'It's me, Harry Singleton. Can I help you, Mrs Billington?'

Betty gave a large sigh of relief and lowered the umbrella, which she'd been holding above her head ready to strike if there had been an intruder. Harry was the husband of the Woolworths cook, Enid, who'd been taken on as a general handyman. 'Hello, Harry, who were you talking to?'

'One of the chaps from a shop down the road. He wanted to borrow a hammer.'

Betty nodded thoughtfully. 'Make sure Mr Billington knows about this. I thought you would have been out with the team as you're now trained as a pall bearer?'

Harry made a show of rubbing his back. 'It's my back. I'm not to lift anything heavy so Mr Billington said as how I should stay here and clean up the yard. I was just getting stuck in,' he added as Betty stepped further into the room to look around.

'Mr Billington's been gone for two hours. What have you been doing in that time?'

'I had to go and collect some more coffin handles and screws,' he said, nodding to where a wooden crate stood open.

Betty looked into the crate which seemed to be half empty and picked up the order form that lay nearby. 'Where's the rest of the stock?' she asked, giving Harry a hard stare.

He pointed to a cupboard at the side of the room. 'I'm just putting the stuff away. Do you have a problem?'

Betty felt her back stiffen. The situation felt uncomfortable. 'Not at all. Do all the staff have access to this store cupboard?'

Harry nodded nonchalantly. 'Mr Billington trusts us to order the stock when it's needed and place fresh orders when we run low.'

Betty nodded her head, trying hard not to show her concerns. Glancing down at the order form that had been with the crate, she could see that the items had been ordered by H. Singleton. 'Get on with clearing the yard. Mr Billington will be back soon and will expect to see the work done.'

Betty had already returned to the office when she realized she'd left Douglas's umbrella in the back room. She'd walked partway back when she again heard voices and this time recognized Harry speaking.

'I reckon she's onto us. You'd best keep clear of here while she's about. The missus said as how she's a sharp one and don't miss a trick. Almost caught her putting a bit of lamb in her bag last week.'

Betty backed away and returned to her desk. Whatever was going on here she didn't like it one little bit.

'Wait up, Vera,' Ruby puffed as she hurried to catch up. 'There's no need to rush.'

'There's every need. I've been a bad woman and it's time I made amends. Whatever must Sadie think of me and, more importantly, what do the people who work there think and will they go home and tell their families? Why, I could be the laughing stock of the whole town, and me, a respectable woman.'

Ruby thought Vera made too much of her own importance but it was best to just nod and agree than to argue the point. Besides, she could hardly catch her breath at the moment. 'Let's have a sit-down for a few minutes before we tackle the last part of the walk. I know I can do with a rest.'

The two women walked over to a wooden bench set in the grass border of the pavement in Avenue Road and let the sun warm their faces while they both composed themselves.

'I came out in such a rush I forgot my gas mask. It's sod's law this will be the afternoon bloody Hitler decides to gas us all,' Vera grumbled.

'Don't be daft. Why, you're one of the few people I know who remembers to carry one these days. Bob said he doesn't even bother to reprimand anyone he catches without one these days and he doesn't know an ARP warden who does.'

Vera sniffed disapprovingly. 'Well, he'll have a smile on

the other side of his face when he finds us all gassed in our beds.'

Ruby didn't even bother to pull Vera's leg about what she'd just said. They still had a bit of a walk ahead and she wasn't looking forward to whatever ideas the woman had in her head for once they reached Oakhurst House. 'So, are you just going to have a little chat with your Sadie then?'

Vera gave her a sharp look. 'What do you mean?'

'I just wondered if you had a plan?'

'Don't be daft,' Vera admonished her as she got to her feet and marched off. 'Are you coming or not?'

'That'll be a no then,' she said to Vera's back as she hauled herself up and followed.

Oakhurst House must have been quite a sight in its day, Ruby thought to herself as she looked up at the grand building. She could just imagine carriages pulling up and the high and mighty of the town visiting for soirees and posh parties. Now it was simply somewhere for unfortunate young girls to go when they'd fallen on hard times and from what she'd heard, they still had a hard time after they'd given birth, with the church taking away their babies before they had time to decide about their futures. 'There but for the grace of God,' she muttered aloud as she followed Vera through the imposing entrance doors.

A woman wearing a severe black dress with a white starched cap on her head stood in their way. 'May I help you?'

'I'm here to see my granddaughter, Sadie Munro,' Vera snapped back, folding her arms in front of her in defiance.

Ruby stood next to her friend and gave a weak smile.

Someone ought to show they were friendly and meant no harm. 'We've just heard Sadie is here and her grandmother,' she nodded towards Vera, 'is worried about her.'

'This is most irregular,' the woman said, giving Vera a hard stare. 'Do you have some kind of proof that Munro is a relative of yours?'

'As if I'd have come marching up here if I wasn't related. Now, are you going to let me see her or not?'

'Wait here,' the woman replied before disappearing into a nearby room.

'I'm taking her home with me,' Vera said aloud as if thinking to herself. 'I don't want no kin of mine being under the thumb of that woman.'

'I'm with you there,' Ruby agreed. 'Whatever it takes, we'll get her out of here or my name's not Ruby Caselton.'

The pair stood in silence for some minutes waiting for the woman to return. Ruby was aware of the many rules pinned to the wall. It was stricter than a prison, she thought to herself.

Both jumped when a door opened and the woman returned. 'You may visit Munro in one month. She's given birth and will be able to receive visitors just before she leaves.'

'She's had the baby?' Vera said, her hard features visibly softening. 'What is it, a boy or a girl? Just fancy that, me a great-grandmother just like you,' she said to Ruby as she reached in her pocket for a handkerchief and blew her nose. 'Just fancy that.'

'It's no concern of yours as to the sex of the child. The people adopting it are the only ones we divulge that information to. Munro has signed away all rights to the child. You may collect your granddaughter on . . .' She opened a file in her hand, looking for the date.

Vera looked distressed. 'What? You mean I don't get to see my own flesh and blood and you intend to give it away? I'm not having that. I want to see her and the baby right now and I'm not leaving here until I have,' she added as her distress turned to anger. 'Now, I suggest you get out of my way so I can go and see my granddaughter right this second.'

'Well, I . . .' The woman stood open-mouthed as Vera grabbed the folder from her hand and pushed past her, marching off down a corridor.

'Thank you,' Ruby nodded to the astonished-looking woman as she hurried after Vera. She could see her friend stopping to read signs on doors as she hunted for Sadie. Catching up with Vera by a pair of double doors marked 'private', she grabbed her by the arm. 'Hold on a minute. Can you tell me what you intend to do?'

'I just want to find her and ask her if she wants to come home . . . and bring the baby with her. We'll manage somehow. I couldn't live with myself knowing strangers were caring for my own flesh and blood. It's the right thing to do, isn't it, Ruby?'

Ruby put her arm round her friend and gave her a hug. 'Of course it is but you must prepare yourself in case Sadie tells you she doesn't want to come home, or she still wants her baby adopted.'

'Oh Ruby, I couldn't bear it,' Vera wailed loudly.

'Shh, someone might hear and kick us out before we find her. You wipe your eyes and I'll take a look and see if I can spot where she might be. Sit yourself in that chair and calm down. Crying is not going to help,' Ruby said firmly. Knowing Vera of old, she realized that the woman could weep and wail for England when the fancy took her and now wasn't the time to draw attention to the pair of them. Anytime now that woman could call someone and have them kicked out.

Quietly opening the double doors, Ruby took a look inside. It seemed to be some kind of sitting room with around a dozen armchairs and a few side tables. She could see a very pregnant young woman reading a book. Closing the door behind her, she approached the woman. 'Excuse me, love, I'm looking for Sadie Munro. Can you tell me where she is, please?'

The woman looked up in horror. 'Oh, sorry, we don't have visitors. It's not allowed. Does Matron know you're here?'

Ruby nodded. She wasn't going to start telling lies. Goodness knows where that would lead. 'Is she nearby?'

'She's next door, in the Hainault. The girls who have problems give birth in the maternity home rather than here.'

Ruby felt her blood run cold. 'Is she all right?'

'She's fine. Rather lucky going into the Hainault as she's treated a bit better in there. It can be like a prison in here at times and quite distressing when the babies are taken away. One of the others got word back to us that your granddaughter had a little boy.'

'Thank you very much, love,' Ruby said, breathing a sigh of relief. She knew the layout of the Hainault having visited friends and family in there over the years. With luck she could get Vera inside to see Sadie without too much trouble. 'Good luck with yours.'

Joining Vera in the corridor, she leant close and whispered, 'Just follow me and don't say anything.'

'But—'

'I've got news but it's best we get out of here without any fuss.'

Vera nodded and the two women hurried down the corridor and past the Matron's office where she could see, through the half-opened door, the agitated woman waving her arms at a man in a white coat.

'Good afternoon,' Ruby waved to them before leaving.

'What's going on? I want to see Sadie,' Vera demanded as Ruby led her a few yards down the road out of sight of anyone watching them in Oakhurst House.

'Keep calm. It seems she's not in there,' Ruby said, holding on to Vera's sleeve as she turned to go back.

'She's not gone back to that bloke, has she? She needs a good shaking if she has,' Vera snarled.

Ruby gave a big sigh. 'Hold your horses a minute. There's no need to start losing your temper. She's not in the home as she's had the baby. Satisfied now?'

'You can't just have a baby and disappear. She'll be laid up for two weeks so what the hell is happening?'

'Just calm down and listen for a minute. She didn't have the baby in Oakhurst House. She had him in the Hainault maternity home next door.'

'Him? She had a little boy?'

'Yes, and that's all I know. Perhaps if you calm down a little bit we could go in and enquire.'

Vera took a deep breath and exhaled slowly. 'I'm calm.

Let's go,' she said, walking briskly towards the maternity home. 'Hurry up, Ruby, for goodness' sake.'

The entrance area of the Hainault was much more welcoming than the church-run home next door. A rosy-cheeked nurse greeted them and when Vera politely explained about her granddaughter the nurse listened and didn't interrupt once. 'We do have some rules where only husbands are allowed to visit once a day. But . . .' she tried to continue as Vera opened her mouth to protest. 'But as so many husbands are in the forces and serving overseas we do bend the rules slightly for mothers and grand-mothers to see the baby. We've put Sadie in a side ward so I can let you slip in for a couple of minutes without being interrupted.'

'Is she poorly?' Ruby asked, as she had never known someone not be on the main ward.

'No, Miss Munro has elected not to keep her baby and as we have the room available, we are able to keep her away from the other mothers until she moves back to Oakhurst in a few days.'

'Oh Ruby,' Vera whispered. 'I never thought that she might give the baby up. I've had all these ideas popping into my mind about her having the back bedroom and me helping the little one grow up, just like you have with your Sarah, and it's not going to happen.'

'Chin up, love. You never know, she may just change her mind once she knows her nan hasn't condemned her to hell after all. Perhaps the nurse will show you where to go while I wait here. Take as much time as you want.'

'Take yourself through to the waiting room and make yourself comfortable. I'm just about to take the tea trolley round for afternoon teas. I can probably slip one out to you,' the young nurse offered. 'Just let me take this lady to see her granddaughter and great-grandson and I'll be back.'

'Bless you, my love. I could just kill for a cuppa.'

Ruby spent the next fifteen minutes watching the world go by. The Hainault was such a lovely place with everyone who passed by having a smile on their face. Occasionally she heard the cry of a baby and got to thinking about her own family. Perhaps before too long Sarah and Alan would have a little brother or sister for Georgina, once Alan was home long enough, that was. She was just contemplating what Bob was up to in the garden when the young nurse appeared with a steaming cup of tea.

'Here you are, nice and hot and strong enough for the spoon to stand up in,' she grinned as Ruby took the cup and saucer from her. 'I thought you'd like to know that your friend and her granddaughter are getting along famously. I take it there had been a falling-out?'

'You could say that. It happens sometimes when a girl brings trouble home. My friend is a respectable woman and she kept this problem from even her closest friends. It's a fluke that we found out Sadie was in Oakhurst House. When do you think we can take her and the baby home?'

The nurse pursed her lips. 'It may not be quite so straightforward. If it wasn't for Miss Munro having minor complications, she would have had the baby in Oakhurst. As adoption documents have been signed she would ordinarily have stayed there long enough for the baby to be deemed fit and healthy before he was handed over to the adoptive parents. As it is, Miss Munro will be here for at least one week before she's moved back to Oakhurst House.'

'She still has to give up her baby?'

'I'm not an expert but having seen a few of the young ladies from the home while I've been here, all I can say is that usually the babies are adopted. If I can be so bold as to say that the administration there is very strict and any girl causing any kind of problems may find herself in hot water.'

Ruby was concerned for Vera and her granddaughter. 'Even if Sadie was to change her mind about adoption, you're saying she may not be able to.'

The nurse nodded her head slowly. 'I shouldn't be saying this, but if I was your friend and if Miss Munro has decided to keep her little boy, it may be prudent for her to avoid being moved back to Oakhurst House. But you didn't hear this from me. Is that clear?'

'Thank you, Nurse . . . I'm sorry, I don't even know your name.'

'I'm Nurse Edwards but the ladies here call me Eddie for short. Being a junior nurse, I'm often younger than many of the mums who come here to have their babies.'

Ruby was lost for words. Eddie? Was this the sign she was waiting for from her late husband? But no, it couldn't be, otherwise what exactly was he trying to tell her? 'Thank you, Eddie, your advice has been extremely help-ful. Once I've spoken to my friend, Vera, it may be that we will be taking young Sadie straight home. When would you advise is the best time for this to happen?'

Nurse Edwards thought for a moment. 'I'm on duty every afternoon this week and towards the end of visiting time I'm often working in the sluice or preparing a tea trolley so wouldn't see someone leaving the ward,' she said, giving Ruby a small wink and a grin.

'I wouldn't like you to get into trouble on our behalf.'

'You won't get me into trouble. I just want to see that baby live with his mother. I've seen her nursing him and I know she loves the little boy. It would be a sin to have him taken from her. Whatever happened to her, she deserves a fresh start, and what better than to be with her grandmother?'

'That girl's guardian angel was certainly helping us when we met you,' Ruby said as she handed back the cup and saucer. 'Thank you from the bottom of my heart.'

The nurse had not long gone back to her duties when Vera appeared, grinning from ear to ear. 'Oh Ruby, he's beautiful, just wait until you see him. I've never seen such a beautiful baby.'

'Welcome to the great-grandmothers' club.'

'Sadie is going to keep the baby. I told her she could come home with me when she was ready, and Ruby, I told her I was sorry for not being there for her when she needed me.'

'I'm pleased for you, Vera,' Ruby said as they left the building and started walking back towards the town. 'However, there could be a few problems we need to sort out before you get them both home safely.'

'There's only one problem as far as I'm concerned and that's there not being a wedding ring on my granddaughter's finger.'

Ruby was confused. 'Vera, I don't think you're going to find some lad to marry your granddaughter while she's still in bed after just giving birth. With the best intentions in the world . . .'

Vera scoffed at her friend's words. 'What I meant was we need to stop off at Woolworths on the way home and buy a cheap wedding ring for Sadie to wear. At least then she'll look respectable.'

Betty slid the bolts across the inside of the shop door and turned the sign to 'closed'. She wondered, not for the first time, if Douglas's business could be called a shop? It was set on a busy High Street in Bexleyheath alongside a variety of retail businesses so in reality it was a shop, but that didn't seem right when one thought of the service being provided.

Douglas, who had not long returned from dispatching his client, was changing out of his work suit ready to return home and collect Clemmie and Dorothy. They planned to take the girls to the cinema to see a musical, which was a rare treat. 'It looks as though you've been busy,' he called from the office. 'I hope you could make sense of my accounting system?'

'Yes,' Betty replied as she returned to the room and straightened his tie. 'I do have a few concerns. Could we spare a couple of minutes to go through them?'

Douglas checked his watch. 'I don't see why not. We can use the work van to go home rather than wait for a bus.' He rubbed his hands together as he walked towards the desk where Betty had made neat piles of invoices alongside a stack of ledgers and a page of neatly hand-written notes.

'I'm afraid you're about to have a shock. I've uncovered a problem.'

'Has my adding and subtraction failed me again? For an accountant I'm always forgetting to double-check my calculations,' he smiled as he pulled out a chair for Betty and sat beside her.

'I wish it were that simple, my love. I've discovered that someone is stealing from the business.'

'What? How can that be? I believed our losses were down to trying to compete with the new funeral directors down the road. I had no idea . . .' he exclaimed, pulling the list towards him and reading through Betty's meticulous notes.

Betty sat quietly by her husband's side. She found no happiness in discovering the discrepancies in her husband's pride and joy. Since meeting Douglas she had admired his keenness to build the business he'd inherited rather than seek his living as an accountant, which he'd loathed. Occasionally she pointed out an invoice or a row of figures before showing him how she'd discovered the initial problem and how she thought someone within the company was stealing. In fact, she was beginning to believe it could be more than one person.

Douglas ran his hands through his short hair in desperation. 'How could I have been such a fool not to notice this? I'm an accountant, for God's sake. Why did I not spot this?'

Betty reached out and stroked his hand to comfort him. 'You've been short of staff, Douglas, and your first thoughts have always been for the families of the deceased. I know how paperwork can slide and be forgotten when one is busy. The customer always comes first in the retail trade, whatever else suffers. Unfortunately this time, someone who is less than honest has seen the opportunity to steal from you.'

'Oh God,' was all Douglas could say over and over again.

14

Freda was late. Her old alarm clock failed to go off on time and however hard she tried, she couldn't get herself moving. 'Serves me right for standing about chatting after my late shift at the fire station,' she muttered to Ruby's dog, Nelson, who simply wagged his tail and curled up even tighter on the hearthrug.

'Eat this before you rush off,' Ruby said as she placed a bowl of porridge on the table. 'You need something in your stomach before you put in a day's work.'

'I might as well. I'm late as it is so if Betty's going to scold me, she may as well do it for fifteen minutes rather than five. I hate being late. I find it puts me out for the whole day. At least I'm working in the storeroom today helping with stocktaking so customers won't see me yawning every five minutes.'

Nelson jumped up and rushed to the front door barking. 'That'll be the postman,' Ruby said, wiping her hands on a tea towel and yelling at him to shut up as she went to collect whatever had been dropped through the letter box. 'There's a letter for you,' she said, placing the thin envelope in front of Freda, who was shovelling the last of her breakfast into her mouth.

'Hmm, it has a Birmingham post mark. I didn't think there was anyone from home who knew where I lived,' Freda said with a frown as she tore open the envelope. 'Oh my goodness!'

Ruby put down the porridge pot she'd started to scrub and sat down opposite Freda. 'Is there something wrong, love?'

'It's my mum. She's had some kind of accident and there's no one to care for her.'

'The poor love,' Ruby murmured as Freda handed the one sheet of paper over for her to read. She had never met Freda's mother but had heard how after Freda's father died suddenly the mother had become involved with a brutal man who dominated her life and made it hard for Freda and her brother to remain at home. Freda's young brother, Lenny, went through a rough patch but was now serving overseas on a ship. Freda had made a good life for herself in Erith. Ruby was worried this might affect the girl's future. 'Who's the person that wrote the letter?'

'Janey used to be our neighbour when I was a kid. I can only think from the few words she's written that our Lenny's been in touch with her. I know last time he was here on leave he said he was concerned for Mum and wanted to know she was well, even though she never got in touch.'

'The chap controls her that much, does he?' Ruby made a tutting noise. 'What is it with some men who use their fists rather than show kindness?'

'A leopard never changes its spots,' Freda said, recalling

233

the slap around the ears she'd received on more than one
occasion when her stepfather came home drunk.

'There's no mention of him here,' Ruby said, checking
on the back of the sheet of paper. 'It doesn't say where
your mother is either. What do you want to do about this?'

Freda's eyes watered as she looked at her kindly landlady, who was more like a grandmother to her. 'Whatever's
happened in the past she's still my mum and it looks as
though she needs me right now. I just can't face telling
Betty when she's so short-staffed . . . and what about my
war work at the fire station? Am I allowed to go off without a by-your-leave?'

'Don't you worry about the fire station. Didn't you say
you're not on duty for a few days? You could go up to
Birmingham and be back again before they know you're
missing. If you aren't, I'll go round and have a word.
They're all family men who once had mothers so they
will understand. As for Betty, don't ever be afraid to tell
her your problems. She's a good sort, is Betty Billington.
Now, get yourself off to work and I'll have your washing
done and on the line so if you want to set off this afternoon, you'll have nothing to do but head to the station. I
suggest that what you do is send a postcard to this Janey
and tell her you're on your way and ask her to find a
respectable lodging house for you. There's no knowing if
you can stay with your mother or whether Janey can put
you up. I've got some postcards in the sideboard along
with a couple of stamps so write a few lines and post it on
your way to Woolies. It'll get there this afternoon.'

*

Betty stared into space, unaware of the hands of the clock on her office wall slowly moving towards half past ten. She should, by rights, be preparing for a staff meeting but her heart wasn't in her job. She kept thinking back to the previous evening and picturing Douglas as he absorbed the information that someone was stealing from his business. Knowing they had to collect the girls to take them to the cinema, they'd begrudgingly stopped checking figures and pointing out to each other how the bank statements didn't match what should have been paid into the bank account after clients had paid their bills. Over and over Douglas kept blaming himself for not taking the money to the bank himself but instead relying on staff members. They packed up the paperwork into a cardboard box to take home. Betty had suggested it wasn't wise to leave incriminating evidence in his office for the time being just in case it went missing.

The telephone on her desk rang suddenly, bringing her back to earth with a jolt. She was relieved to find it was Sergeant Mike Jackson and not head office with a work-related call. 'Oh Mike, thank you for finding the time to give me a telephone call.' She went on to quickly outline why she wanted to speak with him. 'It's just a private enquiry at the moment. We don't wish to involve the police officially until we've collected all the facts as it may alert the thief. Your advice would be welcome if you're able to give it?' Betty listened for a couple of minutes then thanked her friend. 'This evening would be ideal for us. Thank you, Mike.'

Feeling she'd done enough for now, Betty put the problems with the business to one side and thought of happier events. Their trip to the cinema had been hell for Douglas as he'd brooded throughout the whole film, but Betty had been delighted to see how much Clemmie and Dorothy had adored the dance and singing sequences. She had an idea that would fit in with the possible home move as they would be living closer to the town and she would be able to enroll the girls for dance lessons at Erith Dance Studios. She thought back to when Douglas took her out for the first time and they danced the night away at that very same place. She sighed in delight, as there was a polite knock on her door. She called out, 'Come in,' as she straightened her jacket and cleared her throat. Back to work.

'I'm sorry to bother you, Betty. I wondered if I could have a quick word before you start the supervisors' meeting?'

'Of course, Freda, come in and take a seat. We have ten minutes yet,' she said as she glanced up at the clock. Where was the morning going?

'I wondered if I could take a couple of days off? I received this letter as I was leaving for work,' Freda said, shyly handing over the envelope. She hated to ask for favours. 'It says my mother's had an accident and has no one to care for her.'

Betty tried to bury her first thought, which was that she could ill afford to lose such a valued member of staff for even a day, but then she felt ashamed. Freda needed to be supported if her mother was poorly. She knew that Freda had not been home to the Midlands for some years.

Freda fiddled with a button on her uniform as she watched Betty read the letter. 'I wouldn't ask if it wasn't important,' she tried to explain. 'With my brother away there's no one else—'

Betty raised her hand. 'There's no need to explain. This letter says it all. Family is important, Freda. Value it while you can.'

Freda smiled to herself; Ruby had said Betty would understand. 'I'll try to be back as soon as possible.'

'Don't even think about rushing back to us. This letter would not have been written if you weren't needed by your mother's side. Come back when you're good and ready. Woolworths won't collapse without you here. Although we will miss you immensely,' she added as she saw Freda's crestfallen expression. 'Now, here's my telephone number and also the private number for my home. I want you to telephone me each day to let me know how your mother's faring and if you wish me to pass on any messages to Ruby and Sarah,' she said as she wrote quickly on a sheet of paper and handed it over to Freda along with the letter. 'When are you planning to go?'

'This afternoon, if I may? If I can get to London for two o'clock, there's a train that will get me there by teatime.' She went on to explain how she'd already sent a postcard to the lady who'd written the letter so she would be expected.

'Then I suggest that you head off home and prepare for your journey. The sooner you leave, the sooner you'll be there. It's been quiet recently so let's hope your trip won't be broken by air raids. I'll have your pay packet made up so you have some extra money to see you through. I've never had the pleasure of meeting your mother but please do give her my best wishes for a speedy recovery.'

'I will, Betty, and thank you for being so understanding,' Freda said as she stood and hugged her boss. 'I'll do my best to return to work as soon as possible.'

Betty raised her hands to stop Freda's promises. 'I'm not listening. Family comes first, Freda. Always remember that. Now, be off with you before I change my mind.'

Freda left the office, thinking as she went that she'd best stock up with notepaper and envelopes from the store downstairs and make sure she had a pile of pennies in order to make the promised telephone calls.

'Nan, I'm not sure this is legal,' Sarah said as she helped Ruby down from the back of her aunt Pat's horse and cart that had come to a standstill in front of the Hainault Maternity Hospital.

'Don't question what we're doing, Sarah, or you can stay there,' Vera butted in before Ruby could speak. 'I thought you wanted to help us bring my Sadie home to Alexandra Road? Mind you, when I asked you to arrange some transport I never expected your Pat to turn up with a horse.' She glared at Ruby, who was picking pieces of straw off her best coat and straightening her hat.

'There's always Shank's pony,' Pat called from where she was holding the horse steady. 'I hope you aren't going to be too long. I have to collect the pigs' swill bins once I've dropped you all off,' she added for effect, giving her mum a grin.

'Don't worry, love,' Ruby said to Sarah. 'I checked with Mike and he said that Sadie is at liberty to take herself out of hospital whenever she wishes and no one can make her give her baby up. She's moving to a respectable house and living with her own family. We're simply collecting her earlier than planned and without the home for unmarried mothers knowing.'

'And about the word "unmarried",' Vera said as the three women walked into the maternity home. 'I'd prefer it be known that Sadie's husband was killed in action rather than him being a married man who deserted her. She's going to be wearing a ring so no one need know.' She nodded as if the matter was done and dusted.

'How does Sadie feel about all this?' Sarah asked her nan as they followed Vera, who strode purposefully through the corridors of the maternity hospital.

'I've not seen the girl but I get the feeling she doesn't know much about it,' Ruby said. 'Vera's imagination has been running nineteen to the dozen. I'm only hoping she's agreed to go to live with her grandmother and all this is not inside Vera's head.'

'We're going to look rather daft, especially with our transport parked out the front of the building munching on his hay bag,' Sarah giggled.

'Shh,' Ruby admonished Sarah, even though she too had a broad smile on her face. 'The side ward is just up here. You have got everything for the baby, haven't you? It's a bit on the early side for him to be coming home after just one week but Nurse Edwards said he's as fit as a fiddle.'

Sarah patted the shopping bag on her arm. 'It's all here, along with one of Georgina's first pram sets that Freda knitted. It'll be a little on the large side I would think, but at least he'll be as snug as a bug in a rug.'

Ruby nodded approvingly. It warmed her heart the way her girls, as she thought of them, had pulled together for the little madam. Even though Sadie now found herself in a sticky situation Ruby couldn't help think it would take a lot for her to like the girl with her stuck-up airs. But a new baby meant new beginnings, so she'd be generous and keep an open mind. Maisie had handed over nappies and romper suits, saying that little Ruby had far too many, while Freda had started knitting almost at once and had taken it with her to keep herself occupied whilst travelling up to Birmingham. Ruby wondered how the girl was getting on. She had more than a soft spot for Freda and fervently hoped that her trip wouldn't be too harrowing. It bothered her that Freda could be travelling back to where she was in danger, not just from an abusive stepfather but also because it was where her young brother Lenny had got in with a bad lot who had followed him to Erith bent on revenge. She gave a shudder. Perhaps someone should have gone with Freda?

'Here we are,' Vera said as she knocked on the door of the small room and entered. Sadie Munro was already dressed and sitting on the edge of her bed looking tearful.

'Whatever's up, love?' Vera asked, checking that the baby was in his crib.

'I've been told they're coming to collect me to take me back into Oakhurst House. If that happens, I know I'll be made to hand over the baby – they can be so persuasive and I've already signed the papers,' she sniffed.

'We'll be long gone by then,' Vera assured her.

'What, in five minutes?' The girl wailed.

Vera gasped. 'That soon . . . Ruby, what shall we do?'

It crossed Ruby's mind that she was the one Vera always expected to sort out her problems, but she let it pass. 'We need to get a shove on but I'm not sure how the heck we're going to get Sadie and the baby down that long corridor without passing that snooty woman from Oakhurst.'

'Maybe I can help?' Nurse Edwards said, coming into the room behind them, making Sarah jump out of her skin. 'I have a trolley outside. Sadie, if you jump onto it, I'll cover you with a sheet and wheel you outside. They won't think to ask a nurse who has passed away.'

'Oh my, that seems to be going a bit far. Won't it be tempting fate?' Vera asked.

'Needs must,' Sadie said, getting off the bed. 'Nan, can you carry my bags?'

'I suggest you head off now,' Nurse Edwards advised. She pulled off the navy blue cloak she was wearing and passed it to Sarah along with her white nurse's hat. 'Put these on and take the baby. As long as he doesn't cry you should be able to smuggle him out. Hurry.'

Ruby, who had started to hand the bags to Vera, stopped suddenly. 'Won't they think it strange that the bed is empty?'

'That could be a problem,' the nurse said.

'I know,' Ruby said, kicking off her shoes and pulling off her coat and hat before climbing into the bed. 'This'll surprise them when they come knocking on the door,' she added as she pulled the bed covers over her chin. 'One of you tuck me in and perhaps close the curtains before you leave. I just hope I don't drop off to sleep,' she grinned.

Nurse Edwards straightened the covers, gave the room a quick check and handed the sleeping baby to Sarah, who hid him from view. 'Let's get this show on the road, shall we? I'll come back to wake you when it's all clear,' she said to Ruby as she led the others from the room. 'I hope you enjoy your confinement, Mrs Caselton.'

Sarah kept her head down as she hurried down the corridor, her one fear being that the child would wake and start to cry. She left Vera, who took her time stopping to look at signs on the notice boards. Behind her she could hear the squeaky wheels of the trolley being pushed by Nurse Edwards. This was all rather thrilling, she thought to herself. Maisie and Freda will be annoyed they're missing all the fun.

Sarah reached her aunt Pat's horse and cart first and handed over the baby before removing the cloak and cap. She hurried back to where the kindly nurse was helping Sadie down from the trolley and gave back her garments, hugging her and saying thank you. 'I'll bring your nan out as soon as the coast is clear. Now, get yourself gone before you're spotted.'

Pat helped them up onto the back of the cart and Sadie took her baby, who was now wrapped warmly in the shawl Maisie had donated. With Vera joining them, Pat guided the horse round the corner out of view of anyone in Oakhurst House.

Fifteen minutes later Ruby appeared, a big grin on her face. 'I'd say that's a job well done,' she said.

'Did you startle the people from Oakhurst?' Sadie asked.

'I'll say I did, especially with a cushion stuffed up my cardigan. They'd never seen a pregnant woman of my age before. They scarpered pretty quickly when I shouted that my waters had broken.'

Douglas showed Mike Jackson into the front room while Betty checked that the two girls were asleep in their beds. The last thing they wanted was to have them overhearing that their daddy had problems at work. When she joined them, laden with a tea tray, she could see that Mike was taking notes and looked extremely serious.

'Is it as bad as I thought?' she asked, passing him a cup of the coffee that she kept for special occasions. There were times one didn't just offer a guest Camp coffee and this was one of them. 'Please help yourself to a slice of cake. I'm gradually learning how to cook, even with the shortages,' she smiled nervously.

Mike took the coffee and refused the cake. 'Gwyneth said I'll never fit into my wedding suit if I'm not more careful with what I eat,' he said. 'Perhaps later.' He didn't wish to offend Betty.

'Mike agrees with us that there's a problem but has noticed we have more than one culprit.'

'Oh dear, and there was me hoping it was Harry Singleton alone and we could dismiss him and have no further problems. Why is life never straightforward?' Betty sighed.

Mike pointed to a page in a ledger and the bank statement he lined up alongside it. 'This started months before Harry was employed. Look, you can see by matching your cash book entries with what was paid into the bank that not all the cash reached your bank account. Add to that the stock that's gone missing and you have a serious problem.'

'I don't understand why, after all this time, this has happened? Douglas, surely Harry is the only new staff member you've taken on since you inherited the business?'

'I'm to blame. None of this would have happened if I'd stuck to working in the office. When an older staff member mentioned he used to do the banking and ordering I thought it would be rude of me to take the job from him.' Douglas laughed bitterly. 'I even raised his wages for the extra responsibility. What a fool I've been.'

Mike slapped him on the back. 'Don't blame yourself, old chap. If some blighter is out to steal from you, they try every trick in the book. It could happen to anyone.'

'What do you suggest we do, Mike?' Betty asked as she squeezed her husband's hand to reassure him.

'I'm going to suggest doing nothing,' Mike said.

Douglas's expression changed from being upset to one of anger. 'What? You're saying let the blighters steal even more money from me? Do you take me for a fool, Mike?'

Betty frowned. Having known Mike for some years, she knew he wasn't just going to let a thief keep taking their livelihood. 'Let Mike speak, my dear, I do believe he may have a plan. Carry on, Mike,' she encouraged the police sergeant.

'I think there's more to this than petty pilfering. You mentioned you have competition now since another funeral service opened up for business close to yours? Can you recall when this happened to be?'

'I really can't see the connection but it must be around

nine months ago. Hang on, I can check as I still have the advertisement from the *Bexleyheath Observer*.' Douglas went to a bureau and rummaged in one of the drawers. 'Here you are. Grand Opening: October the first 1942. That's a good nine months,' he said, waving the page from the newspaper in the air. 'By Jove, I do believe you have something here, Mike. Are you saying the owners of this new business are stealing from me?'

'No, not directly. I have a feeling that one of your staff will have a connection with this new company and he will be the link.'

'Harry Singleton?' Betty suggested.

'No, he's just a simple fool who's been encouraged to join in with the thefts. We need to establish a link, otherwise you'll not be free of this other company taking your trade.'

'Harry's wife, Enid, is our new cook at Woolworths and I do believe she too is helping herself to company property.'

Mike thought for a moment. 'We can deal with those two separately. Douglas, will you let me see any personal records you have on your staff? I can check them out and also cross-check with the people who have registered the other business. You never know, there could be an obvious link. Once we have enough evidence we can catch the people behind this,' he said.

Douglas looked overjoyed. 'I can't thank you enough, old chap.'

Mike looked serious. 'Hold on, there is one problem.'

Betty was confused. 'What could possibly be a problem once you've caught the thieves?'

'There's more than likely no chance of recovering the money you've had stolen. That's gone for good, I'm afraid. I'm sorry, Douglas.'

It was a glum Douglas who saw Mike off at the door an hour later. Betty could see that even when Mike requested to have Douglas as his best man at his forthcoming marriage it took a lot for him to raise a smile. She cleared the tea things and returned to the front room. 'Douglas, I've been thinking about the new house . . .'

'I'm sorry, my dear, I'm afraid there won't be a new house until this business has been sorted out. Even then money will be short. Why, it could be years before the business recovers enough for us to think about a new home.'

Betty had expected such a comment and in truth was disappointed as the girls were enjoying their new school and she'd looked forward to not having the extra journey each day to see them into their classroom before catching another bus to Woolworths. She knew it was a selfish thought but when she had the solution to their problem she told herself she could be just a little disappointed as she could see the light at the end of the tunnel. 'Douglas, you do trust me, don't you?'

'Of course, my love, I trust you with my life.'

'Then please hear me out. I do believe you have a sound business. You have empathy with your customers at a time when they are feeling deep sorrow. You get on well with fellow traders and you're an excellent employer . . .'

'But—'

'Please, Douglas, I asked you to hear me out,' Betty said sternly. 'I have a couple of items I wish to show you and please don't act like a dominant man when you see what I plan for this family.'

Douglas's mouth twitched as he watched his wife explain her plan.

Betty pulled a small book from a brown envelope she had on her lap along with a sheet of paper. 'This is the house I propose we rent. It's close to where the property is that we'd hoped to purchase.' She held out the page.

'But Betty, I pride myself in always buying property. You know it's a good investment for our future and also that of our children.'

Betty held her hand up to stop him speaking but didn't say a word. Instead she passed over the small notebook. Douglas looked puzzled as he flicked through the pages that held a few words and rows of figures. 'I don't understand?'

'You could say this book lists my worldly worth. I visited my bank manager this morning to check that the numbers were correct. My savings, the money I inherited from my parents and the sale of my little house in Cross Street – it's all here in this book and I'm handing it over to you.'

'Betty, I told you when we married that I have no interest in your money. Ordinarily I could take care of this family. Why, this house alone is worth a hefty sum. I don't understand—'

'What I suggest, Douglas, is that we rent the house you see on this sheet of paper. You sell this house and with the freed-up funds it will not only ensure you recover from the current financial problem but you can make a success of the business. Plus, you purchase at least one more shop, perhaps in Erith as it's a thriving town, and you think about expansion.'

Douglas grinned. 'My goodness, Betty Billington, you seem to have planned our entire life together. However, I am the man of the household and I'm supposed to be the breadwinner. I'm not comfortable taking your money.'

'For goodness' sake, Douglas, don't be an idiot. Have you forgotten our wedding vows already? What is mine is yours? Love, honour and obey? I'm saying that my money is yours and you are to obey me,' she said, trying to keep a stern face but bursting out with laughter. 'Besides, I will no doubt be out of work when the war ends and Woolworths puts the men back in charge. At least I know you'll have a job waiting for me. Is it a deal?'

Douglas swept her up in his arms and swung her around. 'It's a deal.'

15

Freda stepped out of the train carriage onto the busy platform and couldn't believe her eyes. Although travellers were going about their business just as they were in most cities in the country during wartime, this was not the Birmingham she remembered from back in 1938. Bomb damage was in evidence everywhere she looked. Would the city ever recover from this? The journey had taken much longer than anticipated as on three occasions the train had either gone into a siding or stopped at a station due to air-raid warnings. Not once did Freda see or hear a plane overhead but now she felt a wreck from the fear and anticipation. Checking the letter from her mother's friend for the umpteenth time, she decided to use some of her money on a taxi as it was getting dark and she didn't wish to knock on someone's door so late in the evening. A porter hailed a taxi for her and she was soon on her way through the darkening back streets of a long-forgotten town she'd once called home – a place she'd vowed never to return to. The taxi drove past the street where she'd worked on market stalls as a kid scratching for a few pennies or some half-rotten vegetables that could be turned into a meal of sorts that would help fill her little brother's belly, with enough left over for her not to feel sick when she went to bed. Her mother was always out on the town having a good time with the man they had to call Father, although there was not a blood connection to him. Their mother only cared where the next glass of gin was coming from. If it hadn't been for young Lenny getting into trouble, Freda would never have left Birmingham to forge her own path in life. A good life as it turned out, since arriving in Erith, and one she wished never to leave.

'The address you want is just over the road, love. It's the door at the end of the row. You sure you don't want me to take you back to the station?'

Freda peered through the gloom of the evening and could see why he wasn't keen to leave her there. Rubbish heaped in the gutter had attracted rats that ran unafraid across the pavements. Nearby the sound of fighting from the open door of a pub was all too familiar. She was on home ground. 'I'll be fine, thank you all the same,' she said to the taxi driver.

Janey opened the door after Freda knocked loudly. 'Allo, love. You found us all right then?'

Freda nodded. 'I sent a postcard . . .'

'Yeah, it was here when I got home from work. You can stay here tonight if you want to, as it's too late to take you to see your ma. Come in and close the door, then I can put the light back on. I hope you've eaten as I've not got anything in.'

Freda nodded as she followed the woman into a small front room. It was shabby but clean, but going by the lathe and plaster showing through the walls the house had been a near miss from the bombing. 'It's very good of you to let me know about my mum. How did you find my address? Has Lenny been back?'

'No, I've not seen hide nor hair of him since they locked him up. I'd heard he was out and he'd been back to see his friends but he didn't come by to see his mum. Ungrateful bugger.'

Freda let the comment pass. She had nothing in common with these people and had no need to make apologies. She knew the truth of what happened when she was a kid, as did her brother. 'So, who told you where I was and what happened to my mum?'

'It was a chap in the pub who used to hang about with your dad. He knew your mum was on her last legs and that I'd been asking about to find her family.'

'Thank you for caring,' was all Freda could think to say, not bothering to correct her when she said that her mum's partner was her dad. Her dad had died long ago and was a decent man. The thought of her so-called stepfather made her blood run cold. She'd been a bloody fool to leave Erith and put herself in danger if he was still about.

The woman shrugged her shoulders. 'I wouldn't say I care that much but your ma owes me rent and as she named me as next of kin, I didn't want no undertaker landing me with the bill for her funeral.'

'She lives here?' Freda looked around, expecting her stepfather to appear at any minute and give her a good hiding. 'What about her husband?'

'You really don't know what's been going on, do you?' the woman grinned through decaying teeth. 'He's been dead for three years now. Got into a fight and came off worse. Yer ma's lived off her wits since then, if you get my meaning?'

Freda had a good idea what she meant but she was tired and just wanted to sleep. She had no time to play guessing games. 'What's wrong with Mum?'

'What's not wrong with her you mean? All I know is she's in the hospital and won't be coming out and she owes me rent. You can 'ave her room but I want some rent and upfront. No half-promises like I've had from her.'

Freda fumbled in her purse and pulled out ten shillings. 'You can have this for now and I'll draw some more out in the morning when I find a post office. How much does she owe you?'

'Ten quid.'

Freda flinched. 'As much as that?'

'She's not been working for a while. Now, I've got to be off out. Do you want the room or not?'

Freda was puzzled. 'I just gave you some money for the rent so I could stay and see my mum.'

'That was off her debt. You need to pay me upfront if you want to stay. It's half a crown a week.'

Freda dug into her purse for the coins and thrust them at the woman, cursing herself for feeling any form of pity for her mother who had put her in this position. She had four shillings left until she could draw some money out of her post office savings account. Her mum's debt could leave her with very little money to her name if she were to stay here for long. 'This is all I have for now. Can you show me to the room? I'm rather tired after my long journey? Will you take me to see Mum tomorrow?'

'Can't see as how you need me with you. She's at the

General. You've got a mouth so you can ask for yourself. Top-floor room on the left is yours until next week.'

Freda nodded and climbed the steep wooden stairs. She was too tired to argue. The sparsely furnished room was cold even though it was still summer. Placing a chair in front of the door, as there was no lock, she undressed and climbed under the thin blankets, too tired to think straight. However, as sleep claimed her, a whisper of a thought crept into her subconscious and suggested something wasn't right.

'I'm off home, but thought I'd let you know I can work a few more hours this week if it helps, what with Freda away?' Sarah said to Betty as she stuck her head round the store manager's office door.

'You are an angel,' Betty sighed. 'May I be cheeky and ask if you would like to work in the staff canteen?'

'I'll help if I can. What's wrong with Enid? Is she poorly?'

Betty indicated for Sarah to come in and close the door. 'I have reason to believe she's stealing from Woolworths. It's just something I overheard but I think it could be true. Apart from that, standards in the canteen have dropped alarmingly since Maureen left to work on the railway. I'd kidnap her and bring her back to the store if I could,' she added with a wry smile.

'My goodness, do tell what's happened. I had no idea about Enid but then I've taken to not eating the food she cooks. She can even ruin a pot of tea.'

Betty explained about her husband's business problems

and how Enid's husband, Harry, was more than likely involved. 'I also overheard him bragging about Enid helping herself to food from the canteen.'

Sarah looked annoyed. 'That's not on at all. We've done our utmost to make her welcome and feel part of the team. Why not move me to the canteen for a few weeks and I'll keep an eye on her? You don't need this on top of Douglas's problems. I do hope you can save his business.'

'We have the help of Mike Jackson as well as some plans for the future which I'll keep under my hat for now,' Betty explained, reaching for the staff work rota. 'Now, let's see what we can do about our canteen dilemma.'

Sarah left Woolworths an hour later, her head reeling from what she'd been told. It went without saying that she would help Betty as much as she could. She hadn't forgotten the idea she had to put some money aside for when the war was over. As long as she had someone to take care of Georgina she would work all the hours God sent. Thinking of her daughter made her hurry as she crossed the busy High Street and headed to Alexandra Road where Maisie was keeping Georgina entertained while Sarah worked. She was just passing her nan's house when she heard her name called.

'Sarah, we're in here,' her mother-in-law, Maureen, called out. 'I collected Georgina and stopped off at Ruby's for a chat. She's invited us to have our tea with her rather than bothering at home as we're both working women,' she said, giving her a kiss and hug. 'You look as though you've been rushing.'

Sarah followed Maureen into the house. She still could not get used to seeing the older woman wearing the uniform of a porter on the railway. For her, her mother-in-law looked most at home behind the staff counter at Woolworths swathed in a white apron and dishing up delicious food. 'You look tired,' she said to Maureen before being launched at by her young daughter. 'Hello, my love, what have you been doing today?'

'Dress, dress . . .' the little girl chattered excitedly.

'Maisie's been fitting the girls for their bridesmaids' dresses,' Ruby said as she greeted her granddaughter with a kiss on the cheek.

'I don't know how she manages to do so much. I feel exhausted just thinking about it,' Sarah said. 'Do you want a hand, Nan?'

'No, sit yourself down for a while and tell me what's been happening at Woolworths. It's been a while since I've been in to see everyone,' Ruby said as she bustled about in the kitchen. 'We have bubble and squeak and a freshly fried egg for tea. Pat dropped by with a few spare eggs so I thought it would be a treat for us.'

'It sounds delicious,' Sarah said as her stomach grumbled. 'We all miss having a decent meal lunchtimes at work.'

'It's still that bad, eh?' Maureen asked.

'Worse if anything. Her standards are dropping every day. I know you'll keep this to yourselves but Betty has problems with Enid that aren't just to do with her cooking. She seems to think the woman is light-fingered.'

'That wouldn't surprise me,' a voice said from outside the back door.

'Maisie? I didn't know you were here,' Sarah said. 'What do you mean?'

Her friend stubbed out her cigarette butt on the door-step and stepped inside with baby Ruby on her hip. 'Bob offered to take the girls to see the pig so I popped down here for a natter. I daren't tell the kids he'll be on the dinner table come Christmas.'

'It's lovely to see you,' Sarah said, taking the baby from her and lifting her up in her arms. 'Crikey, what's your mummy been feeding you? You're like a little chubby piglet,' she said as the baby gave her a toothless smile. 'So what's this about Enid?'

Maisie leant against the door frame between the kitchen and living room. 'It was when we went up to Canning Town looking for my parents. I told you how we went to the Woolies there to see if there was any news as Enid had mentioned she worked with my mum at the branch a few years back? Well, Freda spoke to a cleaner who'd been there a while who knew Mum but she'd never heard of an Enid Singleton or a husband called Harry, but she remembered a woman with a limp who sounded just like Enid. I'd always thought there was something shifty about the pair of them and that news didn't surprise me at all. I meant to tell Betty but with everything kicking off after that I forgot all about it.'

'It does sound a bit fishy,' Sarah said, thinking of what Betty had told her that afternoon. 'Do you mind if I let Betty know? She may be able to look into their personnel records.'

'Why not? The sooner Betty sacks her and gets some-one back who can cook like our Maureen here, all the better. I know I'm not working there at the moment but when I pop in I like to be offered a cake or biscuit and since Enid took over the kitchen I won't even have a cuppa in there. She can ruin boiled water, that woman can,' Maisie said with a shrug.

'I wish I'd never left Woolworths,' Maureen said. 'I don't really fit in at the railway and it's so tiring. I think I've bitten off more than I can chew with that job.'

Ruby walked into the room wiping her hands on her apron. 'Why not hand in your notice? I reckon Betty would have you back in a flash.'

Maureen gave her a dubious look. 'Do you think so? I thought that when we signed up for war work we had no choice but to stick it out or we'd get told off?'

'There's no way of putting this nicely but you were too old to be called for war work. Was it Irene who talked you into it?' Ruby asked.

Sarah was annoyed. 'Mum did receive a letter telling her she had to sign up for some kind of work. I remember her telling me about it. Don't say she dragged you off to join her?'

Maureen shook her head. 'Please don't blame your mum. I did say that I felt I wasn't doing enough to help bring the war to an end and went to sign up with her. But I'm no spring chicken and I really can't manage this shift work and the heavy lifting that the stationmaster insists we do.'

'That's not right,' Maisie said indignantly. 'You should tell the old so-and-so to go sling his hook.'

Maureen smiled. 'I wish I could. He seems to think we should do the same work as the men we're standing in for.'

Sarah was beyond angry. 'Those men were young, fit

and healthy. That's why they've joined up and are fighting the enemy . . .'

'Or are six feet under,' Maisie added.

Sarah wasn't giving up. 'Maureen, please consider giving it all up and coming back to Woolworths. Think of it as essential war work. If the staff starve to death and there's no one to run our stores, what will the shoppers of England do?'

Maureen gave the women watching a weak smile. She was close to tears. 'I only do a little cooking. You make me sound like Winston Churchill.'

'You're much more important than him. He can't cook,' Ruby said as she went back to her frying pan. 'An army marches on its stomach and, come to that, so do the rest of us. Get your coats off and sit down. Our grub's just about ready.'

Freda crept on tiptoes into the ward, aware of every small sound her shoes made on the polished wooden floor. Around her nurses were going silently about their work, straightening bedding, taking temperatures and carrying bedpans. She was told her mum was in Nightingale ward but which of the beds was hers? The beds lined up on each side of the long ward looked identical and, come to that, so did the women in them. It had been so long since she'd seen her mum that Freda was unsure she would even recognize her. Some of the women had visitors who talked in hushed tones, leaning in close to the sick women. However, the majority of the patients didn't have visitors.

'Can I help you?' a nurse said, coming up to Freda just as she was contemplating leaving the ward.

'I'm here to visit my mother, Mrs Smith? I was told she was here but I have no idea how ill she is or what happened to her.' Voicing her thoughts aloud for the first time, Freda felt like crying as she would have done as a little girl when she wanted her mum to make everything better after she'd scraped her knee or been picked on by older kids.

The nurse smiled politely. 'You must be Freda. We were informed that you would be visiting sometime soon. Your mother is in the last bed on the left but before you go to see her I believe Sister would like a quick word.'

Freda was worried. 'Why would she want to speak to me? I've only just arrived in Birmingham. I don't know anything about my mum's condition. Is there a problem?'

The nurse took her by the elbow and steered her towards a door at the entrance to the ward that she'd just walked past. She knocked politely on the pebbled glass window before replying. 'It's just a formality as you're the first member of her family to visit.' Freda didn't answer as the nurse opened the door and steered her in. 'This is Mrs Smith's daughter,' she said politely before leaving Freda alone in the room facing a nurse dressed in navy blue with the smartest white cap Freda had ever seen; she was fascinated by the starched pleated folds that fanned from the back of the white headdress. However did one keep such a thing clean? she thought.

'Please take a seat. I'm Sister Stuart and I'm in charge of the ward where your mother's being taken care of.' She reached for a pile of buff-coloured folders and flicked through them until she found the one she required. 'Ah yes, Mrs Smith. Your mother is very poorly. She's been here for three weeks,' she said pointedly, looking at Freda through steely eyes.

'I . . . I've only just heard she's been ill. I don't live round here anymore . . . I came as soon as I heard . . .' she stammered.

'You have a brother?' She looked down at a sheet of paper. 'Leonard Smith?'

'He's away at sea. I've not seen him in a while. He always visits when his ship docks. I live in Erith – that's in north Kent. I work there too.'

The woman nodded slowly. 'Your mother has no other family?'

'My dad died when I was a child and she remarried a while back. I heard that he's now dead,' she added quickly.

The woman checked the page and turned it over, frowning. 'There's nothing here that indicates your mother was married. Are you sure?'

Am I sure? Freda thought to herself. The pair were blind drunk most of the time and when, as kids, they were told to call the brute 'Father' both she and Lenny had assumed their mum had married the man. He'd been living with her a few years ago as she'd heard as much when the police came knocking.

Freda chewed her lip nervously. What must this imposing woman think of her not knowing if her mum had a husband or not? 'After our dad died Mum took up with a chap and I always thought he was married to her but we was just kids so I may have got it wrong.' She shrugged her shoulders. 'I'd no idea what happened to him until today but I can find out details if you want me to?' Freda said, wondering if Janey would know how he died.

The sister looked at her for a couple of seconds before breaking into a smile. 'There's no need now you're here. Don't look so worried. I've heard many a story in my time in this job and nothing surprises me anymore. You're here and that's what counts.'

Freda felt her fear melt away. 'Can you tell me what's wrong with my mum, please?'

'Your mother was brought in after an accident. She took quite a severe beating and her legs were broken but she does have other health concerns.'

Freda flinched. 'Beating?'

'She was found in an alleyway early one morning. It's been touch and go for a while now.'

'I had no idea. We didn't keep in touch like normal families do,' Freda replied.

'Miss Smith, in my job I've come to the belief that there is no such thing as a normal family. We all make our own way in life regardless of our upbringing. Some make a go of it and some, shall we say, fall by the wayside.'

Freda nodded. She knew exactly what the Sister was implying.

'With your brother being away at sea we shall have to add you to the documents as next of kin. It's highly irregular but not uncommon in wartime. Now, are you staying locally? I'll need to add an address to the records.' She lifted a pen and waited for Freda to speak.

'The thing is, I can only be here for a few days. I have a job that I can't leave for any longer than that and I'm also a dispatch rider for the Fire Service. I can't let people down.'

The nurse gave her a hard stare. 'Your duty is with your mother. She may not have long in this world and deserves to have you by her side. What is your job?'

'I'm a junior supervisor at Woolworths. We're rather short-staffed at this time and I need to earn my way—'

'A shop girl? There are shops here in Birmingham crying out for staff. I don't see that there is a problem.'

'I don't have anywhere to stay long term. The room I'm in is not . . . is not suitable long term,' Freda said, feeling as though she was making up excuses when the truth was, she dreaded stayed at Janey's house much longer. Nothing had been said, but Freda couldn't help but feel she wasn't welcome and Janey was trying to get her last shilling from her.

The senior nurse gave her a look and although it only lasted a few seconds, Freda felt as though she'd been thoroughly scrutinized. 'Speak to Nurse when she takes you to see your mother. She will know of respectable lodgings.' With that the sister rang a small hand bell on her desk and put the file to one side.

Freda murmured her thanks and left the room. The nurse she'd met earlier was standing outside. 'I'll take you to see your mother. She's awake and just had a nice wash, all fresh and ready for her visitor,' she smiled at Freda before heading off at a brisk walk towards the end of the ward. Freda had no choice but to follow, even though she dreaded seeing her mother and having the past come back to greet her.

'Here she is, Mrs Smith, you must be so happy to see

your daughter. I'll leave you both to have a nice long chat. There's another half hour before the end of visiting time.'

'Thank you,' Freda murmured as the nurse bustled away.

'So you've come then?' Lily Smith said, glaring at Freda. 'You took your time.'

'I had no idea, Mum,' Freda explained, while staring at the shrivelled woman on the bed in front of her. Her mum had aged considerably since Freda had last been at home. Thin grey hair framed yellowing skin and there was not an ounce of fat on the woman's body. She looked more like eighty years of age than in her mid-forties, Freda thought to herself. 'Please tell me what happened to you?'

Lily shrugged her shoulders, which triggered a coughing fit. When it had subsided she spoke bitterly. 'What do you care? I've seen hide nor hair of you in God knows how long. I could have met my maker and you wouldn't have given a damn. Your brother's no better. Where's he? Back in prison, I bet?'

Freda frowned. 'Mum, you know why I moved away. With you shacked up with that brute I had no choice. You may not have worried about him beating you black and blue when you'd been knocking back the gin but I feared for my life. Then when Lenny disappeared I knew it was time for me to leave home and seek him out. But that was years ago. There's a war on and our Lenny is more than doing his bit for king and country. He told me he keeps in touch by letter wherever he is in the world and sends you a few bob. Have you forgotten?'

Lily stared away from her daughter with a vacant look

on her face. 'There's a war on, you say? It must have slipped me mind for a minute . . .'

Freda was worried. How could anyone forget about the war? As if on cue, a siren started to wail and the once quiet hospital ward became a buzz of activity as those patients who were able to walk began pulling on dressing gowns or coats while others were helped into wheelchairs. Lily began to snivel. 'Make it stop, make it stop,' she begged, putting her hands over her face.

'Shh, Mum don't fret. I'll get some help,' Freda said, heading to where a nurse was coaxing an elderly lady into her coat. 'Excuse me, please, what happens to my mum and the lady over there who can't get out of bed?'

The nurse gave her a quick look before continuing with her duties. 'Cover her head with a blanket and you get under the bed. She'll just have to take her chances. I'm sorry,' she added, giving Freda a small nod before helping the patient towards the large double doors at the end of the ward. 'You can come down into the basement with us if you wish?' she called back. 'There's one nurse who will be staying with the patients who can't be moved.'

Freda took a quick look around the ward. Her mum was one of two patients who had wire cages over their legs protecting broken bones, which would have made it almost impossible to move them to safety before the bombs started to drop. Leave her mum and save her own skin? It didn't take more than a second to decide. Lily Smith never once did a thing to help her kids after Freda and Lenny's dad had died at such a young age. She only ever cared for herself, not once thinking what her children were going through. No one would blame Freda if she followed everyone else down into the cellars of the hospital, would they? Just a few steps to walk and she'd be at the top of the stairs and on her way to safety. But it didn't take more than a second for Freda to decide to stay.

'Bert, Bert, help me, for God's sake, help me,' Lily called out, using Freda's dad's name.

She turned towards her mum's bed and hurried back, making soothing noises as she reached the bed. 'It's all right, Mum, I'm here now. You don't have to worry any-more,' she reassured the fretting woman, taking her hand and sitting down beside the bed as the ward emptied bar them and an elderly lady sleeping on the other side of the room.

'Don't leave me,' Lily beseeched her daughter. 'I'm frightened.'

'There's no need to be frightened. The Luftwaffe wouldn't bomb a hospital.'

'You hear of such things . . .' Lily whispered, her wide eyes looking from left to right. 'You got to watch the bug-gers,' she added seriously.

Freda tried not to laugh. 'You just sleep, Mum, and I'll watch out for the buggers.'

'You won't leave me, will you, Freda?'

'No, I'll not leave you.'

'Not ever?'

'No, not ever,' Freda replied, leaning over to kiss the wafer-thin cheek and wondering how she was to survive here in Birmingham for the foreseeable future.

16

Betty shook her head in disbelief. 'I'm not so sure this is a good idea,' she said as Mike helped Douglas into a coffin propped against the storeroom wall.

'Mike's proved that my staff member Martin Chambers is related to people running the new business down the road. We just need to find him with his fingers in the till, so to speak, and our problems will be over. Will you wedge that piece of paper in the lid so I can have some air and also see what's happening? There's no need to be so worried, Betty. It's rather comfortable in here,' he joked, seeing her worried face through the small gap.

'I don't think this is at all funny,' she admonished the two men as she saw Mike trying hard not to grin. 'What if these men turn violent? And before you say another word, Douglas Billington, I don't want to hear that you're in the right place if one of the men bump you off.'

'Don't you worry, Betty,' Mike said, 'I have men outside and I only have to blow my whistle and they'll come running. Now, you take yourself back to the front office and pretend to be dealing with a grieving relative. You do know it's PC Robert and his lady friend Miss Burgess, don't you?'

Betty nodded. 'Yes, it's all been explained to me.'

'Good. Chambers and Harry Singleton will assume you're busy and hopefully use the time to steal the new stock that conveniently came in this morning. I'm hoping that his relative may also arrive to help, which will make our job much easier once they're nabbed.'

'I understand,' Betty said.

'Just make sure to tell them both that Douglas is out on business and won't be back for a while.'

'I can do that but please be careful, both of you. Gwyneth will not be pleased if you're injured. You both seem to be enjoying this a little too much for my liking. This isn't some playground prank.'

Mike assured Betty that no one would be hurt and insisted she went back to the front of the shop and open up for business. 'I'll be just inside this store cupboard and can see everything through the drill holes. Now, hurry before the men turn up for work.'

Betty reluctantly left her husband and friend to return to the front of shop and play her part in what she hoped would be the plan that stopped all thefts from Douglas's business once and for all. She hadn't told the men that she had a little insurance tucked away in her desk drawer. The hammer would come in very handy indeed if anyone dared hurt her husband.

Unlocking the door and turning the sign to indicate they were open for business, Betty busied herself tidying up and doing what she hoped looked like normal every-day work in a funeral director's shop. She jumped as the door opened, looking up with a ready smile expecting her pretend customers. It was Harry Singleton.

'Harry, you know you're supposed to use the staff entrance at the back of the premises.'

Harry ignored Betty's reprimand and headed to the door which led to the staff quarters.

'Oh Harry, Mr Billington has gone out to visit a bereaved family. He asked that you start unpacking the delivery and have it all put away by the time he gets back. Martin can help you as well,' she added, trying to act as though it was a natural request and not one that would trigger a police arrest.

Harry stopped to look at Betty. 'How long before he gets back?'

Betty casually checked her wristwatch, trying not to shake. 'Two hours, I would think. When you finish unpacking the stock you can make a start cleaning the hearse. Tell Martin to help you as we need both jobs done as soon as possible,' she said to his back as he shuffled out of sight.

It felt an age before the plain-clothes policeman arrived with his lady friend, both respectfully wearing black and playing the part of recently bereaved individuals. Betty slipped into the back room to inform Harry and Martin that she was not to be disturbed as she had customers in the front of the shop. She announced this in a loud enough voice to make sure that Douglas and Mike could hear, although she tried hard not to glance towards where they were hiding. Returning to her customers, she quietly locked the door so, if things became violent, Harry and Martin could not escape through the shop. She then updated PC Roberts and his companion with how things stood in the rear of the shop, and they in turn informed her about colleagues stationed in the street outside and also in the narrow street behind Douglas's business.

'There seems to be a lot of police staff involved in this small theft,' Betty said, concerned that police were being taken away from more important cases.

'Mrs Billington, this gang have stolen from many businesses. Your husband is not the only victim. They take over empty premises and then do their utmost to undercut and steal until they close down respectable companies. After that they sell their own respectable business complete with proceeds from the stolen goods.'

'I had no idea it was such a serious crime. One would almost think this was organized crime like what we see in the American films at the cinema.'

'Mrs Billington, this is organized crime and we know that there is a major East End gang behind what's going on.'

Betty was confused. 'You mean Harry Singleton is part of the gang?'

PC Robert's companion, who had said little up to then, gave Betty a sympathetic smile. 'Harry Singleton is one of those, shall we say, unfortunate people who gets sucked into any little scam that makes their working day more lucrative. This time he may have bitten off more than he can chew.'

'One of my staff contacted me to say that Harry and his wife, Enid, may not be all they seem. Enid is our cook at the Erith branch of Woolworths where I'm the manager. She's not very good at her job but needs must. I'm beginning to believe she's pilfering on a small scale from the food meant for my staff's meals. When I interviewed Enid, initially for the position of cleaner, I was under pressure and didn't follow up references after she said they'd earlier worked for our Canning Town branch. It seems no one knows an Enid or Harry Singleton at that branch, although there was a woman working there at one time whose description fits that of Enid.'

The PC made a note of what Betty had said. 'We can look into this and arrange for a local officer to visit you at the store.'

'Thank you. It may be something or nothing but I'm going to be keeping a close eye on her after this. Whatever is that . . . ?' She exclaimed.

'That's the signal we've been waiting for,' PC Roberts said, jumping to his feet as his companion rushed out of the shop and waved to her colleagues. Betty tried to follow but the constable indicated to her to stay where she was.

Betty felt rather faint and sat down again. She could hear raised voices and expletives from the back room of the shop and prayed that Douglas and Mike were not harmed.

It wasn't long before a handcuffed Harry Singleton was led through the shop by two burly policemen, red in the face with anger and shouting his innocence. Betty kept her head down to avoid the man venting his anger in her direction. This was followed by two of Douglas's regular staff members also in handcuffs who were not as outspoken as Harry, although both were sullen and angry.

'Is that all of them?' Betty asked one of the policemen as she wondered if it was safe for her to venture out to the storeroom to see if Douglas was unharmed. She'd not seen Mike Jackson either.

'Yes, madam, we have all of those involved this end.'

'This end?'

'There was a raid on the other undertaker business up the road. You'll likely have no more problems from that gang again. Your husband will be left in peace from now on.'

Thanking the policeman, Betty headed out to the rear of the business and spotted Mike rubbing the side of his face. 'Have you been injured?' she asked, showing concern for their friend. 'Is Douglas still talking with the police officers outside?'

'I caught a stray punch from our mate, Harry, but it was just the one. I reckon I'll have a shiner come tomorrow. Don't worry, it's part of the job. Gwyneth has seen me with the occasional bruise. It'll be gone by the time the wedding's here,' he added, seeing the look of horror on Betty's face.

'Thank goodness for that. It would be just awful if Gwyneth's parents thought you'd been out boozing before the wedding, what with them being chapel and teetotal. Why, Gwyneth's father might well stop the wedding if he thought you were a drunk.'

Mike laughed and then winced at the pain. 'No fear of that, nothing will stop me marrying my Gwyneth. When I look at how happy you and Douglas are I know it's the right path for me. I can't wait to be a husband to Gwyneth and a father to Myfi. Speaking of Douglas, I can't say I saw him during the affray. I do hope he's all right. Douglas?' he called loudly.

Mike was answered by a muffled shout. Betty, along with Mike, approached the coffin where Douglas had gone to hide an hour before.

Mike pulled back the lid and Douglas stepped out. 'Thank goodness for that. I thought I'd be left in there for the rest of my life,' he said, mopping his hot face with a handkerchief. 'The paper must have slipped out so the lid got stuck and I wasn't able to jump out at the required moment to help apprehend the criminals,' he said.

Mike tried not to grin. 'Thank goodness we heard you, old chap,' he said, slapping him on the back.

Betty too was grinning from ear to ear. 'Oh Douglas, you meant well but I don't feel that a life in the police force is for you. Perhaps stick at what you're good at,' she suggested, giving her husband a kiss. 'Now, I really do need to get back to Erith and see what's happened at Woolworths while I've been gone. Sarah is a very worthy stand-in but I do like to keep my hand on the rudder of my ship.' She checked her wristwatch. 'There will be a bus along shortly.'

'There's no need to wait for a bus. We can give you a ride back down to Erith. I promise not to have the police driver ring the bell in case someone thinks we've arrested the respected manager of Woolworths,' Mike said, trying to keep a straight face.

'God forbid,' Betty laughed. 'Whatever will Clemmie and Dorothy think of their father stuck in a coffin, a raid on the business and then their stepmother being taken away in a police car?'

*

Freda replaced the heavy telephone in its cradle and checked that there were no coins to collect before leaving the telephone box. She'd hoped to catch Betty at Woolworths but was told she wasn't expected in the store until later in the day. It did seem strange for her not to be there. She'd try again later after going to the hospital for afternoon visiting. Betty had asked for an update once Freda had seen her mum and knew what was happening.

Taking a piece of paper given to her by the friendly nurse she'd met when first going to see her mum, she checked the address but couldn't recall the road. I'll ask at a shop, she thought to herself before crossing the road and setting off at a brisk pace. The sooner she moved out of Janey's house and found a room to rent, the better. In the twenty-four hours since she'd arrived she couldn't quite say why but she felt it best not to dally too long in the house.

Heading towards the High Street, she suddenly spotted a familiar building. There was a Woolworths store. She knew she'd see a friendly face in there; weren't all Woolies staff eager to help customers? She pushed open the heavy wooden doors that were so like the ones in the Erith store, and stepped inside. Even the smell of floor wax and the goods on sale made her think of her adopted hometown, although privately she thought the window display was a hundred times better in her own store.

'Excuse me,' she said to an older woman who was behind a counter selling fresh vegetables.

'Yes, ducks, what can I get for you?' she asked.

'Nothing at the moment but I wondered if you knew

where this street was?' Freda asked, handing over the scrap of paper.

The woman pulled a face and handed back the paper. 'There's not much of that street left after yesterday's raid. I don't think anyone was killed,' she added tactfully. 'Were you looking for someone?'

Freda felt her heart plummet into her shoes. Was she destined to stay at Janey's place? 'I've had to come home urgently as my mum's poorly in hospital but I've nowhere to stay.'

'I thought I recognized a local accent,' the woman smiled as she started to fill a weighing bowl with potatoes before shooting them into a customer's shopping bag and taking her money. 'You don't live round here anymore then?'

'No, I moved south, just outside London. I work at Woolworths down that way.'

'Blimey,' the woman said with a grin. 'That makes you one of us all right. You say you need somewhere to stay? How long would that be for?'

'I'm hoping once my mum's feeling better I can get back to my job. I'm also a dispatch rider for the Fire Service and I don't want to let anyone down.'

'I'd say your mum's more important than any job or war at the moment. Look, seeing as you're almost family I can let you kip down in my box room if you like. A couple of shillings a week and a bit of food thrown in, that's if you're not too fussy? I take it you've got your ration book and stuff?'

Freda nodded. 'Yes, I brought everything with me.'

'Good, then have a think about it and come back and

let me know. I'm here until half past five today. The name's Doreen West, by the way. They all know me around here. I've worked for Woolworths for the past ten years or so.'

What a stroke of luck, Freda thought to herself. 'I'll know how long Mum will be in hospital once I've spoken to her doctor this afternoon. Can I pop back in and let you know?'

'You're more than welcome. I hope you get good news about your mum,' she said, turning to serve a woman who was checking the cabbages and onions.

'Thank you,' Freda called back before walking over to the small cafe bar in the corner and ordering herself a cup of hot Bovril and a slice of bread to keep her going through the afternoon. The bread was the grey-coloured National bread but it was filling all the same. Hopefully the doctor would have good news. After promising her mum that she'd stay with her for a while she found herself feeling disloyal to Betty and her colleagues as well as to the fire station. But for the first time in her life Freda felt as though her mum needed her and, as Doreen had told her, family is important and she'd never felt needed by her mother before as she'd always had a man around since her dad had passed away. Then it had been the gin bottle she'd taken comfort from. Despite never having felt loved by her mother, Freda knew she would not forgive herself if she wasn't here when her mother needed her. Unfortunately, she might not make her way back to Erith for quite some time.

*

'Hello, Betty,' Sarah said as she spotted her boss hurrying into the store. 'Did you enjoy your morning off?'

'Can you spare me a few minutes?' Betty said as she headed to the stairs that led to her office. 'We may have a small problem.'

Goodness, whatever could that be? Sarah wondered to herself as she followed Betty into the office and sat on the chair opposite watching as she removed her smart jacket.

'I'm rather warm after all that rushing around,' Betty said before explaining her day so far to her astonished friend.

Sarah sat spellbound as Betty described how the problem had started and that Harry Singleton was now one of the men being interviewed by the police. 'How brave of you both,' Sarah said. 'Thank goodness Harry Singleton is under arrest.'

'Mike Jackson's working with the team who are investigating the crime and has noted all we know. It seems that our little business is not the only one to have come a cropper because of these scoundrels. I just wish I'd checked out Enid's references when I took her on,' she said more than a little angrily.

'Betty, you've been under a lot of strain, what with being short-staffed and trying to keep the branch afloat. No one can blame you for not following up a reference for a part-time cleaner, can they?'

'Please don't make excuses for me, Sarah. I know you mean well but it all boils down to me not being on the ball. I believe the Americans have a saying for this. The buck stops here – this time it stops here with me. I made a telephone call to the Canning Town branch before I left

Douglas's business so hopefully there will be a response before too long and we can sort out all of this sorry business. Whatever I hear, it does mean that we will have to let Enid go. We've had suspicions she's a little light-fingered and with her husband having stolen from my Douglas's business, I don't feel comfortable having her here. Whatever will we do about preparing food for the staff? The answer is beyond me.'

Sarah gave a secretive smile. 'You may just be in luck. Maureen is going to come in and have a word this afternoon.'

Betty beamed. 'Wouldn't it be wonderful if she could fit in a few hours each week to help us out? We just need Freda back in the fold and all will be right with the world once more,' she said.

Just as the women were digesting this information there came a knock on the door and one of the cleaning staff stuck her head round. 'Sorry to bother you, Mrs Billington, but someone tried to get hold of you this morning on your telephone. I was told to let you know when you got into work.'

'Thank you, Ellen, who was it?'

'Freda Smith, ma'am. She said she'd try to get in touch later today.'

Betty looked at Sarah. 'I do hope her call will be to tell us she's heading home, then we can relax for a little while.'

'There's something else, miss. That Enid has burnt the staff dinners and people are waiting to eat,' Ellen said before leaving the room quickly in case Betty was angry.

'Oh well, they do say relaxing is overrated. Come and

give me a hand, Sarah. Let's see if we can salvage enough food to keep our staff happy.'

The two friends headed to the staff canteen where they found windows being flung open and staff waving newspapers about to clear the smoky air. Betty marched over to the serving counter. 'Whatever has happened here, Enid?'

Enid gave her boss a surly look. 'It wasn't my fault,' the cook replied. 'I can't be serving and cooking. I need more help.'

'Maureen managed well enough,' Sarah answered .

'She had better food to work with. This is the third time this week I've had to serve up sausages that are more like sawdust than pork.'

Betty frowned. 'I'd made arrangements to have stewing beef delivered today from head office. Did it not arrive?' She knew there wouldn't be much to go round but padded out with vegetables, it would be filling enough for the workers.

Enid shrugged her shoulders and didn't say a word while Sarah stepped behind the counter and reached below to pull out Enid's shopping bag. Tucked inside was a large parcel wrapped in white paper and string. 'This wouldn't be the missing food, would it?' she asked as Enid tried to snatch back the meat, tearing the paper in the process so the red flesh could clearly be seen.

There was an audible gasp from the staff and mutters of 'shame on you' and worse. Enid glared back. 'Don't look at me like that. You'd all have done the same given half a chance. Don't think you're going to sack me because

I resign. I'm sick of this job and being a skivvy to the likes of this lot.'

'I'm afraid it's far too late for you to resign,' a male voice announced from the doorway. 'Mrs Enid Singleton, or should I say Mrs Ellen Sinclair, I'd like you to accompany me to the police station where we are already holding your husband Herbert Sinclair on charges of robbery and also the theft of money from the Canning Town branch of Woolworths in September 1940.'

There were even more gasps, and a couple of cheers, as Mike Jackson led away the red-faced woman.

'I'll take that, if you don't mind,' Maureen Gilbert said, reaching for the parcel of meat. 'I know some hungry workers who'll be needing a decent meal inside them after all these weeks.'

'Gosh, I've never heard so much cheering,' Betty said after giving Maureen a hug and welcoming her back into the fold. 'I hope you're here for good?'

'If you'll have me?' Maureen grinned as she pulled on a clean white apron and started to peel a potato. 'Now, let me get cracking. Spam and chips for the hungry hordes and steak and vegetable pies for tomorrow's lunch should hit the spot nicely.'

Freda sat down in the proffered chair and watched the elderly doctor as he glanced through the notes in front of him. She hoped that his news would tell her that Lily was on the mend and that once her bones had knitted she would only need a little convalescence before resuming her usual life. Freda would then be able to make plans to return to Erith and her own life.

The office was no more than a box room, with windows set high on the wall that would still have let little light in if they'd been cleaned and didn't have brown tape stuck to them in case of enemy action. It was hard to estimate the doctor's age but his fading tweed suit, and the few stray grey hairs on his otherwise bald head, gave Freda the impression that the man had been brought out of retirement to play his part in the war effort. The air was thick with smoke from a pipe that lay on the desk. Both the pipe and the desk seemed to have seen better days.

The doctor looked up at Freda and then down again to the notes. 'Your mother is an extremely poorly woman,' he said without making eye contact.

Freda wasn't expecting to hear this news. 'Yes, she has broken bones but they do mend eventually, don't they?'

The doctor reached for his pipe and, before placing it into his mouth, said, 'Usually, yes, but your mother is not a well woman. Her health was not good before her . . . her accident.' He puffed on the pipe and watched to see how his words had affected Freda.

A frown crossed her face as she absorbed the few words spoken by the man. 'What are you trying to tell me, Doctor?'

'Miss Smith, your mother will never walk out of this hospital.'

Freda sighed. 'For a moment I thought you meant she was going to die,' she said, giving him a small smile. 'It will be a blow to her not to be able to walk properly for a while but I'm sure we can cope somehow,' she said, thinking of how she could possibly move her mum to Erith so she would be able to work back at Woolworths *and* care for her parent.

The doctor placed his pipe down and leant forwards as far as the desk between them would allow. 'Miss Smith, that is exactly what I'm saying. Your mother's heart has been weak for some time, and that's aside from her other health problems. It's a miracle that she survived the beating she took. Often even younger, healthier people don't survive such injuries. However, you must face facts. Your mother is not long for this earth and you must prepare for the eventuality.'

'How long?' she asked, trying hard not to cry. It seemed so unfair when her mum was still quite a young woman.

'A few weeks, perhaps a couple of months at the most, but I can't guarantee more than that.' He looked down at his notes. 'Sister has written that her spirits have risen since your arrival. It would be a sin for you to disappear from her life again and leave her alone in her last days.'

She raised her chin defiantly. 'Doctor, you know nothing of my family's history but be assured I will not leave my mother alone and will be here in Birmingham for as long as I'm needed.'

After a short discussion about Lily's future treatment, which amounted to very little, Freda left the office feeling despondent. In the short time she'd been back in her hometown she'd started to believe she might be able to build up a relationship with her mum and that they'd possibly keep in touch over the years to come. Now that had all been dashed away. She was not only losing her mum but, unless Lenny could get leave, she would be facing her parent's death on her own. But what of her job and duties in Erith, and how would she be able to support herself? Would the offer of a bed from the kindly woman in Woolies extend for weeks, maybe even a month or two, and how could she support herself when she wasn't able to work?

Freda headed to the ward to see her mum, trying hard to pin a smile on her face and not let Lily see her worries. She would really miss her friends down south and possibly even Gwyneth and Mike's wedding. She gave herself a shake for thinking such selfish thoughts. Whatever happened, she would make her mum's last days as cheerful as possible. Every mum in the world deserved that at the very least.

17

'Maureen, I can't say how pleased I am to have you back working here at Woolworths,' Betty said as she helped the store's favourite cook clean up after the panic of a late meal break. 'I do feel that we rather dropped you in at the deep end, what with you just popping in for a chat.'

'I've loved every minute of it,' Maureen smiled as she wiped down a table. 'As you now know, I came in to see if you'd have me back but I didn't expect to walk in on such a drama. Let's hope that it's an end to that family and we can all move on.'

'I'll agree to that,' Betty said, raising a cup of tea she'd just poured. 'Here's to a peaceful few months for us all. Now, tell me, do you have to give notice to the railway people?'

'As luck would have it, they have a new intake of female workers and as I've been so miserable of late and unable to manage many of the tasks given to me, they said they'd let me go. Is it right to be so happy even though the stationmaster deems me to be a failure?'

Betty was aghast. 'However can anyone say such a thing? Why, you are the backbone of this store and we've

283

been lost without you. I've never heard so many cheers as when you claimed back the kitchen.'

'Perhaps if I'd been able to cook down at Erith station it would have been a different kettle of fish. As for humping luggage and the like about and learning train timetables, I was next to useless. There was a complaint last week that I'd put someone's grandmother on a train to the coast when she wanted to go to London. They found her sitting alone in the waiting room not knowing where she was.'

Betty tried not to laugh but failed miserably. After wiping her eyes she said, 'The railway's loss is our gain. Now, I must leave you as I have a hundred and one things to catch up on.'

Betty had no sooner entered her office than the telephone started to ring. 'Oh Freda, how lovely to hear your voice,' she said as she recognized who had placed the call to her office. 'Now, tell me, how's your mother?'

'She's not so good,' Freda said.

Betty could tell the girl was close to tears by the tremble of her voice. Never had she wanted so much to give someone a hug and be there to help. 'Do you have enough coins? Can I call you back so this isn't costing you a fortune?'

'I'm making this call from the Sister's office. She allowed me to use the telephone as it was important.'

Oh my, Betty thought to herself, as she listened to the young woman explain what had happened since she arrived in Birmingham. 'Listen carefully, Freda. However long this takes, believe me when I say that your job will be here for you when you return. I will also take it upon myself to visit the fire station and tell whoever is in command of your predicament. You just need to concentrate on your mother. What has the doctor said about her recovery time?'

Betty closed her eyes with dread as Freda told how her mum's days were numbered. 'My problem is, Betty, I need to be able to earn while I'm here or I'll not have a roof over my head or be able to help my mum with anything she may need.'

'I'll send you some money . . .'

'No, Betty. It's awfully decent of you but I need to do this for myself.'

'I understand what you mean, Freda,' Betty said, although she was cursing her for being so independent. 'Is it not possible for you to stay with your mother's friend?'

Freda did her best to keep her tone light-hearted when she replied it wasn't possible for more than a day or so. She didn't wish her friends to start worrying about her when all she had herself was an uncomfortable feeling about Janey. 'A lady who works in a local Woolworths store has offered me a room but I'm not sure how long she'd be happy for me to stay.'

'You say there's a Woolworths store nearby?'

'Yes, it's not as nice as ours but the staff seem friendly.'

'I suggest that you finish visiting your mother and try to telephone me when you're able. I'm going to recommend you stay at your mother's friend's house for tonight while we get something arranged long term,' Betty said carefully. 'Do you understand?'

Freda felt a rush of emotions flood through her. One moment she'd never felt so alone and the next it was as if

Betty was here by her side holding her hand. 'Yes, I do understand. There's another hour before visiting time finishes this afternoon. Will that be too soon to telephone?'

'An hour will be ample time. Please give my best wishes to your mother and, Freda, keep your chin up, my love.'

The call ended and the line went dead, with both women staring into space and trying their hardest not to cry. Betty gave herself a shake. Whatever Freda said, she would not see the young woman go without. She'd find a way to make Freda's time in Birmingham as pleasant as it could be as she waited for her mother to pass away. Pulling open a desk drawer, she reached inside for a buff-coloured booklet that listed all the Woolworth stores in England. She flicked through the pages until she came to the Birmingham store Freda had mentioned. She picked up the telephone receiver and started to dial.

Freda thanked the Sister for allowing her to use the telephone and headed back to the ward, where she found her mother not only awake but propped up on her pillows chatting to a nurse who was manning a tea trolley.

'There you are, Freda,' Lily said. 'I told the nurse you would help her with the tea round as you have nothing much to do,' she said, much to Freda's surprise.

'Someone has woken in good spirits,' Freda replied, trying to look for a sign that her mum was in fact close to death. Had the doctor got it wrong?

'Mrs Smith has taken her pills and feels much brighter,' the nurse said as if she was reading Freda's mind.

'Mrs Smith can speak for herself, thank you very much, Nurse,' Lily snapped. 'Now, get along, the pair of you, and let me sleep.'

Freda moved along the ward, stopping to hand out drinks and plump pillows. When she was a safe distance from her mum she spoke to the nurse. 'I take it you know how ill my mum is?'

'Yes, we're briefed before each shift. We'll do all we can to make her comfortable. You need not fear anything,' she smiled sweetly, giving Freda a concerned look. 'I assume you'll be here for the foreseeable future?' she asked.

'Yes, Mum only has our Lenny and me and he's overseas somewhere. I'll have to try and get word to him.'

'That would be a good idea.'

'You must have experience of such things. How long can it take?'

The nurse reached out and squeezed Freda's arm sympathetically. 'There's no knowing. I've seen people who should by right have passed away sooner rather than later who seemed to fight and hold on for different reasons, then others who pass away quickly. We have a vicar you can speak to if you feel you need some form of guidance. I believe you are alone in Birmingham?'

'Thank you, I'll bear it in mind,' Freda said. 'Yes, I have to make arrangements to find somewhere safe to live while I'm here and I can see that I'll have a lot of time on my hands when I'm not here during visiting times.'

The nurse did her best to ignore Freda mentioning the word 'safe'. 'Look, my name is Sally. I live in the nurses' quarters. There are a few of us who help out down the church when we're not on duty. We often go to the pub afterwards. Why not join us when you've sorted out living accommodation? We're all away from home so are in the same boat in some respects. Apart from that, you're more than welcome to give us a hand on the ward. Our ladies love a cup of tea and a chat.'

Freda gave her a grin. 'Thank you, I'd like that.'

'So what was that all about? Have you been planning my funeral?' Lily mumbled sleepily when Freda returned to her bedside.

'Don't be daft, Mum,' Freda said as she straightened the white starched sheet.

Lily's hand shot out and grabbed Freda's. 'I'm not a fool, girl. I'm not a fool.'

Freda pulled her hand back and rubbed it where her mum had squeezed it hard. 'I have no idea what you mean . . .'

Lily peered from yellow-rimmed eyes. 'He's done for me this time. There's only so much a body can take and mine's taken too much.'

Freda wanted to turn and run from the ward and never return but knew she couldn't. She owed it to the woman who brought her into this life to hold her hand and soothe her worries until the last breath left her body. It's not about me, she muttered to herself as she sat down and started to talk.

'Freda, I'm so pleased you could ring me back. I have some good news for you.'

Freda was happy to hear Betty's voice. If she closed her eyes, she could pretend she was sitting in Betty's office in

Woolworths and not in a smelly telephone box in a strange street in a town that had become alien to her after so many years. 'Unless you can tell me that this is all a dream and I'm going to wake up back in my bed in Ruby's house I'm not sure I can be pleased about any news at the moment.'

'Oh, my dear, was it that bad?'

'Yes,' Freda replied, feeling her voice start to tremble. 'Mum knows she's going to die. Don't tell me how but she knows and I've been sitting with her trying to make sense of what she has to say and to calm her down. They've given her something to help her sleep so I'm able to leave her for this evening.'

'Good, good,' Betty said in a soothing voice. 'I've pulled a few strings and found you a part-time job in the Woolworths store you mentioned. Mr Gordon, the manager, seems a good sort and said he was calling out for extra help and wondered if you could do a few hours each morning? He said he'd discuss details with you when you go in to see him. I also took the opportunity to ask about accommodation. I said where you were staying was temporary and you were keen to rent closer to the hospital. I did mention the lady you spoke to and he assured me she was a kindly soul and would take excellent care of you with full board. I had a chat with the lady and you can move in this evening if you wish. I've noted down the address. You don't have to pay rent for the first month as it's all been taken care of. I hope you're not angry that I've interfered, Freda?'

Freda felt as though a huge weight had lifted from her shoulders. 'Oh Betty, how can I be angry? You have no idea what a great help you've been. I'll go and collect my few bits and pieces from Janey's and be there this evening,' she said as she rummaged in her handbag for a pencil and paper to write down Doreen's details.

'Mr Gordon has suggested that you use his telephone to contact me each day so that I know you're safe and well. Don't feel for one moment that we aren't all thinking about you and ready to drop whatever we're doing to help you if the need arises. Now, is there anything you need me to do for you, or to send?'

Freda thought for a moment. All of this had taken her by surprise. 'I . . . I don't know. I suppose I shall need some clothing, as I didn't expect to be staying here for any length of time. There is something . . . would you ask David Carlisle if he knows of a way to contact my brother, Lenny? I know he can't drop everything and come home from wherever he is but I'd like him to know that Mum doesn't have long . . .' She fell silent, thinking of her brother and her mum. Although she had the best friends anyone could wish for, it was now she realized the true meaning of family and why it had meant so much to Maisie when she was determined to see her mum in Bethnal Green. She shuddered as she compared the outcome of their journeys as she knew hers wouldn't end happily either.

'I'll do that straight away. Just remember, Freda, you're not alone and I'll arrange the staff rota so the girls can visit you.'

Freda found it hard to speak. 'Th . . . thank you, Betty. I'd best get going and move my things to Doreen's house.

I'll be in touch,' she said before putting down the telephone and cutting off her link to the life she loved.

In the days that followed Freda soon fell into a routine. Doreen's family were extremely welcoming and although Freda was almost never at the house apart from sleeping in the small box room and waking to Doreen calling her for breakfast, she enjoyed their chats on the way to work and how the woman never intruded on her private life.

Working at another Woolworths store was interesting as she was put on any counter that was short-staffed. Most days this was alongside Doreen selling vegetables, which was not the most glamorous position in Woolies but it kept Freda from thinking too much as she weighed out potatoes and cabbage to the queues of women that never seemed to shorten. During tea breaks she found herself to be a magnet for the younger girls, who were underage for joining up and were biding their time eagerly awaiting being able to leave home to do their bit and explore the world. As much as Freda explained that working in a Woolworths store in another part of England was very much the same as working in Birmingham, Freda found she was never alone for long as she described finding digs and what living not far from London could be like for a girl born and brought up in the Midlands.

Freda would grab something quick to eat in the store's canteen before hurrying to the hospital to sit with her mum. Lily had good days when she would chat quietly before dozing off but then there were the days when she was agitated and aggressive towards her daughter, blaming Freda for all her ills. The medical staff assured Freda it was part of the illness and she was in no pain but even so, she ached for her mum to be like she remembered her before her dad had died and before her mum had taken to the drink and they'd been a proper family. True to her word, Nurse Sally had whisked Freda off to the pub to meet her friends and it had been an evening when Freda could forget about her problems and listen to the young nurses talking about their work and lives. Freda had long enjoyed the belief that nurses fell in love and married the handsome doctors they worked with but when she mentioned her thoughts the girls had fallen about laughing. It was explained that many of the younger doctors had joined the services whilst the older ones, and those who had come out of retirement, manned the hospitals back home.

The weeks ticked by and although Lily was frail, her broken leg had healed enough for Freda to be able to help her into a wheelchair and take her mum out into the hospital grounds. It was while sitting there one day enjoying the early September sunshine that she heard a familiar voice. Turning round, she shrieked with delight, waking her mum from a deep sleep while other patients looked to see what had happened to make the girl they'd come to like take on so.

'That's a sight for sore eyes, Freda Smith taking it easy sunning 'erself while we travel all the way up 'ere ter make sure she's all right,' Maisie declared, sweeping her friend into her arms and giving her a tight hug.

They were joined by Sarah and close behind Gwyneth as all the girls jumped up and down in excitement to be together once more.

After introducing her friends to her mum, who eyed

them all suspiciously before going back to sleep tucked up under a pile of blankets, Freda turned to the women with tears glinting in her eyes. 'You have no idea how much I've missed you all.'

'We've missed you too and thought that as you weren't likely to be home soon we'd surprise you with a visit. Maisie's David arranged for us to have rooms in a pub down the road and the landlord is arranging a bit of food for us later on so we can have a little celebration,' Sarah said with a grin.

'Celebration? I'm just so happy to see you all.'

'We thought as how with you not likely to be back in Erith for my wedding next week we'd have a little bit of a do here with you now.'

Freda's face dropped. 'Oh Gwyneth, I'd forgotten about your wedding. Time has passed here and I'd lost count of the days. Apart from working a few hours at Woolworths and going out once or twice with Nurse Sally, I've spent most of my time here with Mum. If it weren't for the leaves starting to turn to gold on the trees, I'd have thought it was still summertime. As much as I'd love to, I'm not sure I can leave Mum to go celebrating, though,' she added wistfully.

'And why not, may I ask?' a deep voice asked from the doorway of the hospital ward. 'I haven't sailed the seven seas to get back here for my sister to refuse to paint the town red with her mates.'

'Lenny!' Freda shrieked and threw herself into the arms of her young brother. 'Where did you spring from? I never expected to see you in a million years.'

'David pulled a few strings,' Maisie said proudly. 'I'm

married to the man and have no idea how he does it but he comes in 'andy sometimes,' she said, wiping a tear from her eye to see her young friend so happy.

'What's all this commotion?' a frail voice enquired from the wheelchair.

'Mum, it's Lenny. He's come to see you,' Freda said gently, knowing her mum could easily be confused. She led Lenny towards their mum, where he knelt down by her side.

'Who's that?' Lily said, squinting against the autumnal sun. 'Bert, is that you?'

Freda thought her heart would break. Fancy her mum thinking her dad was back after all the years he'd been dead.

'Don't be silly, Mum, it's me, your little Lenny,' he smiled gently. 'Are you going daft in your old age?'

Lily frowned and thought for a moment before breaking into a smile. 'Come here and give your mum a kiss,' she said, fighting to free her arms from the confines of the blankets. 'Now, I hope you've been a good boy at school today. No more fighting and getting the cane, eh?' she chuckled.

The tears that had been threatening to fall since Freda was surprised by her chums finally overflowed and ran down her cheeks. Sarah took her arm and led her away. 'Best not let your mum see you upset,' she said, enfolding her friend in her arms and soothing her as she cried. 'We're all here to help you and David's arranged for Lenny to be here for . . . for the duration,' she added, not quite knowing how to put what they both knew into words.

Freda nodded and blew her nose after wiping her eyes with a freshly laundered handkerchief she'd pulled from the cuff of her cardigan. 'It's been happening a lot lately. One moment Mum is chatting normally and the next she's in another time and place. Often she chats as if my dad is at work and will be home soon. She's not had any notion of the war, or that her kids have grown up, for some time now. The poor lamb is petrified when we have a raid as she just doesn't understand what's going on.'

'Is there nowhere that she can be transferred to? A convalescent home perhaps?' Sarah asked, hoping that there could be some help for her friend's mum.

'No, she needs round-the-clock nursing care and the staff here are so lovely. They've done everything possible to keep Mum comfortable. It's just a matter of time now.'

'Poor, poor lady,' Sarah said. 'I wish I could do something . . .'

Freda gave Sarah a hug. 'Just being here is helping so much. However did you manage it? Who has the children and what about Woolworths? I'm still pinching myself to make sure I'm not dreaming. As for our Lenny arriving, well . . .'

Sarah led Freda over to a seat under a nearby tree so they could talk without being overheard. 'Betty has been such a good sport. You know that Maureen's back working at Woolies?' She continued speaking after Freda nodded her head. 'Well, she's not only fitted in moving house but has also taken on a couple of part-time ladies, so she insisted that me and Gwyneth had time off together while David shipped his mother in to take care of baby Ruby and the two girls so Maisie could come along. Nan and

Maureen are caring for Myfi and Georgina between them. Even Vera offered to muck in, although she's very much the doting great-grandmother at the moment. Why, they've all moved heaven and earth so we could spend a few days together. To be honest, after Maisie was away last year on her own for so long we didn't like to think of you being in the same boat.'

'You've all been so wonderful to come and cheer me up as you have, and so close to Mike and Gwyneth's big day as well. That's going above and beyond the call of duty. However did you pull it off for Lenny to arrive with you?'

'That was pure coincidence. As you know, David had done his best by writing letters and making a few telephone calls but he'd not heard anything back. Then this morning as we were preparing to leave, who should come knocking on the door but your little brother.'

'Not so little anymore, I swear he's grown another foot since I last saw him. I can see how Mum thought it was Dad standing there. He does have the same look about him,' Freda added wistfully.

Sarah laughed. 'He's no longer the little ragamuffin lad who turned up on Nan's doorstep and caused us so much trouble. Why, he's a grown man now and I reckon he can turn a few heads when his ship's in port. Look at your nurse Sally. She's not taken her eyes off him since we arrived.'

Sally saw the girls watching her and came over. 'Why don't you head off with your friends, you must have so much to talk about?' I'm sure your brother can manage to keep your mum entertained for a while. I'm on duty for the rest of the evening so I'll keep an eye on the pair of them.'

Sarah gave Freda a knowing smile as Sally went back to the invalid's side. 'It could be handy having a nurse in the family.'

The four girls clinked their glasses of pale ale together. 'To friendship,' Maisie said loudly, causing a few drinkers at the bar to turn and look their way.

Sarah nudged Maisie's arm. 'Shh, or you'll have them wanting to join us,' she said, trying not to look towards the bar. 'We're all respectable married women. I'm not even sure we should be in a bar without a man to accompany us.'

'I'm not married yet,' Gwyneth said, giving Maisie a wink.

Maisie roared with laughter. 'I doubt a man would look my way if he knew how many kids I had at home and what lay on the horizon.'

Freda, who was about to remind her mates she was free and single but didn't take to meeting men in pubs, opened her mouth to speak and froze. 'What do you mean? What's on the horizon?'

Sarah held her breath, hoping Maisie wouldn't give too many details in her reply.

'I just mean that David and me want a few more kiddies and we don't see why we should wait. Especially now we have a nice 'ome.'

'That would be lovely,' Gwyneth sighed. 'I'd like nothing more than to have a couple of babies. Once I'm married to Mike,' she added quickly before turning a delicate shade of pink.

'Blimey, you come here to cheer me up and all I'm hearing about is babies. I feel truly on the shelf when I've not even got a boyfriend,' Freda huffed.

'You're not on the shelf. Why, you're far too young for that,' Sarah said. 'I'd dearly love another baby before Georgina is much older. I always thought my children would be close together in age.'

'You need an 'usband in the same country for that to 'appen,' Maisie laughed out loud.

'I just knew this conversation would turn smutty,' Sarah retorted, reaching for her purse. 'Who would like another one?'

Once the girls had given their orders Maisie, not one to let a subject drop, turned to Freda. 'Look how long Betty waited until she married. There's 'ope for you yet, kid.'

'Cheers, Maisie, I had hoped for a family of my own. That's not likely to happen for Betty at her age, is it? She'll have to stick with caring for Douglas's two daughters. I know she loves them to bits but it's not the same as having your own, is it? A shame she's past the age to have children of her own. Anyway, what's this about her moving house? Has she had bomb damage?'

'No, they're renting a lovely house in Carlton Road. Their own place is up for sale and Betty reckons she has someone interested in buying already,' Sarah said. 'I went with her to take a look. I'd kill for a place like that for when my Alan comes home and the war is over.'

Freda was horrified. 'My goodness, do you think all this

business with those men pinching from Douglas's business has put them in dire straits? It seems strange to go from owning to renting, even in wartime.'

Gwyneth, who'd been listening to the three friends chattering away, gave a small laugh. 'It couldn't be further from the truth. Betty wants to live closer to Erith and she's encouraging Douglas to expand his business. She sees the money from the house as being put to good use. Mike told me. I swear he'd be keen to join Douglas's enterprise if he wasn't married to the police service.'

'I say good luck to the pair of them,' Maisie said, raising the glass that Sarah had just passed across the table. 'It's a good business to be in as everyone needs the service of an undertaker at some point in their life.'

The girls fell silent as Freda stared down into her lap, deep in thought.

18

September 1943

'What a wonderful day,' Ruby said as she removed the hat pin that secured her Sunday best hat to her hair. 'Even the sun kept shining and the Luftwaffe never made an appearance,' she added, not mentioning that she'd been on her knees the moment she'd walked into church on Bob's arm to pray for a peaceful day with no rushing to air-raid shelters halfway through the service.

'The adult bridesmaids didn't keep the younger ones in check,' Vera said. 'The two littlest were running amok while Mike was making his vows. I'd have slapped their legs if they'd been mine,' she sniffed.

'No one seemed to mind and it was, after all, a family service. There was only one thing missing to make it perfect and that was our Freda.'

'It's strange you should mention that,' Vera said as her eyes glinted. 'Her mother's taking a time to die, isn't she?'

Ruby was shocked. 'Vera Munro, that is an evil thing to say! Wouldn't we all cling to life as much as we could if the only other option was meeting our maker? I reckon her having Freda staying nearby and Lenny being there for the foreseeable future has made all the difference. I know I'd hang on if my loved ones were there by my side.'

'Does that include grandson-in-laws?' a man's voice asked.

Ruby spun round. 'Well, I'll be buggered, Alan! When did you get here? Do Sarah and Maureen know you've made it to the wedding? She was that upset knowing you'd been delayed.'

'Crikey, woman, so many questions,' he laughed before giving her a big kiss on the cheek. 'I've just arrived and you're the first of the family I've spotted as I stepped into the pub. Hello, Mrs Munro,' he added politely as Vera, not one to step away during private family moments, was listening intently.

'I was just saying to Ruby that it'll be her and Bob's wedding next,' Vera smiled at the handsome airman.

'You said no such thing, Vera Munro. You were telling me how naughty the bridesmaids were,' Ruby said sternly, although she gave Alan a small grin. 'You'll find your wife over there with her mum and dad. Goodness knows where your Georgina is. No doubt joining in with the older kids sliding on the dance floor. I'll join you when I've seen that Gwyneth's parents are settled. They're pretty decent folk considering they're teetotal,' she said as she pushed Alan in the direction of his wife.

Ruby hadn't taken six steps before she heard Sarah give an almighty shriek followed by Alan's mum Maureen. All's right with the world, she thought to herself. I have my family close and before too long Freda will be home and in the warmth of her friends. She'll need taking care of for a while and that will be my job. A thought struck her. She could do what the younger girls had done a few weeks ago. She could catch a train and go to visit Freda. Yes, she'd do just that, she decided.

'Why, Alan, if you'd arrived an hour earlier, you could have been in the wedding photographs,' Irene Caselton said, giving her son-in-law a polite peck on the cheek. 'George, can you not take a few more of the happy couple with Alan and the family? Surely you can do that outside the pub?'

George nodded enthusiastically, patting his trusty Box Brownie camera before shaking Alan's hand. 'It's good to see you home again, Alan. Will you be with us for long? That's if you're allowed to say.'

Alan tucked his arm back round his wife's waist and the other over his mum, Maureen's shoulder. 'For the foreseeable future, George. I'm back instructing new pilots. With luck it won't be too far away and I'll be home on a regular basis.'

Sarah squealed with excitement. 'You never put that in your letters.'

'I wanted to surprise you,' he grinned. 'For now I'm on leave for a week before reporting to Biggin Hill. I'll know after that what my duties will be.'

'A whole week?' George said thoughtfully. 'Had the pair of you thought about celebrating your wedding anniversary?'

Alan gave him a blank look. 'Wedding anniversary?'

Sarah slapped her husband playfully. 'For heaven's sake, Alan, do you not remember our wedding day, the third of September 1939 ... the day we went to war?'

Alan tried hard not to laugh at Sarah's words. 'But that was three weeks ago?'

'A husband does well never to forget an anniversary,' Irene said as she stroked the head of a fox-fur stole slung casually around her shoulders.

'That's true,' George said. 'Irene had me search high and low for that thing in case an anniversary should come along that I'd forget.'

'I swear the thing is watching me,' Maureen said with distaste. 'The eyes seem to follow me.'

'It's probably still annoyed with our Georgie trying to feed it and dig it a hole in the garden,' George guffawed.

Irene looked indignant. 'I don't see what is so amusing. The child is three years of age. It's time she learnt some discipline. With you all chuckling at her antics she'll grow into a wild child. God forbid what she'll be like when she's an adult.'

'I shall beat her soundly and send her to bed without her supper if I catch her ill-treating another fox-fur stole,' Alan declared seriously.

Irene waved her white gloves at her son-in-law. 'Oh Alan, why is it I can't stay angry at you for long?'

Maureen laughed. 'Is it something to do with him being an RAF pilot? Now, we need to get this show on the road. I'm off to help Ruby sort out the food then it'll be time for the band to start playing.'

'Food? I'm famished,' Alan declared, rubbing his hands together and sniffing the air. 'That aroma doesn't smell like paste sandwiches and trifle. What's going on?'

'Bob decided that as the members of our pig club were all involved in the wedding we should donate the beast to the occasion. So, we've pooled our vegetables together and come up with a tasty meal for all the guests.'

'The apples for the pies come from the trees in our garden,' Irene added.

'You'd best get that photograph taken before Alan has custard down his jacket. He hasn't changed since he was a lad.'

'So that's where Georgina gets it from?' Sarah said. 'What a pair they make.'

At that moment Georgina spotted her daddy, and amongst happy tears and kisses they headed outside the pub. George collected his mother and they all congregated outside the entrance to the Prince of Wales public house so that Alan could be included in the happy celebrations. 'I'd like one of Sarah, Georgie and me with our parents if there's enough film left in the camera, George?'

'There is, Alan,' George said as he passed the camera to Mike Jackson, who was resplendent in his dress uniform for the occasion of his nuptials. 'Come on, Bob, you're as near as damn it one of the family so tuck yourself in beside Mum and give us a smile,' George said as he slapped the older man on the shoulder.

The extended family jostled together in the late September sunshine as Mike instructed them to move closer together and shout *cheese* as he took their photographs.

'That should do it,' he said, handing back the camera to George. 'I need to find my best man and have him announce that the meal is served, then we can have the speeches and start to enjoy ourselves.'

Ruby headed back into the hall with Bob following close behind. She wanted to oversee the serving of the meal and make sure Vera didn't pinch all the crackling. 'It seems to have gone off all right so far,' he said. 'I just wish his mum could have been here to see her boy marry such a lovely girl.'

Ruby agreed with him as she waved to a friend across the room. 'Perhaps if he hadn't waited so long to marry she'd have seen him walk up the aisle. There again, he waited for the right girl to come along and that's as it should be. What is it they say, marry in haste and repent at leisure?'

'Is that why you're still avoiding marrying me, Ruby?' Bob said.

'Please, Bob, now's not the time or place to talk about our plans.'

Bob took her by the elbow so that Ruby faced him. 'It never is, though, is it? A man can get tired of waiting, you know.'

Ruby laughed and gave him a quick hug. 'It's a bit on the late side to be saying that, Bob Jackson, now that you've given me a bad name by living under my roof and putting your slippers by the hearth.'

Bob spluttered with indignation. 'It's all above board and respectable. The neighbours all know I've moved into the room that Gwyneth and Myfi vacated so that Mike can start off his married life without his old dad living with him. Even Mike has slept on your settee for the past week while Gwyneth and the girl settled in over the road. Why, I'd call any man outside who was saying that anything untoward was going on.'

'What about women?' she said, nudging him pointedly as Vera came into sight. 'There's someone who could make an angel look as though she'd supped with the devil.'

'Blow Vera Munro. It wasn't so long ago she wanted to drag me up the aisle but I was having none of it,' Bob said, feeling a little hot under the collar. 'All I'm saying is I want to make an honest woman of you, Ruby Caselton, and the sooner, the better. You said as how you were waiting for a sign from your Eddie. Is there any chance he's sent it yet?'

Ruby did feel guilty. Perhaps she was expecting too much but deep inside she couldn't help but think she wanted her late husband's approval before she wed again. 'I'm being a daft old woman, Bob, but it means a lot to me to know Eddie is giving me his blessing. I'll understand if you won't wait for me. I know I'm being unfair.'

Bob sighed. 'No, it's me being pushy as usual. It's all this wedding malarkey that's doing it. Our Mike and Gwyneth are so much in love that it made me think I want the same,' he sighed.

'Love changes as we get older,' Ruby said. 'It doesn't mean we feel it any less but it shows in other ways. We make a good team, you and I, and in time we will walk down the aisle together but for now let's leave things as they are, eh?'

Bob sighed. 'I'm fine with that but it'll be your loss if some Hollywood starlet snaps me up,' he grinned, once more becoming the Bob she knew and loved.

'If that happens, I'll pay for the wedding licence myself,' she laughed. 'There is one thing you can do for me, though,' she said as a serious look came over her face.

'Just name it.'

'I want to go away for a few days and thought you'd like to accompany me?' she said, trying hard to choose the right words. 'And you can take that gleam out of your eye. This is all above board.'

'A man can dream,' he said. 'We're not off to Cornwall again, are we? It was a bit of a do last time we went down there.'

'No, I want to go and see how Freda is faring. I've missed seeing her today. She's a big part of our lives and I'm worried for the girl. It's a lot to face watching a parent as they pass away and she's not much past being a kid. I know the girls went up to see her a few weeks back and her Lenny is with her but I want to see her for myself and for her to know she's being thought of. What do you think?'

'I think it's an admirable idea. I'll get the train tickets organized and we can try and book into the pub where the girls stayed. They said it was comfortable enough. Now, let's get this meal served before Vera becomes even more agitated.'

After an enjoyable meal and much joviality as Gwyneth's father opened the speeches, Mike got to his feet to make his. Sarah found herself wiping a tear from her eye as the shy police sergeant spoke of meeting the love of his life when she moved to Erith and lodged across the road at Ruby's house, and how they planned to stay in the same location with Gwyneth having moved to his side of the street. He then thanked Maisie for making the bride's attendants look so beautiful and the guests all cheered when he suggested she should start her own bridal gown shop in their hometown, as she was as good as any London-based couturier.

'Get away with you,' Maisie shouted back, although she was thrilled that her part in Gwyneth and Mike's special day had worked out so well.

'Please raise your glasses and toast the bridemaids,' Mike said as he led the toast.

It was then Douglas's turn to speak. He got to his feet and cleared his throat. Betty beamed with pride as her handsome husband praised the happy couple before accepting the toast on behalf of the bridesmaids. Everyone laughed when Georgina shouted 'cheers' from where she was hiding under the top table.

Reaching into his pocket, Douglas withdrew a telegram. 'Sadly we do have someone missing from the celebrations. Our friend Freda cannot be with us today and I know that both the bride and groom miss their young friend being part of their special day. Can I ask that we toast our absent friends?'

It was a more subdued crowd who rose to their feet and said as one, 'Absent friends.'

'Aunty Fweeda,' called a little voice from under the table, which again caused mirth with the guests.

'I'm thinking we should rent out our youngest bridesmaid for functions and parties,' Douglas smiled.

'But not funerals,' Bob shouted out, much to Ruby's disgust as she swiped him with the napkin she had on her lap.

'As I was saying . . .' Douglas said, trying to regain the attention of the guests. 'Freda was not able to join us today but I know Gwyneth was thrilled with the gift she sent.'

Gwyneth held aloft a silver horseshoe decorated with wax orange blossom attached to a white length of ribbon for the bride to loop over her arm. The women present collectively sighed with delight.

'Freda also sent a telegram, although I do wonder if her sailor brother had something to do with the rhyme.' He again cleared his throat. '*Today's the day, tonight's the night, we shot the stork so you're all right.*' He folded the yellow piece of paper and handed it to the groom with a grin.

'You did a fine job,' Betty said to Douglas later as he steered her round the crowded dance floor. Maureen had joined the small band on the stage to much cheering as the bride and groom led the dancing.

'I must say, I was rather nervous. In my line of work I tend to be in the background rather a lot so to suddenly have to speak up and be jovial came as a shock.'

'No one would have known. I'm sure Mike will give you a reference if you wish to become a public speaker,' she added, smiling up into his eyes.

'No thank you, I'm more than happy with my lot. The business is doing well and we've all settled into our new home. What more could I want than my lovely wife and our beautiful daughters? This war can't last for much longer and then we can look forward to our old age and a peaceful life.'

Betty sighed as she closed her eyes and thought about everything she had. She just had this nagging feeling that something was missing and once she found it she would be perfectly happy with her life.

Elaine Everest

'Oh, I do love this song,' Gwyneth sighed as she listened to Maureen singing the well-known Glenn Miller ballad 'Moonlight Serenade'. 'It's the perfect song for my wedding.'

'Our wedding don't you mean, Mrs Jackson,' Mike said tenderly as he held her gently as they danced.

'That does sound funny, Mrs Mike Jackson,' she laughed gently.

'It's too late to change your mind now. I'll never let you out of my sight for as long as I live,' he said. 'You know, this song could be about us, Gwyneth.'

'Why do you say that, Mike?'

'Listen to the words,' he said as he gently murmured the refrain. '*I stand at your gate and the song that I sing is of moonlight . . .*'

'That's beautiful, but I don't understand . . .'

'You have no idea how many times I stood at the gate of number thirteen thinking of you inside and not having the nerve to knock on the door and speak to you.'

'Oh Mike, I'm so pleased that you did. I can now confess that I too hoped you would be on the beat or walking down Alexandra Road so we could pass the time of day,' Gwyneth said with a small sigh.

'Thank goodness we managed to meet,' Mike laughed, 'or we'd have spent our old age glancing across the road at each other and never the twain would meet. What a pair we are!'

'Are you sure this is the right pub?' Ruby said, peering up at the boarded-up building.

310

'The sign says it's the Golden Goose and look, they've painted "business as usual" on the wall here by the front door. Come on, let's go in,' Bob said as he nudged the door open with his elbow since it was the only part of him he could use due to carrying their two suitcases.

Ruby blinked as they went from the sunny street into the semi-darkness of the public house. 'Hello, is there anyone at home?' she called out whilst holding the door ajar, not only to let in a little light but also to make for a quick getaway if needs must.

'Welcome, welcome,' a short weasel-faced man said as he appeared from behind the bar. 'I take it you're Mr Jackson and his lady friend?'

'We are,' Bob said as he glanced at Ruby, warning her not to say a word. He could tell by the look on her face that she wasn't keen on being called a 'lady friend'. 'It looks as though you've had a visit from Hitler's air force?' he said, nodding to the boarded-up windows. 'That must be a bit of a problem in your line of business?'

The landlord agreed. 'This lot happened last night. It's not the first time it's happened, though, and I reckon it won't be the last. I did think about not bothering to glaze the windows again but the wife wouldn't be having any of it. She said she was off to her mother's until it was fixed. I reckon I can hang it out for a week,' he laughed as Bob joined in.

Ruby coughed politely. 'Are we still able to have our rooms if it's not too much of a problem? That was two rooms,' she added pointedly.

'The rooms are ready,' the landlord replied. 'You'll be pleased to know that the rooms at the back weren't affected by the blast so you can see out. Not that there's a lot to see around here apart from bombsites and rows of old houses. I'll just finish serving these gents and then I'll show you up. Would you care for a drink?'

'No thank you,' Ruby replied before Bob could speak. 'We'd just like to unpack and freshen up before we visit our friend at the hospital.' She took a seat at the side of the room and Bob joined her.

'A half pint wouldn't have hurt,' he said with a glum expression.

'Later, Bob. I wanted to get out of the way before those blokes spotted us,' she whispered, turning her back on the room.

'Who's that then?' Bob asked as he tried to peer around Ruby.

'Don't let them see you're looking at them,' she hissed. 'I swear it's that chap who broke into my house and tried to catch Lenny a few years ago. What was his name . . .' she murmured to herself. 'Whiffen . . . that's it, he's Tommy Whiffen and I thought he was locked up for what he'd done. He's a nasty bit of work all right and here he is right back in the area where our Freda and Lenny are staying. Whatever are we going to do?'

'Do you reckon he'll know who you are after him being locked up?' Bob asked, concerned for Ruby's safety.

'Oh, he'll recognize me all right. He can't have forgotten how I floored him with my frying pan before your Mike took him away in handcuffs. He's a nasty so-and-so. We need to warn Freda in case she and Lenny come here to meet us.'

Bob thought for a moment. 'I'm all for letting the local bobbies know as well. From what I recall at the time, I'm surprised he's even out of prison. Whatever we do we need to act calm and not alert them. Let's get unpacked then go and warn Freda and the cops. I may just give Mike a telephone call as well.'

'Mike's on his honeymoon, Bob, but you could speak to the desk sergeant at Erith police station. He'll have a record of what happened. Why don't you ask to use the landlord's telephone? It'll save time?'

'What a daft pair of beggars we are,' Bob laughed quietly. 'Me for forgetting that Mike's not on duty and you for suggesting that I ask to use the landlord's phone.'

Ruby looked confused. 'What do you mean?'

'He could be a mate of theirs and for all we know he could be part of the gang. We could be in the midst of something very tricky here.'

Ruby gripped her handbag close to her body. 'Bloody hell,' she whispered.

'Just keep out of their line of sight until we get upstairs. Here, take this newspaper and read it until we head up to our rooms. After the journey we've had I'm not fit to protect you should the man attack in any way.'

Ruby leant over and kissed his cheek. 'Don't you start worrying about me, Bob Jackson. I can take good care of us both. I just wish I'd packed my heavy frying pan.'

'So you have a lot of people stay at the pub, do you?' Bob said to the landlord as the man placed Bob's suitcase on the bed.

The man shrugged his shoulders. 'Not as many as I'd like. People don't travel as much in wartime and this area of Birmingham hasn't much to offer unless you know folk living here. I'd prefer a place by the sea but the wife's not one for changes. Why do you ask?'

'No reason,' Bob said, going over to look out of the one small window that overlooked a yard at the back of the pub. 'I was thinking the chaps you were serving were staying as well and as how it must be nice to run such an establishment. I fancied it myself at one time and like you, I could see myself down at the coast somewhere.'

The man laughed. 'No, they're locals celebrating a mate's return to the area. Are you in the pub game?'

Bob wasn't about to tell the man he was a retired copper. 'No, I never did settle to much. A bit of this and that, you know what it's like,' he said, copying the man's casual attitude. 'Well, I mustn't keep you from your guests. I'll be off out shortly to visit my lady friend's family. I wonder . . . is there a side door we can use? She's a bit on the timid side for walking through busy pubs. You know what the ladies are like with their strange ways.'

The landlord laughed in agreement. 'You can say that again. Turn left at the bottom of the stairs and it takes you through the snug and out to the street. Your lady won't be bothered with crowds if she goes that way.'

Bob inwardly thanked his lucky stars as he nodded his head. 'Cheers mate, that'll more than keep her happy.'

'Are you sure you know the way to the ward?' Ruby asked nervously as they approached the large Victorian building.

'That's the second time you've asked me that and for the second time I'll say that yes, I know the way. Freda wrote it down in her letter and she said there was a large noticeboard just inside the main doors. She also knows when we're arriving and said she'd try to slip away to meet us so stop your worrying, woman. And before you ask, I also know where the air-raid shelters are and I've remembered to put a note in my overcoat in case I get blown to smithereens and need identifying. Are you happy now?' he added good-naturedly. If truth were known, Bob was as nervous of going into the hospital as Ruby. In his experience nothing good ever seemed to happen inside these places.

'I know I've never met Freda's mum but I feel after all these months of the girl writing to us and keeping us posted on what has been happening that I know her. Is that daft of me?' she asked as Bob took her arm to help her up a flight of steps that led to the front doors.

'No, it's not daft at all, love. In a way I feel the same. Freda's part of our family and I've missed her cheery face around the place. Even popping into Woolworths hasn't been the same since she left Erith.'

'I know just what you mean, but we can't wish her home with us as it means she'd have lost her mum and I'd not wish that on my worst enemy. Speaking of which, did you manage to get in touch with the police station in Erith?'

'I did it while you were unpacking. I spoke to Mike's boss. He remembers the case and agrees with me that Whiffen would have gone down for longer than a couple of years. He's going to check it out and suggests we keep our heads down as much as possible to be on the safe side.'

Ruby looked worried. 'I don't like the sound of that one little bit. I think we should just go home. We can say hello to Freda and Lenny and warn them Whiffen's back on the scene and then we leave for home.'

Bob opened the door and they entered the large entrance hall to the hospital. He wasn't so sure that Ruby was right in what she said. He couldn't go home to Erith knowing that Freda and her brother would be alone in Birmingham with their very sick mother. The pair of them weren't much more than kids and he felt responsible. Ruby would agree with him once she'd calmed down and had a think about things. He ushered Ruby inside and stood looking at a board hung from the ceiling with arrows pointing to the wards. This was certainly a large building, he thought as he scratched his head.

'Ruby! Bob!' They heard a shout as heads turned to where Freda came running towards them. 'Oh, it's just awful. Thank goodness you're here. I don't know what to do.'

'There, there, my love, I'm here now. Whatever is the matter?' Ruby looked at Bob and raised her eyebrows as she held Freda and soothed her with words of comfort. Perhaps they were too late and the girl's mum had passed away. She didn't expect Freda to react so badly, though.

Bob carefully led them both to a wooden bench and helped Ruby sit down whilst still holding on to the sobbing Freda. 'Now, perhaps you can let us know what's happened,' he suggested softly whilst patting her back. He felt so helpless.

Freda looked up at Bob. 'It's Lenny, they've taken him away.'

'Who?' Ruby and Bob asked at the same time.

'That Tommy Whiffen. He's back and he's got hold of our Lenny. After all this time I thought he was safe but the man's back and blaming Lenny for him going to prison.'

As Ruby and Bob looked at each other, not knowing what to do or say, a young blonde nurse came hurrying down the corridor. 'Oh Freda, there you are. I've been hunting high and low for you. Someone told me that Lenny was in trouble and then I couldn't find you . . .' The young nurse looked distressed.

Freda noticed Ruby's puzzled expression. 'This is Sally. Our Lenny's been stepping out with her since he's been home. Sally, this is Ruby and Bob, you've heard me talk about them. They're like family to me. I don't know what I'd do without them.' She started to cry again. 'I feel such a fool. I told Lenny it would be helpful for him to go to the pub and see you for a drink, Bob. Then he could bring you back to the hospital. Mum's not so good today so I didn't want to leave her and come myself.'

Bob frowned at Ruby. So Lenny could have bumped into Whiffen while they were all in the pub. 'We never saw your brother, but we did see Whiffen talking to the landlord, along with a couple of other rough-looking chaps. We were coming here to warn you.'

'How do you know that they have Lenny?' Ruby asked.

'He made a phone call to the hospital and one of Sally's colleagues gave me the message. He said he was going to watch the man and follow him as he had a gut feeling he was up to no good and he was also muttering bad things about Lenny. That was over three hours ago now and he hasn't been back or contacted us. What if Lenny's been injured? Tommy Whiffen must be as angry as hell with our Lenny.'

Sally looked at Ruby and Bob and could see how worried they were. 'Lenny told me what happened to him when he was a youngster. He said that this man is dangerous and was pleased he was behind bars. Why is he back, do you know?'

'I thought the same, lass, and that's why I made a telephone call to Erith police station to ask them to enquire about this chap. Something's not right here. Do you think I could use a telephone to let them know what's happened? It's been no more than an hour since I spoke to them but it's best they know that Lenny is missing. They should be able to contact the local bobbies to help us.'

Sally agreed. 'We have a telephone that relatives can use. It should be working as there weren't any raids last night. It's always touch and go whether the thing works after a night of bombing. Follow me,' she told Bob.

'She seems a nice girl,' Ruby said as she took a handkerchief from her handbag and wiped Freda's eyes. It broke her heart to see the girl so upset.

'She is and our Lenny's very fond of her,' Freda said with a watery smile.

'I'd best get my hat trimmed ready for another wedding,' Ruby said. 'It met with a bit of a disaster after Gwyneth and Mike's wedding.'

'Why, whatever happened? I'm so sad to have missed it.'

'You was missed,' Ruby said, patting her hand. 'Your telegram caused a laugh, though.'

'It was Lenny's idea,' Freda said. 'I thought it was a little risqué. What happened to your hat?'

Ruby sat back on the bench seat and laughed. 'We went back to our house afterwards for a drink and a chat. I wrote that Gwyneth's parents stayed at our house? Well, we was having a bit of a chat and I'd left my hat on the side in the kitchen when I'd put the kettle on. I sent Myfi out to see what Nelson was up to as he was so quiet and she came in with my lovely hat minus the feathers that Maisie had so carefully stitched to the band. That dog knew he'd done wrong as he crept off and didn't even come begging for a biscuit.'

Freda burst out laughing. 'I do miss Nelson. He would always sleep on my bed. In fact, I miss you all and really want to go home to number thirteen. Is that really awful of me to say so?'

'No, love, it's not bad of you at all. You must feel torn at the moment but just remember you're a great comfort to your mum at a time when she needs you. Now, would you like to take me to meet your mum?'

Freda nodded sadly and they headed to the ward where Lily's bed was hidden behind a curtained screen. Freda pulled back the curtain and ushered Ruby forward. 'Mum, this is Ruby, the lady I live with in Erith. She's come to see you.'

Lily's eyes fluttered and opened slowly. Ruby had never in her life seen such a gaunt face or thin skin on a living human being. It was as if she was looking at a living skeleton. 'Hello, Lily. I'm so pleased to meet you,' she said, sitting down on the chair by the bed.

Lily's eyes flickered from Freda to Ruby before she

whispered. 'Get me . . . some . . . clean water, please . . . Freda . . .'

Freda took the jug by the bed and did as she was told, closing the curtains as she left. Lily reached out to Ruby who took her hand and leant in close, listening hard as the woman tried to speak. 'I'm pleased you came . . .'

'There's no need to speak, love. Save your strength for trying to get well,' she said, knowing that was never going to happen.

'Take . . . take . . . good . . . care . . . of . . . my girl.'

'Shh, I'll always be there for Freda. Don't you worry yourself,' Ruby said, trying hard to blink away threatening tears. Here was she, an elderly woman fit and well, while this poor slip of a woman was fading away in this hospital bed. Life was so bloody unfair at times.

Lily clawed at Ruby's hand, gripping it tighter than a vice. 'Tell her . . . tell her I'm sorry . . . for not . . . being a . . . a good mum . . .' she gasped. 'I love . . .' Lily's eyes fluttered and Ruby watched with wonder as what life was in this poor wretch of a woman simply switched off and the fingers gripping her hand went limp. Eyes that had been watching only seconds before stared into nowhere.

Ruby leant over and carefully closed Lily's eyes before kissing her cheek. 'I'll care for them both as long as I live. Never you fear, my love, never you fear.'

Bob bumped into Freda as she was returning to the ward with the water for her mum. 'Can you tell Ruby that I'm heading back to the pub to see what's happened to your brother. The local police will be there soon so she doesn't need to worry about me. It seems the bloke has escaped from prison and they've been looking for him for the past week.'

'I don't know, Bob. That Whiffen chap can be pretty violent. Ruby will never forgive us if anything happens to you. Hang on a minute while I leave this by Mum's bed and then I'll come with you.'

'No, you can't. You might be recognized, then we'd be in even more hot water with Ruby.'

Freda chuckled. 'You do realize we're more frightened of Ruby than we are of a criminal?'

'I'll go with you,' Sally said as she joined them. 'I'm about to go off duty and I couldn't rest knowing Lenny may be in danger. None of them know me and if anyone gets hurt, I'd come in handy. I can run fast too,' she added, seeing Bob's worried look.

Bob thought for a moment. 'That would make sense. The landlord knows I'm visiting family so we can say you're my daughter if he should ask.'

'I'm still coming with you,' Freda said obstinately. 'I can hang around at the end of the street and call the police if anything should happen.'

Bob nodded his agreement. 'We'd best get cracking.'

Freda handed the water jug to a passing nurse and asked her to let Ruby know that they'd be gone for a while, unaware that behind the curtain at the end of the ward Ruby was holding her mum's hand as Lily slipped away.

'So, what's the plan?' Sally asked as they arrived at the end of the street.

'Freda, you're going to stay here and if anything happens, use the phone box over the road and ring this number. Ask for Sergeant Charles Nugent. He's aware of the situation and will pass on the information to his boss,' he said, handing Freda a piece of paper and a pile of coins. 'We're going inside the pub to have a drink and keep our eyes and ears open. No one is to be brave and attempt anything, regardless of what we witness. Is that understood?' he said, giving them both a hard stare.

'How about a signal if something should go wrong?' Freda asked.

Bob chuckled. 'You've been watching those Johnny Johnson crime films again, haven't you? I tell you what. If one of us should wave something from the door of the pub, you're to go into action. Is that good enough?'

The girls nodded and Sally took Bob's arm as they headed into the pub.

'What would you like to drink, my dear?' Bob asked as they stood at the bar together.

'A small glass of bitter would be lovely thank you, Granddad,' she replied with a grin as he looked taken aback. 'I'm too young to be your daughter,' she whispered as the landlord turned away to get a glass.

'I'll have the same. Best not have too much or my lady friend will be upset,' he said as the man returned.

'She's not with you, sir?'

'Off doing a bit of shopping,' Bob said.

'And your granddaughter's a nurse? You didn't mention that earlier.'

'Most of the family are in the profession so Granddad wouldn't have thought to say,' Sally said sweetly. 'Can we sit down over there, Granddad? My feet are killing me after my long shift.'

'I'll bring the drinks over,' the landlord said.

Bob led her to a seat on the other side of the room, where she nudged him and nodded to where a group of men had their heads together talking quietly. Amongst them he spotted the chap Ruby had said was Whiffen.

'I can't see Lenny,' Sally said, trying not to stare too much in case the men noticed. 'This is a nice pub. Do you have many guests?' she asked the landlord as he appeared with their drinks.

'No, love, just your granddad and his friend,' he said before returning to the bar.

'Now what do we do?' she asked Bob.

'We sit and watch,' he said with a smile. 'Why don't you tell me a bit about yourself while we bide our time?'

They'd finished their drinks and nothing much had happened apart from the landlord occasionally going down into the cellar by the entrance at the side of the bar and then returning empty-handed with a worried look on his face.

'That seems strange,' Sally said. 'Would he not come back with bottles or stock? It's almost as if he's checking on something . . . or somebody?'

Bob raised his eyebrows. 'You could have something there. Do me a favour and keep the landlord distracted while I take a look.' He reached into his pocket and took out a ten-shilling note. 'Buy some more drinks and keep him talking.'

Sally did as she was bid and watched from the corner of her eye as she talked to the man about the hospital and the war. He was flattered by her attention and paid no notice to the rest of the bar until there was the sound of something crashing to the ground in the cellar.

'What the . . . ?' he shouted as he headed in the direction of the noise, leaving Sally alone. It was then that she spotted that Whiffen and one of his mates were missing.

Without stopping to think, Sally headed to the outside door and whipped off her navy blue nursing cape, waving to Freda, who gave a thumbs up and went to the telephone box. Going back inside, she wondered what to do next. The door to the cellar was a solid wooden affair with metal bolts. Perhaps if she locked the door at least the villains couldn't escape? But what about Lenny and Bob, would they be safe? They were already outnumbered three to one if she was to include the landlord. Yes, she'd lock the door, she decided, as she headed in that direction. In the corner of the pub the other two men were watching her closely. 'I'd scarper if I was you,' she called over to them. 'My friend outside has called the police and they're on their way.'

The men got to their feet and left the bar almost at once. Sally reached the door and was pushing it closed when someone on the other side gave it a shove and she went sprawling onto the hard wooden floor. Lenny came through the entrance followed by Bob, who turned and securely bolted the door.

'What are you doing down there?' he asked as Lenny helped Sally to her feet and swept her up in an embrace.

As the police took Whiffen and his men away Freda explained how the force had arrived just as the rest of Whiffen's gang had left the pub. 'It's such a relief to know the man is back behind bars,' she sighed. 'I suppose we'd best get back to the hospital to see Mum and Ruby.'

'I'll use the landlord's telephone to let Ruby know where we've been all this time.'

The youngsters sat down and chatted excitedly as Bob went to find the telephone. Freda could see how much in love her brother was with the bright-eyed nurse as they sat holding hands.

A sad-faced Bob returned holding a tray containing four glasses of brandy. 'You'd best drink this as I have some sad news for you.'

19

July 1944

Betty walked around the busy store. Even though it was summer her thoughts were never far from the next season and that meant cold months approaching. She was more aware than ever that Woolworths should play its part in keeping shoppers warm and happy. A stock of army blankets was due in any day now and she was keen to make a display that would attract her customers to the many uses of these drab-looking items.

'Sarah,' she said as she approached the supervisor instructing two new staff on how to display crockery on a counter without causing the items to crash to the ground. 'Would you be able to accompany me for a few minutes?'

'Certainly, Mrs Billington,' Sarah said, and after a few words with the two young women she followed Betty towards the large shop windows. 'Are we planning a new display?'

'No, although I would like us to think about what we can do with that stock of blankets that are due in. Stacking them up on a counter and watching them sell seems so uninspiring. I feel as though I want to add a dash of fun to the store for once. It seems so long since we did something exciting. Perhaps we could put our heads together and try to come up with some ideas?'

Sarah thought for a moment. 'We need input from Freda and Maisie. They're the ones who come up with all the good ideas. I'm just the girl who does as she's told,' Sarah said. 'Even Gwyneth is a dab hand at making things these days since Freda roped her into helping out with the Brownies.'

'Then we should have a cosy afternoon thinking up ideas and perhaps eating a few cakes and drinking tea. Why don't you all come along to my house on our next half-day and we can sit in my garden and put our feet up? Maureen has been giving me lessons and my baking skills are improving all the time. Douglas says I'll make someone a perfect wife one of these days,' she laughed.

Sarah smiled, thinking back to the stern woman who employed her when she first came to Woolworths. Who knew that this warm, friendly family woman was hiding underneath that stern exterior of a committed spinster? How our lives can change, she thought to herself, and she placed her hand gently on her stomach. 'You certainly will,' she agreed.

Betty frowned as she glanced at her young friend. 'Is there a secret you've not shared yet?' she asked.

'Oh Betty, trust you to guess. Yes, I'm expecting. Isn't it thrilling? I've been dying to tell you all but wanted to wait until I felt the time was right and with Alan off on his latest training course it was only right for us both to give the good news to our parents together before I tell my friends. We told Mum and Dad and Maureen last night. They're overjoyed, although Mum said it made her feel old to be the grandmother of two children.'

'That sounds like Irene. What did Ruby say?'

'Nan had guessed. Nothing much gets past her but she kept quiet, knowing how we had to tell everyone in the right order. I'm surprised no one has noticed as I've either been bursting into tears or wanting to sing from the roof-tops. My moods have been so changeable.'

'I'm truly thrilled for you and Alan, and of course Georgina. I wonder what she'll be like with a baby brother or sister?'

'I'm hoping that with her being four by then she'll understand about the baby and be a little helper for her mummy.'

Betty took Sarah's arm and moved her to one side as a customer bustled past with a basket on her arm. 'When is "then" to be?'

'Not until the new year. My doctor said that being my second, and with Georgina coming early, I could even have a Christmas baby. Wouldn't that be wonderful?'

Betty smiled with delight. 'It certainly would be a joyous time of year to welcome a child. You are truly blessed, Sarah.'

'Who knows, the war may even be over before this little one arrives.'

Betty nodded her head in agreement. 'We can but hope. The invasion of Europe has brought the end of the war so much closer that Ruby's yearly prophecy that the war will be over by Christmas must come true very soon.'

Sarah giggled. 'We do rib Nan about that but I have a

feeling that life will soon be much happier so she may just be right this year.'

'Now, let's make arrangements for you all to come to my home and we can celebrate in style with one of my cakes. Make sure Gwyneth accompanies you as well.'

'I'll do that and we'll look forward to your baking. But Betty, please not rock cakes if you don't mind?'

Betty pretended to frown although her smile betrayed her. 'They weren't a great success, were they? It may have been the lack of dried fruit.'

'Or replacing the margarine with lard,' Sarah said, wrinkling her nose.

'That could have been it,' Betty laughed as she watched Sarah head back to her work, her smile slipping for a moment to show the sadness she did her best to hide from others.

'Are you decent?' Ruby called out as she tapped on the closed door of Bob's bedroom. 'I've got your clean washing here and I've darned the toes in your brown socks, although there seems to be more darning wool than original sock. You might think about some new ones. I'll see if they've got any wool in Woolworths and set about making you some.'

The door opened to a grinning Bob. 'Do you always talk to a closed door?' he said. 'If you'd not been chattering away so loudly, you'd have heard me say I'm decent and come in.'

'I'm not stepping over the threshold of this room, Bob Jackson. It's not done, what with us not being married.'

Ruby bit her tongue as soon as she realized what she'd said. They'd been ticking over nicely together since he'd moved into Gwyneth's old bedroom. Now she'd gone and brought up the subject and he was bound not to let up about them getting wed.

Bob raised his eyebrows and gave Ruby a sad smile. 'Don't worry, Ruby Caselton, I'll not bother you with that question ever again. When the time is right, that's if you haven't changed your mind, you can do the asking. For now I'm comfortable seeing you every day and living under your roof. Why, I may even do a little bit of decorating. That's if you're agreeable to me doing some bits and bobs around the house?'

Ruby felt as guilty as if she'd murdered the man and planted him under her gooseberry bushes. Bob was a decent man and she truly loved him. Try as she might, she couldn't get this silly thought out of her head about her Eddie giving her a sign. 'Bob, I should be apologizing to you for keeping you dangling like this. I should also say that if you change your mind, then I'll not hold you to your promise.' She looked down at her hand where the ring he'd placed on her finger shone brightly. 'I should give this back to you, it's only fair,' she said, starting to remove the ring.

'Don't be daft, woman. What would I be doing with something like that? It's a gift so should never be returned. It's also a token of my love and admiration and as long as you can see it every day, then it'll remind you of me. If I see the ring's been taken off, that will be my sign to pack my bags and go.'

Ruby thought for a while before sliding the ring back

down her finger. 'I don't need a ring to remind me of you, Bob. I think of you when I'm cooking your meals and I think of you when I'm knitting your socks.'

'And when you go to sleep each night?' he asked gently.

'I can hear you snoring through the wall so I'm not likely ever to forget you.' She didn't add that she saw him in her dreams and her heart beat a little faster whenever she spotted him across the room. That was for young girls, not for grandmothers and women who'd been married before. He'd think she was such a daft old thing and that wouldn't do at all.

'I didn't expect the bus ter take so long to get us to Betty's,' Maisie complained. 'I swear my ankles have swollen ter ten times their size. Betty had better have the kettle on as I'm gagging for a brew. Now we've got all those steps to climb to her front door.'

Freda grinned at Sarah and Gwyneth. They were walking several steps behind their friend who'd not stopped complaining since they'd met up to catch the bus to Betty's house. 'Anyone would think you'd not had a baby before,' she joshed Maisie.

'It was nothing like this last time, I can tell yer,' Maisie said, stopping to rub her back before starting the climb up the steep steps. 'Carrying our Ruby was as easy as pie. This one's like an elephant in comparison. It's got to be a boy, what with all the indigestion I've had as well as trouble sleeping. I'm so hot I reckon you could fry an egg on my forehead.'

'Well, I think you look wonderful. I only hope I look half as glamorous when my time comes,' Gwyneth said.

'You're not, are you?' Maisie said, turning to look down the few steps she'd already climbed. ''Cos if you are, I can pass on my frocks if you want ter borrow them?'

The girls all stopped and looked at the pretty Welsh girl with excitement.

Gwyneth's eyes lit up. Maisie had used her sewing skills to great effect making loose cotton summer dresses that still had style while covering her gradually expanding girth. 'That's very kind of you and I can't wait to use them but for the moment I have no need of them. One day soon perhaps?'

'I'll pack them away and put your name on them as the next user,' Maisie said as she started to climb the steps once more, giving a sigh as she reached the top and tapped on the door.

Sarah took a deep breath. 'Actually, there is someone else who would quite like to borrow them if you don't mind?'

Freda whooped with delight. 'You're not, are you?'

'Oh, that is wonderful news,' Gwyneth beamed. 'There's nothing better than lots of babies amongst friends.'

Maisie looked down the steps to her friend and grinned. 'I thought you were starting to fill out your Woolies overall rather quickly,' she said before bursting out laughing. 'Freda, you'd best start knitting faster.'

'Whatever is all this commotion?' Betty said as she opened the front door. 'I could hear the excitement right through to the back garden. Come along in, Maisie, you're the colour of a beetroot. This sun can't be doing you any good at all in your condition. You can have the garden seat under the apple tree and put your feet up for a while. I'm still getting over you almost giving birth to your first child in my store. I'm not ready to repeat the process yet and most certainly not in my own home.'

Maisie hooted with laughter. 'I don't know, it is rather a nice house. I wouldn't mind a couple of weeks here being waited on hand and foot,' she added as they walked through the large open living room towards the door which took them out to the grassed garden. 'You could start a maternity home for Woolworths workers the way we're starting to breed.'

Betty looked to Gwyneth, who was admiring the view down the garden. 'Not you as well?'

'Sorry, not guilty . . . well, not for the moment anyway,' she smiled at her boss.

'She's still practising,' Maisie said, giving Betty a wink.

'Is it only me who feels uncomfortable when you come out with your little sayings?' Betty asked.

Sarah had also turned a little pink. 'I'll never get used to what comes out of Maisie's mouth,' she giggled. 'But we do love you for it,' she added quickly in case her friend took offence.

'So it is just the two of you expecting happy events?' Betty said, trying to move the conversation on.

'You knew?' Freda said, looking disappointed.

'Only for a couple of days. Sarah was looking a little peaky at work and it came up in conversation. I can assure you Sarah said she was not going to make any announcements for a while.'

'Apart from with my friends today,' Sarah said, giving

Freda a quick hug. 'I didn't want to tempt fate by saying anything too early. You never know what can happen.'

'Don't I know that,' Maisie said a little sadly as she sat in the comfortable garden seat while Betty tucked cushions around her. 'But everything turned out for the best,' she added, not wanting to worry those present who'd not yet had experience of carrying a baby.

Sarah stretched out her legs and sighed as the sun warmed her face. 'This is how I imagine being on holiday would feel like,' she sighed. 'No air raids, no fears and just . . . well, just nothing to worry about. Perhaps now that Hitler's on the run we can start to think about holidays,' she said dreamily.

'I can't think of holidays, not knowing my David's up in London most days with the wretched buzz bombs coming over,' Maisie said fearfully.

'Do you mean the doodlebugs?' Gwyneth asked. 'Mike said there's been some awful injuries from them and the worst thing is you don't know they're going to hit until the sound stops.'

'David's heard a few and said all you can do is take cover and pray it coasts over but then you know some other poor soul's going to cop it.'

The girls looked up to the white clouds overhead and fell silent.

Freda could see that she was going to have to cheer up her mates. They'd gone above and beyond the call of friendship when she'd been in Birmingham and after her mum died. It was only right she did her best to keep them cheerful now. Especially with Maisie and Sarah adding to her list of godchildren and nieces and nephews. They might not be blood relatives but to the children in the care of her friends Freda was known as their aunty. 'So, Sarah, when can we expect to hear the patter of tiny feet?'

'Early in the new year, or if the baby is as eager to come as Georgina, it may even be sometime over the Christmas holiday.'

Freda sighed. 'I love Christmas and to think we could have two more babies in the family by then is so exciting. I'd best get knitting.'

'And I'd better knock up a few more frocks or we're going to be fighting over what to wear with us both expecting at the same time,' Maisie said. 'Besides, if I don't start sewing soon, my expanding tummy won't let me close enough to the sewing machine to make anything and the girls are growing so fast they need new stuff.'

'We need to pool our kiddies' clothing,' Gwyneth suggested. 'I have a perfectly good coat that Myfi's grown out of that would fit your Bessie or Claudette.'

'I have a pile of clothes Clemmie and Dorothy have grown out of,' Betty said as she approached with a laden tea tray. Freda jumped up to help. 'We could start our very own children's clothing exchange between us. Why don't we go upstairs and have a sort-out after we've had tea? I can have Douglas drop the clothing down in the hearse when he's next heading your way,' she said as she started to hand out plates.

Sarah gave a shudder.

'Whatever's wrong?' Betty asked. 'You've turned rather pale.'

'I felt someone walking over my grave,' Sarah said,

giving herself a shake. 'I've not had that feeling for years. Not since before Alan was lost in action.'

Gwyneth looked puzzled. 'What do you mean, someone walked over your grave?'

'It's a saying,' Freda explained. 'When you feel as though something is going to happen but you're not sure what.'

'Oh my,' Gwyneth said, looking worried.

'Oh, come on, girls. Don't start believing superstitious nonsense. It was most likely me mentioning Douglas driving the hearse.'

Maisie peered at Sarah. 'Well, it didn't affect her that time. Let's have a slice of your cake. That'll cheer her up.'

'Don't talk about me as if I'm not here,' Sarah said as another shudder ran up her spine. She placed her hands across her stomach protectively and tried to pretend nothing had happened. My nerves have been up and down since expecting this baby. That's probably all it is, she thought to herself.

'There's some lovely bits and pieces here,' Maisie said as she held up a pretty navy blue coat and matching hat. 'I reckon it'll fit Claudette a treat. Are you sure I can't give you a few bob for this little lot?' she asked, looking at the pile of clothes heaped on the children's beds.

'Good grief, Maisie, after what you've made and altered for us over the years this is only a little of what I feel I owe you. Seeing Bessie, Claudette and Myfi make use of this lot is payment enough.'

'Shall we take them downstairs?' Freda asked as she started to pile dresses and jumpers into Gwyneth's arms.

'Yes, please do, then Douglas won't forget to take them with him tomorrow.'

Maisie started to laugh. 'I can just imagine Vera's face if she sees a hearse pulling up outside my house. She'll be hot-footing it up the road as quick as her little legs can carry her to find out what's going on.'

'Poor Vera, I do wonder if she will ever change her ways,' Betty said with a smile.

'Bless her, she's not been so bad lately since her Sadie and the baby have come to live with her. Nan said Vera has her hands full now that Sadie is talking about going back to work to pay her way,' Sarah said. 'Here, Freda, give me some of those and I'll help you both downstairs,' she added, taking some of the clothing from her friend and following Gwyneth and Freda down the steep stair-case.

Maisie got up from where she was sitting on the corner of a bed and went to help but Betty held her arm. 'Wait a minute, Maisie, I wanted to ask if there was any news from your brother? Did your David get word to him about your mum and his girls?'

Maisie shrugged her shoulders. 'Not a dickie bird. David's written everywhere and anywhere but we've not had an ounce of luck. The only consolation is that he can't be dead or he'd be on a list somewhere.'

'So the girls will continue to live with you for the fore-seeable future?'

'It looks like it but to be honest, I'd be upset to see them go now. It's as if they've always been part of my family. It's been four months now and I just love 'em to bits.'

'You're a good woman, Maisie . . . Whatever is Freda screaming . . . ? Oh my God . . . !'

Betty and Maisie clung together as they heard the angry sound of what sounded like a low-flying plane approaching, making the strangest *phut phut* sounds. 'It's got to be one of those doodlebugs that have been exploding all over London,' Maisie said, trying to take command of the situation. 'We've got to get downstairs and take cover. If that thing's engine cuts out, then it'll only be seconds before it hits the ground and explodes from what David's told me. Come on, Betty . . .' she said, grabbing her friend and dragging her towards the stairs. Pregnant or not, Maisie flew like the wind with Betty close behind, knowing they could be killed at any moment.

'Where's your shelter?' Freda asked as the girls all bumped into each other at the bottom of the stairs.

'Shh, listen,' Gwyneth said. The colour drained from their faces as Freda, who was closest to the back door, looked out and shouted. 'I can see it and it's almost overhead. Get down, all of you, now!'

Betty kicked open a nearby door. 'Down here, there's not much room but—' She never did finish what she was saying as an almighty roar, louder than thunder and more earthshaking than any bomb they had experienced since the beginning of the war, shocked their very souls.

Betty came to, gasping for breath and wondering what had happened. The air was full of dust and she couldn't see a thing. As her mind cleared she remembered Freda calling that she could see the doodlebug and then nothing. She pulled herself to her feet, aware that the hallway wall where she'd been standing ready to lead her friends to the cellar had gone, as had the outside wall as through the cloud of dust she could see daylight. A groan from nearby brought her to her senses. 'Maisie . . . Sarah . . . Freda . . . Gwyneth . . . please let me know you are all right,' she called out through fits of coughing. She waited with bated breath, praying that all of her friends would reply.

'I'm over here and I'm fine,' Sarah called from somewhere in the region of the front room. 'How about the rest of you?'

'A few grazes on my knees where I landed but I do believe that's all,' a wobbly-voiced Gwyneth called.

'Maisie, Freda, please answer me,' Betty shouted out as she regained her strength. Silence.

'Maisie, please let me know you're still with us?' Betty called again with fear in her voice. The dust was starting to settle a little and as the sun began to shine through the debris she scanned what was once her beautiful home looking for the people who mattered so much to her. 'Maisie . . . ?'

'Bloody hell, I thought I was a goner there,' Maisie said as she struggled to her feet with a bundle of the children's clothing still under one arm.

'How do you feel?' Sarah asked, climbing over lathe and plaster that had fallen from the ceiling and walls, until she reached her friend. 'Is the baby all right?'

Maisie laughed as she wiped her face with her one spare hand. 'I landed on this lot. You could say that our children's clothing exchange softened my landing and saved my baby,' she grinned, before bursting into tears as she felt a small kick. 'Thank goodness.'

Gwyneth climbed over to Maisie. 'It's best we get out

of here as soon as possible,' she advised. Between them the three women helped her towards the back door at the same time as calling out for Freda and hoping against hope that she'd not been badly injured – or worse.

'Look. Down there.' Gwyneth pointed before running to where Freda lay on the grass close to where they'd all been sitting earlier. She knelt down by the young woman and took her hand to check for a pulse. 'Freda, speak to me,' she cried out.

'I'm fine. There's no need to check to see if I'm dead. I'm winded after flying from the back door. It's not an experience I wish to repeat,' she added weakly as the others reached her side and helped Freda to her feet. 'I'm going to be bruised all over and not be able to sit down for a while.' She winced as she rubbed her backside.

Betty uprighted the garden seats and urged her friends to sit down and rest.

'Oh Betty, your beautiful house,' Sarah said as they gazed back up the long garden. Windows were missing; there was part of the roof gone and a side wall only partially remaining. Only two houses away there were large gaps where homes had once stood.

'We've got away with our lives,' Betty replied stoically. 'I fear some of my new neighbours may not have been so lucky. A home can be repaired or rebuilt but I imagine that in this street this afternoon some people have lost their lives.'

'We should go and help,' Gwyneth said, getting to her feet.

'No. You stay here and wait. There's an ARP post just

up the road and I can hear bells from the fire station so help will be here soon for those poor people.'

Sarah rubbed her ears. 'Everything sounds muffled to me.'

'It will be the force of the blast,' Freda explained. 'Give it a few hours and your hearing should be back to normal. I do suggest you two rest up for a few days. The shock of what's happened could affect the babies. We've all been through enough these past years so let's hope this is the end of any problems for us and our families,' she said with a sad smile.

Sarah nodded her agreement but even as she did she felt the familiar cold chill creep up her spine. She closed her eyes and prayed.

20

November 1944

'One month to Christmas Day, where has the year gone?' Maureen asked as she sat down next to Irene at the back of the bus.

'At least we're here to celebrate the occasion with our families. My blood runs cold every time I think back to the narrow escape the girls had when that doodlebug exploded near Betty's home,' Irene replied as she handed over coins to the conductress and thanked her for the tickets.

Maureen nodded. 'All's well that ends well and Betty has already moved back into her repaired home. Her neighbours weren't so lucky, though. They do say that if your name's on a bomb, there's nothing you can do about it.'

'That's stuff and nonsense and you know it, Maureen. We all have as much chance of being killed as the next person,' Irene said, putting her friend in her place. 'Look at poor Freda's mother. She died young and the war played no part in that. You just don't know what's around the corner.'

Maureen nodded her head. 'That's very true and it's why life must go on or Hitler and his cronies have won. At least our girls are playing their part by bringing new life into the world. Maisie is due anytime now and if what Sarah says is right, she could well give birth by Christmas rather than the new year so we'll have lots of babies to cuddle during the festive period.'

Irene laughed. 'Oh, you and your cuddles. You've always got a child on your lap.'

'You've softened as well, Irene Caselton. Why, I've even seen you sitting on the floor playing with our Georgina.' She patted her friend's knee. 'We're a lucky pair of so-and-sos, aren't we?'

'You've never said a truer word. We'll be even luckier if Woolworths has any of those pots and pans in stock by the time we get there. Thank goodness Betty gave us the tip-off that the New Cross store were expecting a delivery. It's a shame, though, that the Erith branch didn't receive them as it would have saved us this journey.'

Maureen grinned to herself. Irene could always find something to moan about. 'I'm enjoying the trip out. It was nice to get the train to New Cross and the bus won't take long. It's good to see new areas.'

'Even if so many towns are bombed to smithereens? It is interesting to see these places in real life, though, rather than on the Pathé News at the cinema. I can see Woolworths up ahead. Look at the queue . . .'

*

Betty watched as Sarah rushed from the office. No amount of persuading would stop her from accompanying Freda on her motorbike to the New Cross branch of Woolworths. At over seven months pregnant Sarah should not be doing such things but anyone in the same situation of knowing that their mother and mother-in-law could be in danger would have done the same. Freda had assured Betty she would take good care of their friend.

Betty sat down at her desk and thought for a moment before picking up the telephone and placing a call through to Vickers in nearby Crayford, where she asked to speak to George Caselton. She quickly informed him of what she knew. The stunned man thanked her and promised to keep her informed of any developments. She stared at the receiver before making a second call to David Carlisle. If there was one man who could move heaven and earth to help her friends, then he was the person. The call remained unanswered. She reached for her coat and headed out of the office door. Stopping off to collect Gwyneth who was working on the Christmas goods counter, they hurried to Ruby's home in Alexandra Road.

Arriving breathless on the doorstep gasping for air, Gwyneth hammered on the front door.

'Hello there,' Bob said as he opened the door with chubby young Ruby under his arm. 'I take it you've heard the news?' Seeing their puzzled faces, he added, 'Maisie's up at the Hainault giving birth to this little one's brother or sister. The last we heard David was pacing the floor in the waiting room hoping for news. Ruby's just getting herself ready to go up there and keep him company.' He looked at the white face of his daughter-in-law, Gwyneth, and frowned. 'It's something else, isn't it? Has Mike had an accident?'

Shaking her head, Gwyneth took the baby from him as they went into the house.

'Ruby, you've got visitors. You'd best get yourself down here,' he called up the steep staircase. 'I managed to pick up a few rolls of wallpaper from Misson's Ironmongers so she's started to strip the walls in my bedroom. I said I'd do it but you know what she's like . . .'

Betty tried to smile but the rush had made her feel dizzy and she sat down suddenly and closed her eyes. 'I'm sorry, I'll be all right in a few minutes.'

'I'll get you a glass of water,' Bob said, hurrying from the room. Passing Ruby in the doorway, he gave her a frown and nodded back at the two women to show he was concerned at their arrival.

'Hello, my loves, this is a funny time of the day for a visit when you should both be at work. Has Woolworths fallen down?' she laughed at her own joke.

Betty put her hand over her mouth and dashed from the room and out the front door that was closer than the back garden. She could be heard being sick in the small front garden.

'What's happened?' Ruby asked as both women got to their feet to go and check on Betty.

After they'd helped Betty back inside and made her lie down on the settee with her feet up and a cold cloth on her forehead Gwyneth explained as much as she could about the situation.

'You say Freda and Sarah are heading there on Freda's motorbike?'

Gwyneth nodded her head. 'That was around half hour ago so they must be well on their way. Head office may know more by now,' she said, looking at Betty who was struggling to her feet.

'I've got to get back and see if I can find out more,' she said, still looking a ghostly shade of white. 'Trust me to feel poorly at a time like this.'

'You're going nowhere,' Ruby commanded. 'Gwyneth can go back to Woolworths and ring head office. She can tell them that you've been taken poorly and you've put her in charge. Gwyneth, Bob will go with you to relay any messages back here. I'm needed at the maternity home to be with David and Maisie.'

'What about young Ruby here?' Gwyneth asked as she put the struggling toddler on the floor to play. 'We can't expect Betty to help with her feeling poorly.'

Ruby thought for a moment. 'I'll rally the troops. Vera can come and give a hand. In fact, I'll take the youngster up to her house on my way out. If we're none the wiser about developments, when the girls all come out of school, I'll have her feed them and keep them all entertained until it's all right for them to be in their own homes. My gut is telling me this house is not going to be the right place for kiddies at the moment.'

Betty wrote down some instructions for Gwyneth and asked her to let Douglas know about the situation. 'Please let your Mike know as well. We need family and friends close at this time,' she said before collapsing back on the settee.

'You need to see your doctor as well,' Ruby instructed, giving Betty a knowing look.

'I have an appointment this afternoon. I've not been feeling right for a couple of weeks now.'

Ruby nodded. 'Gwyneth, can you make a telephone call to Betty's doctor when you get to Woolworths? He can make a house call here.'

'Oh, but—'

'Stay where you are, Betty, we've got enough family in hospital at the moment without you ending up there as well,' she commanded. 'Bob, get some tea made before you do anything else. You'll find a bit of sugar in a tin at the back of the pantry. Now's a good a time as any to use it.'

Gwyneth looked out of the large bay window as a van drew up with the Vickers company name written on the side. 'George has arrived. He seems to be using a company vehicle.'

Ruby held her breath and tried to remain calm. She felt that the news they would eventually hear would not be good and she would need to be the strong one in the family for her son and granddaughter, as well as for Alan, once they heard if Irene and Maureen had been injured – or worse. She went to the door and greeted her son with a hug and a kiss as he joined their friends and family to decide what to do and to wait.

'Are you sure you're all right?' Freda asked as she helped Sarah climb off the motorbike. 'I'm an utter fool allowing you on this motorbike. Alan will have my guts for garters when he hears about this.'

'I've never been a good passenger on a motorbike. That's why you never used to see me on Bessie that much. I prefer four wheels or two feet,' Sarah said as she held on to Freda while gaining her balance.

'I was thinking more of the baby.' Freda nodded to Sarah's spreading girth. 'You've already experienced that doodlebug at Betty's house, now I've shaken you up all the way here. We've still got a bit of a walk as the air-raid precaution people have put up barriers at the end of the street.'

'I can do this, don't worry about me,' Sarah said determinedly.

Freda thought for a moment. Since becoming a dispatch rider for the Fire Service she'd come across some pretty awful situations. Thankfully the firemen, police and ARP wardens never let her close to any horrific sights, but she knew they were there just the same. The last thing Sarah needed was to see anything upsetting in her condition. 'I want you to stay here until I've found out what's happened,' she instructed her friend. 'There's a WVS canteen over there. I'll get you a drink and you're to stay with my bike while I see what's happened to Irene and Maureen. You can keep an eye on my bike as well in case someone tries to steal it,' she said.

'You will tell me what's happened, won't you? If Mum and Maureen are hurt, I need to know.'

Freda nodded and walked over to the WVS women at the mobile canteen. After requesting a mug of tea for Sarah she leant close to one of the women who was serving. 'I wondered if you would keep an eye on my friend over there. She's expecting and I have reason to believe that her mum and mother-in-law may be down there.' She nodded to the other end of New Cross Road where smoke could be seen rising from what was left of a row of buildings and shouts and commotion from the rescue services could be heard.

'Of course I will,' the woman said. 'It's supposed to be pretty grim up there with many lives lost. They say it's one of them new-fangled German V2 rockets come down on Woolworths.'

So it was true? Freda closed her eyes for a minute and breathed deeply. She had to go and see if there was news of Irene and Maureen. She owed it to the people she thought of as her family.

'Are you all right, ducks?' the woman asked. 'You're no more than a kid. You shouldn't be going down there. It's not a sight for a young girl.'

Freda gave the woman a wan smile. 'I'm small for my age and tougher than I look. The Fire Service wouldn't have taken me on if I were a weak kid. I'd best be off. My friend's name is Sarah, by the way. I'll try not to be too long.'

With warnings to take care ringing in her ears Freda set off at a trot towards where the New Cross branch of Woolworths was supposed to be.

'Oi, where do you think you're off to?' a policeman shouted out to her as she got closer to the scene of the explosion.

'Fire Service dispatch, sir,' she said politely, hoping she'd be allowed to get closer. 'I'm looking for two women. Their surnames are Caselton and Gilbert.'

'If they were in the vicinity of Woolworths, then I'm afraid you'll not see them alive if you see them at all,' he said. 'Why the rocket came down here and not on London I have no idea but it's ruined the lives of many local families who'll never forget this day for as long as they live. Where do you expect to find your folk?'

Freda shrugged her shoulders. 'They were coming up to Woolworths to buy pots and pans. They'd have got the train to New Cross station and then the bus to the store. I'm hoping they didn't get as far as Woolworths and may possibly be trapped or injured . . .' She could see from the incredulous look on his face that she was being too hopeful. 'There's a bus just up there. I'll take a look anyway,' she said, ignoring him as he shook his head in disbelief.

As she approached the bus Freda was surprised to see people still sitting in the seats. The bus had turned grey from the amount of dust in the air and there was an unnerving stillness about the scene. As she walked towards the rear of the bus she came across an ambulance crew standing on the platform passing bodies out to colleagues. It was then it hit her – the passengers were all dead. Killed by the blast from the explosion. She'd heard of this happening but had not come across such a thing since starting her Fire Service work. 'Excuse me, where are you taking the injured?' she asked a nurse who was assisting the ambulance staff. 'I'm looking for my friends.'

'There's a first aid station over there,' the woman said, pointing towards a church hall. 'They may be able to help you.'

Freda crossed what had been the main road only a couple of hours before and entered the hall. She could see walking wounded as well as people lying on stretchers. No one took any notice of her as she walked up and down the rows checking the shocked faces.

'Freda,' she heard a frail voice call out. Turning and checking the stretchers she'd just passed, she spotted Maureen being tended by a doctor.

'Maureen,' she shouted and rushed to her side, taking the hand that was reaching out to her.

'It's Irene, she . . . she . . .'

Freda looked about her as she tried to listen to Maureen. Irene had to be close by if the women had been brought in together. 'I can't see her,' Freda said, turning back to her friend.

'She didn't make it,' Maureen whispered. 'I tried to help her but it was too late . . .'

'I'm sorry, miss, we have to take this lady to hospital immediately,' the doctor said as he waved to stretcher-bearers standing nearby.

Freda watched as Maureen was taken away. She thought of Sarah waiting for her by the WVS van and George and Ruby back home. How could she tell them they'd lost one of the people they loved most in the whole wide world? Little Georgina had lost her doting grandmother and could possibly lose her second nanny, Maureen, as well. She thought of Ruby and how this would affect her and then Alan, who was somewhere fighting for his country and could lose his mum. It was then she spotted one of Maureen's gloves lying on the floor. She'd knitted it herself as a gift last Christmas. Sinking to her knees, she reached for the glove and silently sobbed. Life was so bloody unfair. So bloody, bloody unfair.

21

Christmas Eve 1944

Ruby gazed out of the window of her bedroom. It was Christmas Eve and no one in the Caselton family felt much like celebrating. Outside snowflakes were starting to fall like frozen tears from heaven. How her extended family clung together and coped over the sad weeks since Irene's death she couldn't understand, but cope they did. When Freda had made her frantic telephone call through to the police station at Erith Mike had moved heaven and earth to get Sarah back to the warmth of her family where she'd grieved for her mum. The child she was carrying was safe and gave hope to them all that the circle of life would continue.

News from the maternity home late the same night was that Maisie had given birth to healthy twins, a boy and a girl – a secret she'd kept for the past months as a happy surprise for her friends and family.

Bob had been the backbone of the family, as along with Douglas he'd helped George with all the arrangements for Irene's funeral. It was George who insisted that they wait so that both Sarah and Maisie were strong enough to attend the service and interment at Saint Paulinus Church, where Irene was to be buried close to where Eddie was at rest. Maureen would also be at the church. Alan had been allowed to collect her from hospital for the day so she could say her goodbyes to the friend she had tried to save by dragging her from the bus.

There was fifteen minutes before the car arrived to take the family to George's house where they would walk together to the church to say farewell to Irene. She looked out the window and spotted Freda coming back down the road from Vera's house and greeting Betty at the gate. Vera and her granddaughter, Sadie, had come up trumps, offering to care for the children and to shield them from the sadness of the day.

Picking up her black gloves and handbag from the bed, she headed towards the stairs as she heard Bob call up to her. 'Ruby, would you bring my black tie down, please?'

'You'd forget your head if it wasn't nailed on, Bob Jackson,' she replied as she entered his bedroom. The walls were still half stripped since the day of the rocket attack at New Cross, Bob having diverted his attentions to caring for the family. Perhaps in the new year they could get the job finished between them? That flowered wallpaper had been on the walls since Eddie had decorated the room nigh on twenty years ago when it had been their Pat's room, she thought as she picked up Bob's tie where he'd left it draped over the washstand. Going to leave the room, she couldn't help but tug on the edge of a piece of the peeling paper. It came away easily between her fingers and disclosed several rows of neat writing on the plaster underneath. 'What the . . . ?' Ruby said as she stepped closer to read. 'That's Eddie's handwriting,' she whispered to herself as she read aloud the first line.

'*Look for the silver lining when ne'er a cloud appears in the blue . . .*'

She hummed the tune of what had been her late husband's favourite song as she followed the words written on the wall.

'*. . . So always look for the silver lining, and try to find the sunny side of life.*'

Ruby allowed the tears to run unchecked down her cheeks. 'You took your time, you old bugger,' she laughed quietly, 'but perhaps it was meant to be found today of all days. I'll take that as my sign, thank you.'

Going downstairs once she'd wiped her eyes, Ruby bumped into Betty in the hall. 'You look very smart today, Betty, and you've got some colour in your cheeks at long last,' she said as she gave her a welcoming kiss.

'I know it's not the day for good news, Ruby, but I wanted you to know that you were right. I'm not too old to have a family,' she said, her eyes shining with happiness.

Ruby hugged the woman close. 'It's always the right time for good news like that. I'm so pleased for you. When?'

'Early June. It's going to mean some changes but I can't wait,' Betty declared.

'It will be something to look forward to. Now, go and sit yourself down and rest your legs while you can,' she said, ushering Betty into the front room. 'Bob, can you spare me a minute of your time?' she called to where Bob was slipping a small bottle of brandy into his suit pocket.

Bob came out into the hall, closing the door behind him. 'Now, before you say anything, Ruby, this is just to warm the cockles while we're in the churchyard. It's freezing out there,' he said, knowing that he'd been caught red-handed.

'Oh, stop your rambling, Bob,' Ruby sighed as she put his tie around his neck and knotted it neatly before straightening his collar. 'I was thinking that Easter would be a good time.'

Bob was puzzled. 'A good time for what?'

'For our wedding of course.'

Bob frowned. 'You've had your sign?'

'Eddie was always saying we should look for the silver lining in our lives and you are mine, Bob Jackson. I don't know what I'd do without you.'

Bob grinned. 'I know it's not the done thing considering where we're about to go but come here, Ruby Caselton,' he said as he pulled Ruby into his arms and kissed her tenderly. 'Nineteen forty-five will be a year to remember, a bloody good year indeed.'

Acknowledgements

Writing used to be such a lonely profession. Writers would sit in their garrets and write by the light of a candle – if such stories are to be believed. These days we are in contact via social media, meeting for talks, conferences, award events, writing retreats and afternoon tea. Book launches and other successes are celebrated with bubbly, and a week doesn't go by without invitations to at least one 'writerly' event. Thank you all for your company.

When we aren't celebrating we work hard with edits and promotions for our books, along with producing words for the next, but one of the most enjoyable treats is getting out to meet our readers at workshops and author talks. I've been privileged to meet not only those who enjoy my sagas but also the people who remember Woolworths and the areas where my stories are set. Thank you all for loving my stories.

I'm lucky to have such a wonderful publisher. The Team at Pan Macmillan go beyond the call of duty to help polish my books before they are presented to the world. Also the wonderful PR team at ED Public Relations, who work so hard to promote my books – you are a joy to work with. Thank you.

None of this would have happened if it were not for my agent, Caroline Sheldon. Thank you for having faith in me and being there to answer my many questions.

Last but not least, a big thank you to my husband, Michael, for reading my work and taking an interest in story outlines and research.

The Woolworths Girls

Can romance blossom in times of trouble?

It's 1938 and as the threat of war hangs over the country, Sarah Caselton is preparing for her new job at Woolworths. Before long, she forms a tight bond with two of her colleagues: the glamorous Maisie and shy Freda. The trio couldn't be more different, but they immediately form a close-knit friendship, sharing their hopes and dreams for the future.

Sarah soon falls into the rhythm of her new position, enjoying the social events hosted by Woolies and her blossoming romance with young assistant manager, Alan. But with the threat of war clouding the horizon, the young men and women of Woolworths realize that there are bigger battles ahead. It's a dangerous time for the nation, and an even more perilous time to fall in love . . .